CARLY'S PEOPLE

11155-BARR

CARLY'S PEOPLE

ANN HILDRETH

CONTENTS

11155-BARR

1

Dreams, according to Freud, are either wishes or fears based in one's subconscious. Are we limited to those choices only? Can they ever be something else?

She seemed to slip out of the limbo of deep sleep into a place of light and activity. It was like being born, maybe. Newly created, then, she found herself to be a small thing in this place with walls that were so high they were in almost complete shadow at the top. Tall arched windows framed with gossamer curtains let the sunlight angle its brilliance onto the marble floor. Swirling there and mixing about, the afternoon's light gleaming off their brocades and jewels as they moved, were men and women each so magnificently dressed, bejeweled and powdered she couldn't fully comprehend their beauty. It was too much. Music and words and laughter and sounds of petticoats and brocaded shoes lightly skimming the marble came on a rush of air to her there at their feet. There were no words within her to speak, though she tried to utter something, anything. What could she do, then, bark? No, that didn't seem right, yet there she was, small among them and like a puppy, wanting to join with them and do as they did. Then, upon realizing that she was, in fact, with them, there in the forbidden place of the marble floors, she became afraid and frantic.

She waited to be found out, not knowing how to move or where she might go, even if she could push into motion the strange little body she'd recently assumed. Surprisingly, no one came to arrest her and no one of the elegant beings seemed even to notice that she was there. But it was so that she was in their midst. That was proven to her as she touched a satin coat richly embroidered with gold and silver threads, the tails of it passing by her face as its owner whirled to the music. Then, as they turned she could watch the ladies with their fans and feathers and; she could hear the swishing of their skirts and smell the perfumes coming from petticoats and pantaloons and even their feet! What beautiful feet they had, so exquisitely dressed in shoes of gold and velvet with little turned up toes, the lace from their petticoats teasing the tops of them. How incredible they were and how excited she was to be among them. The master of the giant windows and marble floors would soon come, though, he would recognize her presence and he would rage at her once again. So; it would seem she was not new after all, but one who had knowledge of things beyond the moment of this place.

Suddenly there came the raspy voice of Madame Cook and the hideous fat charwoman who hated and bedeviled her incessantly: "Where are you lurking, you ugly thing? I have a stick for you!" Madame Cook sang out. And the charwoman chortled, "And I have a mirror for you, mon petite idiot. Boo!" And the awful laughter began moving over her and there was no one to help or who would shelter her from the assault.

Frantic now, she pulled on the satin skirt of the nearest superb being who smelled of Lilacs and Gardenias, and with massive effort, she cried out of a strictured throat: "Help. Help Julie!" Could she look pathetically up at this amazing creature of beauty and make her wish to help an ugly wretch, to whisk her away from the cruelty and the pain momentarily to be hers? But no, the woman did not feel the tug on her skirt nor did she hear the pleas of help. Where to go, what to do? Hide behind the man with the lace coming out of his velvet sleeves; no, no, that would be bad.

She urged herself to stand, to try to run but her feet were wrapped in rags and they were like stumps of wood that wouldn't bend. Madame Cook and the charwoman came inevitably after her. She could hear them marching against her, the clip-clop of their heels on the marble and their raspy voices cursing her ugliness and her stupidity an assault from behind her. Which did they hate the more? The laughter came more loudly then, closer and closer. The beautiful guests ignored her presence in their midst and she wondered how *that could be when she admired them so? What was her crime? How had she made her way to that place when always it was forbidden and she had never before dared venture there? What rip of fate's curtain had placed her in the midst of the celebration of the higher beings, as she surely had not the will to overcome her place alone. Who would save her, who would hold her?*

Where is the mother? Where is she who cradles her and sings to her and keeps her warm in the night and safe in the day? Finally, without knowing how she did it; she ran, clopping her wooden feet on the marble floors, trying to see beyond the forest of hosed legs and skirts and knowing the two were just behind her, Madame Cook's stick menacing the air. Run and run and run but still she had not made it to the end of the room. If she could just get to the outside. Outside in the air where she could run to the river and the rock; if she could go back there, she would be safe. She could find the mother and the mother would keep her safe.

At last there is the door, there is a slit of the light of the outside. The door is huge and she cannot open it. It is wood of such a weight as to be stone. Open, open door! Tug and pull and push but it will not budge and the stick is heard again, swishing like when Cook chops the chicken heads off. By magic, the door opens enough to let her little body squeeze through and at once, she is in the open air. She can run to the river and the rock and find the mother. The running seems interminable but at last she is there at the river and the rock. She can only move slowly now, her wooden feet exhausted and her sausage legs quivering as she stands before the place she once played. She waits for the mother to come but there are only ashes and black logs where the home was and she cannot think why that might be. Was not everything forever?

Madame Cook and charwoman pounded the earth beyond the hill; they were coming and they, like forever, would not stop. What could she do without any thoughts except fear? She must wait for the mother. The mother would make Madame Cook and the charwoman go away, the mother would make the home come back; she would tie the pretty ribbon in her hair and comb it with her beautiful ivory comb. All the noises of Cook and her awful stick and the charwoman and her frightful mirror would be nothing more than the tinkle of the river moving always. She must wait. She must wait.

But the mother didn't come, only two horrid ghosts moved by her touching her in bad places and still, Madame Cook and charwoman pounded ever closer. All because she'd fallen into the midst of the beautiful ones in the marble palace. She sat still by the river, huddled against the mean spectres, staving off their touches and their terrible smells, waiting to be rescued. But the ghosts persisted and came ever more strongly, tugging at her arms to open them, tugging at her body, then they held her there and she couldn't move even her wooden feet. Madame Cook came and charwoman held the mirror so that all could see Madame Cook beating her with the stick, each blow as raucous as her voice, mounting to a cacophonic crescendo of tormented mind and spirit. As she knew it would, there came the pain of being without beauty or spark and having to watch her own mindlessness in the dark mirror.

Coming awake is the hardest thing a person has to do in life, Carly thought, especially when something terrifying jars the mind. She had heard an awful noise, hateful laughter and she remembered someone held her down while she struggled. She had left the dream with a bad feeling and as with all the dreams she woke from, good or bad, she could never go back and fix it if it was bad or enjoy it if it was good. Then, there was another disturbing overlay to it. This morning, a Saturday, should not have begun by being startled awake so early. It meant she would have to endure the hangover in its entirety that much longer. It had already begun its descent onto her and it was this part, the first part of its realization in the brain, the face, the back of the neck—that was always the worst of it. It was not anything she wanted to list as an accomplishment, but it was so that her experience with hangovers was consummate. There was no aspirin, ibuprofin or motrin that could patch the awful crack in her skull—there was no toothpaste virulent enough to eliminate the burnt rubber taste of dead alcohol in her mouth—no homeopathic fur of the canine powerful enough to make it all grand and smart and perfect again. But as it always did, the day would advance, and later, she would either be cured or back in the bag. Either way, the prospect was better than the present reality.

Wish your life away.

The memory of her Friday night was typically fuzzy but she had the sense that the dream and her Friday night activities were connected in some way. It was an emotional connection; she had no skills or the will to isolate it at the moment. She simply followed her morning routine, annoyed. The tall door of the bar at the Wiltshire Hospitality Suites out by the freeway appeared starkly in the front of her mind as the tooth-brushing ritual began. Cap off, squeeze toothpaste onto brush, insert and rotate on teeth still even, still white; consider the door. *Did I go there last night? Was that the last place I went? Or the last place I remember?*

An image of tall arched windows came into her mind; tall windows that had not worn well with time. Marble floors and tall windows, then bang! like a sound, the image and the essence of it vanished and in its vanishing, pierced a place in her gut.

La idiot terrible!

Carly pulled the toothbrush from her mouth, rinsed it and tapped it twice on the side of the sink. Floss; consider the window. It's the window across from the big door in the bar that looks out on the airport's south runway. But why was that image so powerfully emotional? Why so charged with

13

self-loathing at the same time? It was just a window in a bar. *What did I do last night?*

"Nothing you weren't really good at." Wicked Sister laughed, a knowing chortle that signaled some kind of triumph. Carly's heart sank.

"Oh, don't go all wimpy on me, Carly. My God, it's not like it was the first time, for Chrissake."

Carly sighed. "It's not enough that I have this hangover and you don't, I have to put up with your remarks and innuendoes. You know I don't like that. It bothers me."

Another laugh, this one edged more closely to anger. "You don't want *remarks* and innuendoes then, Miss Prissy Butt? How about the fuckin' facts? Hmmm?" Wicked Sister did not wait for Carly to resist, apologize, or reconsider. "He was in the bar, he bought drinks; we drank. Then we went to his room. We got him ready—I tell you, I thought he was going to explode." She laughed again, recounting, "It took the better part of an hour but he was begging—begging, like on his fuckin' knees, he was begging! 'Please Carly please oh please let me do it to you, let me touch you please oh please—'"

Hearing the laughter, Carly looked up to see her own face in the mirror, the green toothpaste foam around the edges of her mouth, eyes bleared, making a clown's face. She forced a wide smile to assure herself that at least her teeth were pretty. Then, she caught a glimpse of Wicked Sister behind her, a fulsome wraith, hated and loved for her freedom to be here and not, wild and beautiful, unaffected by any of Carly's self disgust and insecurities and as brazenly amoral as Carly had no emotional dexterity to be.

Carly rinsed her mouth and patted it dry with the hand towel. "Just shut up and go away, okay? I don't want to hear you today."

"Ha! Touchy, aren't we?" Wicked Sister smiled, enjoying herself.

"Well, you would be too, if—"

"—if what? If I'd spent the night fucking my brains out with a man old enough to be my father?" a snicker of the worst kind, "And then leaving him—"

"Don't!" Carly wanted to cover her ears but she knew it wouldn't do any good. Wicked Sister could always penetrate the pitiful blocks Carly offered. "I don't want to hear you and I don't want to see the pictures."

"Okay, okay. I'll be nice." Wicked Sister said, now cajoling. "I just want to talk about it, that's all. It was oodles and boodles of fuckin' fun. I know you don't remember but you ought to."

"No!!!" then more evenly, "no. I just want to know— if—was he—did he—"

"What? Come? Explode? Die?" Wicked Sister laughed. "Yes to all of the above except the last. We haven't killed anyone—yet."

Carly released a sigh, "God, one of these days—. We've got to stop this. These lost nights are—"

"More fun than anything!" Wicked Sister whooped.

"No, they're dangerous. My God, Sister, what happens if—well, if I run into a client, maybe and I don't recognize him—I could lose my job! What if I can't make it home some night? What if I'm too drunk?" Carly's agitation was building, "—and these dreams. They just keep piling up and I don't do anything about them."

"And why should you? They're just dreams, for Chrissake. It's not like it's the fuckin' Golden Tablets being handed down to you from on high—" Wicked Sister was good at scoffing Carly's annoyance away. She made her smile; their humor impeccably joined and a saving shield against all that was unjust that fell upon them.

Carly set the toothbrush paraphernalia aside, pulled a regular brush through her hair, flipping back the annoying fall of it into her face. She thought about a haircut—something

15

short and severe, more in keeping with her job, maybe. "God, I hate this do," she said.

"You hate it because it's sexy. I like it. If you change it, you'll be sorry." Wicked Sister was smiling, Carly knew, but she meant what she said.

"Just quit, okay? I said I don't want to deal with you today." Carly's defense was puny, but it was what she had. She put the brush down on the vanity counter and looked again in the mirror for Wicked Sister and seeing her posturing naked by the shower, quickly left the bathroom and shut the door. She could hear Wicked Sister's laugh, though, as once again she had shot Carly through with her outrageousness.

And last night. What man was it? Old enough to be her father? Foreign? French, perhaps. Wasn't there an echo of French spoken to her last night? Had the man been tall with pale blue eyes? No, that was Victor. No, not Victor. It was the master of the marble floors scowling and sending his minions to destroy her because she'd sullied his celebration with her ugliness. Carly shuddered, remembering that snippet of the dream. *Trouble, trouble, always trouble.*

No, it had been an older man with sagging skin and the miracle of an erection that he adored and marveled at—and so begged to use. And then, awful images came into her mind of bodies grappling with each other, cavorting in a gruesome sexual discordance.

Carly shook her head and squeezed her eyelids tight, willing herself to think of something else. Something uplifting, a rescue, an escape—it was then that she saw the huge glowing blue light for the first time.

2

The father passes along only sin with his seed. The mother curses generations with the many creative ways of doing it.

It was a cosmic question that could perhaps never be answered to anyone's satisfaction, certainly not to Carly's: why was that hateful woman her mother? If Carly ever questioned that there was a God, she questioned it when she looked at Betta Mary Kincaid and let the essence of all her memories of being with her and not being with her trail along. That she, Carlen Ann Worthington, should have slid out of that woman's body 43 years ago to be thence connected with her forever was the cruelest of ironies. Carly knew very well that she was incapable of seeing Betta Mary in an objective light, and she knew too that how she did perceive Betta Mary was through the filter of her reactions to the woman. But the truth was what it was, an aggravation. No, worse, a stigma—Betta Mary was now and always had been a slut, an alcoholic, a neglectful mother, a user and a manipulator. It gave her perverted pleasure to impose herself on Carly, the one, the only child and in short, the only one left in a family once vital and roundly populated now virtually doomed to extinction.

"Thank God for Sister!" Carly thought loudly, not caring if Wicked Sister heard her. Surely, if she was listening, such a prayer would go directly to her already outsized ego, then it would course its way unabashed to the core of her, that tenacious strength that was Carly's greatest buffer, again and again. She was Carly's most perfect friend, protector, mother, sister and best of all, even after all these years, Betta Mary only suspected there might be another one, but she was never

17

quite sober enough to say with absolute certainty. This gave Carly power. It was the finest, most quiet and killing kind of revenge, no matter that it only lasted for the second it took her to think it.

But that was a philosophical analysis, a thought process that only Carly engaged in; Betta Mary was not an abstract thinker. She was a person ruled by physical actions, reactions and sensations. It would not occur to her that there was another way to be or think or feel; she was untroubled by other's needs and perspectives. Her own were sacrosanct. As was exactly reflected in the current state of things with Betta Mary. On Friday night, she had left her favorite drinking place, Barney's Sports Cabin at Crego Lake, made it to her car and there, she had passed out on the front seat. Barney found her when he came to open up Saturday morning. He called Carly to come and get her mother.

There was nothing to do but drive out there and retrieve the old woman and hope, once there, that she could recruit someone to help her with Betta Mary's car. Wicked Sister was once more virulent in her outrage. "That bitch! That fucking old bitch!" she railed. "You are going to have to take care of it, Carly. Believe me, if I get my hands on her, she's fuckin' dead meat! God, I hate her!"

"Please stop. That doesn't do any good," Carly said. "It doesn't do *me* any good. I hate her, too, but there's nothing else to do but take care of it. I mean, I can't leave her there."

"Why not? She left us all over the place. Just dumped us off—you know, you remember! Left with people who didn't give a goddammed shit about us!" Wicked Sister was not finished with her tirade. She would spew the bile until they got wherever they were going, then she would sulk in the back seat of Carly's car. "Do you remember that asshole she left us with back when we were 4? God, he stank! I think we've been rubbed, felt, poked, and diddled by every old fart from three counties out!"

"I don't want to remember that stuff. I don't know why you make it a point to bring it up, then rub my nose in it. All I'm trying to do is just get through this thing and I don't need that." Carly didn't want to be snappy but that's the way she felt. "And I shouldn't have to remind you that Grandma and Grandpa did care for us. They really loved us!"

Wicked Sister did not respond. Carly went on. "If you think all that poking and diddling is funny, it's not! If you think—well—you're the one whose always out there, doing exactly what Betta Mary's done all those years—you're the one who falls all over those old men, gets them all—and does—whatever you do—God!"

Wicked Sister gave her a wounded look, "Hey! That's not fair! Don't tell me you're not interested in getting your licks in. Every time we're out there, you're the one who's all pissed because it's not a Victor night—and you're the one who's looking around at all the crotches in the joint. Working up a little vengeance, there are we?"

"Never Victor, I love him, but maybe you're a little right on the—um—crotches part," Carly conceded, "but you're the one who always goes for the oldest man in the place."

"Well, shit. Sue me." Wicked Sister turned toward the window, "I don't know what we're arguing about, for Chrissakes. If we don't stick together, Carly, she'll have us at each other's throats. Just the very thought of being around her gets us into the same fuckin'crap every time."

"Sometimes, you can be right." Carly smiled.

"You better fuckin' believe it! And what's this 'sometimes' shit?"

They both laughed.

It was a hot day and the parking lot at Barney's Log Cabin smelled like a tar boiling pot. The odor did not mix well with Carly's hangover and her stomach pitched into itself, so she had to stand unmoving for a moment beside her car. Her

19

mother's old Chevy was parked at the side of the log structure, the front bumper menacing the middle of a log. She wondered if Betta Mary had once again driven into the building. Maybe not this time, there was at least an inch of clearance between the bumper and the log. Betta Mary was not a good driver anyway, her stature an issue—like a lot of old people, she sat scrunched in the seat and looked through the steering wheel to see the road. Which, of course, was impossible since the road was well below her scope of vision. So; when Betta Mary drove, she more or less aimed her car at the right hand lane and if it was a "less" day, well then; it was up to the rest of the traffic to make way. Carly had bought cushions for her and all sorts of elevating contraptions but Betta Mary only smirked at these offerings.

"Think I can't drive, goddammit?" Betta Mary had scowled at her and spat through toothless gums, "I can drive! I can drive better'n you drunk or sober!"

It was useless to argue with her as she was always best, better, had more power, more craftiness, was more physically able, clever, witty or whatever other quality Carly might be accomplishing or threatening to accomplish at the moment. And if that didn't properly subdue Carly, then came the standard, "After all I've done for you—"

But Betta Mary was short and now at 70, she was shorter than ever, her bones having settled in on themselves. Carly tried not to think about her mother's motivations to punishing Carly one way or the other, but the fact that Carly's 5'9" presence towering over Betta Mary's 4'11" was one that was too obvious to ignore. That was one thing her mother could never do—be as tall as Carly. There was some satisfaction in that for Carly, but nothing of a significance great enough to make a difference to Betta Mary's more powerful and practiced perspectives.

Carly put her hand up to the window of the car to shadow the glare as she peered into the front seat of it. Betta Mary was not there. But of course! She was inside repeating herself. Hoping Barney hadn't served her but knowing he would have just to shut her up, Carly went inside. Stale beer and fermented tobacco odors filled the vestibule but going through the doors into the interior, it was cooler, a nice contrast from outside and the closer she got to the bar, the better it smelled. Hamburgers were cooking on the grill, fries bubbled in the fryer, covering over the standard unpleasant smells of old drinks and old drunks.

"Well, wouldn't you know! The old bitch is downing her fourth goddammed beer and trying to pick up that old groper sitting next to her." It was Wicked Sister. Carly was surprised.

"I thought you were going to stay in the car."

"I was, but I decided you might need help. Both of us know how the fuckin' old bitch gets when she's on a roll."

"Mighty generous of you." Carly said.

"No need to get sarcastic. I meant it." Wicked Sister said, "I'm here to help. She beats you up and gets away with it."

"And you're just itching to get your hands on her, aren't you?" Carly countered. Wicked Sister was silent but gave Carly an overly pleasant ingratiating smile. "And how did you know it was her fourth beer?"

"I don't know, it just looked like it on her face—you know, going all fuckin' stupid like she does. And 'itching' is not the right word—what does 'fuckin' hold me back' say to you?"

At the bar, Betta Mary waxed animate, giving the pot-bellied farmer on the stool next to her the full assault. He seemed properly enraptured. Carly went to the other end of the bar and caught Barney's attention. "What does she owe?" Carly asked when he came over to her.

"Just $8.50 for today, but she left a tab last night. I tried to make her understand that she owed a tab but she was too far gone." He rifled through the grease stained checks and came up with one. "This is it. $37.35. Someone bought her some drinks or it woulda been more."

21

"Barney," Wicked Sister said in her most confidential voice, "We'll pay for today's tab, but let's get something straight. You know and I know that you shouldn't have served her today, let alone last night. You let her go to that car, knowing she was too drunk to drive—she was probably too drunk even when she came in. So don't come on to me about some past sins tab, hmmm?"

He grumbled but took the ten Wicked Sister held out to him. "Keep the change," she said, lightly, then to Carly: "Okay, you better handle Betta Mary. I'll break her fuckin' neck if I have to so much as look at her."

"I thought you said you were going to help." Carly was annoyed now, having taken Wicked Sister's earlier insult about being a pushover.

"I did help. You didn't see a fifty going out the window, did you? That was a ten I gave Barney."

Carly came around the bar to present herself in front of Betta Mary who was turned toward the pot-bellied farmer. "Time to go, Mother." Carly said, unsmiling, toneless.

Betta Mary turned a killing look on Carly, "What the hell are you doing here?" Carly could hear Wicked Sister in the background, "Jesus, I hate that bitch."

"I'm here to take you home." Carly said as evenly as possible, "you slept in your car last night."

"So?" Betta Mary leaned further into the pot-bellied farmer as if he were a coveted game piece and she, the master player. He was beginning to falter some and lean away.

"So; you probably stink, for one thing." Carly said. "You look awful for another. You need to get home and get cleaned up."

The farmer was no fool. He could see that his position of being in the middle of the two women was not going to work out well for him. He slid off the stool ungracefully and faded to the other end of the bar, taking his beer with him.

It was all Carly could do to keep Wicked Sister from

hauling Betta Mary by her hair out of the building to the car. Help indeed. "Just so you know," Carly whispered, "beating the ca ca out of the mother is called 'parental abuse'. They have laws against that these days."

"Yeah, well, too fuckin' bad they didn't have laws against kid abuse in *those* days!"

It was a nasty trip back to the old farm, only 12 miles but dense with emotional electrons ricocheting about in a chaotic flurry. Betta Mary wandered in and out of consciousness, swearing about her car and her conquest of the fat farmer having been cut short. Then she lolled into sleep again and drooled on the upholstery. Carly had to engage Wicked Sister's attention during the long twenty minutes in order to keep her from raging Betta Mary out of her sleep altogether.

"It would be something like trying to teach a little kid a lesson by paddling them when they're asleep for something they did hours before." Carly pointed out. "All you do is wake them up, they don't remember what they did and nothing is gained. She would never remember."

"Well, where did you get all that grand logic, Miss Knowitall? It wouldn't be like that," Wicked Sister countered, "it would be sweet revenge–and trust me–she'd fuckin' know what it was about."

When they got to the farm, Carly pulled the car alongside the path that led up to the back porch. She tried to wake Betta Mary but was only partly successful. In the end, she took Betta Mary forcefully out of the car, roughly locked her arm around her waist and hauled her up the steps, her mother muttering then laughing. "Legs won't lock," words slithered over by a thick tongue against toothless gums, "they too woozy."

"She'd know!" Wicked Sister repeated.

Once Betta Mary was in her bed, Carly went into the kitchen to look for a drink. It was dank in the old place, even though the heat outside should have warmed it up and dried it out. It smelled like the bar but without the redeeming aromas of hamburgers grilling and fries frying. What was it about old folks who drank and smoked? They always had everything all shut up, not a breath of air stirring. Maybe it was a mindset peculiar to that generation before air-conditioning had become so available. Still, you'd think—

Carly made the rounds of the windows in the big kitchen and opened the side door onto the front porch. There was only a little breeze but the cross ventilation let the fresh air come in and would soon improve the smell, at least, if not the mess. Ashtrays were piled full of cigarette butts and half-empty coffee cups next to empty beer cans and whiskey bottles crowded the table top.

"You'd have to get a goddammed backhoe in here to clean this shit up." Wicked Sister commented.

"Oh, you're back. Well, just in time." Carly said, "You can help clean this up and then—lucky us, we get to clean her up."

"That's what you think. If I touch that old whore, it'll be to pull her fuckin' brains out through her eye sockets." Then Wicked Sister laughed. "You're the one who said you had to do the right thing or whatever. So fuckin' do it, huh? I'm gone."

And so she was. It was a lonely afternoon, made worse by having to clean up after Betta Mary. Her mother snored and moaned by turns and Carly put off cleaning her up until just before she was ready to go. By that time, she'd had a few drinks, which soothed her hangover and kept it from pounding her brain so insistently, and she could work her way through the awful task of undressing the old woman, bathing her and putting her back to bed. Betta Mary smelled of perspiration and unwashed places and her breath, when Carly was close enough to her to get a waft of it, was burped out of hell itself. Having to touch Betta Mary reminded Carly that she was of this woman; that she was destined to be like her and there was no use to fight it. The thought made her cringe with real nausea. It was then that Betta Mary woke and leered at her, rheumy eyes bulged and glaring. "What the hell're you doin'? Get me a drink! Goddam, get me a drink, willya?"

Carly turned away. "I can't do this," she whispered. "I thought the Scotch would make it okay but I just can't."

"Not to worry." Wicked Sister's voice was strong. "Take a break, Sis. I'll handle it."

Carly knew what Wicked Sister intended and she wanted to have renewed energy, rehabilitated purpose or guts or courage or whatever it took to stop her, but she simply didn't. All she could muster in the way of protest was: "Don't overdo it—okay?"

Wicked Sister didn't answer but set about her business in a methodical way. "You want a drink, do you, old lady? Okeedokee, you got it! One big fat fuckin' drink coming up!" Wicked Sister laughed in a low monotone and Betta Mary, some inner memory signaling her to fear, opened her eyes wide and crossed her hands in front of her face.

"No don't!" Betta Mary rasped, "I don't want no drink. I don't."

"Too late now! Ye asked and ye shall fuckin' get your fuckin' drink!" Wicked Sister took the half bottle of whiskey from the night stand and with her left hand grabbed Betta Mary's jaw and held it open while she forced the neck of the bottle into her throat and poured. Betta Mary gagged and flailed by turns and the moments of the action, though only seconds in the real, seemed to move to a slowed beat. Wicked Sister pulled the bottle out of the old woman's mouth and had it poised to bring around to the side of Betta Mary's head in the perfect swing. But she saw that Betta Mary was too involved in gasping for breath through the gurgles of whiskey to know what was coming, so she set the dripping bottle back down on the night stand and stood back, smiling.

25

"Okay," she said, sweetly. "I'm done now."

Carly bent down to help Betta Mary back into the bed, and let her slip onto the pillow, still wheezing the whiskey. She patted her back while the old woman looked fearfully at her, unable to draw enough breath to speak a protest. The moments of watching Wicked Sister force the bottle down Betta Mary's throat were alive in Carly's mind and she felt awful that she must be the focus of her mother's frightened look. But she knew it had to come to that. It always did. Wicked Sister was only trying to watch out for Carly, to help her, that's the way they'd always been together. Maybe Betta Mary would think twice before getting snotty with Carly again, cussing at her and ordering her *goddammed* around.

Carly calmed Betta Mary, patting her back until she went to sleep again, then she changed the whiskey sodden pillowcase, cleaned off Betta Mary's chin and neck and went back into the kitchen. It smelled a lot better with the windows opened and the ashtrays cleaned. And her grandma's kitchen table was back to its former dignity of bearing only a tablecloth and the sugar bowl and salt and pepper set. The glow of the Scotch was amiable in her now and she smiled a bit as she thought of Wicked Sister's overkill approach to everything.

"Mmmm, that was fun, wasn't it?" Wicked Sister mused proudly.

Carly just smiled and sipped her drink.

"C'mon. Admit it," Wicked Sister cajoled, "no harm done and we had fun now, didn't we?"

"Well, it was a little scary at first—but I guess—well—I guess it was kind of gratifying."

"Whew! Talk about forcing a compliment!" Wicked Sister laughed. "You loved it you know you did! Now, time to finish that drink and let's get our butts over to the Lost Limbo or maybe out to the Hospitality again."

"Oh, no," Carly said quickly, "I'm not going there again

so soon. Besides, we might as well go on over to Barney's and see what we can do about Mother's car."

"Mmmm, well, okay. Anything's good with me as long as they serve booze and offer a dick of the day, a handsome little cucumber we can make ripen!"

"Incorrigible." Carly laughed. "But I doubt there'll be anything interesting over there. You know what the usual clientele is like."

"Yeah, like the guy with the belly that Betta Mary was putting the moves on?" Wicked Sister made a snorting noise, like a pig, then she laughed too. "And how desperate are we today?"

"Not that desperate! But there's Scotch to be drunk and me to drink it. Who knows what we might run into—the night is long, huh?"

"That's my girl!" Wicked Sister hovered eagerly while Carly grabbed her keys and purse. Then they were out the door, into the car and on their way to somewhere else.

3

You would think a person's ability to draw well would make them popular and sought after . . . but you'd be wrong.

Carly was not the typical artist. She didn't have her office decorated with avante garde cutting edge cutesy decorative gee-gaws. No clever quips were framed and hung attractively amidst awards. There were no awards. Her office was plain, almost sterile, except for the file folders of current jobs she stacked on her desk in a neat order of priority. Her pen caddy was dust and eraser-shavings free, her drawing board was the home of one set of triangles, a layout pad and was set at exactly a 90 degree angle to her desk. Her computer was angled on her desk at the other end and its screen-saver was a plain black square. By comparison, Emily Hanford, the other art director, had an office loaded with flea market art, some of her own capricious little drawings, plants and candles and a warm lamp that sat on an ornately cirlicued wicker table between two wicker chairs stuffed with wildly flowered puffy cushions. Her desk was a mess of files and busy-ness and her drawing board was never in the same place on any given frenzied day. Her monitor's screen saver was a photo of her making a pudgy cute face as Tom Cruise contemplated bosoms belonging to the body of his *Top Gun* costar. People liked to go there and see what neat things she'd found at some little corner antique shop or what whimsy at what out-of-the-way galleria. Emily was 26, she was blonde and cute and she was a shopper! Carly was 43, her hair was dark with threats of iron gray streaking from her hairline; she was not cute, not even good looking and she was not a shopper—she was a drinker.

Carly knew very well she should not let herself get into comparisons, especially with an Emily-type. Emily had been hired last year and that alone had thrown Carly into a pit of angst. Carly had been the only art director CSG had ever had and it had taken her almost twenty years to achieve that exalted position. Why another art director? Why, indeed. It was very clear to Carly that Harold Seckinger, son of the Carl Seckinger of Carl Seckinger Graphics, Inc., did not like Carly even a little bit. Exactly as soon as his father had retired, Harold had hired Emily, as if she'd been waiting in the wings.

"He is a fuckin' toad, Carly. Goddam! Why do you worry about that shit? He's not going to fire you. He doesn't know his ass from a hole in the ground when it comes to this place. He's a shithead who's grabbed up all the awards your projects won—do you think he's going to risk losing that over some overweight craft farting blonde bimbo? I don't think so." Wicked Sister could just blow it all off, like so much sawdust in a fat wind, but not Carly. It stayed with her, and as resolutely as she put the comparisons away, they insisted themselves back into her considerations and they smelled bad. In those moments, she wondered if an involuntary passing of gas had insinuated itself upon her presence. That then, troubled her even more. Could other people *smell* how she felt and what she was thinking, too?

She had asked Wicked Sister if she thought Harold was maybe having an affair with Emily. Wicked Sister's guffaw shattered sound barriers and rattled plate glass windows. "What a picture!" she hooted. "Goddam! Can you see that wimpy little weenie trying to make it into that piece of blonde marshmallow? Fuck, they'd stick to each other like so much wet dough if he ever tried to pork her."

"You are graphic, I'll say that for you."

"Yeah, I am, aren't I?" Wicked Sister was pleased with

herself. She paused a minute, eyes sparkling, then she went on, "You remember how he was in high school, don't you, Carly? He wouldn't walk across the hall to feel up a naked girl, but he sure pined away for Victor!"

"Shut up! That's not even funny." Carly shook her head to rattle out the quick picture of bloated, damp Harold Seckinger and his aching longing for her own Victor Precznikov.

"Well, you get my point, don't you?"

"Umm—you mean because I went with Victor then." Carly looked at Wicked Sister, sitting un-demurely in one of the plastic chairs she'd brought from the cafeteria. "If he only knew about now." A tingle manifested in her lower regions as she thought about last Wednesday night and Victor—long, tall madly handsome Victor—irresistible, naked on her bed.

"But he doesn't." Wicked Sister snapped impatiently. "Married Victor. Cheating Victor. Stupid Victor. He'd never have made it through college if it hadn't been for us! Then look what he did! He is a user, Carly, a goddammed whore, worse than that because he fuckin' lies about it. I did not like him then, I do not like him now."

"I don't know what I'd do without Victor." Carly said, turning her head back to the layout she was working on. "I—got over—that *thing* a long time ago. It doesn't do me any good to remember it. It's not going to change. And I'm not going to kick him out or ask for my keys back."

"That *thing* was the lowest fuckin' point in your life—our life! I mean, you really had me scared."

Carly put the pencil back into the caddy on her desk. It was useless to think she could work when Wicked Sister was around. She smoothed the still blank paper on the layout pad, as if that would magically make the pictures appear on it. A blue light appeared in the middle of the newly straightened paper, hovered in it or on it or over it, Carly couldn't tell, then it was gone.

"What was that?" Wicked Sister asked, an odd sound to her voice, a tenor Carly had never heard before.

"I don't know. A blue light or something, I guess." Then, glad they weren't talking about the *thing* anymore, she remembered to add, "I saw one the other day, too, only that one was a lot bigger."

"You should have told me. Those things are bad, Carly." Wicked Sister was uncommonly serious. "They're evil."

"What? How would you know?" Carly smiled at the thought, "Have you been going to church or something when I'm asleep?"

The phone bleated and as Carly reached to pick up the receiver, she recognized that Wicked Sister was genuinely frightened.

"I just know, that's all. It's bad. Bad for us." Then she was gone.

The phone receiver felt cold next to her ear. The air vent had been blowing cold air on it for the last half hour. It made her think of Wicked Sister's extremes for some reason. But there was little time to think; the voice at the other end of the line was Harold Seckinger's and it said, in an aggressive impatient tone: "Carly, my office *now*."

A typical command from little Harold, his voice just barely deeper than hers, trying to be stern, to command authority. What his voice couldn't be, his tone could. He clattered the receiver at his end and it snapped loudly in Carly's ear. "Now what!" was all she could think, feeling an awful unsettled aggravation. As she sighed, she could hear her voice quiver. She felt suddenly very insecure, much more than usual.

Trouble, trouble, always trouble.

She met Emily coming around the corner of Harold's secretary's desk. She had a palpable fingers-in-the-pudding grin on her face that became a whole chubby smile when she

31

saw Carly. Millie, Harold's secretary looked objectively away. "Your turn, huh, Carly?" Emily's voice was throat-y with some kind of triumph and it wiggled with her excitement.

Carly chose to address Millie: "Shall I go on in?" She knew that ignoring Emily was childish, but it was simply out of her control. No, actually, the truth was that she did have control and it told her that she didn't want to look at Emily just then. She knew that if she looked at her she would feel something bad. Wicked Sister may have gone but Carly could feel her hovering and her mood was not good.

Millie simply gestured toward the door, gave Carly a non-committed look, obviously not risking any involvement in what was going on. Carly went to the double doors but just before opening the one that would let her enter Harold's office, she heard Emily whisper none too quietly, "What's her problem? You know? Who does she think she is anyway?"

Carly tried not to let the words stab at her, or conjure the immediate memories of a friendless childhood, shunned, of other girls in high school turning cold looks at her, saying similar things. "What's her problem? So? She can draw, so what? Who does she think she is?" She knew who she was, there was the problem. She was the daughter of Betta Mary Kuhns Worthington, Ramirez, Pettinger, Stanton, Kincaid, oft-married whore and drunk and everyone knew it. Small town, small minds, big mouths. She would be just like her mother, the one person in the world she most wanted to be unlike; yet it was an inevitable outcome. No one ever gave her a chance to be Carly.

"Cool it." Wicked Sister whispered, "get a grip. That little twit is worthless. It doesn't matter what she says. She can't draw her way out of a wet paper bag and she knows it. She's just jealous and we'll deal with her later. Now come on, buck the fuck up and let's go see the toad!"

"'Buck the fuck up'," Carly smiled at Wicked Sister. "You have a way with words, you do."

"I know. And you can draw." Wicked Sister laughed lightly, "We should collaborate on a children's book. Let's see—we could call it, 'The Fucking Counting Book' or 'Learning Your Fucking ABC's'." Another light inner laugh and now imbued with renewed stature, Carly opened the door to Harold's office and strode across the deep pile carpeting, making herself as tall as possible so that Harold would have to look even further up than usual to address her. But Harold didn't look up from the desk drawer he was rifling through. Knowing she was there, he said: "Sit down, Carly."

"No thank you." She said.

Still looking through the file drawer, his tone up a decibel and acappella, "I said 'sit down'. We have some things to talk about and it's going to take a while."

Carly sat down, not feeling any of the momentary confidence Wicked Sister had just moments ago instilled. Where did it always go so easily? Harold emerged from his drawer search with a folder in hand. "This is what I was looking for," he said. "Good. Now, Carly, tell me how long you've been with CSG."

"We both know I've been here since—before you were here—twenty three years." She added in a tinny voice as if it might matter to him, "Your dad hired me."

"Right. He did." There was just the slightest pause before he went on, "I did not. Twenty-three years is a long time. It can be a lifetime in this business. You have to be sharp, stay on your toes, keep up with the cutting edge of design, thought, marketing trends. After awhile, that gets harder and harder to do." Harold smiled, knowing he was stirring her insides with hot sticks, enjoying it.

Carly could say nothing. Wicked Sister said nothing. There was nothing to say, the only thing to do was to look at his pouty lower lip, fat like a sausage in a casing, and watch it glisten.

"I've had an offer to sell CSG. It's an attractive offer but

—

33

I've got to clean up a few of dad's mistakes around here first—" Again he paused, letting the implications eat at her. "Yes, I'm sure you know that I think you're one of dad's most glaring mistakes. But I'm not going to do anything drastic about that at the moment. I want to keep things status quo but show an upswing in production while negotiations are ongoing. The first of the steps I have already taken in this is to appoint Emily as Senior Art Director. She's a very capable young woman and devoted entirely to CSG and to my authority."

Carly felt a sharp aggravation burn at her throat. She did not look up but kept her eyes on her hands resting together in her lap, waiting for the next blow. It came.

"The firm that's interested in buying CSG is Bickham Enterprises. You know who Frank Bickham is, don't you?" He put his hands together on the desk in front of him, a hated gesture, reminding Carly of an interview with the principal. It reduced her to a juvenile mindset.

"I know you know his Executive VP, Victor Precznikov." Harold went on, "Didn't you used to date him in high school?" It was as if he knew that they went well beyond high school, Carly thought, as she watched him haplessly. Like a cat, he smiled, the mouse securely in his paw, talons poised and glistening. He patted the file on his desk, the one he'd searched so diligently for, then he opened it slowly.

"Here, Carly, is a little report an agency has gathered about some of your off-CSG time activities." He smiled down at it and rattled the papers in it. Carly could feel the surge of blood thrusting upward through her neck veins. There was an awful shot in her gut. Wicked Sister was still quiet. The sense of it all was overwhelming. She couldn't look at the report, there were too many pictures there. Or were they in her mind and she projected them onto the pages held in Harold's pudgy fingers?

He smiled up at her, gloating a victory. "Yes, indeed, Carly, you're a busy person when you're not here, aren't you?"

She thought about Victor, about their affair, their twenty two year Wednesday night affair. Did he really know about Victor? If he did, and he told or even threatened to tell Victor's father-in-law, Victor would leave her. He'd be gone from her life and then where would she be? She felt prickers and ants marching along her spine then move relentlessly through her veins. She had to stand up. She was on fire. "Stay sat!" Wicked Sister ordered in a rough whisper, "He's playing you. He's a toad, a snake." Carly sat back down.

"It says here you drink a lot," he looked up at her again, menacing still. "Actually, you get drunk, very drunk. You frequently do not go home until the early hours of the morning. You pick up a different man every night. This cannot help your alertness at CSG." He paused again. " Did you have sex with my father? Is that why he kept you here so long?"

Carly let an audible croak slip past her lips; intended to be an outraged "no" it dissipated into a sound of misery in her uncertainty. Perhaps there had been some expectation of her all these years; perhaps she was guilty of somehow abusing that expectation to keep a job she probably wasn't qualified to do. As the silence ticked away the moments of an awful defeat, Carly felt a stirring. Against all the hard and fast rules Carly had set in concrete, it was Wicked Sister who stood and finally spoke:

"Let's recap, a minute here, Slime Boy. Where do you get off making unfounded accusations about us? Do you know you can be sued for this kind of harassment?" She rested her thigh against the edge of his desk and leaned into it, making him stretch his short neck to look up at her, his Adam's apple a pitiful little bobbling knob in the middle of it. It was not surprising that he said nothing. He had never seen Wicked Sister. She smiled down at him now, and as if she had a grip on his genitals, he dared not move. The left side flip of hair that Carly so disliked fell across Wicked Sister's face, the shadow of it all the more emphasizing the casually menacing look that mated with her smile. Harold dumbly wondered what to do that he might regain control of the interview.

"Well, little Boss Man, my advice to you is to put that gossip-y report away, kiss your ass for the loss of whatever you paid its originator, and don't think a thing about us fucking your dad. It'll just drive you nuts for wondering—did she? Didn't she?" Carly's heart was hammering as she turned to go, but Wicked Sister wasn't finished yet. It was she who turned back to eye fiercely the wet faced Harold, pink rimmed eyes ogling up at her.

"What, my little man, have you got down there in that desk drawer you were fumbling through when we came in?"

"Don't, please don't." Carly whispered but she knew Wicked Sister wasn't listening. She had already quickly moved to block Harold's attempt to lock the drawer. She pinned his wrist against the side of his chair and the tiny key dropped to the floor. He may have whined an 'ow' but both she and Carly were too intent on the tape recorder whirring away in the middle of the drawer to hear anything except that. Carly was surprised, but Wicked Sister laughed knowingly as she let go of Harold's wrist and picked up the tape recorder. "What a grade B movie thing to do, you fucking little rat sneak, you!"

"Oh god." was all he said.

"Another infringement against our rights, recording a conversation without our knowledge. You are a bad little boy, aren't you?" She continued to smile at him as she took the tape out of the recorder, reached her hand into her blouse and secured it in her bra. "Because we're a good employee, a thoughtful and considerate friend, we're now going to fucking save you from your fucking self. We'll pretend none of this ever happened. Okeedokee, Harold? Ummm—and it won't happen again, huh? Because we've got this nice little bit of evidence here of your first offense—"

Carly was literally shaking when her hand finally felt the

doorknob of Harold's office door. He couldn't see it and she was glad; glad for her and for him because she knew very well that if he sensed any kind of a fault in Wicked Sister's performance, she'd be back to improve on it and that wouldn't be good. It was a long time later that she remembered to be concerned about the sale of CSG to Victor's wife's father.

4

*Blue light specials rarely occur twice in one day. When they
do, it's a good thing to take the bargain.*

*"Dreams are the damnedest things," Carly thought in the midst of
her dream. As she walked along a hallway, faces she had never seen
but that looked as familiar as her own, flashed smiles of
encouragement from behind little windows in wooden doors. She
marveled at the clarity of her vision in the dream, noticing details
on the wallpapered walls and the patterns carved into the doors.
As she reached the end of the hallway, she realized that it was not
wallpaper she was noticing, but murals like the hieroglyphic tomb
paintings of the ancient Egyptian Royals. The doors, too, were not
simply decoratively carved, but were written in a strange geometric
language that spoke, that she heard but couldn't understand, yet
they too were as familiar as the words in her own vocabulary.*

*The end of the hallway was before her and it was inevitable
that it would open to something else because she couldn't go back
right now, that she knew. The hallway was purposeful, but had
been hers for only that moment, now it must be another thing. When
the new scene appeared before her, it did so as if it were the unseen
Disney artists laying the brushes here and there and like magic,
letting the dribbling paint unfold into a exquisite scene. It amused
her that as she stood at this strange and beautiful threshold, she
could think abstractly of Walt Disney and of her interest in the
techniques of animation. Again, she marveled that this was occurring
in a dream that she was as aware of as if she were awake, standing
on her living room balcony, seeing the courtyard two stories below.*

*She stepped lightly from the hallway onto a marble-like plateau.
Marble-like? She smiled to herself. It was real marble, that she could*

see with the still clarified vision. Streaks of blue gray igneous matter ran helter-skelter in veins across it. As she admired it, the blue-gray veins changed to gold and assembled themselves in an orderly geometric pattern, reminding her of the carved patterns on the doors she'd seen in the hallway. It was all very odd, but odd things in a dream were not uncommon, she knew, and though she was in its grip utterly, she did not feel frightened. To the contrary, she felt unusually confident and secure.

Within moments of that thought, a glow of blue, a light, vibrated its vigor into the area surrounding Carly. The light was warm in some way, though she wasn't sure that it was a felt sensation. It seemed more of a known sense of warmth, some condition she'd been sure about all along, but had never occurred to her as an idea. She peered into it, looking for something she sensed was there, another knowing. Upon her mind's articulation of that, the blue light became a group of people, and exactly as soon as she recognized that it was several, it became one. But when she started to address the one, it reformed itself into a group again, but with the one to the front of the rest. Carly tried to see the changes, to identify the dynamics, but she could only recognize the change itself, not see it happening. In the moment that she wondered if she should speak to it, concerned that it would change again; it spoke to her.

"Carlen, we are teachers. We are with you." Then there was a long string of words spoken that were, like the carvings on the doors, familiar to her but not understood. The voice that spoke was as if many voices had been keyed together in perfect harmony and synchronization to present a beloved song, distantly remembered but from so far away, so long ago, it could only be heard, not known. Why could she hear them distinctly say the first part, understanding that they identified themselves and were with her there, but the rest of it simply fell away into a pleasant hum.

Carly could feel the end of the dream approaching, the enhancing warmth of the blue light and the people on the marble plateau receding and the chill of who she really was crowding forward. So seldom she had a nice dream, she was saddened to let it go, but her grip on

39

it was as nothing. Quickly she wondered if she would at least go back through the long hallway to the hated place where the woman Carly lived—perhaps see the smiling faces again, encouraging her or that she might remember the exquisite murals. There was a moment, then, as she felt herself being snatched from the glow of blue, that a face becoming a whole figure swept by her or she it. It was a statue, a figure painted as in the hallway murals, but round with dimension. It was a woman, tall and graceful, with long dark hair and eyes so dark that dots of light sat against them like diamonds. In the moments it took Carly to realize that the blue robes painted on the statue were fluttering outward from its body and that the sparkle in the eyes was life, the visage turned to her and smiled slightly.

Carly felt herself pulled out and away from the walls of the dream and she awoke that instant, still seeing the face of the woman. As it faded out of her waking reality, she thought how much it looked like Wicked Sister. And the Blue People! What else was there? Words spoken that she couldn't understand and carvings and beautiful pictures. Her eyes came open to the day.

Barely morning, she had slept in; the clock on her bedside table digitally displayed 10:38. If she had slept in, that meant it was a Saturday or Sunday and she had not had to set her alarm the night before. She tasted her mouth and yes, there was residue there, bad, but not as bad as it had ever been. Not really knowing, but comfortable with the weekend time scenario, she closed her eyes and rolled over, seeking that half hour more of sleep. It was with the most abrupt shock that her body ran into another half way into the turn. She stopped herself before she collided with it altogether, and in one frantic motion, sat up, grabbing the covers around her. She realized she was naked and a horrid wave of nausea struck her midsection. Hangover. Who had she let into her apartment? What day was it? What had she done?

Hoping against hope that it might be Victor, that this was

a Thursday morning, a holiday perhaps, and Mandy and the children were gone to visit her great aunt in Massachusetts, Carly squinched her eyes tight and waited until the nausea settled. Carefully, she looked back at the body in her bed. With some small relief she saw that it was breathing, but she immediately recognized that it was not a body she knew and certainly not a body that belonged in her bed. Its back was freckled and was more square-ish than Victor's. The hair on its neck was grey and needed a trim. There was a hole of bald on the top of its head and she could see that it had three gold rings on one of its hands that was stretched out across her Ralph Lauren sheets.

"Oh God, Sister, what have you done?" She slid off the bed not wanting to disturb the man to wakefulness, to have to see him or confront him. Maybe this was just the backside of the dream and she would wake up and go to work or go tend Betta Mary and be good. She grabbed her robe and went into the bathroom. "I will throw up. I'm going to."

"No, you're not!" Wicked Sister declared. "You know I hate that. It's giving in to that crap. Ride it out for a minute; you'll be okay."

Carly sat on the toilet and held her head. She felt bleary all over. "What happened? Why is—that man—here? You promised you would never—"

"Hey, don't blame me, Sis. You were the one that wanted to hump the guy—and there was nowhere else to go. He's not exactly my type, ya know. Under 50. Too young!" Wicked Sister laughed at her joke. "Not that I didn't enjoy it, mind you. He was a pretty good fuck."

Carly could not assemble her thoughts. She couldn't think what to do with the man in her bed. She had to get him out of there. It must be a Saturday. She struggled to think what she had done the day before, the night before—what had led her to agree to couple with such a homely, tasteless creature.

"Good fuck, like I said." Wicked Sister laughed again.

41

"Carly, don't be such a prude. Jesus Christ, it's not like you don't want to—you love to fuck, just like me. I just like it a little bit harder and older than you do, that's all. The older the guy is, the harder it gets and the longer he can do it. Of course, there is an age limit there; sometimes—"

"Oh, God, just shut up, please." Carly was undone, fraying the substance of herself away; thoughts conflicting with themselves in busy little anarchic groups.

"Come on, Carly," Wicked Sister cajoled, "it's okay to like to fuck. It's natural. Just because you don't know the guy doesn't make it bad. I mean, he was good—he didn't squeeze or pinch or yelp or do anything we didn't like, ya know?"

Carly looked at her hands. Long slim fingers tapering to prettily shaped nails, her best feature. Wicked Sister liked them, but sometimes, what she did with them—Carly shook her head to make the pictures go away.

Think of something else.

"Do you know what day it is?" Carly asked.

"Yes, I do," Wicked Sister said, "but do you really want to know? Wouldn't it be more fun to go back in there and play with him? You know how good it feels to fuck when you have a hangover; how playing makes it go away."

"Gud, no!" Carly said through clenched teeth, it made her sick to think about it. "I just want to know what day it is."

"It's Wednesday. I already called in sick for you." Wicked Sister was at the bathroom door, the robe draped loosely over her body. "So, you see, we can go play with him for a long, long time, nice and sweet."

Carly knew very well that Wicked Sister would have her way and at that, she gave in to the thought of the comfort, now that she was awake and not drunk anymore. She wouldn't have to look at him, or talk to him. She would let Wicked Sister do that, she was so much better at it than Carly was, anyway. She would just go to sleep a bit and when she woke up, she would feel better and Wicked Sister would be quiet when Victor came over later. So yes, that would work. But she had to brush her teeth first.

"Well, hurry up, for Chrissake!" Carly could see that Wicked Sister was eager, her nipples edged themselves hard against the silk of the robe. For some reason not at all known to her, Carly felt it imperative to hide her thoughts about the dream from Wicked Sister. It was amazingly easy to do when Wicked Sister was in a stirred frenzy and impatient with her. As she brushed her teeth quickly and rinsed with mouthwash, she let herself be pleased at how much of the dream she recalled. The hallway, the doors and the people smiling behind them, the marble plateau with the Blue People, and finally, the tall woman who looked like Wicked Sister but wasn't. Even at that thought, Wicked Sister didn't pick up on it. She stood by the door, looking into the mirror at Carly, her eyes lustrous with her urges.

She didn't even see the blue light that exploded into being at the side of the mirror, then lingered sweetly as Carly tapped her toothbrush twice on the side of the sink.

"About time!" Wicked Sister chafed, "Let's get to it!"

Carly smiled sleepily, "I wonder what his name is. Do we know?"

5

The straw that broke the camel's back has been momentarily misplaced. The camel moves on, burdened, alone in the desert.

Harold Seckinger had a dilemma of gigantic proportions on his hands. Having appointed Emily Hanford as Senior Art Director, having made that announcement in an interoffice memo and having shown his hand to Carly Worthington, who had responded in a way that utterly shocked him, he was now locked into an executive nightmare.

How could he have ever known that Carly, quiet, secretive, desperately seeking approval Carly, would have ever jumped up and smote him the way she did. He shuddered, thinking about how he had felt when she stood up and leaned over him. She had called him "Slime Boy". She had so easily discovered his plan to tape record some kind of confession that he had forced out of her with his simpleton investigation report folder. He had to wonder if she'd been drinking. But for her to have changed so suddenly, so acutely diametrically different than any way he'd ever seen her before—he had no answers and even his questions were without merit. It seemed to him now that he must have been under some kind of influence himself, to have thought such a plan would work in real life. But in reality, the influence was only his desperation to have her out of CSG and out before the final meeting with Frank Bickham and Victor Precznikov. If he'd had to write a memo on his reasoning for that, he couldn't have. He had no means to analyze his motivations. It had something to do with his father, with his father's long time fascination with

Carly and his barely civil tolerance of Harold. Beyond that, he could not go.

He thought now of how to get rid of Carly. Not why he should but how. And how, indeed, in the space of a few short days, because it would be just that, a few short days, after the meeting scheduled for that very morning with Frank and Victor. After today, all that was left to do was to negotiate the final details and the length of time his position would be secured with the firm. Surely, there would be some opening of some kind to signal the way to Carly's dismissal. He was usually lucky; so he would stay alert and advance on the opportunity when he saw it.

He'd had Millie ready the large conference room, and checking everything over, he was confident it looked good. There were touches that he had made to it during his tenure there; to the entire office for that matter. It was he who had redone the reception area and the executive offices to reflect the stature of an agency that had national accounts; not very many left now, but still, there were some. It was not that he had ordered the renovation done by an interior decorator firm, he himself had designed then overseen the project. He had a flair for it. As a matter of fact, after high school, he had wanted to go to the prestigious New York Academy of Design, but his father sent him to Brown instead. It was while he was in his second year at Brown that Carly had graduated from Mitchell School of Design in Detroit, a good school but certainly not NYAD and just a short time later that his father had hired her. The only thing that saved him from complete jealous self-destruction was the fact that he knew she was insecure in her job, not sure of herself in the sophisticated agency atmosphere and then, there was something about Victor breaking up with her. That had been the icing on the cake.

It was strange that he understood some of the connections that he and Carly had had since high school and even consciously acknowledged them, but it was impossible for him to relate in any way to them in empathetic terms. Carly always had been the enemy, just as she was now. It was imperative to him that he now rub her nose in the misery she had caused him over the years by being his father's favorite. Maybe it wasn't fair of him, and he acknowledged that, too, but there were greater matters to be settled and it was fairness to him that most concerned him. His father, now 75, suffering from advanced Alzheimer's disease, had held on too long to the operations of the agency and had lost half of its accounts before Harold and his mother had taken things into their own hands, retiring him and committing him to a nursing home. In Harold's mind, and now his mother's as well, it was Carly Worthington who'd had the old man's ear and who'd somehow, probably through her sexual charms, he was convinced, manipulated him into promoting her and prolonging her job. That had brought the agency down to its current status; not the powerhouse it once was, but mediocre, creating mediocre campaigns that said nothing but average. Now getting only the dregs of the GM work and what was left of the Fischer Body work after Detroit's MediaMart had skimmed off the cream.

It was an idle thought but a constant one that Harold wondered why it was that instead of inheriting the genes necessary to make him good looking and aggressively charming like his father, he owned the genes that gave him his pudgy mother's wiliness and feminine perseverance. Not since high school had he allowed himself the fantasies of coming together with a tall man like his father, of somehow earning his pleasured approval. Harold couldn't go to the places he was convinced that Carly went to do that; another good reason to hate her. But of course, he couldn't tolerate knowing that about himself.

In Hamilton, the only caterer was Phillipe who owned the one haute cuisine restaurant in the town, *d'Oscar*, and which, conveniently, was two doors down from the CSG building on Michigan Avenue. Millie had seen to it that Phillipe had the breakfast buffet set up, coffee was French, hot and strong and a white coated server stood ready behind the long white clothed table burdened with silver chafing dishes and Louis XIV crested dinnerware. It was class that counted, and Harold had an abundance of that. He smiled at the server, a thin young man with an elegant neck, pleased with the look of things and most of the morning's thoughts. Moments later, Millie ushered in the other two celebrants, Frank Bickham and Victor Precznikov.

Emily Hanford felt very close to Harold Seckinger. She felt as if they had become not just good friends, but great friends. She was a bubbly person, she made that effort—it was something her mother had told her: "Be cute and witty, and with your talent, you'll always get along." So far, it was excellent advice. It had gotten her through school, through Chicago Institute of Fine Arts and then through the touch up course where most of the Institute graduates found themselves in an effort to put their skills to commercial use, Great Lakes Tech. She had interviewed with Harold just after graduation, having put her resume out to every agency in Chicago, Grand Rapids, Lansing, Ann Arbor and Detroit. Her plan not to stray too far from home kept her pretty much along the I94 corridor, then someone had mentioned that there was a major agency in Hamilton, Michigan, a town strategically connected to Detroit and the auto industry. One agency more, one resume' more. It was a fortuitous choice.

"Emily," Frank Bickham spoke her name, breaking her momentary reverie, "how would you feel about moving to Detroit to service certain accounts in that area if we asked you to?"

Emily allowed the question to stew into an answer. "Why would you want me to move to Detroit? Wouldn't that be the

job of the account exec? Why would an Art Director—"
Suddenly Emily realized that it wouldn't matter in what
capacity she moved to Detroit, whether or not she would be
willing to was the issue. She smiled a dimpled smile, "Yes, of
course, I would, if that was required."

Harold looked pleased, she thought. That was good. He
would get her through this, and she would be an asset to the
sale and to his plans. Maybe some day, it could go further
than that. Maybe, their friendship might blossom—

Victor, who had been quiet through the whole of the
interview until now, its ending, spoke up. "I understand
you've been appointed Senior Art Director. What role do you
see for yourself with CSG down the road?"

Emily smiled cutely again, assessing him, thinking how
she might impress him for Harold's sake, "Yes, I was pleased
with the promotion but confident I can do the job. As you
know, we have a staff of five illustrators, two designers, six
copywriters, one Senior Copywriter, five production staff,
including a photographer and three people in the processing
plant. As Senior Art Director, it's my job to oversee all the
projects brought in by our account execs and that includes
the liaison work with the Creative Director, who is sort of my
aide de camp, you might say." Emily gave a tiny sugary laugh
as humility emphasis before going on, "I have my hands full
right now, but I see myself down the road as an Executive
Director of the creative portion of the agency's work. Then,
promoting Niles Parker, the current Creative Director, to
Senior Art Director as soon as I would step out of that position.
I believe I have a lot to offer a renewed CSG and I'm eager
to prove it."

Victor looked at her steadily with eyes so light blue, they
were unnerving, almost surreal. Naturally, she was
uncomfortable, but she felt she had made a good case for
herself, and for Harold having promoted her. She continued

to smile and brightly be the fix of his gaze. His next question surprised her.

"There is another Art Director on staff, Carly Worthington. Have you eliminated Ms. Worthington in shifting positions and creating new ones within the company?" He asked it evenly, but there was an edge to the question that Harold thought he recognized as attending that long ago affiliation with Carly. Emily simply was stunned and unprepared to answer.

"I—well, I actually—um—I didn't think about Carly. I mean, she's very quiet, and, well—she hasn't really participated in—umm—team projects." She faltered, trying quickly to review what she was saying and not seem controlling or overly grasping at authority. Another cute smile came quickly to Emily's features, giving her substance again. "Carly doesn't seem to get involved. She mostly likes the individual projects, those that she can handle on her own. She keeps to herself a lot." Emily's head nodded for emphasis.

Victor sat back in his chair, a non-committal look across his handsome face. "Thank you," was all he said. Harold was afraid to look at him. Frank Bickham, on the other hand, was not.

"We haven't met Carly Worthington yet, have we?" Frank smiled at Victor, his face a study in laconic curiosity. "Do you know her?"

Victor was quick to answer and smoothly explained, "Yes, I went to school with her." He looked over at Harold, "As did Harold. High school. I think you were a couple of years behind us, right Harold?" Without waiting for an answer, Victor turned back to Frank, "Actually, I've taken the liberty of doing an independent investigation of CSG, its employees and the level of satisfaction, loyalty and turnover in the last few years. Important to the overall financial health of any enterprise in the current state and to enable projections for the future."

"You're right about that. Good job, Victor." Frank seemed

49

the soul of sincerity, smiling still, as he addressed Emily. "Thank you, Emily, for your help this morning in clarifying your goals in common with the agency's goals."

She was dismissed. She felt the server move to her right to gather her coffee cup and napkin to swiftly remove any signs of her presence from the shiny table.

"And thank you, Mr. Bickham, Mr. Precznikov—Mr. Seckinger." She stood and smiled, dimpling at each of them in turn as she said their names, then she moved quickly out of the room. A little chubby, maybe, but still, smooth as silk; she congratulated herself on an interview well handled. She was confident Harold would praise her.

As soon as Emily had closed the door to the conference room, Frank said, "Is Carly Worthington some sort of pariah around here, Harold? A ghost, perhaps. I think it's time we met her."

Harold knew it was inevitable that Carly be a part of the process of the transition, on some level, anyway. It was something he had striven to avoid as long as possible, but that time was at an end. At least, he had gotten his agenda out there first and Emily had performed beautifully. So, perhaps it would be to his benefit to have the two men make comparisons while the strength of Emily's interview was still fresh with them. Harold picked up the phone and punched in Carly's 3 digit extension.

6

The dimensions of a right triangle can be determined if the length of one of its sides is known. A romantic triangle's dimensions can never be determined; even if all sides are known and especially then.

On the way to the conference room after being called there, Carly was amazed that she was still employed by CSG after Wicked Sister's Tuesday night, Wednesday morning fiasco. Calling in sick was a new thing for Wicked Sister. She'd never been so bold about managing details of their career life before. But by some grace of his being too busy with the sale negotiations, Harold had somehow not noticed or fired her, though she realized now that getting rid of her was toward the top on his priorities list. Pulling that stupid investigation ploy was only the first attempt, she was certain, and she was grateful to Wicked Sister for catching on to it. But his next move would be smarter, she knew, and more difficult to detect, even for Wicked Sister's uncanny ability. Neither of them liked the whiny, round little man, but both acceded that he was capable in some ways, and certainly, as a schemer.

Carly had acted quickly yesterday morning to move the man out of her apartment as soon as Wicked Sister had roused him and done her will. She had then cleaned the apartment and herself thoroughly, removing every conceivable speck of evidence of his being there before going to work for the afternoon. Wednesday night would soon be at hand. That was Victor's night and she belonged to him then. She would cleanse her intentions by accomplishing twice as much at work and would be pure and whole again by the time Victor arrived

11155-BARR

at the apartment. Wicked Sister would stay away, that was the pact. She'd had her fun.

As soon as she walked into the large conference room, Carly felt as though she were walking into thick warm soup. The room was air-conditioned, but it was not a physical sensation that created the feeling of being swamped by heavy warm liquid—it was the thickness in the room, a dynamic of energies. Over the years of their "arrangement", it had been seldom that she and Victor met in public. There were no connections between their worlds. Victor's life was taken up with job and family and a lifestyle that far exceeded Carly's humble 2 bedroom apartment and her $30,000 a year job. Anytime they found themselves in a public situation, it was a simple nod that would be considered acknowledgement of once having had an acquaintance, then each moving off into individual worlds. Carly never mentioned any such meeting to Victor when they were together in the careful world of her apartment, nor did Victor. It was simply not anything either of them wanted to look at, to consider in any terms whatsoever.

Victor was immediately first in her vision, as always and exactly as always, she felt the sexual arousal his presence invariably produced in her. But this time, it wouldn't be a simple nod, then pass along into whatever event or moment that was on their individual agenda. She would have little problem hiding her interest; she was a woman. She wondered how he was reacting. What would he do to displace his excitement—as he never had to do in her apartment? And in her apartment, his arousal was immediate and insistent.

Victor stood up when she came into the room as did the others. She glanced quickly at his crotch, knowing the delight that rested there, but now seeing no stirring of it. She wasn't sure whether she ought to be happy that he showed no outward signs of his passion for her, or disappointed that it was under control. Maybe men had some kind of turn off switch that was a necessary part of their more protrusive anatomy, she mused to herself, whereas women could just throb to their hearts' content and send out their wanton signals indiscriminately. She smiled inside herself, allowing a tiny twitch of it to appear on her face. Victor looked over at Harold.

"No need to introduce Carly," Victor said, "I remember her well." Then to Carly, smiling smoothly and politely, as if they hadn't been impossibly gripped together, sweating in their frenzied lovemaking just hours before, "How are you, Carly? It's been awhile."

He took her hand and shook it firmly, and as she smiled woodenly, not answering, Victor turned to his father-in-law and said, "This is Carly Worthington—" he paused to let them regard each other, "—and Carly, this is Frank Bickham of Bickham Enterprises."

It had not occurred to anyone there that Frank Bickham would be so instantly and obviously attracted to Carly. Naturally, things like that cannot possibly be anticipated. No one, not even Carly, especially not Carly, had noticed when she walked into the room, that his expression changed, the sharp business mindset erased from his features and unabashed interest settling on them.

"I'm very glad to meet you, Carly," he said, in a baritone voice that was deep but not harsh. It caught Carly's attention and there was an extension of the energy of it as he took her hand. She was warmed by his touch and recognized something descending on her, like the wrap of protection that Wicked Sister sometimes gave her; a not-alone feeling. Suddenly, the warm soup overlay changed to the sense of a gentle breeze, a seachange that should have relaxed her but instead, confounded her. She had no concept of where these emotions originated.

Harold who had said nothing up to this point, became vocal, his already high pitched voice a notch up. Almost whining, he said: "You can sit over there, Carly," he motioned at the chair opposite the threesome. "This won't take long."

To Harold's great chagrin, and Carly's continuing surprise, Frank maintained a hold on her hand and taking her arm as well, led her to another chair, closer to his seat at the conference table, "It may take a little longer than anticipated by Harold. I have some extensive questions about your work and your place at CSG and I'm sure Victor does as well." He smiled over at Victor quickly then turned back to Carly as he pulled the chair out for her. "Care for some coffee, or a beverage of some kind?"

At the mention of coffee, the server was there with a cup and saucer, a linen napkin and a silver spoon. "Do you care for sugar or cream, miss?" the thin young man asked. "The brew is a special French roast, and it's quite good."

"Okay, thank you," Carly said to the server, "just black, thanks."

"It's strong, too," Frank leaned over and said in an intimate tone, "you should try some cream with it."

Carly looked up at him surprised to find his face so close to hers. He had his hand on the back of her chair and now he touched her shoulder. "Thank you," she said, looking back to the server, "Cream then, thank you." And a gold rimmed cream pitcher on a tiny glass coaster was set in front of her.

"Um—and thank you, too, Mr. Bickham." Carly wondered how many times she'd said 'thank you' since she'd been in the room. She felt stupid and awkward, until Frank ran his hand along her back as he moved toward his own seat—then she wasn't sure how she felt.

"Call me Frank," he said.

"The interview went well, don't you think?" Wicked Sister asked sweetly when Carly entered her own spartan office. Wicked Sister was once again sitting in the plastic cafeteria chair, but this time, her legs were crossed elegantly and she sat upright, like an attentive client, important to the firm and serious about it. Carly smiled at her and that was all it took to dispel the posture, the sweet voice and modest countenance. Wicked Sister whooped, "Oooooh, baby! I could get next to that big ol' hunk in a New York minute, I could! Fuck! Did you feel his hand? If his pecker is as strong as his hand, I'm on it!"

"Good grief, Sister, will you settle down, please?" Carly moved around to her desk, and turned her computer on. "I've got work to do."

"Don't you try that with me, little missy!" Wicked Sister pointed her finger, "This is someone I could take a real interest in. We *are* going to talk about it."

Carly was always unsettled when Wicked Sister did not use profanity. It meant she was dangerously serious and Carly completely understood the ramifications of annoying her at that point. "I have to be honest, Sister," Carly began with purpose, "I think he's attractive, too. But I know he's married, for one thing, and it was you who debased Victor for being married. 'Married Victor, cheating Victor, stupid Victor'—?"

"I don't care if he's married. That's his wife's problem. I can handle it." Wicked Sister let her words create an idea before she went on. "You, though, have a problem with Mandy Bickham Precznikov. You have a problem with Victor not being married to you. That day—that fucking day—you almost lost it and you put us both in jeopardy."

Carly fixed her gaze on the blue monitor screen, rolling the mouse around, watching its little arrow try to find an icon to click on and open. She tried to focus on some task she might take up on the computer to better ignore Wicked Sister. She did not want to go into that ugly place where her heart was shattered and her soul had left her. But she felt it coming for her, the memory thundering into her consciousness, as vital and hideous as it had been the day of its beginnings in that reality then. As the memory overcame her barriers to it, its life renewing in the hidden places where it had once lived, it brought with it, the awful spilling through her of the poison she had felt on that day and reminded her of her own insidious sense of oncoming disaster.

It was Christmas break of Victor's senior year at MSU. Carly had been at her job as illustrator at Carl Seckinger Graphics exactly six months. Their plans were on schedule as far as she knew and even Wicked Sister was to some extent, content, quiet and in the background much of the time. Carly had finished the two year course at Mitchell School of Graphics Design in Detroit and though she'd had to waitress for three months while the job at CSG opened up, she nonetheless got it, all according to plan. Victor would have a business degree when he graduated in the spring and though he hadn't made an impression on the NFL during his tenure with the Spartans as a running back, always a dream of his, he seemed not at all disappointed. Carly thought nothing of it, nothing at all, as they lay in bed after making love in the new apartment she could now afford. Victor talked about things, but she only half heard what he was saying. She wanted to touch him again, to fondle him and make him move. It had been months since she'd seen him, since they'd made love and once with him only lit more fires in her. Carly was stirred and insistent. Her part in their plans were secure, she was confident of their future, he'd get a big job, it would be perfect, but now, she wanted more of his wonderful strong body.

"I spoke to Frank Bickham today," he said, taking her hand away from his penis. It was clear to her then that something was out of the ordinary about their lying around. *When Victor wanted to talk over her touching him—and why would he see Frank Bickham over holiday break?* Nobody did anything serious during break. Jobs really wouldn't come up until the following semester. *What is today?* she asked herself, then answered: *The 23rd of December. Why would anybody be talking jobs two days before Christmas? But what else was there he would talk to Bickham about?*

Carly tried to be cautious; edgily making her way over a course that felt increasingly threatening. Her mind followed a tenuous line of reason, an investigation into some illogical chaos and there, so engaged; she sensed a terrible thing, but could identify nothing more than that with a deep-set, unwholesome dread. "What did you talk to Bickham about?" she ventured.

Victor didn't answer right away, but stared up at the ceiling. She watched his profile and saw that the usual placid grace of being handsome was disrupted by something tormented. She drew back from him and sat up. A gruesome fear was on her; her hands went numb and she began kneading her fingers to get some feeling back in them. He took both her hands in his one and said, "Stop it, Carly. Don't do that."

"What did you talk to Frank Bickham about? What's he got to do with anything?" Her tone was sharp and insistent. She could hear it being shrewish but she couldn't soften it, the pounding of her heart hurt and crowded the sound out of her.

"He's got a lot of companies," Victor said, still holding her hands. He looked at her then; she instantly recognizing a terrible truth in his eyes. He went on quickly, before she could speak or do something physical. "It's nothing, really. Just a job. I mean, I'm going to go to work for him. It's a great job, Carly and a lot of money. I'll start as a vice president, managing Bickham Paper."

She said nothing. She narrowed her eyes and peered into him to see what more there was, but she knew with a certainty from his tone, by his not telling her, that everything about them was ending. Her fingers still felt numb. She had an overpowering urge to get out of the bed and go running from the apartment, naked, into the snow and run and run and run

57

until she didn't feel this hateful worthlessness on her. But she sat there, peering, waiting.

He sat up, releasing her hands and put his arms around her shoulders awkwardly and heavily, like they were two long tube socks filled with clay. This was it. She knew it now for certain. He was going to cut her open and leave her to bleed out plan and purpose until she was nothing. What would she do? What could restore her? Could Wicked Sister? She had no time to wonder. She had to have action. She pushed him away from her. "I don't want to hear this," she said. She leaped from the bed and went to the closet, groping in the dimness for a robe.

"How do you know what you don't want to hear?" Victor came from the bed and followed her to the closet. He tried to pull her to him, but she ducked out of his grasp and with a robe, she hurried into the little kitchen.

"I know. That's all. I know." And worst of it was, she did know and it made her throat constrict from shoving tears back. She hurt everywhere.

"Okay, listen to me. Listen," he said, following her, his voice an insistent plea, "I can't help it, Carly. It's Frank Bickham, it's the only way I can get that job. I mean, she just told him that we'd—that—I mean—"

Carly opened the refrigerator and clanked bottles around so she wouldn't have to hear him. She knew what he was saying and that was enough. She brought out a bottle of beer, uncapped it and took a long swig, looking at his misery the whole time. Things turned then. Wicked Sister was there. Carly felt her beside her, but for the first time ever, Carly shoved her back. She felt a power in the hurting and the pain suddenly became irresistible. She wanted to know everything and feel it hit her and slash her insides and she didn't want to be saved from it.

"And *she* would be—?" Carly asked. She used a hard voice, leaning in against the counter, beer in hand, tough, eyeing him coldly. She was Wicked Sister. "Mandy Bickham?" Carly knew about Mandy Bickham, a stupid little blonde thing, still a teenager who had too much money and no controls.

Victor seemed to collapse a full inch when Carly said the name; his misery was a live thing. He reached for her again, but she put the cold beer against his belly and shoved him back. She went to the table and sat down.

"Yes. Mandy Bickham." He virtually choked out the answer. Caught, he couldn't look at her. "I don't even know how it started. She just showed up everywhere I was. At games, at hangouts, even at my dorm. It was just—" He sat down and put his head in his hands. "She just fell over backward and opened her legs whenever I was around. She was just there—and you weren't."

"Oh no! Don't you goddam smooth it over! I *wanted* to be there, but you said you always had to study so I couldn't be. I'd distract you, you said. Hah!" Carly took another long swallow of the beer. She would drink and drink so she wouldn't cry. She was going with the pain, letting it rule and in it, she was empowered.

His eyes flickered as he looked off in the direction of the sink.

"So?" She let her voice vibrate with the venom she felt. "You are fucking Mandy Bickham now. Getting a nice job at Daddy's nice company, and—?"

He shook his head, closed his eyes and sighed his words. "She's pregnant."

There was a rush of hate and anger that fell on Carly so virulently it moved her in her chair. *I will gut her,* she seethed in her mind, glaring at him. Wicked Sister was with her, a true force, an affirmation. *I will disembowel the bitch. Then I will tear off her scalp and tie her fucking blonde tresses to the doors of Bickham Enterprises, then I will throw buckets of her blood at the windows. Victor is mine. His seed is mine!* But all she could say was: "You fuck. You stupid fuck."

———

59

Carly only partly remembered the days in the hospital after the receptionist and another illustrator from CSG had found her on her couch in the apartment, near death from alcohol poisoning. Three beers for starters, one fifth of gin, and a half pint of vodka had mercifully lightened her mood after Victor had gone, the more she drank of it, the lighter it got. At the last, her body had tried to vomit the alcohol from its system, but it was too late. She struggled to take that last drink from the pint, and struggled not to vomit and not to cry.

7

Reasonable guilt is most unreasonable. It leaves us with few alternatives but to take our punishment.

Carly drew back from the computer and turned to look at Wicked Sister. "I didn't want to do that. Why did you make me?" Carly pulled her chair over to her drawing board now, still seeking a focus. "I got over it. Now, I have to put it away all over again."

"I didn't make you, Sis. You made you. Why do you always blame everything on me?"

Carly brought a piece of charcoal from the caddy and put it to the layout pad. There was some kind of artsy scribbling that she wanted to use for the Legends graphics, maybe now would be a good time to scribble wild strokes on the pad. Be loose, let it out, not care. "I don't always blame everything on you. But I do when you do things. Like that." Carly added with a sigh, "That hurt all over again. I didn't need to do that."

"You know Frank Bickham is attracted. He's going to make a move." Wicked Sister came closer to Carly, "You let those memories come up because you wanted an excuse to see Victor in a true light and let Frank Bickham in. There's nothing wrong with that."

Carly sighed again. "Yes, there is something wrong with that. Don't you get it? I love Victor. I have since the first time I saw him in 11th grade. My God, how much plainer can I make it? Wednesday nights are everything to me."

"Fuck you." Wicked Sister said, angrily. Then she left and Carly felt bad, unsettled. She tried to concentrate on the

61

scribbling for the Legends thing and even took one of the scribbled sketches, scanned it, opened it in Photoshop and saw right away, it was a junior piece of work, unsuitable for the envisioned ad. Carly looked at her watch. It was only 2 P.M. She would try again. "Maybe if I use a marker," she thought, "maybe that will work better."

This time, she used a double wide nib green marker and the flow of it on the paper was satisfying to her. The marker was working. "You are a good scribbler," she said to the marker. "One thing accomplished today, anyway."

She placed the piece in the scanner, and started the scan. The phone rang.

"Carly Worthington." She absently identified herself as she watched the scan unfold on the screen.

"Frank Bickham here, Carly." There came the careful baritone into her ear, down through her system, touching a place somewhere close to her spine, some core place. She thought minutes passed before she mustered an acknowledgement.

"Will you have dinner with me tonight?" There was no small talk, just that abrupt proposal. No reasons laid out, no pretty talk, just that low voice managing all sorts of sensations inside her.

Carly tried to think quickly, to weigh her options. To ask all the questions and examine all the issues and agendas potentially connected with such a meeting. *Danger, danger, Will Robinson!* seemed to be the best she could come up with and she laughed at herself. Before she could stop her, Wicked Sister answered him.

"I'd be delighted to have dinner with you." *Victor, what about Victor!* Carly threw her anger back at Wicked Sister. *Victor can have dinner with Mandy!* Wicked Sister replied smartly, then into the phone, to Frank, she said: "Shall I meet you?"

"No," he said, "I'll pick you up. There's a great little

restaurant at the lake. Sits out over the water. I'd like to take you there."

"You mean 'The Aerie'?" she asked. "That's out in my neck of the woods. I grew up near there."

"Yes, that's it. If you grew up around there, you had some beautiful country to play in." His voice sounded pleased, interested, intelligent and Carly felt herself being lulled and coaxed and squeezed by that and by Wicked Sister's response to it.

"I need an address," he said, "give me that and I'll pick you up at 6. Is that enough time for you?"

"No," Carly answered, "I—uh—I have to go—um—see my mother—"

"You bitch, you!" Wicked Sister was livid, *"Erase that, change that now, or else!"*

Carly sighed, continuing, "—but I can do that and get back—by 6:30 or 7. Maybe if you pick me up at 7?"

"Excellent! 7 it is. Now, all I need is an address. Wait," he said with a laugh, "I have your personnel file here. 800 Parkview Apartments, 2D West, right?"

"Yes." Carly felt tugged by his voice and its tone of happiness. *Is that real? Did I do that? Or is it Sister?* "Come to the west building, to the center door. That's where the buzzers are. You'll see my name then just push the button there."

"I'm looking forward to seeing you, Carly."

Carly put the phone receiver back on the desk plate, looking for Wicked Sister, her thoughts racing around the notion of Victor's father-in-law. Victor's father-in-law. Mandy Preczinkov's father. Her father. Married. Husband. Father, father-in-law.

"Why does it matter to you that Frank is married and is a father and it doesn't matter that Victor's married and is a father?" Wicked Sister, still a little angry, was sharp in her tone.

"Because Victor was mine before he was hers." Carly

answered simply. There was that logic that had been with her always.

"And you can go out and do one night stands , fucking a thousand guys on a thousand nights and that doesn't impact fucking Victor?" Wicked Sister hurried to her next point, "But one simple little dinner date with a hunk who happens to be connected to Victor is a fuckin' sin? Tell me why, huh? Tell me goddam why!"

"Don't you swear at me, goddammit!" Carly said, then started laughing.

It took a second, but Wicked Sister joined in. Finally, she said: "We can't argue, you know. If we lose each other, we lose everything we've got."

"I know it, Sister," Carly said. "I'm sorry. It's just that I panic when I think about Victor leaving me again—"

This time Wicked Sister sighed. "I know, and I don't know what to do about that."

"Don't do anything. I don't want to go through that again. I have him on Wednesday nights, sometimes when Mandy's gone, he gets to stay over and that's a bonus. That's what I have of him and it's my whole life. I have to keep him. If I lose him again—"

"Yes, I don't want to go through that again, either. But I don't want to be tied down to a fuckin' pretend one goddam day a week marriage. We're not getting any younger, our goddam mother is taking the pee out of us every goddam week now—there's always something! What happens when we get really old? We don't have a job, we don't have any money, Victor's fuckin' retired and gone off to live with Mandy in Arizona. Then what?"

"I don't know. But I know that fooling around with Frank Bickham isn't going to help." Carly realized the sharp edges were coming back to their discussion. "Let's not argue anymore, Sister. I've already accepted that we'll go to dinner with him. Let's just keep it quiet, simple and a one time deal, okay?"

"Okay on two of those counts." Wicked Sister agreed. "I'm going to go take a fuckin' nap. I'm beat!"

Carly turned back to the monitor, moved the mouse around to bring the screen graphics up again. A large luminescent blue light hung there just off to the left of the full screen. It stayed for what seemed a long time while Carly tried to center her gaze on it and see if it was real. It couldn't be real because there was no such thing as floating blue lights. Yet there it was, there it stayed and in her mind, was remembered as fifth in a series and subject of a dream only slightly recalled. Glad that Wicked Sister had gone off for her nap, Carly took those moments to allow the blue light to be and to think about why it might be there. Did it have a purpose other than to mystify her? Maybe it was evil like Wicked Sister was so certain it was. If it was, why wouldn't she, Carly, get that sense of it? *Maybe because*, she answered herself, *my senses are completely unreliable.*

The blue light faded out and skipped off to disappear in the light of the one small window of her office. Glad not to be further disturbed, Carly went back to the Legends ad art, deciding just how she would doctor it. Then, how she would fade it to the background, letting the shadowed type follow the chaotic background pattern to a perfect, organized conclusion at the bottom, carrying the message right to the Legends logo. Great! She felt good again, focused, accomplished.

The earlier sense of control and structure she felt at her computer had dissipated to almost nothing by 6 o'clock, having been replaced by a tangle of unnamed fears and insecurities. Because of the—thing—dinner date—she felt stupid calling it that—she had resisted her usual routine of having a Scotch and water upon arriving home, always followed by at least

11155-BARR

two more before she went out into the night where she and Wicked Sister might get lost. It was a routine they hadn't changed for years. Wednesday night was sacred; she stayed home for Victor and often had only two or three drinks during the entire evening. It was nice, waking up on Thursday morning, having been thoroughly and splendidly made love to by a man who would have been her husband if he could have been, and waking up sober without even a trace of a hangover. Other nights were vacant and needed filling. Wicked Sister was very creative about doing that. And that was one of the questions Carly had about tonight's dinner with Frank Bickham: Why had Wicked Sister all of a sudden decided to put a face to the faceless; to risk feeling something for someone, when everything was going along so established and regulated?

"I don't know!" Wicked Sister said, edgily. "I'm feeling my age, I guess. I mean, you have Victor. I don't share in that and I don't want to. I hate him. But I want something, for Chrissakes! Why shouldn't I have something, too?"

"Are you saying you want me to stay away, tonight?" Carly was trying to understand, but it disturbed her that Wicked Sister was somehow separating from her, building a bond, or wanting to, somewhere else.

"Maybe. What would be so wrong with that? I do it all the time." Wicked Sister was becoming exasperated and angry again. "Maybe it's my turn. I've always stepped back when you had things to do, but I've always been there for you—always! Goddammit, Carly, don't tell me you don't remember, that you don't want to remember. Don't block stuff out—that's not fair! You blame me for everything and I get credit for nothing!"

It was Wicked Sister's insistence, Carly thought fleetingly, that was going to bring on another of those hated memory machines. They advanced relentlessly on her, overcoming her consciousness and making her be again the worthless rejected creature that she'd so long masked and made to be still and quiet, not to cry.

Her mother's perfume, a cheap scent, wafted over all in the car—all across Carly's little flowered overnight sack with her jamies and panties and socks in it, sinking into it. Then it would crawl over to her with the mix of cigarette smoke and be in her hair, twining into the loose dark braids she herself had done and the Mommy smell would be on her, hated and loved and so longed for when it went away.

Carly was a big girl for her age, she'd be six next November, but she still couldn't see the road when she sat in the passenger seat. It was extra low down to the floor; the car was old and the seat had been worn; that and the dashboard which didn't wear in the same way the seat did, was extra high. The car putted loudly as it made its way over the country roads and Carly was doomed to look only at the sky, the tops of the trees or her mother's face, now all made up and excited because, Carly knew, Betta Mary had a "date." That's why she was going to stay with Aunt May and Uncle George for awhile. Why the date would go on for more than one night mystified Carly. She could remember when her mother was married to Horehay, and they went out all the time and let her sleep in her own bed. That was okay. They came home always, sometimes not until the next day or so, but they did and she always could make her food and play just fine and watch TV when she wanted. She did not now know why she had to go and stay somewhere else. It made her mad.

"We're getting dumped, that's what." Wicked Sister was always saying stuff to her secretly, always so their mother couldn't hear. "She's not going on a damn date, she's gonna get married again, I betcha."

"No, she's not." Carly whispered behind the flowered night sack. "If she was gonna, she'd of said."

———

67

"She lies all the time. She's a damn liar. Don't you know that?"

"Nuh-uh. She's not." Carly put her thumb in her mouth and started to suck on it noisily.

"Get that thumb outta there. Shit Carly, you're gonna make our teeth stick out."

Carly pulled the thumb from her mouth reluctantly. She looked up at her mother, one moment hoping she'd heard the exchange between her and Wicked Sister and the next, hoping she hadn't. There'd been no need to wonder about Betta Mary's attention. Her eyes wandered over the road but were seeing some private excitement ahead. Her being was focused on it and tensed for it, obliterating all else.

It had only taken a few minutes for the old puttering car to turn into Aunt May's driveway, for Betta Mary to grab all of Carly's things, yank her out of the car and march her to the house. Only another half minute to shove her inside the door as soon as Aunt May opened it, handing the sack and the suitcase to Aunt May, who glared at Betta Mary, saying: "You'd better get in here and stay a minute with your little girl."

That had not taken much time at all. Not the minute Aunt May had ordered, for sure; Carly knew it only took seconds for Betta Mary to pat her head, straighten her braids and say, "Bye Carly." The perfume-smoke smell from her gloves lingered around Carly's face. It was in the next moment that Betta Mary was leaving, in spite of Aunt May standing sentinel to the scene, arms folded in stern disapproval. Carly knew what was coming and it was like what *the end* might be like, maybe even *death*. She didn't want the moment to go forward; she wanted to be magic and still it forever, holding Betta Mary there so she couldn't leave her ever. But she couldn't, she was useless, the end of all was near and Carly started to cry.

"Stop that." Betta Mary ordered. "I'm going anyway. And you'll just make your nose snotty by crying."

It was Wicked Sister who stopped the crying then, and who took that one quick giant step over to Betta Mary, faster than anyone could think and grabbed the pointing gloved finger and twisted it hard. "Go ahead and go, you goddam shithead! We don't care! You're just a damned ole whore and you're mean to us, anyway!"

"Goddam you!" Betta Mary yelped and struck Carly across the cheek. "You wicked little sister, you!"

And it was Wicked Sister who took the blow and snapped her head back around, snarling at Betta Mary, "Goddam you right back, you old ugly, you!"

Aunt May drew a long shocked breath, then releasing it, turned to her sister and said, "You'd better get going, Betta Mary. If Dad could see you now—"

"Don't tell 'im, don't tell 'im, May, please." Betta Mary was on the porch. "It's not my fault. She's just a wicked, wicked girl."

Aunt May shut the door and Carly, so condemned and rejected, fell to the floor whooping uncontrollable sobs. Aunt May stood looking at her for a moment, then called to her husband, "George! Come in here. Take care of this child! I've got supper to get!" Then she stepped over Carly and disappeared into the kitchen three rooms away. Carly's sobs diminished as she heard a man's footsteps come closer to her. Big George swooped down and picked her up and Carly felt like a kitten as he began to stroke her. "Uncle George loves ya, honey. Don't you worry. Uncle George loves ya real good."

He took her into the living room and sat down, still holding her, in the big recliner rocking chair. He rocked her for a long time, saying little whispery things to her until she stopped crying altogether. She was tired, then; the rocking made her sleepy. The TV was on and a Howdy Doody rerun was sending its noise out through the doorway. It made a hum in her brain that called for sleep. Sleep. She let her head loll onto Uncle George's chest and she slept.

69

She heard the TV noise again as she felt Uncle George moving his hand underneath her bottom and her legs. She heard a muffled pop, pop and suddenly, between her bare legs, there emerged a big hard piece of his body that he moved up and down, squeezing her legs tight around it. He whispered at her, "Good girl, good girl. Oh yes, Uncle George loves ya." She wiggled, trying to get away, but he held her there, his big hand holding her legs around the thing that now poked up against the skirt of her dress, his other hand holding her belly. The harder he breathed the more he whispered, "Oh, Uncle George loves ya, Oh pretty girl, pretty girl, Oh honey!"

Then his mouth came down on her shoulder and his left hand grabbed her tummy hard and suddenly all kinds of warm wet stuff was all over her legs. She hadn't peed her pants, she knew, but she didn't know what horrid thing she had done. She started to cry again, so she didn't feel him putting the thing into his pants. Pretty soon, Uncle George stood up and carried her to the kitchen doorway, "Look, May," he said, "she's puked."

"Well, for God's sakes, take her in and clean her up." Aunt May snarled, without turning from the stove to actually look. "Can't you see I'm busy?"

And at that, George took her into the bathroom, humming all the while he wasn't saying, "Uncle George loves ya, honey." Neither Carly nor Wicked Sister remembered throwing up.

It was later that Wicked Sister figured out that the warm wet stuff came from Uncle George and a long long time later that Wicked Sister figured out what to do about having to sit on his lap two or three afternoons a week while Aunt May got supper. They'd always had nice strong teeth, and now that the big ones had come in, Wicked Sister made her plan. Carly didn't want to know. She hid on the afternoon Wicked Sister said she was going to do it.

Pop, pop, the buttons of his pants came undone and

Wicked Sister could feel the thing crawl out of the hole and come up between her legs, growing harder and harder. He'd been whispering his usual "Uncle George loves ya, honey," cooing into the back of her neck. She hated all that slobber, but she smiled anyway and turned around to him and asked, "Do you want me to kiss it, Uncle George?"

"Oh, yeah. Kiss it, honey, kiss it."

Exactly as fast as she'd gone the one step to grab and twist Betta Mary's finger, she bent her body down over the big red thing, took it in her hands and clamped her teeth onto it, biting down hard, like on chewy beef. She felt the warm liquid in her mouth but this time, it wasn't "puke", it was blood. "Oh, God!" he cried softly, not daring to shout. She felt him shudder and his hand came from around her belly to grab the thing, now gone all soft. Wicked Sister wiped her mouth with the back of her hand, and climbed off his lap. He was helpless to stop her; he had both hands at his crotch, eyes closed, praying she hadn't bitten it clean off.

"C'mon, Carly," Wicked Sister said, going off to their bedroom, "you can come out now. It's okay. We don't ever have to watch Howdy Doody again!"

11155-BARR

8

Sometimes, when they make puzzles, they don't give you all the pieces. You have to see the gods of puzzles for that.

Carly calmed down after the remembering about Uncle George. Wicked Sister was right about always being there for her, and Carly told her so. It was almost 6:30 and she hadn't had a drink, yet, but thought that one wouldn't hurt while she showered and changed her clothes.

"Plenty of time, Sister." She said, taking the glass with her to the bathroom. The ice cubes made little crystal clinking sounds, tunking against each other in the pale golden Scotch. "You get to say what to wear. Better be thinking about it."

"Yeah, there's that black thing with the low square neckline. I like that. It's sexy."

"Okay, good enough—but maybe a little dressy for the Aerie," Carly said, trying to compromise between their tastes. "But if you want to wear—oh, I know. What about the black pant suit. That's smart. Then, the drapey white blouse with the ametrine lavaliere—just perfect."

"You think?"

"Are you being sarcastic?"

"No, fuck no! I really want to know." Wicked Sister was impatient, "You're the one that walks around the business world all day, not me. You think I pay attention to that shit?"

"Okay. The black pantsuit it is." Carly started the shower and peeled off her clothes. Glad to be changing, it was still hot out there and she felt a little gamey. "Did we ever decide if you wanted me to go away or what?"

"No, we didn't." Wicked Sister was nervous, Carly could

tell. It was rather unnerving for her when she was so uncertain. Wicked Sister was the lightning rod, if she fizzled—well, anything could happen.

"Don't you think we should get it figured out?" Carly asked, stepping into the shower, letting it warm her skin, grown cool under the blast of air from the AC fan in the bathroom ceiling.

"I'm not sure I want to be completely by myself, Carly. I mean—I want to enjoy him, but you know my fuckin' mouth." Wicked Sister smiled, then Carly laughed, as they both got the picture of Wicked Sister in control, chatting on about fucking CSG, fucking Harold, and their own dear fucking mother. "Maybe, we should let you start."

The Aerie was a lake person hangout, not a white tablecloth restaurant but classy, because the theatre groups hung out there, the Yuppies and Tekkies from Ann Arbor. They were the young nouveau riche who strolled around, letting everyone know they were on a first name basis with Bill Gates or Steve Jobs at the very least. True, it was several cuts above the pizza popcorn parlor on the other side of the lake that catered to the barely drinking age college kids and the public beach boaters. But to Carly, it would always be "The Stilts", a shabby roller rink and sometimes teen dance hall where the "Screaming Angels", a local rock band sweat out the night on the stage while she and Victor and fifty others like them swayed to the slow ones with bodies locked together.

It was no surprise to Carly that the decor replacing the wooden walls and slat boards that pretended to be the Stilts' windows, was now richly done in muted purples and grays, like something Harold and Emily might dream up. She smiled to herself and Wicked Sister smiled with her. What did make an impact upon her in a unique way was the head-turning and veiled ogling of her and Frank when they walked through to be seated at their table by the window. *It's because we make a stunning couple,* Wicked Sister remarked and Carly countered with, *No, it's because they know he's a married man.* After she thought it, she was sorry and said so; but she was not convinced it wasn't true.

He ordered a bottle of wine, a Cabernet, but Carly knew nothing about the quality of the vintage, or how to taste it or even like it. Scotch was her drink and she knew she was out of her element with anything else.

"If you don't care for the wine, Carly," he smiled, knowing, "I'll order something else. Wine before and during dinner is a social dictate, nothing more. Human beings, their tastes and personal preferences are a diverse lot and that interests me more than appearing socially suave."

"I would like just a tall Scotch on the rocks, please, a splash of water and a twist." *Brave girl,* she thought, then Wicked Sister said, *Try the wine. It might be tasty.* "No, nevermind. Let me try the wine."

"Are you sure?"

"Yes, I'm sure." She wasn't but Wicked Sister was and that would be how the evening would go, Carly was determined. In her recollection, there had never been a time when she and Wicked Sister had made a pact to work together, to appear together at once. It was an odd feeling and one Carly wasn't sure would ever become comfortable or workable. With every move of his hand or smile or tilt of his head, Carly would chastise herself for the appreciation and the sensations it created in her. She would be thinking of Victor, of all they'd meant to each other over the years and how this meeting, this date with his father-in-law would hurt him deeply if he knew. Wicked Sister would be thinking of how Frank's brown eyes seemed so open and vulnerable, how the gray hair growing back from his temples was a dear feature that promised gentle wisdom. That his face, his smile, every bit as handsome as Victor's but in its way was far more sanguine, far less slick and to her, threatening, and finally, that after all these years, she might have someone who liked her brashness, her beauty for its sake and hers.

At last, after dinner and after all the questions and probing he had done about her life, whether it was based in genuine interest or a desire to determine whether she would be acceptable as a plaything, Carly felt it was time to ask him some probing questions in return. In a rare moment, Carly realized the roles she and Wicked Sister traditionally assumed were, at least for this night, reversed. She would be Wicked Sister's protector and advisor.

"You are married, Frank. Is that correct?" Carly took a sip of the Cointreau he had ordered for her, and watched his face. With some satisfaction, she noted that his color changed slightly, a flush under the tan, but his eyes kept steady onto hers.

He didn't hesitate to answer, but his voice was low. "Yes, I am married. A fact for the past thirty years."

Thirty? That seemed unlikely to her, knowing that Mandy was close to forty. *Is that a lie?* She wondered and immediately, Wicked Sister responded, *Give him a break, huh, Carly? Maybe there's something we don't know.* Carly was quiet then. He seemed to want to go on, so she let him.

"I know you're doing the math in your head," he smiled at her, "I can see calculators going click-click in your eyes. You have the most beautifully deep dark eyes I've ever seen— whether you think so or not, they hide very little.

"But that's not what you want to know, is it? No, of course, not," he answered his own question. "Okay, here's my story: Mandy's mother was an incredibly bright and beautiful woman when I met her. I was just starting law school at University of Detroit and she was the daughter of one of my professors, a law judge who'd sat on the bench for forty years. She was a wild thing, erotic and like nothing this old farm boy had ever seen before. She was eight years older than me, but that wasn't a factor at the time. Professor Hartley, her father, was a widower and was absolutely opposed to any relationship between us, she already had Mandy and, I never really knew for sure, but I think he was afraid we would all leave him. We wouldn't have. Well, I wouldn't have, but as it turned out we had no choice. He disowned her and kicked her and Mandy out of his house when we announced our plans to be married. As I said, he'd been on the bench for forty years and that left little diversity in the man's personal viewpoint. The law's a habit if you let it be, and he did. Enough said about that." He looked at Carly's face as she sipped on the liqueur. Her eyes looked hurt to him. He reached for her hand across the table, letting his fingers rest there. "Are you sure you want to hear this?"

Carly had been letting Wicked Sister listen and flow along with the story; but she, too, had listened and felt Wicked Sister's rare softness. "Yes, I'm sure. I—would like to know." She said, letting the fingers of her left hand remain under his.

"Fair enough. I can't say that I was in love with Beatrice, I was fascinated with her, she was incredibly uninhibited and that certainly swayed my young libido. And given the fact that I'd just started law school, I was looking at another solid two or three years, then the bar, before I could practice, so; it had to be enchantment overwhelming good sense. We didn't have a penny, not a shiny dime. But by the time Professor Hartley closed his doors to Beatrice and Mandy, I had taken on the role of protector-hero-provider. And that's about it. I finally earned my law degree when Mandy turned fourteen, after I'd made my first three million out of the first two companies I acquired—with a little help from my parents. I passed the bar and still have an office, just not a practice. Interesting how the years and events change personal goals."

"That's a nice story, but it doesn't say anything about your *marriage.*" Carly was quick with the remark, Wicked Sister had no chance to stop her. *Shoe's on the other foot,* Carly

---

smiled inwardly, then remembering her promise, she apologized again.

"Touche'. It doesn't." He took his hand back and signaled for the waiter. To him he said, "Coffee and the check please."

Wicked Sister was struck. *Now, see what you've done. He hates us.* Before Carly could answer, Frank spoke.

"It's just that it's not easy to talk about. It sounds almost concocted telling it, saying it all out loud. I don't talk to anyone about it. At least, I haven't up to this point. I'm not sure I know what to say. I'm still married, yes. Mandy is legally my daughter, I adopted her when she was seven, almost eight. Beatrice is—well, to be blunt—mentally unsound. She's been in and out of a variety of institutions, alcohol and drugs played a part in her mental diminishment, but I'm not sure any of the doctors know which came first, the addiction or the emotional disorder. Because Mandy wanted it, Beatrice is at home now, in her own suite with around the clock attendants—"

The waiter came with the coffee and the check and Carly was glad of it. Now, she wanted the story to stop. Every time Frank said "Mandy", weaving her into his story, he added a humanness to her, an empathetic connection point that Carly wanted no part of. All these years, she had thought of Mandy Bickham Precznikov as a loose teen ager, wanton, throwing her money around to get what she wanted, getting pregnant to trap her man. Victor came to her, Carly, every Wednesday night to confirm that truth. She had no interest now in letting a mutual pathos like a disturbed mother create a different light on the woman. *No, no, no!*

But Carly, maybe Mandy is the human one, maybe it's Victor that's—

Stop it! Victor loved me and showed he loved me long before he ever got caught by her money! Carly looked out across the lake, trying to mask her expression as she argued with Wicked Sister. *I know you when you're on your best behavior, not cussing, being sweet. Mother called you Wicked and you surely can be. I agreed to go out with Frank tonight, just for you, but let's leave Victor out of this. I'm not going to let him go again, and that's final!* There was no answer, but contention within remained.

"The lake is beautiful at night," Frank said, "I've really enjoyed myself this evening, Carly. I hope I haven't put you off too much by the fact of my—marital status, or the almost unbelievable story that keeps me there."

"No," Carly replied, again trying to mask her now troubled expression, "I guess not."

"Something's the matter," Frank said, connecting with her eyes, "I can see that something's wrong. What is it?"

Carly sighed. She couldn't tell him what was really wrong; that she was turbulent inside because she was historically involved with his son-in-law or that the attraction to him was creating a deadly chasm and she wanted a Scotch to make it smooth out. "Well, you are married, no matter what kind of marriage it is, and—well, maybe *I* should be blunt now—" she felt Wicked Sister hammering at her, but she went on anyway, "—it's a little too close to my job. You're about to become my ultimate boss, Harold Seckinger is still going to have control over my status with the company and he hates me—Victor is an old acquaintance—I don't know. What are the day-to-day implications here? It's all just too—complicated."

He considered his coffee, but Wicked Sister saw his eyes and their look of submission to fate touched her indelibly. "But it's not—mmm—" she was going to say 'fucking' but Carly, even in her snit at being cut off, stopped her, "—insurmountable—I mean, umm—as far as looking into things. I mean, exploring—what there might be—if anything—"

"You'll consider—seeing me again?" He brightened.

Wicked Sister smiled broadly, beautifully. "That would be just dandy!" She took the last sip of the Cointreau. "I like this stuff. It's pretty damned good, as a matter of fact. And just so you know, the wine wasn't all that bad, too."

Frank laughed. "I'm very glad, Carly. I—find you very attractive—and I want you to get to know me—who I am."

"Yeah, I'm having a good time, too, Frank." Wicked Sister smiled back at him, "I can't promise anything, you know? But it'll be a gas finding out, huh?"

"A gas it is, then!" Frank reached across and touched her hand again and this time Wicked Sister quickly entwined her fingers in his and let the warmth of him flow through her, hoping Carly would feel him, too. She did not take her eyes from his.

9

---

*Just when you thought it was safe to get normal; Mother
Abnormal reminds you of your heritage.*

Frank drove her home and took her to her apartment door,
took the key from her hand and unlocked it for her. She
watched him in wonderment. She wasn't so countrified and
socially retarded as not to know that gentlemen did that, but
it amazed her that someone so attractive to her was treating
her like a lady. It was a new experience and it made Carly
question her earlier condemnations; as for Wicked Sister, she
was a puddle of tingling awe. *Now, of course,* Carly reminded
Wicked Sister, *here comes the part where he sashays on in, sleeps
with us and we never see him again. A good thing for me, but I
don't want you to be disappointed, Sister.*

Frank handed the key wordlessly back to her and with
the slightest sigh, he stepped back, taking her hands in his.
"I can't say in words what this evening has meant to me,
Carly." He lifted her right hand, put it to his lips and kissed
her fingers lightly, "That someone like you, beautiful,
intelligent—and fun—will take a chance with me to find out
where we might take—whatever it is."

Wicked Sister moved close to him, that's what she knew
how to do, how to express, but it was Carly who turned her
face up and kissed him lightly on the cheek, then stepped
back. "Thank you for a wonderful evening, Frank."

"May I call you? Will you have dinner with me again?"
He kissed her hand again, not letting her go.

"Oh yes, I will!" Wicked Sister smiled, taking his hand
and kissing it right back, "The sooner the better!"

"You are refreshing," he laughed again, and said, "Goodnight. I'll call you tomorrow." Then he turned and walked down the hall. Wicked Sister lingered at the door watching his stride.

"My dear fuckin' vibrating Miss Pussy! What a hunk, I want, I *want*!" She said to Carly, "See there? That wasn't so bad, huh? He didn't say 'let's fuck' the whole night long and neither did I. That's got to be a record!"

"Well you just broke it," Carly laughed, relieved to be home. "And yes, it wasn't so bad, but I'm glad it went without incident."

"You mean without Victor finding out." Wicked Sister said tartly as she followed Carly into the kitchen.

"That's part of it, yes." Carly answered, reaching for a glass, then grabbing some ice cubes out of the freezer. Clink, clink, ker-plunk! Then she poured the Scotch over and watched it cascade its magic oils over the shining cubes of ice. "But there's more to it than just that. What if it gets around that I'm seeing the man who's buying the company. Whether I'm sleeping with him or not isn't going to make any difference to how good I am at my job, or how consistently I do it. That's in enough question right now—thanks to your little calling in sick trick the other day."

"Oh, for Chrissakes', Carly, would you get past that? Jesus, all I did was *save* your fuckin' ass. You're the one who wanted to bring that bozo home." Wicked Sister sat at the passthrough on the living room side of the kitchen. "I don't know what you were thinking. Except throwing something into Victor's face without really doing it, then saying it was my fault. Just because I fucked him once he was here doesn't make me the bad guy, ya know. I just like to fuck, that's all."

"And I don't? Anyway, I didn't bring him home. That's a fact. I wouldn't do that."

"Here we go again. For Chrissake, Carly, why would I lie about it? I mean, it's not like I'm trying to save my fuckin' virginity in your eyes or somethin'. Like, I got big secrets from you, huh?" Wicked Sister was getting exasperated again. "Jesus Christ!"

"Okay, okay." Carly took a drink of the Scotch. "We won't argue about it anymore. Let's see if we can figure out what to do now. It's only 10 o'clock. How about a quick run out to the Hospitality? You like that place."

"Why don't we just watch the news and go to bed?"

Carly laughed. "Are you kidding? You're kidding, right?"

"Not really. Let's just get cozy in our 'jamies, you can have another Scotch and we'll find out what's on the boob tube at this hour. A fuckin' novelty, huh?" Wicked Sister looked at the couch. "Only you work the remote. It's a goddam mystery to me—punching those buttons."

"Oh, no you don't!" Carly said, a knowing coming over her, "You think if *you* stay here, *I'll* stay here and eventually I'll get so—bored—I'll let you do it with Frank."

Wicked Sister looked at her, but Carly couldn't tell whether the look was puzzled or whether it was a caught look. The phone rang and it startled her, throwing questions out of her consciousness for the moment. *No one calls here at this hour, or rarely, anyway. Who could it be?* They both thought the same thing, but then their thoughts split, Carly hoping for some miracle allowing Victor to call on a Thursday night, and Wicked Sister sure it would be Frank, calling to say a sweet goodnight with that baritone voice that stirred her so.

"Mrs. Worthington?" Not a baritone but a crisp tenor male voice asked.

"This is Carly Worthington, yes." Never a Mrs.

"This is Sergeant Blackman at the State Police post on Warren Road," he said it as if it was a question, but then his tone changed to firm and assured. "I have your mother here, Betta Mary Kincaid. She's been arrested for being Drunk and Disorderly, for Assault and Battery against an officer and she was too drunk to make her phone call. I managed to find your name and number in her personal effects as the next of kin. You are her daughter, correct?"

"Yes, I am," Carly said reluctantly. *Trouble, trouble, always trouble!*

"Normally, we would leave her in the drunk tank overnight until she sobered up and arranged for bail in the morning, but two things—" Trooper Blackman said. "One is that in deference to her age and condition, we don't think the tank is the place for her and second; it's pretty crowded in there now. Race weekend started today."

"Condition? You mean her drunken condition?" Carly asked.

"No. That is, she's drunk alright, but she seems to be having some other difficulties that we can't determine the nature of. I don't know, " he said. "I'm no medic, but she's having a problem with her feet or her legs. She said she was paralyzed, but she's drunk and she's been talking nonsense— somebody locked her legs, she said, and she seems unable to move them."

"Oh, she's just drunk, that's all," Carly said, disgusted. "She says that all the time. Some kind of excuse she makes for being drunk. Like you're going to believe that someone locked up her legs. God!"

"We need to have you come and get her," he said, somewhat emphatically. "If you don't have the $500 cash for her bail, we'll waive that until tomorrow morning, but you'll have to leave a check then retrieve it with cash at the District Court by 9 AM."

Carly wondered what they might do if she didn't retrieve Betta Mary. Leave her in the lock-up for once. "That fuckin' bitch. At it again! Jesus Christ, how many times is this that we've had to go get her?" Wicked Sister was once again at her peak annoyance point.

"Ma'am?" There had been a silence or had Wicked Sister actually spoken?

———

83

"I'll be there in a half hour," Carly said and hung up the phone.

"Well, here we fuckin' go again," Wicked Sister railed, "Goddam bitch is going to—Jesus Christ! I hate her!"

"Listen to me. Just quit it." Carly searched the key basket for her car keys, "We've got to go get her and get her home. There's no one else to do it. It doesn't help when you get so angry. It upsets me."

"I know it." Wicked Sister admitted, "I know it. I'm sorry. Honest to Jesus Christ God I am. But Carly, think about it. When is this fuckin' shit going to end? Will she keep on doing it until she's worn us out and we're blathering nut cases?"

Carly found the keys and grabbed the black suit jacket and her purse. "Good thing we didn't get into our 'jamies, huh?"

"Don't change the subject. You know I haven't said anything, ever. But it's been right underneath the surface— what do you suppose your precious Victor would do if he found out your mother's not exactly socially acceptable?" There it was again, Wicked Sister not cussing. A bad sign.

"Are you planning on having him find out?" Carly asked, then added, "That would be a novelty after all these years. And you know, it wouldn't break me up to make the announcement to Frank that *I* couldn't see him anymore because my mother's an alcoholic madwoman and so is his wife!"

"Go ahead!" Wicked Sister countered quickly. "He finds out, Victor finds out."

Carly pulled the car out of the parking lot and headed down Winter Street to the highway, she'd pick up Warren off the freeway. "You know, I've said it a hundred times, but I'll say it again," Carly mused. "Every time Betta Mary does something like this, you and I are at it. She brings out the worst in us. You said it last time. We've got to stick together."

"I know it. You're right. It's just that fuckin' feeling—you know? It's like no matter what we're doing or where we are, we're powerless if she wants to make it so." Wicked Sister sat back in the front seat and sighed. "We're goddam what? Forty-three? Almost forty-four. Shit. I'm tired of fighting that old bitch. She always wins, no matter what! It's just got to stop, Carly. It's got to."

"Well, I don't know what there is to do about it." Carly pulled onto the highway and into westbound lane. The lane would move them onto the freeway in about a mile. Carly always thought it was like cars on rails. You went there no matter how you steered, the traffic just swept you along. And the traffic was heavy tonight. "Start of the Race Weekend," the trooper had said. Carly made a mental note to stay away from this end of town for the next three days. Race weekends could get annoyingly over-attended.

Wicked Sister had been quiet for a few minutes, but then she said, "I know what there is to do about it."

Carly turned around to see if she could read her. Nothing. "I'm not sure I want to hear about this."

"You don't have to listen. I mean, it's nothing. Just that one of these days, she's going to pile into something, drunker than a skunk with that fuckin' old car of hers."

"What are you saying, Sister?" Carly was alarmed.

"Hey, calm down. I'm just saying she's going to end up doing us a favor by driving off the road one day in that old clunker." Wicked Sister's voice was low, "I just hope when she does, she doesn't take some poor innocent bystander with her, ya know?"

"As if you gave a fig about a poor innocent bystander!"

Carly chose not to think about what Wicked Sister was saying, not any aspect of it. She let herself wonder what Victor was doing at that moment. Then, deciding that was not a good subject to escape with, she turned back to the dinner with Frank and his story. Immediately she didn't like that, so she settled on Harold and Emily and what they could possibly be planning for her now. That subject wasn't good, either. Wicked Sister started to laugh.

"What's so funny?" Carly snapped.

"You are, you dits! Did you just see yourself running around in all kinds of frantic little circles, trying to avoid stepping in puddles and getting into muddy fuckin' trenches instead?"

Carly smiled. "Yeah, I guess there isn't much really good to think about, is there. That doesn't say much for life, huh?"

"Hey, I'm not complaining! Well, maybe a little. Let's just get the old bitch out of jail and get it over with. Maybe tomorrow will be better. Right now, I'm really sleepy. Wake me when we get there, will ya?"

"You know I will." Carly promised, then waited while she felt her slip away. There really wasn't much to think about, when it came right down to it. Especially with Wicked Sister asleep. She did keep things lively. She wondered what she would have done with Frank's invitation if it hadn't been for Wicked Sister. Turned it down for sure. It would be trouble, she sensed it; but now there was that connection. Was it with Wicked Sister exclusively?

A very large blue light shaped like a triangle bathed the front seat of the car in its exotic vibrant blue glow for the tiniest moment. Then, did she hear something?

"Carlen we are with you. We are with you."

Or was that Wicked Sister dreaming?

10

The righteous are unaware that they smell bad. They think the stink comes from the people next door. They keep moving because of the stench, but all the people next door keep on stinking. Duh.

Victor was untroubled by life or any of the times it threw at him. He was confident he'd managed everything very well and would continue to be effective in his life. It was true that he'd only made state awards as a running back but by the time he was in his senior year at MSU, he was almost positive that not getting drafted to the NFL wasn't going to be an issue at all. By that time, he was clear about his relationship to football and to Vietnam. No injuries, no maiming and no death was his goal. Obviously, in order to cement a clear pathway to attaining that goal, he would need to seek immediate employment; the job had to be excellent and he would have to find a way to avoid the draft after graduation. At one point, he'd considered getting Carly pregnant to avoid the draft, but that seemed too limiting, with overtones of finality. As much as he enjoyed that almost addictive sexual interplay they had going, he knew they weren't going anywhere particularly as a couple. It annoyed him that she thought in such narrow terms. Just get a little apartment, a job, get married, have kids and there's happiness on a plate. His concept of maturing was doing it in a huge mansion with servants, wearing $500 Italian suits, driving a Porsche to the Club for golf and a Rolls to the Club for dinner. He hadn't been much concerned about whether this scenario included a woman, a family—but if it did, it certainly couldn't be Carly.

She simply didn't have the class to walk alongside him in that life. So; he hadn't even had to think about it when Mandy Bickham entered the picture; she and her situation were ready made for his ambition as well as for his interest in avoiding Vietnam.

He had waited until she was seventeen before he made love to her, smart to avoid the statutory rape pitfall, then he did it as often as his schedule allowed. By the time Christmas break came, she was well into her third month. Frank Bickham had not been pleased, but Beatrice Bickham was and that's what counted. Bickham would do anything to keep his wife calm and steady and catering to Mandy was first on her list of things that made her placidly non-contentious. Victor hadn't planned it out in such detailed terms, really, but he certainly worked it, once it fell into his lap.

Looking out the window of Harold Seckinger's office and seeing the traffic, the verve, the busy-ness of the uptown section of Michigan Avenue, he was in a state of thorough self-satisfaction. It had all worked out so very well. Even to continuing to enjoy the long-legged pleasure Carly Worthington offered him. As a wife, she'd have exasperated him to fits, as a lover, she was absolutely yielding and respondent and was nicely tucked into a corner of his life that was all indulgence and no maintenance. From time to time, he'd ventured out to see what sleeping with a model might be like, or an ingenue and sometimes, just whoever was the attraction of the moment. And that was always fun, but the sex with Carly was hands-down unbeatable. And there she was every Wednesday night. It was a great life!

He smiled slightly as he acknowledged he ought to be thinking of something else. Thoughts of Carly brought arousal. Frank and Harold would be back soon and he ought not to have a monumental erection when finalizing the CSG buy. He laughed to himself as he turned back to the inner office, thinking about what he'd said to Frank as they wound up

Emily Hanford's half hour. "—doing independent research into employee satisfaction and loyalty levels—" Carly and he on her bed, playing, stroking, little kisses on the neck, talking about her job, the atmosphere at CSG. It was easy to get her to talk openly with him, they'd been together for so long. And it hadn't been a lie, employee satisfaction was an issue. And satisfaction with Carly was definitely a two way street. He laughed out loud this time.

"What's so funny?" Frank opened the door in time to hear Victor's laugh.

Smooth as always, Victor replied quickly, "Not much. Just thinking about something cute your granddaughter said the other day."

"I see. Well, you can tell me about it later," Frank said, "It appears the lawyers are waiting for us in the conference room."

"Okay, let's go." Victor was eager to get the final papers signed. It meant an interesting change in his function as an Executive VP with Bickham Enterprises and greater enrichment, if he could make everything at CSG work. The two men walked out of the office that would soon become Victor's and down the hallway to the large conference room. That, too, was situated at the front of the building with windows overlooking Michigan Avenue.

"Are you sure Harold's okay with this new twist?" Victor asked Frank. "Myself, I hate surprises and I don't trust that little—man." He'd been about to call Harold a "toad," one of Carly's favorite terms for him.

"If he's not," Frank replied in a low tone, "then the deal is off. He knows that and he wants to close worse than he wants to be top exec. He'll still be in charge of most of the operations, he does know a few things, but he'll answer to you as President of CSG. It'll be up to you to make sure he keeps his books straight and his staff relationships strictly professional."

89

"Not hard to do. I think there is some favoritism toward Emily Hanford, but remember, Frank, I know him from way back." Victor spoke in a low voice, too, as they stood in the hallway just outside the closed conference door. "If he has an interest in Emily, it's platonic, I guarantee you. I don't think Harold is actively homosexual but—"

"I understand. In any event, his personnel management skills will need watching. Together, the two of them seemed bent on excluding Carly Worthington from any participation in CSG current and future projects."

Frank looked down the hallway toward Carly's office, then back to Victor, "It's my opinion that Carly has a gifted mindset and she's very talented. Considering her veteran status at CSG, I feel she is a tremendous asset and I think it's wise to cultivate that. But we'll talk more about that later."

Frank looked back at Carly's office before turning to go into the conference room. Victor, not a sensitive man, nonetheless felt some niggling annoyance at—what? He couldn't define any one thing out of the several that may have penetrated, but there was something. It was not his nature to delve into things too deeply, and he was good at making his life work. Whatever it was that had bothered him would either surface or go away. Trusting that, he followed Frank into the conference room. He smiled. In less than a half hour, he would be President of CSG, Inc.

Frank had tried to think of any number of reasons he might amble down the hall toward Carly's office and seeing her there, just lean inside the door to say a friendly 'hello.' He had promised to call her and he would, but it was being here in the same building with her, on the same floor, probably not thirty feet from her office, her presence, that made him seek to see her face and have her smile at him. He understood perfectly well that he was utterly taken with her, there were a hundred things he wanted to give her; a million days he wanted to spend with her—and he understood, too, that being with her was completely unfair. Beatrice may be demented, but she was as healthy as any 61 year old had a right to be. She smoked, she drank, her body was saturated with all kinds of drugs, yet there she was, well and able, either having a violent episode or vacant of any expression. And he would be sadly so connected to the woman until she died, an event that was many years in the future.

"Are you ready, Frank?" It was Victor standing in the doorway of the conference room. The attorneys had gone on to the club, Harold with them and Victor and Frank had promised to join them after stopping by the Paper Company offices. "Shall I get my car?"

Frank turned back from his watch on Carly's office. "Sorry. Just thinking about how you might effect some re-arrangements here."

"Yes, I've had some thoughts on that, too. But we ought to get moving if we're going to stop at the plant before lunch." Victor felt again that tiny disturbance of his righteousness, then as was his way, he dismissed it. "I can drive, if you want."

"Umm—no, I think I'll drive out there myself." Frank said. "You go ahead, you're the one who has to stop at the plant. I want to do a couple of things here while they're fresh in my mind. I'll join you and the others at the club."

"Okay, see you there." Victor left the doorway and pausing just the slightest bit to look down the hall, he made his way out into the main reception area of the executive floor. He could now see Carly every day of the working week, plus Wednesday nights. Maybe he could install a couch in his new office, a lock on the door—and have Carly in for a working lunch. The thought excited him and he had to turn it off.

Frank watched Victor step into the elevator and as soon as the doors closed, he turned down the hall toward Carly's office. He would be free now to see her for a moment. He looked quickly at his watch; eleven forty-five, wondering what time they went to lunch at CSG. Twenty steps to her office. Would she be there? Had she gone to lunch? Would she be glad to see him if she was there?

The door to Carly's office had a glass panel the length of it and as he came up to it, he saw her, chin in hand, leaning over her drawing board. His heart leaped as he saw that fall of dark hair curling about her left hand. He wanted to touch it, to touch her. He opened the door, disturbing her concentration and she looked up to see him standing there. He felt like a gawky teenager.

There was a look that passed across her face, recognizing him, something like a caught lamb might look, he thought, then came the smile and everything else was out of his mind. "Frank!" she said. "I—expected you to call."

"I would have, but this is better." he said, smiling, hands in pockets to keep from reaching across her desk and touching her all over, scaring the dickens out of her, he was sure. "We completed the transaction this morning and the rest of them have gone on to lunch. I have to join them soon, but I wanted to stop by and say 'hello' as long as I was in the building."

"It's nice that you did," she said. Then again, he saw that charming little metamorphosis that came over her features as she laughed, lightly. "I'm glad. It's—exciting to see you. You look good."

She said it like she might be contemplating the perfect steak and he felt again that marvelous sense of primeval rightness in wanting her. In that moment fairness or not ceased to be a consideration. "And you are luscious." Frank said, "Can I see you tonight?"

"Yes, uh-huh! Emphatically yup!"

He laughed. She made him feel very welcome. "I'm completely enchanted, you know."

"Yeah, me too," she laughed again and with him. "I wasn't

the witch on this job, though. I don't know who set it up, but I'm damned glad the magic is working!"

"I hope the spell continues," he said in earnest. "I'll pick you up at 7? You have to see your mother again?"

"No," her eyes sparkled as she said it, "I—took care of that last night. 6 is great if you want."

"I want. 6 it is." He reached across the desk and quickly touched her hand, "I'll see you tonight. Dress casually, we'll go to a little harbor bar for dinner on the big lake."

"You mean Lake Michigan?" she asked. "That's kind of a jog, isn't it?"

"A short flight and a half a boat ride, that's all." Frank watched her face as she managed the itinerary. She was like a little girl on her first carousel ride. "Is that okay with you?"

"Damn straight!" she said. "I'll be the height of casual!"

He laughed again. "I know you will. See you at 6."

"I can't wait," she said to him as he left her office. He strode to the elevator feeling like the cock of the walk, the man of the hour, the King of Hamilton. "My God, you make me feel good," he said inside of himself to that Carly he carried there now.

93

11

Pleasure acts as if it's going to be there forever, but it is a temporal thing. Don't be fooled.

Carly had not really agreed to the three day trip, but Wicked Sister's excitement had been so unbounded, she'd been swept along by it, not taking the chance for a protest until later, when they were out on the boat. She noted with a mixture of awe and insecurity that the boat was more yacht than boat, a seventy-five foot cruiser, complete with two bedrooms, one a master suite, a galley and a bar, it had a captain, a cook and a steward. Having her own bedroom allowed Carly the privacy of a protest, which on Saturday morning, may have been a little late but no less vigorous. The first thing she said to Wicked Sister was: "We are out of our element!"

"Just because he's got all that money and can do things like this," Carly pointed out, "doesn't mean *we* can do things like this. We don't have the upbringing—besides, we have obligations and responsibilities. What if something goes wrong with Mother? What happens if Victor—"

"Goddammit, Carly!" Wicked Sister said, emphatically setting the tone, "Don't give me that Victor shit! He hasn't come around on a weekend in ten years, since the last kid was born and then it was only for three hours. Jesus Christ! What'd'ya think? There's gonna be a miracle all of a sudden and he's going to come and carry you off on his big fuckin' white horse? I don't think so."

Carly pursed her lips and looked out the cabin window at the endless dark blue of Lake Michigan's horizon. The boat rose and fell, rocking slightly with the swell as it motored slowly, hugging the Michigan coastline. "Listen," Wicked Sister softened her approach, "I don't like being so damn hard on you, but you got to get with the program, Sis. Jesus, here's this man who's my God falling head over heels for us, he's got all the money in the world, he's sweet, he's tender, he's considerate, he's so goddam good looking it breaks my heart! And you're pissing it all away on a guy who wouldn't—*hasn't*—give you the courtesy of one loving word in over twenty-two years. I mean, why was it we had to find out from Harold that Victor was involved in the CSG buyout? Why wouldn't Victor share that with us? Because, you don't mean shit to him, that's why. You're his Wednesday night fuck, his diversion from his fuckless Mandy marriage. Look at the picture, Carly. I mean fuckin' *look* at it!"

"I have looked at it! That's all I *do* is look at it!" Carly jumped out of the chair and went to the bed. She thought about throwing herself onto it, pounding it with her fist and bursting into tears like the people in the movies got to do. She couldn't do that. There would be no crying, now or ever. She sighed as she lowered herself into a prone position. "But— I know this, Sister—jumping from that frying pan into this fire isn't going to help anything."

Now it was Wicked Sister's turn not to say anything. She was not skilled at analyzing actions and outcomes or sparring with Carly's brand of logic. Carly went on, her tone controlled, but almost at a submissive level. "I also know that there's nothing to do about 'the old bitch'. Betta Mary does what she wants to do when she wants to do it. I don't think she even thinks about it, about any of it, it's just standard behavior with her. She could no more not do it, than she could *not* breathe. I suppose you'd call her a survivor. If she kills her only child to survive, if that's a requirement, she'll do it. I don't think I want to fight it anymore."

"What are you saying, Carly?" Wicked Sister spoke now, alarmed, "That's goddam not fair! I've got a stake in this, too, ya know." She let that thought linger there before she went on, "If you give in to that fuckin' old bitch's demands, and you let yourself be the weekly pound of an asshole who doesn't give a shit whether you live or die—well, what have I been doing all these years!?! Goddamit, Carly, give me a break here, huh?"

"I'd like to," Carly muttered, sleepily, "I really would. But I'm probably not up to it—"

"Carly!" Wicked Sister said, loudly. "If you fall asleep, goddammit—" Then she thought how maybe Carly falling asleep and taking a little nap wouldn't be all bad. Maybe she was just being nice, and after all, giving her the break she'd asked for.

Wicked Sister got up off the bed and took a quick look in the dresser mirror on her way out. Beautiful! She tucked the fall of hair back behind her ear like Carly did, pulled the beach robe back and assessed the impact of the body in a bikini, and went out the cabin door, knowing she was a knockout. It was time she and Frank got together. He'd been too much the perfect gentleman, hadn't even kissed her on the mouth, but there was desire there and it was time for consummation. She was now conveniently convinced that this was why Carly had so sweetly and quickly faded into sleep. On some level, Wicked Sister was certain, Carly wanted Frank as badly as she did.

Wicked Sister went up the three steps to the deck. The bridge was forward and she looked at the windows there but saw only the captain. Where would Frank be? Fishing? No, not off a boat like this. She walked along the deck, holding onto the deck rail, realizing her skimpy sandals probably weren't the best foot attire for boating. There was a glorious breeze and it smelled like sea; she stopped a moment to breathe it in, realizing as she did, that it was a rare time that she thought to indulge in benefits of the upper senses, like smell or taste. That was usually Carly's domain.

"Hey there." It was Frank's delicious baritone beside her ear. He wasn't touching her but he was close; she could feel the tingling as she reveled in his body heat. She turned quickly, smiling up at him, trying to be Carly-like. "Hi, I was looking for you."

"I'm here," his voice faded off as he looked down at her body exquisitely spilling out of the bikini. He couldn't seem to stop himself from lifting his hand and touching her breast. The moment rushed through them, holding them there as if they'd been struck by the electricity exuding from the touch of skin on skin. He pulled his hand back, "Carly, I'm sorry," he said.

Carly woke to look up at him, to see the look of shock and desire mixed on his features. Wicked Sister tried to maintain her hold but Carly quickly pulled the beach coat around her and looked away from him. "Please don't do that," she said, still hearing Wicked Sister's protests and feeling that deep unsettled urge that was her signature. She wasn't sure to whom she had addressed her plea, Frank or Wicked Sister.

"I am sorry if I offended you," he said, "but I want to do it again. Then more. I want to feel what it would be like to be next to you—"

"Frank, please stop it." Carly turned to go back below deck, but he took hold of her arm, carefully bringing her back to the mid ship's railing.

"I won't do it again. I promise." Then he smiled. "Today, anyway. Come on, let's get dressed and go out to dinner, okay? We're about to put into Frankfort, we can drive up into the Leelanau Peninsula for awhile, take a look at the dunes, then stop in for dinner at Le Bear. It's a beautiful spot overlooking Lake Michigan. What do you say?"

Carly smiled back at him. "It sounds wonderful," she said. As he took her hand to lead her to her cabin, she felt herself being drawn to his warmth. Wicked Sister's thoughts of touching him, arousing him, were suddenly wildly vivid in her mind and she took her hand away from his and hurried off to her cabin. "I'll be ready in a half hour," she said lightly to Frank. Then to Wicked Sister, she muttered, teeth clenched, "What are you trying to do, kill me?"

"No, just trying to get you fucked by a good man for once."

Before anyone wanted it to be, Sunday evening was upon them. Frank had all their gear out on the deck and he stood looking down at it like a lost pup. She came up the steps dressed in slacks and a blouse, just what she had worn when they'd started their adventure. He turned around when he heard her come onto the deck, "God, you're beautiful!" he said.

"And so are you." She didn't smile, neither she nor Wicked Sister. "I mean it. It's been a wonderful time. Thank you."

He came over to her and touched her face, "Don't sound like this is the end of it, Carly." He kissed her forehead, "It's not. It's the beginning."

She didn't say anything for a long time, confused by the sensations created by his light and considerate touch. But she had to make it clear to him. "When it's over, I can't help it—I just have to turn off and get ready for—um—everyday life."

"Don't say that. Please."

"I have to. It's what's real." She smiled this time, but pulled away from him, "*This* is pretend." She could feel Wicked Sister angrily poking at her, there were words but she didn't want them right then. They could argue later, when they got back to the apartment. Then there would be Scotch and regular things and in just a couple of days, there would be Victor and it was Victor, after all, who was real in her life, who she knew would always be there on Wednesday nights. And no matter how many men Wicked Sister had sex with, the only man Carly had ever made love to was Victor. That was her commitment.

The flight back was mercifully noisy, so no conversations were possible, but at the airport and on the way to the car, Frank was persistent. "Carly, I know I should never have asked you out in the first place," he had her arm as they came to car. He opened the door for her. "But by the same token, you could have turned me down."

"Would you have taken 'no' for an answer?"

He smiled a half smile as he got into the driver's side. "I would have been prepared to, eventually. Here it is, Carly, this is an attraction with a meaning, with an intent. It's much more than just a game or a lark, kidnapping you and setting a mood so that I could have my way with you—which, as you know, didn't work anyway."

"I know, Frank," she said, "I really do know. But it's over. We're back to our other lives. Almost, anyway."

He sighed. "There can be other weekends, weeks, nights—" he reached over and took her hand. "I know it's not ideal, but I do have time to be with you and I want to. I want to very much."

"You don't understand, Frank," she said, her hand still in his, "*I* have obligations."

He could only muster an "oh". He was silent until they pulled into her parking lot and stopped the car at the end of the west building sidewalk. He turned the engine off. "I'll help you up with your things."

"Thank you," she said. They both got out and he brought her luggage out of the trunk. They went together up the walk and as she started to insert the key into the outer door, he took it gently from her.

"That's my job," he said. He put his hand alongside her face and turned it up to him, "and I'd like to keep it."

She sighed again. "I don't know what to say, Frank."

They went through the door and started up the stairs. "Carly, I'll take what I can get. Whatever of your time you can give me." He waited until they came up to 2D and once again, he took the key from her hand, and he said, "Please think about it, will you?"

He opened the door and she went inside; he followed with her bags. "Where would you like these?" he asked. "The bedroom?"

She turned to look at him. He was such a puppy, a hopeful wag-tail look on his face, she smiled, then she started to laugh.

"It's funny?" He was sure her laughter wasn't derisive, but after that, he was lost.

"Yes," she laughed. "To the bedroom. Come with me."

"Gladly, I hope?" He was smiling.

In the bedroom he set the bags down on the carpet, looking at her face in the dimness, trying to see her expression. She seemed to be waiting for him to come to her. He moved quickly across the bedroom to where she was standing and embraced her. "Please let me love you, Carly," he whispered.

She could feel his arousal immediate and strong against her abdomen and without thinking anything further, still silent, she pulled him toward the bed. Their clothes seemed to fall away and they were close, body to body, and she moved carefully with him as they were together, wondering why he felt so sweet in her, his little cries seeking her insides and exploding there.

"I love you, Carly," he whispered, and it washed over her that what she was feeling was different than the urges created in her by Victor; that maybe this was the magical wind and sky and earth and lightning that had so eluded her. Perhaps it was his feeling for her that created her perfect response; a complete union, a give and a take, trust and caring. There was a spirituality about it, an almost sacred essence. Wicked Sister was quiet except for sighing the words he'd said again and again but Carly could say nothing, so choked she was with her own unworthiness.

12

A torrent of fate is a life storm that few can ever bear.

Carly could still smell his aftershave on the pillow. A gift, he would be with her then awhile longer. She reached for the pillow and pulled it closer to her. What time was it? How long had he been gone? Not long, she was sure, she could feel him around her still. Hugging the pillow, she turned over to see the digital on the bedside table. 12:03, it said in its red brilliance. That meant it was Monday already and in just a few hours, she would have to go to work—but maybe she would get a glimpse of him there. Maybe he would have to take care of more of the closing, more of the details of transition. Something to look forward to. Her eyes closed again and she thought about putting away the luggage, the new luggage he had bought for her, and all the beautiful clothes. She felt warm again, grateful and still in the circle of enchantment.

"He's here, Carly, I can hear him breathing." It was Wicked Sister, her voice a strident whisper. Carly's heart began to hammer, the voice was a danger warning voice that Wicked Sister had seldom ever used.

"Who's here?" she whispered back. Her eyes now were wide open trying to search the dark of her bedroom and she lay very still, as if moving would give her position away.

"Victor. He's here. He knows."

"What? What does he know?" Carly scanned the room, eyes adjusting to the dark. She saw no movement. Nothing out of order. "He isn't here, Sister. What's the matter with you?"

101

"Yes, he is!" She insisted, "He knows about Frank."

"What about him?" She didn't have to ask. If Victor was there, and he knew about Frank, he knew she'd made love to him. What would he do? Her mind hadn't grappled with that concept, yet, though as an outcome, it had been begging to be addressed. In the last two hours, there had been the glossed over hope that she could maintain Victor's Wednesday nights and whatever other time she would have with Frank would not touch Wednesday. Neither would be the wiser. Because for her there was always a consequence, eventually there would have to be one, but—so soon? She wasn't ready. She had no story and no guile to create one.

She heard the refrigerator door open and a clatter of ice cubes against glass. In a moment, she saw the kitchen light go on. "Come get your drink, Carly. I've got a Scotch waiting for you." It was Victor's voice. Then a stirring of the ice cubes. "We have to talk."

"What should I tell him?" Carly was frantic, trying to find a night gown, a robe. Her clothes were all over the floor, so unlike her usual fastidiousness. If he saw that, he would know. "Why is he here? It's a Sunday night. Sister, where are you? Will you help me?"

"I'm here," Wicked Sister said, but Carly felt her uncertainty which made her own intolerable. "Let's at least go in there, so he doesn't come in here."

"Carly. Are you coming in here or do I have to come in there and get you?" Victor called. His voice wasn't loud; it was lackluster, without depth, like softly banged tin.

She let the nightgown fall over her head, grabbed a robe from the closet and hurried into the kitchen. Her feet were bare.

"Surprise. What are you doing here?" She tried to insist the quiver out of her voice. "It's Sunday night." She looked at him as her eyes adjusted to the light. He was wearing a jogging suit, running shoes and his hair was mussed, out of character for him. His eyes were slate and expressionless, and his features were locked into an unchanging look that might have been the photo of a movie star, it was so still and handsome. Carly was afraid. She wasn't sure whether it was out of fear for what he might do about how much he knew or if it was the guilt of it written all over her body. Could he see Frank's handprints on her?

"Here's your drink," he said. He handed her the glass and to her horror, she realized he had gloves on and there was a stick, like a policeman's billy club in his belt. As she connected with the observation, she could feel Wicked Sister's frantic thoughts racing to try to outrun the surge.

She took the glass and sipped at it, trying a twitch of a smile, while her voice ranged unstably. "You didn't say what you're doing here. What's going on, Victor?"

He hadn't smiled and grabbed her, kissing her, thrust her onto the couch and began his first wave of lovemaking, his standard greeting. Fear was guilt and guilt was fear.

"Where have you been all weekend?" he asked, his voice still a low monotone.

"Away." She said with Wicked Sister, heart hammering but casually taking another drink. "That's allowed, isn't it? I don't ask you where you go on the weekends."

"Who were you with?"

She looked away and set the drink down on the counter. "I don't want to drink this. It doesn't taste good."

"Who were you with?"

She started to move out of the kitchen. "I've got to get up in the morning. I have to go to work."

"No, you won't be going to work," he said. His expression hadn't changed.

"Why not?" She turned back toward him again and as she did, felt his gloved hand grip her arm. It did not surprise her that he did it, but it hurt. "Why not, Victor?"

"You don't work there anymore." He said it without

inflection but his hand tightened on her arm. "You were with Frank. I saw you."

"Saw me?" She tried to back out of his grip but it was relentless. "What are you doing, Victor? You've got things wrong."

"I saw you fucking him and I heard you fucking him." The whole of it washed over her then, like a bath of acid, it burned her outsides off and with ugly realizations, one by one, ate slowly away at her center. He had been in the apartment the whole time Frank had been there.

She was dizzy with it; she had cuckolded her lover with his father-in-law while he watched and listened. It was outrageous and terrifying to the bone.

The stick he carried clattered to the floor as he dropped it and raised his fist all at once. It was Wicked Sister who realized the first blow was coming and she cried, "Watch out! O my God, Carly!" That one laid across Carly's forehead, just above her left eye; she felt blood warm the sudden wound and foolishly she thought about the leather gloves, wondering if they were a gift she had given him. After that, there was a mass of pummeling, and as she reeled from the blows, neither she nor Wicked Sister had any cognizant thoughts. At the last of it, she heard him speak, his tone unchanged.

"Goddam whore get what you deserve." Then he threw her down and she sprawled on the kitchen floor, legs akimbo. Before she could gather herself at all, he was on her, grabbing at her bloody nightgown. He ripped it from her body, hands still gloved and soaked with her blood, then he gripped her left breast and pulled at it as if to tear it off. She screamed with pain and he brought his hand to her mouth and held it there while he rammed his erection into her. "Fuck him fuck you bitch you bitch you bitch."

Just before she lost consciousness she heard him gasping his orgasm, sobbing out, his voice now round with his rage, "Goddam you to hell Carly!"

———

Carly felt keys drop onto her chest from a height that insured a buildup of gravitational momentum and they hit her hard, stirring her to wake and try to find the source. The shadow of Victor was all she could see through the blur of the one eyelid she could open. She moaned as she tried to move, to sit up and take stock of her body. The keys fell across her left breast, stunning her into an awful awareness of pain and a fear of what Victor would do next. Yet, she was glad that he had not left her; that he was still there—that meant there was hope. If he didn't love her, he wouldn't have reacted. If he didn't love her, he wouldn't have awakened her, wanting to make up to her for what he had done. But the keys? Why the keys?

"Just so you know," he said, his voice once again even, almost ordinary, "I'm giving your keys back. I don't do whores."

She made her way up to one elbow and gingerly felt of her breast to assure herself that it was still attached, though the pain was declaration enough of that. She struggled the rest of the way to a sitting position and then to her knees. A warm gush of liquid dribbled down her inner thigh and trickles of blood continued to line her face, but she tried not to mind; it was important to make sure Victor knew she was sorry so that he'd stay. "Victor," she croaked, "I didn't want to do it. It was—I didn't mean to. I'm so sorry, Victor. You know I only love you."

Carly looked up at him but couldn't see the glaring eyes or the smirk on his handsome mouth. "You are a whore, Carly. I don't give a shit who you fuck."

She knew what he said was true, and she'd been deserving of the beating. She had gone where she had forbidden herself to go; and she had to make him understand it was an accident. She couldn't let him leave her. As he turned to go, she grabbed his leg, wrapping her arms around it in a vise grip. Her face pounded and her body was a mass of unidentified anguish

105

but the grip was like holding onto life—she must not let go. "Don't leave me, Victor. Please don't go."

He laughed, a gruesome sound but Carly was oblivious. Keeping him there was her only focus. She couldn't hear Wicked Sister loudly insisting that Carly release her grip on his leg.

"OK, bitch, you want to ride, huh?" He laughed again, "I'm leaving one way or the other."

"Victor, don't leave, me, please, please, please don't go!" It was an awful moment but Wicked Sister was forced to endure it anyway, being blocked from escape through some mechanism Carly had in place suddenly. Victor, strong and athletic, kicked at Carly with every step he took toward the door, laughing as if it was a contest. Could she, would she hold on until he reached the hallway? Then, would she allow herself to be dragged, bloody and half-naked down the hall to the stairs? No matter what, Victor would win and there was nothing else to him, ever, that mattered. At the apartment door, Carly's grip fell away and she lolled backward onto the carpet, sobbing.

"You used to be a good fuck and worth the trouble," he said enunciating each word carefully, uncharacteristically. "You disgust me now." He moved his foot to give her one last jab for emphasis, but amazed, felt his foot held by two strong hands and saw the deadly stare of the one good eye. There was no sobbing suddenly and a force came out of the grotesquely beaten body that prickled his backbone.

"You'd better fuckin' mean it, Victor," Wicked Sister said. "It's not like you can it take back, ya know."

He was surprised again as he felt his foot twist and his weight thrown to the side and backward. He smashed into the door with a crack of elbows and skull.

"Now you can fuckin' get your ass outta here," Wicked Sister said, laughing softly. "I'm done."

———

Carly had never endured a pain so deadly and all encompassing. She could not feel if anything was broken, the pain so vigorous it masked any inventory. She wasn't even sure why she was moving, or trying to, then the sound of the phone came into her awareness. It was an insistent demand, the ringing phone, no matter what the bell sound, and all are programmed to respond to it, almost instinctively. She couldn't take stock of her face, but in the pain throbbed a tightness of it and her left breast was a solid ache. She tried to look at it, but her left eye was swollen shut and her right eye seemed to have something obscuring the left part of its vision. Out of the narrow scope of sight she saw blood on her inner thigh but she wasn't alarmed at that. Her nightgown was in shreds and her robe was splattered with drying blood and that was alarming. It would never come out. Amazing how the phone kept ringing.

It stopped as she managed to stand up. The robe slipped over her shoulder and threatened to fall off. She pulled it up and around her, then she started to shake. The phone had stopped ringing and was now busily taking a message. She must get to it. Maybe it would be Victor, telling her that none of this had happened and she would wake up in the morning and laugh at this bad hangover dream.

It was moments, minutes, hours later that she reached the phone, red message light blinking, on the pass-through counter. She punched in the message retrieval button and a voice she hated came into her ear:

"Carly, this here's Norbie Kincaid. I's with your ma tonight at the Cabin and she's tellin' a story, you know, like she does and she just fell down and couldn't breathe. We got the 911 and they come out and took her t' the hospital. Can you come here? The doctor says you should come on."

The line clicked over to dial tone and Carly tried to think if he had said which hospital and how would she ever get there? Then the machine beeped, the tape started to whir

107

again and his voice came back, "Uh—it's St. Lizbeth Hospital, Carly, I forgot. Come on to here."

She turned back to the kitchen and through her one half good eye saw the mess on the kitchen floor—blood and semen and dirty nightgown scraps, a bloody billy club. It must be cleaned up before she could leave for the hospital.

13

One thing's for sure in life; you're not getting out until you're done with you.

She couldn't believe it was only 1:35 AM. It was hard to look at her face in the mirror. Wicked Sister was wretched with remorse. "I'm sorry Carly. I should have done something more than I did. Knocking him over was just fuckin' puny! Maybe I could have grabbed a knife and stabbed him when we were in the kitchen. I saw it coming, I knew he was going to go off like that. God I'm so sorry. Look at us."

Carly thought about Wicked Sister's picture of stabbing him in his lean torso, thrust that knife in and pull it out and do it again and again! And make him hurt and bleed. She felt the anger and the remorse and the sad, sad, Carly sorrow. And now, Betta Mary in the hospital—*trouble, trouble, always trouble*. But, hating her; she had to go there.

"No, you don't have to, Carly. Look what's happened to us! Let the old bitch die!"

"I have to go, Sister. There is no one else."

"How will you drive, for fuck's sake? You can't even see!" Wicked Sister was stridently vigorous in her protests. "Call the hospital and tell them you can't drive! Good Christ, even God wouldn't expect you to go!"

"I can drive. I have to go." Carly said, poking a q-tip at the gash above her closed left eye. The pain, cleansing in its intensity, clarified her.

"Look, look! See what he's fuckin' done!" Wicked Sister railed, "He's cut us, made us ugly! Now Frank won't ever—"

"Shut up!" Carly said without even slightly raising the

tone, "Frank would never do anything again with us anyway. We are stupid to think anything like that could ever work out. It might have gone on for a couple more weeks but that would have been it. We are who we are, remember? Gramma said that, and she was right."

"No, Carly, he said he loves us!" Wicked Sister's voice weakened all of a sudden, and even she knew, as she repeated her own words, that there was no use to wish for the impossible. "He did love us, though. He said he loved us."

"Yeah, well, everybody gets something in life; we got our fifteen minutes and now it's over. We should never have expected any more. It's all just too much and I'm so damned tired."

"Well, let's just go to bed, then. We need some rest. Come on, Carly. It's not good to talk that way." Wicked Sister had little memory, as she was the pro-active one, but she tried now to connect with Carly's rememberings, to bring up something that would bolster her, cheer her or maybe even make her laugh. For the first time, she found the memory box was locked and no matter how deftly she manipulated it, she couldn't make it unlock.

"I know what you're doing, Sister. It's not going to work; it wouldn't anyway. There's nothing in there but ugly horrid things—things we've done—telling who we are. Whore. Like Victor said. Disgusting. We are who we are." Carly brushed her hair back and surveyed as best she could with the one good eye, the swollen, bruised mass of flesh on her cheekbones, around her nose and mouth and eyes. Never beautiful, but acceptable, her countenance now was exactly what she was, a grotesque visage that reflected the very core of Carlen Worthington.

Charwoman's mirror.

"I'll see Betta Mary through this hospital thing," she said to Wicked Sister, "then I'm done with it. I can't do it anymore."

"Quit talking like that, Carly." Wicked Sister's tone had changed from worry to quiet and orderly. That was one thing Wicked Sister could never do; hide who she was and what she felt. "I'm not fuckin' kidding, you know."

"I know. But it doesn't matter what you say or what you threaten. I'm finished with everything. I'll manage this Betta Mary thing, then I'm done."

There was an awful deadness in the room then, Wicked Sister could not find a sparkle anywhere about the contorted aspect that looked back at her. Her own wild beauty had been overwhelmed by this wretched ugliness and it seemed it would never be right again. A large blue light glowed from the mirror but neither Carly nor Wicked Sister paid any attention to it, so lost they were in their trouble.

Wicked Sister was right. She shouldn't be driving. Her insides were tormented by a painful looseness, as if her guts had been left in disarray and needed reforming. Her left eye was now throbbing, her cheekbones hurt and the right one felt as if it was growing erratically under her eye, sending bone spears into the orb to bedevil it. She could barely see the road for the blur. It was in her favor that it was 2 A.M. and that there was an abundance of streetlights and little traffic.

"Jesus, Carly, we'll be lucky if you don't kill someone." Wicked Sister said, "I hope that was a curb you went over back there and not a fuckin' body!"

"Right now, I don't much care."

"Well, I do! I don't want to go sit in some cell for the rest of my life and have some fuckin' goon woman come on to me." Wicked Sister went back to the moment of the first few blows. She had always been able to dodge things like that;

111

always able to figure things out and to counter with better than what was coming at her. It disturbed her in ways she could not articulate; her particular failure in that moment and then, in trying to escape from it, being indelibly locked to Carly's moment, too. She had never hated Victor more. "We're going to call the cops on Victor, Carly. I goddammed fuckin' will if you don't."

Carly turned the car into the hospital emergency parking lot but she couldn't see well enough to fit the car into the one available parking space between two other cars. She parked in the handicapped spot, knowing very well that she'd be ticketed. Getting caught at anything she did was inevitable, but it was beginning to be true: she didn't care much. "Go right ahead. As soon as you do," Carly said, "guess who's going to be one of the first to find out his son-in-law has been arrested for the assault and rape of the woman he spent the weekend with. How do you think that will play with Mr. Frank Bickham? Or Mrs. Frank Bickham for that matter."

"I see what you mean." Wicked Sister was quiet for a minute.

"He knows I can't do anything about it. He knows I probably wouldn't anyway, even if I could." Carly thought about Victor's leaving her apartment and it was like a blow all over again, then she wanted to be back to that non-caring level. "I am always his, still, always losing him. He would never have done this if he didn't love me. But I couldn't keep him there, after what happened. He's done with me now. And who would blame him?"

The car's wheels rammed into the cement parking barrier and the car jolted to a stop. Carly turned the engine off, picked up her purse, eased it over her left shoulder and got out of the car. She did not acknowledge Wicked Sister; nor did she care whether or not she would come with her.

"Goddammit, Carly!" Wicked Sister came close to her, "You have got to get a fucking hold of yourself. Don't you see that worthless asshole is *married*, for Chrissakes? Beating you—*us* to a bloody pulp doesn't mean he cares! It means he's fuckin' crazy, is what! Jesus Christ!"

Carly didn't respond. She opened the doors to the Emergency Room entrance and made her halting way to the reception desk. Wicked Sister kept at her: "Nobody beats someone up, Carly, then fuckin' rapes them, if they're sane. That's what criminals do. Perverts. If Victor loved you so much; then why didn't he ever say so? Or why doesn't he ever ask about you; how you're doing? What do you want? What can he do for you, for a fuckin' change? Huh?"

"He does that. All the time." Carly snapped, "He asked a lot about work, and was I happy there—he cares—well, he did, anyway."

"Don't be stupid, Carly. He asked about work because he wanted to know what was going on there, not because he fuckin' had to know you were happy. That was all just to impress Frank with how much he knew about CSG and won't he make a fine corporate president."

"It doesn't matter anyway." Carly said, trying to read the signs over the reception window. "He's finished with me and nothing else interests me enough to care."

"I know you felt close to Frank." Wicked Sister softened her tone. "I felt what you felt. You want to love him and he loves us. We can get through this, Carly. Frank isn't like Victor."

"I told you it doesn't matter. Now, leave me alone, I've got to get this done and over with."

As Carly stood at the receiving window, waiting for someone to come and help her find Betta Mary, Wicked Sister felt the barriers close around her again. She had been closed off before, she had gone away voluntarily when things were going on that she didn't like, but she'd never felt so barred, without the luxury of movement or access or even escape. It was at once maddening and frightening, two sensations that

Wicked Sister had little experience with. She watched as best she could while Carly dinged on a little bell at the window, then pushed a buzzer, but she couldn't move or speak. Carly had effectively cut her off.

A harried looking woman, short and stout and with irreverent curly red hair came up to the window from the other side. "Yes?" she said. "May I help you?" Then she saw Carly's swollen beaten face, buzzed the door open and said, "Come in through that door and sit in one of these chairs. I'll get someone."

Looking out from the face, only feeling it from the inside made it difficult for Carly to comprehend the woman's reaction, then, when it descended on her that the woman was going for someone to help her with her injuries, Carly called out, "No, wait. It's my mother—" But the red-headed woman was down the hall, already disappearing into a room. Carly looked around, trying to think what she should do to find Betta Mary. She couldn't sit down as the woman had instructed, she had to keep moving and not think about anything except what to do. She felt a little stream of blood tickle her cheek again and she became annoyed. It was from the cut over her eye and it was supposed to have stopped. She felt for a tissue in her purse and coming up with one, she forced it against the swollen area and pressed hard into the cut. "Stop it! Stop bleeding!"

"Hon, it's not going to stop bleeding if you don't stop poking at it." A firm voice came from behind her as someone took her arm, gently moving her hand away from her face. She turned around to see who might be so accosting her but all she could determine was that it was a squarish young man just an inch or so taller than she, with light colored hair, who seemed to exude grins with his voice.

"Now, come with me and Nurse Ratchett here will take your stats while I'm stitching that cut and checking out your fight schedule." His voice smiled again, "I want to see the other guy."

Carly then became confused; perhaps she had come to the hospital to be treated. It seemed that way, but no; there was the Betta Mary thing. "Is this St. Elizabeth's?" she asked as the young man led her to a small room.

"Yes, this is the Trauma Center. The only one in Hamilton, which is probably why you came here, huh?" The young man steered her to a narrow bed or table, it was difficult for her to distinguish, then he said, "I'd like to have you lay back here and I'll get at that cut and take a look at the rest of you. Oh, by the way, I'm Dr. Steele. William Robert Steele, but my friends call me Billy Bob."

The red-headed nurse giggled as she did every time he made the joke, then as Carly made a move to get up, the nurse came to stand beside her and pressed her hand lightly on her chest, urging her to a prone position. Carly cried out, surprised, as the pain from her left breast came to life again.

"What's this?" Dr. Steele asked. Then to the nurse, he said, "Don't you think you ought to get the ward clerk? This patient has to be admitted in some form or another."

"I don't know where she is—" the nurse began.

"Get her anyway," he said. Then once more turned back to Carly, "What's your name, beautiful?"

"Carly." It was as much as she wanted to say.

"What happened to you?"

"I fell down in the shower," Carly said, surprised that she could lie so quickly. "But I'm not here to get treated. I can live with the cut. I came here because I got a phone call from my mother's ex husband. She's supposed to be in here."

"Okay. What's your mother's name?" He asked evenly, preparing the cut over her eye for stitches. "And by the way, you can fool some of the people all of the time and all of the people some of the time but you can't shuck this ER doctor

───

115

who's seen every possible kind of domestic and not so domestic violence injury. Hon, what you got is *not* the result of a shower related accident. Hold still, this is going to sting a bit." He pushed the plunger on the syringe filled with a local anesthetic.

She muttered her mother's name. "Betta Mary Kincaid." Too much for Carly, she lay still, not caring again.

"I'll get that checked out for you." He deftly brought the needle to the lip of the wound and connected it to the other, "don't want to purse them lips—that can make for a nasty scar. I coulda been in plastics—" He laughed, then asked quickly, "Were you raped tonight?"

"NO!" She said too loudly, then more calmly, "Why would you ask something like that?"

"Because your slacks are bloody at the crotch with a mix of fluid that looks remarkably like semen, starting to dry. You're cut and bruised from a beating and that nasty bruise on your left breast is showing on your chest and neck. I'll bet money that if I examined you, I'd find that you've recently had sexual intercourse and in a way that wasn't fun for you."

"It's personal and it doesn't matter anyway," Carly said, sighing. "I'm just supposed to find my mother. I don't know why she's here. Probably drunk."

"Okay, Nurse Ratchett will check on that, too."

Carly tried to think back if she'd heard him say anything to the red-headed nurse about her mother, but she couldn't remember. The sting the doctor had predicted was now turning into tingling at the edge of an ever-widening circle around her eye, its lid and her cheekbone. It felt strange, then stranger still as the doctor began to stitch the gashed flesh back together, like he was pulling on a piece of leather that had somehow got itself attached to her face. Wicked Sister was roiling around somewhere, but Carly put her back and closed that place. She knew that for Wicked Sister it would be like watching a movie with no sound. She didn't feel badly about doing it, though. She didn't feel anything.

Yes, you do. You're hiding it. Charwoman's coming.

"There, that's about it. Just one little clip," the sound of a snip accompanied his announcement, "and we're done. Now, anything you want to report? Name, rank and serial number?"

"No." Carly said simply.

"Well, I have to have something here," the nurse was back waving a clipboard. Carly wondered how long she'd been standing there. How long had the stitching taken? Had she fallen asleep? "And by the way," she said, "your mother is up in CCU. She came in with Congestive Heart Failure and had quite a time, but she's stable now."

"What's Congestive Heart Failure?" Carly turned to look at the nurse, but the doctor answered instead.

"It's a conditional heart attack, more or less. For whatever reason, the heart isn't pumping in regular beats and when that happens, the blood doesn't carry oxygen through the system, so it starts to shut down. Fluids fill the chest cavity and the abdominal area sometimes, too, but the lungs are the vital organs affected. The patient can't breathe; one bad thing leads to a worse thing, the heart is crowded and its erratic pumping is affected even more adversely. It's a condition that can be remedied to some extent, depending on the patient." Dr. Steele looked over at the nurse, "Who's the attending on this one?"

"She doesn't have one. Dr. Mitchell took it. He said he's going to consult with Dr. Rosen in the morning." The nurse held up her clipboard again, and nodded her head toward Carly, "But I really need *her* name, address and hospitalization. Beth's over on south hall with that van-car head-on. There's eight of them with only two insured. A nightmare."

Dr. Steele looked at Carly and smiled again. "All of that means that our ward clerk is busy, so we have to know who you are so we can bill your insurance company. Okay?"

117

"Who's Dr. Rosen?" Carly asked, then, "When can I go see my mother? I have to get that done with."

"Dr. Rosen is a heart specialist and you can go see your mother as soon as I get your stats and make up my mind if I'm going to report this as an assault and battery or as a sexual assault." His voice was smiles, but his words were trouble. "I'm obligated to report these kinds of traumas just as much as if you'd been shot or if you were an abused child."

"Why?" Carly asked, now wary, feeling imprisoned with his intent. Was he lying to her, trying to get her to give him a name? "It's my business, not anyone else's."

"Because if there is potential criminal conduct here, even if you're into something very consentually kinky, the people who grant my license to practice medicine in this state don't care. Not to mention that the police are interested in DNA samples, in identifying serial rapists, and in having some evidence on file in your case if this thing happens again. The kind of beating you took tonight could easily have killed you. Domestic violence has a tendency to have very lethal outcomes." Smiles again, "But you know what, hon? I would much rather simply chat with you, get to know what you're about, than force you to violate some kind of sacred code thing you've got going on with the bozo who did this to you. In any case, I need your name, address and insurance provider. Nurse Ratchett, here, seems quite without recourse. Hey Lucille?"

He turned toward the nurse with the clipboard who stood inside the doorway watching them as she might a segment of *Days Of Our Lives*. She laughed at him and came around by the other side of the table Carly was on, to her good eye side. "You know, dear," she said to Carly, "you have to watch him. He's dangerously funny."

"I don't know why anyone would want to talk to me. I have nothing to say." Carly didn't directly address the nurse or the doctor, but spoke to the door jam beyond them, a place where her one eye's vision had fixed upon. Then without changing tone, she recited the litany of her self; name, address, employment, insurance and didn't watch while the nurse wrote it down on her clipboard. She didn't see the doctor in her narrow scope of vision so she assumed he had gone on to other patients. It surprised her mildly when she heard his voice again.

"Some people might want to talk with you to find out how in the dickens you got here. Take a cab?" Dr. Steele said, his voice alive with a sense of fun that Carly found almost depraved at the moment, and it irritated her. "Other people might want to chat with you to find out why an obviously intelligent woman such as yourself would throw herself around in a shower that way."

The nurse, Mabel, laughed again. "See?" she warned.

"Well, I don't think that's funny. I'm going to see my mother." Carly said, rising to a sitting position at the edge of the table and once again, feeling the warm gush of liquid begin to soak her slacks even more. In her mind, she chastised Wicked Sister for distracting her so that she didn't think to use a pad. Her head pounded and she felt weak-kneed but she slid off the table anyway and stood straight, hiding her agonies. She was determined to walk out of the room, head up, find her mother in CCU, wherever that might be and get that obligation over with so she could get on with what she intended.

"Okay, that's it." Dr. Steele said, moving toward her, "Mabel, get her a gown and help her off with her clothes. There's something very wrong here."

"Right." Mable said, looking at the wide circle of blood at the edge of the table where Carly had sat for that moment. It was then, seeing both of them look, that she turned around to see that the paper coverlet she'd been sitting on was soaked with blood, glistening wet and red under the bright fluorescent lights.

119

Suddenly, there were no bones in her legs. She let go of her purse and it clanked to the floor, keys jangling. The only reason Carly did not follow the purse just as noisily, was because the young Dr. Steele caught her on the way down.

"Jesus, Carly!" Wicked Sister was finally free to speak, "What the fuck did that goddammed Victor do to us?"

14

A stitch in time saves nine; but who knew time was torn?

Wicked Sister was with Carly now, hovering, watching the doctor as she performed the surgery. Wicked Sister said nothing, though, because Carly was in a black closed place and she couldn't be heard without at least some of Carly's will involved. Just as Wicked Sister did not indulge in the alcohol Carly seemed to need, she was equally unaffected by the anesthetic but Carly was out, lank and like the dead. Wicked Sister did not like the feeling but conceded to herself that it was better than Carly wilfully shutting her off. She promised herself that she would remind Carly about that and in no uncertain terms when the drugs wore off. It was just not fair.

The doctor performing the surgery was not Dr. Steele, who, Wicked Sister had learned was not a surgeon, whose specialty was trauma. This doctor, a woman, was a surgeon who specialized in gynecology. Wicked Sister had never paid much attention to any of the problems involved in Carly's physical situations, development, the menses, the pathetic little urges she had to get pregnant. "That's not fucking going to happen now," Wicked Sister mused to herself. Carly had passed out back in the ER but Wicked Sister had stayed awake, not thinking much, just listening to the medical staff diagnose the problems the hated Victor had imposed on them.

"That animal really did a number on her," Dr. Steele said, as he examined Carly. "My God, she's torn all the way up to her chin, practically."

"A bit of an exaggeration, doctor?" Lucille asked.

"Not much of a one. Hey, where's the gynecologist? Wasn't she supposed to be in the hospital?" Dr. Steele worked swiftly to swab the bleeding vaginal area. "We've got to get this woman to surgery and get the bleeding stopped. Did you schedule the OR?"

"I don't know, doctor and yes, doctor and yes, I did, doctor." Lucille said, taking the bloodied gauze from the floor, out of his way, to the disposal bin. "I'll page Dr. Lefkowitz again."

A woman came into the room, a stethoscope dangling out of her lab coat pocket. "Don't bother," she said, "I'm here. Got held up on four. Sorry. What have we got, Bill, do you know?"

"Hi Rachel. What I know for sure is that someone really did a number on her. She just wandered in here looking for her mother who was brought in for CHF and look at her. She wouldn't let us examine her, but I insisted on stitching the cut over her eye; then the proverbial feces hit the fan and here is what we've got."

"I see you've started packing her. Where are the tears, specifically?"

"All the way up the vaginal wall. I think the cervix is ruptured. I was going to try cauterizing, but the tears are too deep and I can't stitch her up here; she needs more anesthesic than I got—but there's more." He pointed at the nurse, motioning her to get the orderlies and the surgery cart. "By the way, you're scheduled for OR2, it's free. She's had her left breast maimed and I've been so busy with the other end, I'm not sure to what extent. You'll probably want to look at that, too. It's your call, but I don't know, get a cosmetic guy in here maybe?"

"Has she been to C-scan?"

"Dr. Lefkowitz, I'm hurt, dismayed!" He smiled, watching the orderlies move Carly and all the tubes and the blood drip to the gurney and wheel her out. "But yes, we did a C-scan.

C'mon, I'll show you what there is—it's your field. You'll know a whole lot more than me when you see the pictures. Oh, yeah, her cheekbone's cracked, too. I think her vision will be okay in a week or two, but I've asked Terry Peeks to stop in and take a look at her. Isn't that funny? Dr. Peeks, the ophthalmologist!" He laughed. Dr. Lefkowitz didn't, so focused she was on the C-scan results.

Wicked Sister did not at all like seeing their body placed in such a position without the benefit of a man on top of it and his best part in it. "Of course," she conceded again to herself, "that's what got us into this. That fuckin' Victor. One of these days I'm going to get rid of him once and for all."

Wicked Sister slept for awhile; there wasn't anything else to do. The operating room had been bustling at one time, but then, when the damage had been repaired, Dr. Lefkowitz called it good. Nothing else going on. Carly was still out. Wicked Sister couldn't feel a stir of consciousness, a breeze of a thought but she couldn't leave their body to go anywhere else. It was boring.

When she woke up, they were in a big room, some sort of group place, she thought. She heard the nurses talking. At least something was going on.

"This one's had a unilateral mastectomy and implantation." The taller nurse said.

"You mean a one-sided boob job?" the dark haired nurse chuckled.

"Oh, nice! You take lessons from Dr. Steele, did you?"

"Actually, I did work with him in Trauma when I first started. I couldn't take the action, though. It's a wizzy-wiggy atmosphere down there!"

"Okay. I forgive you then," the taller one said, "the chest and breast tissue is still swollen but Dr. Celez did a great job matching it with the one they didn't have to take off. Look." The nurse pulled the cover back and lifted the gauze covering over Carly's left breast. "He's a great surgeon. If I ever decide on a face or a rump lift, he's the one to do it."

"What happened to her?"

"That goddamned Victor happened to her, is what." Wicked Sister said angrily, but they couldn't hear her.

"She was raped. The man beat her up pretty badly, I guess. Torn vaginal wall and cervical rupture and—"

"Yeah, I saw that on the chart. But the boob." The dark haired nurse looked quizzically at the traumatized tissue around the breast. "What did he do, tear that off, too?"

"Almost, I guess. I don't know. Dr. Steele treated her when she first came in. He was up here a few minutes ago, but he didn't say much. He wasn't cracking jokes like he usually does, you know?"

"I don't get how any guy can do something so horrible. I mean it's just—deranged. Criminal. That poor woman."

"Yeah," Wicked Sister agreed, "that's what I said. But can you believe she wants to fuck him some more. Good Christ!"

The two nurses had only Carly and two more patients in the Intensive Care Unit. They kept a check on vital signs, drips, color and the general well-being of their patients and once in awhile, they had a conversation. Inane for the most part but if they turned to a subject Wicked Sister could relate to; she became alert, trying very hard to become a part of what they were saying; trying to be heard. Hover though she might, she could not get more than a couple of feet away from Carly. It had never occurred to her that she had less than a grip on the body; that it ruled her, rather than she commanding it. She was without voice as long as Carly lay in a drugged stupor. She could not move arms, insist on toes wiggling, a leg bending, or bring the torso forward to a sitting position. Even the beautiful hands, circled now with the bruises from Victor holding her wrists, would not move, not a twitch. Wicked Sister had only once gone beyond the moment

---

124

when Carly wasn't with her, a part of her, asleep, maybe but alive and interested in their life together.

Now morose, she lay back on the bed with Carly. She could never take an initiative in acting out the life. She came and went as she pleased, but always there when Carly needed someone brassy, gutsy—someone who could do what was necessary to get through the many tough moments that had been thrown at them by life. She'd never done it alone, though. Not once had she taken the actual first step. Carly had always been there, exactly beside and behind her, thinking, maybe even arguing but sharing warm thoughts, admiring her. Even when she was outrageous, even when she was at her wildest, Carly was always there to chide her, to disapprovingly approve. Wicked Sister was not capable of thinking beyond the moment, nor had she ever really known fear. Carly did, however. Carly was almost always afraid of something or other. But this new feeling for Wicked Sister, this way of being, was without description. It went beyond Carly fear because Carly now seemed unafraid. And it wasn't the drugs nor was it the pain they conquered. It was something about what Carly had been thinking. Getting it done with. Seeing to Betta Mary and then, that's it. Victor didn't love her anymore, we are who we are, things like that. Slut. Disgusting. Not caring about Frank. Being ashamed and remorseful of making love with him. And wanting Victor more than life.

That was the fright within Wicked Sister. Victor would win. Laying back down with Carly, hovering over her a forearm's length away, she couldn't help but speculate about what would happen to her if Carly did it again. And that speculation was utterly new to her; to think in terms of actions and to project consequences of those actions. If Carly did that drinking thing again that had sent Wicked Sister into a place of half world, where all was quiet, no one to talk to, no way to move, but only to be alive without life. Forever connected yet detached. Like when Gramma had been buried

125

in the box, unmoving dead, expressionless. Would she be in a box with Carly, in the dark without voice? Would she be there forever, looking at the white satin puff surrounding their body growing darker with mold as each day kept the sun from her? Who would she talk to if Carly couldn't move? Who would she be?

Oh, it was all too much to think about! "Wake up, Carly!" Wicked Sister demanded. "Come on, wake up!" She moved around her trying to find the box with the memories in it, to grab something important and force it into her; anything to wake her up. "Carly, it's me. Come on, Carly, wake up. Wake up, wake up!" There was the box and it wasn't locked this time. Wicked Sister insisted the lid open and horrified, saw there was nothing there. "Nurse, nurse, nurse!" she cried. "Come look at Carly. Come see her, tend her. She has no memories! Hurry!"

But neither of the nurses turned away from their station. No monitors beeped an alarm to tell them that one of their patients was in trouble. The drips were secure, their vital signs were each exactly registering as they should be and certainly, Carlen Ann Worthington, the poor woman who'd been so brutally beaten and raped wasn't due to wake out of the pain killing drugs for another 3 hours yet.

No memories at all in the box and now, there came a full and glowing blue light that moved carefully to wrap itself around Carly's bed. The nurses didn't see it at all, but Wicked Sister was so afraid.

15

Here's a riddle: In the distant woods, a tree falls and no one is within earshot. Is there a sound? Answer: Not if the neighboring trees catch it before it hits the ground.

"Carlen, we are here. We are with you." Carly looked up to see the group of glowing blue entities, spearheaded by the one Blue One, smiling countenances all, floating just above the floor. She was laying on her side in the hospital bed, a light blanket over her legs, the hospital gown tied loosely in the back. She touched the pillow to be sure she was really there in the bed. It was not puffy like her pillow at home and it felt crisp almost. She wiggled her toes and looked at her hands. There were bruises on her wrists which reminded her of Victor, but that was just a passing thought, not the spear through her middle like before. She felt of her face and sure enough, there was the lump on her cheekbone, the bandage on her forehead, but she could open both eyes with almost full vision and she felt great; just great!

"This is a dream, right?" She wasn't sure to whom she should address the question; to the whole group or just the one blue man in front. She raised herself up on one elbow with the intention of sitting up, but immediately fell back when a sharp pain tore through her gut then the genitalia and her left bosom felt as if it might fall off. "No," she conceded, "Not a dream, or I wouldn't have felt that."

"That is correct," the one answered. "You now experience a conscious level that is neither dream nor the material reality to which your human body is accustomed. Though, as you have discovered, the current level of reality allows you the

127

sensations commonly experienced in the flesh, if such is chosen. This is so that you may assume a comfortable normalcy."

"Who are you?" She attempted to sit again, and remarkably, this time there was no pain. "I've dreamed about you before, though, haven't I?"

"We are the teachers," the one smiled and moved closer to the bed. As he did, the whole group moved with him, like a wave of blue would surge across the ocean. Carly tried to allow the concept of their vastness fitting into the small hospital room not to challenge her perspective. She looked to the next bed, the curtain pulled half way between the two beds with someone obviously in it, feet covered over by only a sheet and wondered how it was all of them could be in the cramped two bed room at the same time.

"The time/space grid is flexible in this density vibration," the one answered her unspoken wondering. "It moves as we ask it to move and it accommodates our request according to the laws that rule on this level. You also, are able to make such requests and within the laws, such will accommodate your perspectives. And indeed, you have dreamed interactively on the true dream level of our group many times in the current life."

"Well, why are you here now? I mean, if you're here at all, why now, exactly?"

The blue one laughed a real laugh and Carly had the concept of a mouth with teeth and twinkling eyes, a presence, human-like, in blue robes who, along with the rest of the group, emanated a glowing blue luminescence. "We are here, Carlen, you may be assured of that. More here than here is, to be precise, but that is a concept of levels, aspects and perceptions that we must leave until later. To respond to your question, we are with you now in conversational form of energy, to assist you in coming to an understanding of your directions, of your commitment in this life and to be with you for the duration of these times of choosing."

Carly pulled the needle out of her arm and let the tubes fall from the stand at the bedside. She felt of her left breast and was shocked to see the yellow paint of the disinfectant and the ugly stitches around the areola and coming up around the breast from her armpit. "What's this stuff? Why do I look like Frankenstein's bride?" Then she looked up at them, "Choosing? What do you mean?"

"Again, Carlen, this location, if you will, is a place between levels, a bridge plane, and in it, there will be material items and physical sensations to whatever extent they serve. In this moment, you have discovered the results of a surgery done to you to repair the damage the entity whom you know as Victor inflicted upon your body. If you touch the stitches with a mindset of the healing power of your own essence, you may see them disappear."

He paused, seeming to wait for her to follow through with the process he had described. Carly looked down at the stitches and back at the blue one, "That's ridiculous," she said, "there they are. Nothing can change that. If Victor pulled it off, I couldn't stick it back on again anymore than I can make the stitches on it go away. I mean, only Christ can do miracles like that, huh?"

"That, Carlen," the blue one said gently, "is why we are here. We are the teachers, and our group is vast in the Universe; at our core is the very essence of the Christed Ones, those who have evolved in the teachings in a most perfect and orderly way and those whom we emulate. The one of those to whom you make reference regarding the activities of the healing ritual would be Jesus of Nazareth, the Anointed One, but all are one and the same with him, they are the Christed Ones. We are here to teach you among other things, that you may, in whatever terms you choose, heal yourself. A simple means with which to begin is to touch the stitches there on the body lightly and while doing this activity, in the powerful intellect, envision the wound as diminished. To whatever extent you imagine the tissue healed; the body will follow likewise, as that is its promise and it never fails. As you will it, you will see and feel the healing unfold and healthy tissue and color replace the crude gash."

Carly, more curious than anything, moved her fingers along the line of stitches around the areola, then down the incision at her armpit. Then not thinking about doing it, as she was too busily engaged in willing her mind to make pictures of healthy skin covering healthy tissue, she allowed the hand to become a being itself, and it moved flat across her entire left bosom about a half inch above it. In no more than three seconds, it was done and Carly took in her breath as she saw the stitches fade, the yellow disinfectant stain vanish, while pink healthy skin resumed its place on her bosom. She looked up open mouthed at the group. "It's doing it," she said softly, a half smile of amazement turned toward them, "this must be a dream."

Again, a laugh from the Blue One, "No, Carlen, it is not a dream. It is as we explained it to you. However, in the reality to which you will shortly return, there will be to whatever extent there will, some ramifications of this activity here and you will recognize this as a first step, of sorts, a beginning that precedes the Initiation."

Trying to absorb what he was saying and still reeling in the amazement of the self-ministrations, Carly studied the rapid metamorphosis of tissue and skin without responding to him. The Blue One went on, "To respond to your question about choice, choosing and the like as we referred earlier; what this intends regards the life contract. To simplify; each entity, upon entering a body, makes a contract to achieve certain goals that are, when achieved, an enhancement to the spirit as a whole. Due to the myriad of energies, directions and choices of other entities that may or may not enhance one's own position, individual choices are offered. As each entity chooses its pathway, the direction can become more clear. Not all are of a level where they can discern the remedies or the conflagrations resulting from a choice, but choices are inevitably made nonetheless. It is the one who chooses upon whom the duty of clear perception falls. We are aware of a critical place of choice for you currently on the level of reality occupied in the life and that, Carlen, is why we make our presence known to you in a more pronounced fashion at this time."

"You are the blue lights I've been seeing in the past few weeks, then?" Carly was suddenly aware of the blueness of them, and of the dream where she had gone with them to a plateau. "Yes, but I didn't relate that to anything. I mean, I guess I thought it might be eyestrain or whatever. I couldn't remember the dream much, but that's why you seem familiar to me, huh?"

"Familiar, yes, but the expanse of our acquaintance, if you will, defies the time boundaries of the one life. You are unaware yet of the connection between us, its import to each and what is intended by virtue of our bond. You have much to consider and to define in these critical times—and yes, we know of your many questions—but in the interest of your making the appropriate and unsolicited choices in the current dilemma, we leave you to discover what of this makes impact. Know this, however, it will be revealed in good time."

"What will be revealed?" Carly asked. And they smiled outrageously blue glowing smiles, warm and glorious and rich within her as she received them; then they were gone.

"You can't do that," Carly demanded, "come back here. You can't just leave a person like that after you've started something!"

But they didn't come back. There was no blue light piquing a corner of the room with its exotic brilliance. There was only she and the two beds and the other person lying there in the one.

"And be mindful, Carlen, nothing is by accident and only nothing. All else is by divine design." The words of the blue one swept into her consciousness and she was strangely satisfied that what had been started was not necessarily over by the abandonment of their presence. She lay back on the bed, and knowing she must, reinserted the needle into the vein in her arm, then wanting sleep, she went into it wondering if Wicked Sister had heard them.

"Carly, Carly Worthington, wake up." It was a nurse, a pretty thing with dark curly hair, shaking her shoulder lightly, "Carly, it's time for your meds. Wake up, Carly."

Carly let her one eye come open but the other was stuck shut. Her mouth was sand dry and she ached in every place there was on her body. "Drink," She croaked.

"Well of course, dear, I'm not going to make you take your meds dry," the nurse laughed. "I'm Karen, your floor nurse on second shift. It's 3:30 Carly, and you have to take your pills." She handed Carly a paper cup of water with a bendable straw. Then with the little cup of pills and capsules still in her hand, she went to the end of the bed, bent down and pushed a button and the bed began to whir and tilt Carly's body up and forward. Carly held the cup with both hands, trying to steady it. It felt as if it weighed 5 pounds. She sipped at the water through the straw as the bed jolted to a stop.

"Is this Monday?" Carly asked.

Karen smiled, "No, it's Tuesday afternoon. You had your surgery Monday early morning, then you spent some time in ICU and you came down here this morning on first shift. Here, take this one," she handed Carly a little red pill, "it's Darvon, it'll help the pain."

"What surgery? What for?"

"Now, take this one. It's for building your blood." Karen

handed her a white pill that was more capsule like, "and don't drink too much of that water, or you'll have an upset stomach. Your surgery was to repair—a few problems—you'll have to talk to your doctor about the specifics, though. She'll be in later to see you."

Carly remembered the dream then, where she'd been with the Blue People again and she'd healed the ugly stitches on her breast just as they'd said she could. She opened the gown and looked down at it, but the gauze dressing covered the area and she couldn't determine if there were stitches or not. She saw only the skin of her chest above it, nicely colored and with only a mild bruising. Just a dream, she mused.

"You're doing remarkably well," Karen went on, "Dr. Celez thinks you're his wonder patient, and Dr. Lefkowitz who did the surgery to repair the other damage, is pleased at your progress, too. They were both here this morning, don't you remember?"

"No. The last thing I remember was—" In that instant, Carly remembered it was her mother whom she'd come to the hospital to see. Then all the incidents of that Sunday night and Monday morning unfolded to her again, one by one, each seeming to squeeze into life out of the other recalled.

"Where's my mother?" Carly looked at the nurse, trying to see an expression that would tell her Betta Mary had died or recovered fully and gone home. "Betta Mary Kincaid. Here in the hospital. What's happened to her?"

"She's doing some better, though she's still in CCU. You shouldn't worry about that, Carly, she's getting the best of care." Karen remembered Dr. Steele's aside about Betta Mary and her relationship with Carly. She suppressed a smile. "There is no way you would ever relate those two," he'd said. "Someone in Creation Genetics left his post to take a crap and look what happened. You gotta watch those genetics guys every minute."

133

Carly didn't care about her mother's health; it was simply a focus that had arisen the night Victor did what he did. Something she had to take care of. She had to follow through, then she could do as she pleased about her own life. Choice, the freedom of choice. There was something about that thought that made her feel warm, enriched and even purposeful. That was not how she wanted to feel.

"We have to get you up tomorrow," Karen said, "and perhaps, in a couple of days, you can go see your mother. In the meantime, we'll keep you updated on what's happening with her condition, okay?"

"I guess so." There, that was better, Carly thought, letting the trapped, frustrated feeling return; knowing that the only way out of it was simply to get out of it. Death. There, she'd said it. Betta Mary's death. Carly's death. The last of Gramma's children. She felt very sorry that there would be no one who could appreciate the tragedy of that. Carly set the styrofoam cup on the bedside tray and looked out the window, summarily dismissing the nurse, her ministrations and her Betta Mary report.

Karen, 12 years a nurse and having known all kinds coming and going, went into her classic nurse demeanor, the routine she called Nurse Nighty-gale act, the chipper fixer-upper. She pulled back the curtain between the two beds, talking as she did so.

"This is Doris Patrick, Carly, your room-mate for the duration. Doris is in here for a well-deserved hysterectomy, and just in the nick of time, too, huh, Doris?"

Carly did not look over at the other bed or at its occupant, but Doris spoke as if she had anyway. "Hi, Carly. Believe it or not, we were actually in ICU together. Neither of us knew it at the time, but there we were, free-basing Sodium Pentathol."

Karen laughed, but Carly refused to turn around. "Anyway, Doris here had a tumor the size of a watermelon in her uteris,"

Karen said. "Another few days and it would have been a spinal injury."

"Yeah, my daughter was born smaller than that." Doris laughed. "Not getting around so good right now, but I'm sure thinner than I was."

Her words did nothing but annoy Carly. She continued to look out the window.

"Well, you two gals have a great chat. Dinner's in an hour or so. I'll be back. Buzz if you need me for anything." Karen left, her shoes making the rubber on tile sound, squeaking and scrunching in communion with the floor.

"What's your birth sign, Carly?" Doris asked as soon as Karen had left the room.

Carly turned to Doris and scowled. Her voice was acid. "*What* is a birth sign?"

"A sun sign, where the sun was located in the zodiac on the day you were born." Doris answered. Her voice was husky for a woman's voice, but it was animated and insisted on attention to it. That further annoyed Carly, yet she couldn't resist it.

"How would I know a thing like that? I don't believe in that stuff." Carly laid her head back on the pillow, disinterested again.

"Your belief is not a requirement, Carly. The stuff, as you put it, exists in any case and whether you like it or not or believe it or not." Doris' voice didn't lose its appeal as it clipped along, putting Carly in her place. As Carly turned to look at the woman again, she saw that she was smiling, one eyebrow raised, an impudent look.

Again, it tweaked Carly's annoyance back to full pitch. "Fine. You know so much, you tell me."

"No problem." Doris said, "Of course, let me qualify that with 'it's rather difficult to tell by your appearance', as I suspect the guy who raped you altered the face a bit, too."

"Nobody raped me. I fell in the shower."

135

"That's your story and you're sticking to it, huh? Sounds like a Scorpio to me, intense, stand-offish, intelligent but a fixed sign, the most fixed of all the signs."

"When's Scorpio?" Carly asked, now intrigued.

"A Scorpio is born during the last few days of the month of October and the first 21 days of November. Does that fit?" Doris asked, knowing the fact of it was either Scorpio or Taurus, this woman was not an easily negotiated sign.

"Yeah," Carly said. "How do you know stuff like that? I mean it had to be a lucky guess."

"I think all of the psychic tools we use have to be treated like the wands of Dame Fortune. It's all pretty much a guess, isn't it?"

"I don't know. I've never been good at guessing about anything. I—couldn't have—I mean—" Carly fumbled with her vocabulary access. She had started to say that she couldn't have guessed that Victor would ever harm her but it was only a thought, quickly crossing her mind without the substance of words and then it receded to its hiding place. "How do you know how to make lucky guesses, then?"

"That particular lucky guess," Doris smiled, her voice smiling with her, "was borne out of 40 years of studying the scientific art of Astrology. Everything about it, Astrology, after the precision calculations made to determine the positions of the stars at any given time of day or night as they aspect any given position on the earth within seconds, is simply the art of the educated guess."

Carly gave her a lopsided smile. "And you call it a psychic *tool*?"

"I do." Doris said, "And I do because that's exactly what it is. It's what the bones and feathers of the Voodoo priestess are, the Tarot cards, the I Ching, the Ouija Board, the bumps on your head as read by a Phrenologist and it's been that way for centuries, for all time, probably. It's said that in the time before this one, eons ago, that mind-reading or telepathy was

---

136

a common practice; simply a means of communication between humans. Call it an understanding, maybe, but I believe that telepathy is possible today—real mind-reading, not the tricks pulled by stage psychics and phony healers."

"Interesting. But come on," Carly said, trying to look cynical in bandages, "mind-reading? That's just not possible. You couldn't read my mind, my thoughts are private."

"Yes, you're right, your thoughts are private, but there are things you telegraph, Carly, when you speak. I admit that it's harder with you right now because your face is distorted by the beating you took and I can only see one eye—eyes are the window to the soul—but still I can sense a conflict in you."

"Everyone has some kind of conflict at one time or another, don't they? Isn't that how psychics do it? Like they feature on some of those expose' shows, they just pick up on key words or key phrases? Like you would have picked up on my mother—"

"No, it's not your mother I'm picking up on. It's some man," Doris looked down at her hands in her lap and let her eyes close slowly, then they came open again just as slowly. It seemed an involuntary movement and there was nothing pretentious about it, like a momentary tic. "Some man and another one and a very great conflict in this—hmmm—not a triangle. No, I see a quadrangle that started out as a triangle and it wants to reshape itself even more. And there's the conflict, but I also see a balance—um—an opportunity to balance. A lot of blue light surrounds you, Carly."

"Blue light?" Carly saw them, then, the whole vast group spearheaded by the one blue one, smiling with a real mouth and real teeth. "Nothing is by accident, Carly, nothing."

———

137

16

Honor thy father and thy mother. But if you can't do that,
then you are obligated to pretend.

Betta Mary tried to sleep, as she didn't like to think. Thinking
without the benefit of booze and smokes was either very
frightening or very boring. She was not a woman who liked
to philosophize; she didn't like to project in the abstract and
there was very little left for her to think about besides her
condition or memories. This was the frightening part. Only
two things she didn't like to think about and all the rest was
boring. When she wasn't thinking about her condition, or about
the other and the boring came into her mind, as a consequence
of a lifetime of creating excitement to defy boredom, the
excitement of fear of what was going to happen to her because
of the condition replaced boring. Or the wrench of regret of
times past replaced the thinking about her condition replaced
boring. And so it went when sleep wouldn't visit.

Betta Mary begged the nurses for a cigarette, for just one
little drink, an afternoon cocktail to relax her, a beer to kill
her thirst. Instead, they gave her pills and water and no salt
crackers and tea. Tea, the accursed drink of the goddamned
snooty Worthingtons. She'd rather drink lye than drink tea.

Those goddamned snobs shoving that shit down my throat at
their dumbass tea parties, killing people with all that boring talk
about politics and church and all the goody two shoes shit charities
they did. Oh, I ain't forgot. Nosiree. And him, Jeffery Carlen
Worthington. Think he'd help me out? Shit no! He was just as
goddamned bad as they were. Snooty assholes. Thought they was

138

better than everyone else. High and goddammed mighty mucky-much, he was even fuckin' the maid. Got her pregnant, too.

This was the part that made Betta Mary start breathing hard into her oxygen mask, steaming it up. She didn't like thinking about the Worthingtons, about Jeff and that time of her innocence ruptured because it always brought the same poignant stab that insisted her innocence had not been so violated after all. But here she was, doing it again, coming so fearfully close to death like she did the other night and still, none of it would stop coming into her mind. As soon as she put it out of her mind, switching venues; thinking about how much fun it was going out to the Cabin. Thinking about the place, pictures tumbling into her mind; there she was surrounded by all her friends, having a nice drink or two and telling stories about the old days. Laughing and ordering another round. It even made her feel nice about Norbie, that old sweat hog. Then for no reason at all, some story she'd told or some comment by one of the others remembered came into her mind and boom! There it was again, right back on her doorstep. And damned if that didn't lead right into Carly. Then she did feel bad.

It was a mixed up thing, that was. Sometimes you just had to think about it, to get it out of your head, once and for all. She could never claim as hers the once and for all part, though. Maybe if she thought about it all the way through, if she let the damned pictures into her head, let them right on in there, maybe she could stop feeling bad about it and maybe, please Dear God, the fear and the low-down feeling would go away.

All she had ever wanted was just to be happy. She was nothing but a dumb farm girl, born last into a family of eight children, 4 sisters 3 brothers, and a dad that thought Betta Mary was just the berries! Of course, her ma didn't think so much of her when she would run to Pa and get petted like a favored kitten whenever she'd done something wrong instead

139

of taking her punishment like the others did. She had never felt bad about that before, but now, seeing the faces of her brothers and sisters as their resentment settled in, she was sorry. She never wondered why she might be sorry either; that was just what hit her, that's all. Then she'd try to think about something else. Sometimes it worked, sometimes it didn't.

In those days, there wasn't any TV, damn little radio at least where they lived out south of Hamilton on a big old farm down in the southeast corner of the county. The lines didn't come through for the electric until the forties, but even then, Ma didn't want to have that evil stuff in the house, absolutely certain it would come out of the wall and kill them all in their beds. When the war came, though, you almost had to have a radio and one that would plug into the electric, because the batteries just weren't strong enough to last and to get the good stations in. Old WJR over in Detroit was a good one to listen to. It brought Pa and Ma the news about the war and it had the Lone Ranger, the Squeaking door, the Green Hornet and all kinds of other stuff for the kids. Betta Mary was just eleven years old when the war started; well, America's war anyway. Her brothers all went off to fight and only Teddy came back, and him with no legs and sick as a wasted dog. He didn't live out the war. There was awful sadness in that, even Betta Mary felt it, but Ma went into the parlor alone where the stars were in the window and grieved every night for all her boys. Pa was stoic and went on about doing his business. Cows don't wait, pigs don't care and neither does the seed growing in the ground. Sometimes in the winter when there wasn't a lot to do, he'd go off for a week or so and come back when he'd drunk himself out. Ma still grieved in the parlor alone.

Then the girls got married, one by one. May Lee married George Wallin, Carol Dolly married Sam Wheaton, Barbara Ann married Len Pruden and Laura Lottie married Charley

Allen. Betta Mary wanted to find a husband too. Laura Lottie was only four years older than her and at sixteen she was a whole lot more ready than Laura Lottie was at twenty. The soldier boys were coming home from the war and it was great fun to go to Hamilton all dressed up and go down by the train station to watch them coming in. Pa never knew what she was doing. She told him she was going to the library, which was the only one in the county then; that she had to study things because she wanted to be a teacher. Ma knew, but she only guessed and couldn't say for sure and besides, she never cared for Betta Mary anyway. She would be glad to get her out of the house.

It was her 10th trip to the train station to watch the boys coming home, and already she'd met five nice boys who she'd gone to the bar with. She liked the feeling of giddiness that drinking alcohol gave her; she became more grown up, wittier, prettier and everybody thought she was cute and innocent, a pretty little farm girl. She could see why Pa liked to go off on his drinking times. It made you not who you were and you could do anything you wanted and then, you could go back home and nobody was ever the wiser. The first time she did it with one of the boys, it had been awful and it had hurt like hell, but he liked it and that registered with her. So; when he wanted to do it again, she made him buy her things and buy her drinks. After a while, and after a couple of different boys, she started to like it, too. Then it got so she liked doing it so much she thought she ought to find one of them she really liked and settle down and get married like Laura Lottie. Then she could do it all the time, drink when she wanted to and not have to worry about getting caught. As luck would have it, on that 10th trip into town, that's just the moment when Jeffrey Worthington stepped off the train, looking like a million bucks in his navy dress uniform.

After that, it was all downhill. That was the stuff Betta Mary didn't want to think about and if she did, she wanted only to think about the good parts. How was she to know that Jeff was already married? The Worthingtons were all from over to Port Huron. Nobody from Hamilton, least of all anyone in a little farming community 15 miles southeast, knew anything about the high muckey-mucks over there. Jeff had come over to Hamilton because the family had sent him there, to see if he could get himself straightened around after the navy mustered him out, and work a regular job his dad had got him in a feed and hardware store. They figured if they took the boy out of the way of the Detroit bookies, the gambling dens and the loose women, the boy would get straightened out as a matter of course. Once that was done he could come back to his fancy wife, his cushy life and start taking over the family grain business. When Betta Mary discovered that Jeff was from money, especially then, she set about changing at least some of those plans. Of course, he didn't tell her about the wife until she was pregnant the first time. Just her luck, that one had taken a good hold, too. Jeff found a doctor who liked to gamble and together they made a deal—Jeff would get his dad to pay for a new car which would turn into a debt payoff for the doctor and in turn, the doctor would take care of Betta Mary's problem. And there was money to spare.

The second time, it wasn't so easy. The doctor had since died, Jeff was tapped out with his father and they were on their own. "Then, marry me, Jeff," was Betta Mary's solution.

"I can't. I'd be a bigamist." He said with a wink.

"What's that?" Betta Mary had no problem being ignorant of things. It added to her resume'.

Jeff thought she was cute, being so stupid. "That's someone who's married to two people at once without benefit of a divorce somewhere in there." He laughed.

"What's so bad about that?" Betta Mary said, snuggling up to him, like she knew he liked. "You don't ever see her anyway. You could marry me, we could have the baby and just keep on the way we are."

"You are funny, you are." He kissed her nose. "They tend to put fellas in jail for such a thing, Bet. We can go ahead and have the baby and keep on the way we are, but I'm not going to jail for marrying two women."

"Am I the best gal you ever had?" Betta Mary started to undo his pants buttons. "Don't you just love gettin' in me?"

"Come on, Bet," he started laughing, "you know I think you're aces, but I'm not going to jail just so—now, quit that!" He laughed some more, but soon, Betta Mary had him in the place where she knew what to do with him and he stopped laughing.

"You want to keep that, doncha Jeff, honey?" she whispered. "Don't it feel wonderful?"

"You know it does, baby."

"Then you have to marry me if you want to keep me makin' you feel good, huh?"

Betta Mary worked him over every chance she got until he finally agreed to divorce his wife and marry her. By the time the divorce was final, Betta Mary had given birth to a stillborn girl. She grieved for weeks; she was inconsolable and Jeff was, poor addictive Jeff, guilty for not divorcing sooner; guilty for not marrying Betta Mary sooner. If she'd not had the stress of carrying a child out of wedlock, the baby would have been fine. So; he married her and she was happy Betta Mary again, all cuddley and cute and stupid, like he liked. But not one of the other Worthingtons liked anything about her at all.

They moved to Port Huron and lived in that big old house on Chicago Street and didn't do anything all day long except sit around and talk and drink tea and have folks over who planted phony kisses on your cheeks and gave you phony hugs and talked some more. Jeff was gone all the time because he hated it there, and she was stuck with the rest of them.

143

She hadn't been drunk in a year, the only way she could have a cigarette was to go to the kitchen and smoke in the pantry. She never got cuddled any more, Jeff was gone and when he did get home, he was either disinterested or drunk or both.

Finally, it was Jeff's uncle that solved her problem. Visiting from New York, Jeff's mother's brother, Austin Carlen, brought a spark to the boring life around the Worthington mansion. He was full of stories about his adventures during the war, being in the Intelligence Service and working with the Brits. It was like a movie come true to Betta Mary. He was older but still handsome and virile and what a romantic figure he was. Like Robert Taylor or Tyrone Power. Betta Mary, for the first time, began to enjoy the teas Mother Worthington hosted, because he would be there, telling of exotic things, surrounded by the ladies of culture, but always with a wink and a private smile for Betta Mary.

It didn't take long at all, really, for Betta Mary to make it more than plain that she was a lonesome wife of a man who never came home and she would be pleased to entertain some secret moments. That was the first time Betta Mary had ever been gripped by something she couldn't work to an advantage. She hadn't thought a thing about it, going into it, just fulfilling her desires was what she figured it would be. But that wasn't the way it turned out. He had her turned inside out; she was hungry for him, maddened by a closeness that she couldn't own. Every time he made love to her, it was like her drug and as soon as he was done, she had to have more.

"I'll be back, little sweetie, you know I will," he'd said so smoothly. "But someone may come in or someone may wonder what we're doing in the guest house—" or the library, or the laundry, or the boat house or his rooms. "If we want to keep seeing each other, we've got to be discreet. You've got to keep your head about you when I'm around. You do want to keep on, don't you, little sweetie?"

Oh my God, more than life!

When Jeff came home she was cold to him and he was indifferent to her. "But I have someone," Betta Mary consoled herself in her secret world, seeing there Austin's tall body with the precious line of hair that led to—"a wonderful man who loves me."

Then she got pregnant for Carly. That was the worst time. Austin had immediately cut her off, angry that she let herself get pregnant when she wasn't having intercourse with her husband. She had made the announcement to him, just as they were about to make love in the boat house. He was kissing her neck and fondling her breasts, seconds from being inside her and she thought it would be the best time, as he wouldn't care. They would just go ahead and make love and he'd be so happy with her again, so madly in love with her that he'd be glad they were going to have a baby. He'd insist on her divorcing Jeff and they'd go off to New York and live happily ever after. But instead of completing their lovemaking, he pulled away.

"How could you be so stupid?" he railed in a hoarse whisper. He didn't look at her, but got up and hurriedly put his clothes back on. "You're married to my nephew, you twit. Don't you understand what that implies? Are you an idiot?"

Betta Mary started to cry, lying still in the surrender position, so ready for him to be with her. "But I thought you'd be happy! I thought you loved me," she wailed.

"Shut up, you miserable slut. Voices carry out over the water." He bent down and put his hand over her mouth, while he pointed at her with the other hand. " Now, you listen to me." His rough whisper killed her heart, "This never happened. None of it. You go back to the house, and as soon as you possibly can, you find Jeff and make him screw you. I mean it, make him think he's never made it like that before. There's your baby's father, not me."

And that was the last Betta Mary saw of Austin Carlen. When Carly was born, her dark hair and eyes were just like

145

her grandmother's. Mother Worthington was so pleased that the dear child took after her side of the family; she named her Carlen, as was fitting. Then Jeff got the maid pregnant and one day, when Carly was six months old, Betta Mary just packed up, took the baby and left in a taxi.

Where in the hell did I think I was going then? Betta Mary looked out the window of her hospital room, tears stinging her eyes and running down her cheeks, making them itch. She tried to remember where she had gone before she ended up back at the farm, with a kid and another new husband. *Oh, hell, it was Arizona first, then I don't know, Colorado, then New Mexico? I guess. That's where I met that old fuck Jorje Ramirez. What a old horny toad he was! I always liked it but he liked it three times worse than me. 'Course there was Carly and I did have to watch out for her. What a pain in the ass! Always wantin' something. Never leave a body alone long enough to take care of a body's needs.*

Betta Mary remembered the times when Carly came into their bedroom crying that she didn't want to be left alone, then seeing her and Ramirez doing it, she'd wail all the more, scared, probably, but still, when you gotta quit in the middle of it to tend to a brat—.

"You are a wicked sister! You get your ass back there in that living room right now! Jesus Christ! You got TV, you got toys, you got your precious drawin' pads and crayons and every goddamned thing other kids are beggin' for. You hear me, you wicked sister, you! You get your ass outa here and leave us alone. NOW!"

Then finally, she'd get to go back to Ramirez and finish up. Poor Carly, she didn't know what was going on. It was the best thing, though, after Ramirez and before she married Bud Pettinger that she took Carly over to May Lee's to stay for a bit. It was Pettinger's fault that she couldn't go back and pick Carly up right away; he was just so jealous of Betta Mary paying any attention to anyone else. Besides, Pettinger traveled all the time and he liked to take her with him. What kind of life would that be for a child? There were lots of times she asked herself why she'd taken Carly with her when she left the Worthingtons in the first place. They would have gladly kept her, doted on her, given her all kinds of things and sent her to the best schools and all that Betta Mary never had.

"No kid of mine's gonna grow up thataway. Spoiled and hoity-toity. Nosiree! I'll take her with me and she'll be just fine." That's what she told herself at the time, but now, feeling miserable with her heart lagging behind the beat of the rest of her body, she knew very well why she'd taken the baby with her. Because she belonged to her and Austin, not her and Jeff, that's why. And because she was hurt and angry and taking Carly away from them was the only way she knew how to get back. She imagined Austin coming for a visit wanting to see Jeff's child that he knew was really his and being hurt and miserable and regretful and anguished when neither Betta Mary or Carly were there. Then there'd been the money, too. They were always good for a few hundred sent to a Post Office box in New Mexico or Alabama or Kentucky or wherever she was. "Carlen Ann needs—" And in a week or two there it would be, a check for $500 or $600. Even when Carly was at May Lee's and George's, she'd sometimes get them to send money. She supposed they did it so as not to have to put up with Betta Mary, but she always wondered why they never fought for Carly. Never came after her, never sent a note with the money, and even once they knew Carly was over at the farm with Ma and Pa, they still didn't contact her. That was a mystery and now, same as always, thinking about it set Betta Mary off.

She could feel her breath getting more and more shallow and there was less and less fog on the plastic oxygen mask. And there it was again, that awful full feeling that went right up to her chin and that terrible weight was on her chest again, pulling at it from the inside out, pulling down, cutting the air off. Soundlessly, her eyes bugging wide, toothless mouth agape, Betta Mary felt at the side of her bed for the call button. *Where did that fuckin' thing get to! God, I don't want to die. I ain't ready! Oh God no! I need to see Carly first.*

17

*You are under the impression that it's okay to let it all fall
into your lap. Then they make you stand up and you lose
your lap.*

Carly had been in the hospital for three days. There was a
phone now at her bedside on that roll-around tray but she
couldn't think who she could call. She had no job, so there
was no use calling CSG to tell them she wouldn't be in for
awhile. She had never, in all the years they had been lovers,
called Victor. That was forbidden. It stunned her to think
that, in all of her life, through school and even over at Mitchell
Design, she'd never made friends with a woman or with
anyone, for that matter. As a child, she'd been placed around
in various childless aunt's homes, here to there, no time, no
instincts to friendship. Then, as if by vicious design, the short
time she'd had with Grandma and Grandpa Kuhns was
dominated by Betta Mary and her needs and demands. After
that, her life had been completely devoted to Victor, and when
he wasn't around, she filled it with hauling Betta Mary out of
trouble, tending to her needs and hassles and whatever time
was left over, Carly did whatever Wicked Sister wanted to
do; drink and go find men. It was a strange feeling to talk so
openly with someone as she had talked to Doris Patrick in
the last two days. Their conversations alleviated some of the
ache she felt about Victor and how he'd left her. She couldn't
bring herself to mention Frank. If she didn't have to think
about him, all the better. But Doris knew. Not the details; not
the tawdry nature of her cheating on Victor with him, or the
fact that he was the father of her lover's wife, but Doris knew

149

anyway, just not enough to amaze Carly with her knowing. It was just a guess, but perhaps, that was what was keeping Wicked Sister away. She hadn't been around since the night they'd come to see Betta Mary and Carly wasn't sure why. It bothered her.

She looked over at the other bed and saw that Doris was asleep. She'd had a big day. Her first solid foods after the operation and up and out of bed this morning for a walk down the hall. "I never nap," Doris said just after lunch, "but I feel one coming on. What an old lady, huh?" Then she laughed. Shortly afterward, she was making a delicate little snore.

Carly had not had the nerve to look in a mirror since the "incident" which was what she had decided to call the unthinkable, unmentionable block of time during which she had somehow fallen in the shower. All of that would have to be dealt with at some later time. It was not a thing she could gather into her perspectives. The moments of it she had faced could not be assessed and she was incapable of repairing any of it; so it was better to heal her body at the moment, and take care of the obligations she understood. Betta Mary.

Doris said she didn't look bad at all; that every day, her appearance was improved and closer to normal. Everyone, especially the doctors, seemed quite astounded by the accelerated healing of the tissues surrounding her left breast. Carly questioned that it was accelerated at all, that it was probably only a normal programmed function occurring because she'd had that dream. And now, sober for days, she was able to recall more and more of these wispy trails of thoughts that when brought together like so many puzzle pieces, began to make a cognizant picture. She smiled to herself, thinking of Doris' monumental contribution to her bolstered mood; and her declaration of the presence of the blue lights. "It's always a comfort," Doris had said after their first few of these conversations, "to have someone else to be crazy with."

———

150

Karen came bustling into the room, the tread on her white nurses' shoes squeaking like a demented bird. Her face was grim at first, then she rearranged her expression to be compassionately serious. "Carly, I'm not going to beat around the bush here, but I don't want you to be alarmed, either. Your mother has had a setback, and her doctor has called down to ask if we could bring you up to CCU. Do you think you're up to sitting in a wheelchair? I couldn't get hold of Dr. Lefkowitz but Dr. Steele said if you felt up to it, it wouldn't be harmful."

Carly tried to think what that might mean. Wheelchair to CCU to see Betta Mary? A setback? As she searched Karen's face for impossible information, for perhaps a look at how a visit with a mother whom she couldn't love would play out, there came a blue light, a teeny one, but wildly glowing its luminescence, and like a butterfly, perched on the tip of Karen's nose. Inappropriately, Carly smiled, then corrected her visage, saying simply, "Let's go then."

The smell in the room was unmistakably that of feces and Carly couldn't understand why they hadn't cleaned it up. This was a hospital, an antiseptic hotel, where to violate the code of sterile was unthinkable. She looked up at the nurses' aide, who'd brought her to Betta Mary's room. "Do you smell that?" she whispered to the aide.

"Smell what?" The aide looked perplexed. "I don't smell anything."

Carly wondered if it was her thoughts, like sometimes before, when she'd had bad thoughts, she could actually smell them, like gas passed and circulating in the air. She reviewed, had her thoughts been bad? She did not want to be here, doing this, but bad? No, she didn't think so. Why, then, would she smell the awful smell? They came closer into the room and the nurse and the two doctors tending Betta Mary looked over at her. "You must be Carly," the male doctor said to her, then to the aide, "See if you can bring her closer to this side of the bed."

As the doctors shifted positions, Carly saw her mother for the first time in weeks and the impact of Betta Mary's altered appearance made her fix her look immediately on her mother's eyes. Rheumy with lids half closed, the only sparkle there was from the light glancing off the tears that filled them. Betta Mary's skin was yellowed and hung from her bones in lifeless dry folds and Carly thought she couldn't weigh over 70 pounds, yet her belly looked as though it might weigh half that. It was a gruesome sight and instantly came a word to her, "death" and she knew then, where the smell had originated. It was the smell of death. Hours seemed to pass as Carly communed with that thought and all its portent. What shall I do? How should I be with her?

"I'm Dr. Mitchell," the male doctor went on, uninterrupted, bringing time to its proper reality, "and this is Dr. Rosen." He nodded his head toward a short woman with dark curly hair worn too close around a face that would have been pretty except for it being too small and an overly large nose shadowing the lower half of it. *A rich doctor,* Carly thought fleetingly, *why wouldn't she have that nose done?*

"Sylvia Rosen," the woman smiled and offered her hand to Carly. Carly took it and mumbled an acknowledgement.

Dr. Mitchell then nodded to the aide and said, "Let's take this outside, for now. Mrs. Kincaid is stabilized again, but it will be awhile before she comes around."

Once in the hall outside the door to Betta Mary's room, Dr. Rosen abruptly took center stage, "I'm your mother's cardiologist and surgeon, Dr. Mitchell here, is a general practioner." She said it as if it were a position at least three levels beneath her own exalted one, "This is the second setback for Betta Mary in as many days, Carly. We apologize for not filling you in earlier, but it was our understanding that you were undergoing your own trauma."

"Okay." Carly acknowledged the political apology, making way for Dr. Rosen to continue.

"Your mother's condition is not limited simply to CHF, but is exacerbated by a severe diabetic problem, a compromised liver and some arterial and venal problems. However, we feel that it would be prudent to consider a remedy to the heart condition, which could, in turn, alleviate some of the other problems she's experiencing."

"And what remedy would that be?" Carly wondered what she looked like to them. She sat in the wheel chair in a hospital gown and hospital robe, positioned gingerly on one hip to stave off inner pain, her hair unwashed and her colored gargoyle face, looking back, trying to assume an intelligence of which she was utterly unsure. She had to not care; not let it be a point or she would miss what they were saying.

"That would be a pacemaker." Dr. Rosen went on, "Your mother's heart has a good pump, but a slow beat. When it's left to its own devices, so to speak, it simply can't keep up with the rest of the body's need for blood and the oxygen and nutrients it supplies to the rest of the system. If we implant a pacemaker, that will regulate the beat more to normal and help the body deal with its other problems."

"You said 'arterial and venal problems'. What does that mean?" Carly glanced back into the room at Betta Mary who seemed to be in some dazed world, the dull look still an expression. "Exactly." She added.

"Exactly. Well, exactly, that is—um—Dr. Mitchell, I believe this is your area?"

He smiled, a gentle looking older man, a Norman Rockwell country doctor characterization right to the full rosy cheeks and the white hair. "What we're talking about here, Carly, is basically, that your mother's veins are about 70-80% closed with plaque. I'm sure you are aware of her lifestyle. Alcohol and cigarettes are the culprits for the most part, here. Over the years, these agents have helped to create a buildup of materials deposited in the veins by the residue in the blood as it passes through and finally, it builds to the point where it closes off any useful flow to the system. Of course, this affects the major organs, the extremities particularly. With her level of diabetes, it's amazing that she still has her feet."

"What? What do you mean?" Carly shook her head, not understanding.

"Typical of diabetes, the extremities often are starved of nutrients because of the affect diabetes has on the circulatory system, then add the rest of the venal problem and when the blood flow is cut off entirely, the tissue becomes gangrenous, pustules appear, then it turns black and dies."

"That's why she always wore socks, then." Carly said it mostly to herself, remembering the times she and Wicked Sister had picked her up from a bar or the jail, took her home and cleaned her up. Always, she wore socks that came to her knees, but not once had Carly removed them when she put her to bed; interested only in doing the least in the least amount of time and not touching her any more than she had to. "Are her feet—um—"

"Actually, considering everything," Dr. Mitchell said, "her limbs are in relatively good condition. There is the onset of problems evidenced in the heightened redness of the tissue from her calves on down into her feet and toes, which is a preliminary sign, but as of yet, there are no open sores or pustules."

"Well, then, tell me this, Dr. Mitchell. Why would you want to put in a pacemaker that's going to make blood flow through veins where it can't flow? Wouldn't that make it worse for her?" Carly caught his look of acknowledgment the seconds it took for him to look away. Dr. Rosen stepped in again.

"That's my department, Carly." She smiled her plastic bedside smile, "Her pump is good and a pacemaker will help the rest of her conditions by letting the blood get to the extremities."

"But that's not answering my question." Carly wondered why she was annoyed with this woman, and in her response, why she was so uncharacteristically dogged. "What I asked is, wouldn't that make it worse for her in terms of blood trying to go where it can't go? Wouldn't that be prolonging the inevitable? Painfully?"

Dr. Mitchell fixed on Sylvia Rosen with an almost satisfied look but she was unaware as she herself was fixing a gaze on Carly that was narrowed and angry. With a raised eyebrow and cocked head, she looked down at Carly.

"Am I understanding you correctly, Carly? You would rather we did nothing and let your mother die after going through who knows how many of these assaults on her system?" she snapped, emphasizing the word 'die' with a crisp drama.

Carly wondered what she might say now. The truth? She did want her mother to die. Then she would be free, no longer attached in the eyes of the world to Betta Mary Kuhns who had thrown her away and made her into the miserable alcoholic slut Victor said she was. But did she really want to see Betta Mary suffer? There was the conflict. She quickly thought back to the times when Wicked Sister had tormented the drunk Betta Mary and she, Carly, had felt hateful and exhilarated at once.

"I don't know," Carly answered truthfully, "I really don't know. I was asking you."

"Well, I'll tell you, then. The decision has been made, actually," Dr. Rosen snapped. "I don't have to sell it to you, I was merely being courteous. Your mother has already given her consent and Dr. Mitchell and the nurse were there to hear it. The sooner we operate, the sooner her system can start responding. As soon as she stabilizes, we will schedule the surgery." Slyvia Rosen looked coldly at Carly then at Dr.

155

Mitchell. She turned and walked swiftly away, her lab coat moving in the breeze she made.

Carly looked back at Dr. Mitchell. "Is that true? Did Betta Mary really give her consent? I mean, how could she? If she was having an attack, how could she think clearly enough to make such a decision?" Then she said, "Nevermind. It doesn't matter. Dr. Rosen's going to do the implant anyway. Just answer this, please. How much is this going to cost? Betta Mary has no insurance, you know, and she's on limited Medicare."

Dr. Mitchell smiled slightly. "I don't know Carly, you'll have to contact Dr. Rosen's office to find that out. I apologize for what must seem an intrusion on your sensibilities, but Dr. Rosen is—um—passionate about her work."

"Yes, well—everything that goes around comes back around." Carly said, then immediately wondered from what tiny corner of her past that little homily emerged. Grandma Kuhns. Yet another blue light sat on Dr. Mitchell's shoulder for a millisecond before it rose and with no time/space restrictions, slipped past Carly's right hand, touching it ever so lightly as it did, and came to rest on the wound above her eye. There was an instant of the tiniest recognition in Dr. Mitchell's eyes and Carly was overwhelmed with a sense of empowerment. A tick of a smile passed between them.

18

A close encounter of the third kind means a real sighting;
but then, there's the no remembering rule. Remember that.

Again, Carly didn't think she was asleep, but here she was again, in that dream place, where the room she and Doris were in was suddenly filled with countless blue entities, so vast were their numbers they went over the hospital's horizon to an infinity that couldn't be seen. It came to her attention immediately that the room's light was only that of the moonlight outside; the only manufactured light was from the hall and the nurses' station, yet it was like daylight in the room. The one blue one, standing again in the forefront, smiled a greeting. Carly looked over at Doris to see if she was awake.

"She will not view this gathering," the one blue one said, "though she is aware on a level that pertains to her current personality expression. Good evening, Carlen. We are pleased to find you well."

"Is this like before? The dream that's not a dream?"

"It is indeed. Now that you have come to a place of acknowledgment of our existence and your connection with us, we will be steadily increasing our presence with you that will, at the same time, serve to increase the level of the learning we are to teach."

"Teachers. That's right." Carly again sat up in the bed without a twinge of pain and looked at her wrists. They were without marks. For the first time since before the incident, she picked up the hand mirror from the nightstand drawer and looked at her face. There was a thin red line above her left eyebrow, but other than that, her face looked as it had

---

157

always looked. Except that there was an expression there that she had never worn before. It made her look—attractive.

"You *are* attractive, Carlen, in the flesh and in spirit." The one Blue One smiled.

"No, that can't possibly be so. Sister and I have done a lot of bad things, really bad."

"If you insist on carrying the negative aspect of these activities about with you, holding them to your bosom stingily, you will own them and they will be with you until you discard them." Still smiling, he went on, "It is the same premise with bruises and the physical damages to the body. If these marks have importance to you in whatever ways you consider them, that is how they will be regarded by the body, which simply follows the commands of the essence. Release them, as you have done here, and they can no longer be manifest with you."

Carly considered that, looking at her wrists and feeling of her left breast. No bruises, no scars, no pain. "How do you know that's how it—works?"

"We are given the Law."

"What law?" Carly stood up and flexed her arms and her legs, feeling the freedom of it, the joy of being unfettered by pain.

"The One Law of the Law of the One, the Infinite Universal Law that describes in its brilliant simplicity, the purpose and dynamics of the Universe and all in it. That Law is: Increase the Light."

Carly was still then, captured by the essence of what they were saying, locked into their eminent logic which at that moment, she could virtually see unfolding in pictures before her. "Unbelievable!" she said, "but it's too simple, isn't it? Shouldn't God be more complicated than that?"

"Why would that be, Carlen?" the Blue One asked. "Think, if you will, of the moments of your own consternation at the complications of faith, mystery and duty as presented to you in the form of religion and as you've resisted it and discarded the postulation. Is the simple, pristine pathway to Increase of Light not that which you have sought in the life? As the Carlen personality, you have evolved to this place, this moment, if you will, where Higher Self has insisted upon a choice of direction, a clarification of purpose of the whole essence. To enable you to make an appropriate choice, you are allowed these times of exploration and of exposition. We cannot effect your choice, nor are we allowed to unduly influence. Your will to choose is a sacred thing; and we are allowed only to demonstrate to you certain truths, to lead you to the places where you may explore your past, to evaluate your essence, its purpose in the present and thereby to find the perfect future."

"Oh, this is all too much. You must have the wrong person. I'm not at all who you think I am." Carly sat back on the bed and as she did, she experienced a pain in her insides; a sharp poking at the cervix and suddenly her breast felt heavy and sore.

"We know exactly who you are, Carlen, in this moment, moreso than do you. However, it is not our aim to upset you, or to lead you into places you are not ready to experience. But it is this: The mother entity is soon to cross over and there is much to resolve on this experiential level as well as others to which we have yet to introduce you before this event can occur in the impeccable terms contractually ordered. Also, there is conflict within and without that must be appropriately resolved and as all these events, conditions and situations are interdependently to occur, your awareness is required. Recognize, confront, forgive and release. Abandon all else."

"And what happens if I can't become aware? What happens if I'm right and you're wrong and I'm, we, Sister and me, are not the ones you think we are?"

"That is not a consideration, Carlen. We are perfectly

mindful of your essence, your Higher Self, the soul progenitor and of all the personalities from lives past, including the present incarnation as Carlen Worthington and the shadow entity whom you call Sister."

"Shadow entity? I wouldn't call her that, if I were you. You understand, don't you, that you don't want to make her angry with you." Carly was serious and spoke from grave experience.

The Blue One laughed gently. "We do not desire to anger any entity on any level of expression. It is true that the Wicked Sister persona has an ego, however undeveloped, that is separate from yours; but as an actual mind/spirit entity, she has no authorization to develop, nor does she possess the skills, the motivations, the consistencies necessary to attain a spiritual beginning. The Wicked Sister persona is an outcome of labeled behaviors that has existed for you as a protective mechanism from the hardships of a difficult and loveless childhood. She is a foil, a counterpart who reflects a strand of the whole cloth."

Carly considered that momentarily and immediately rejected the analyses. "Then how come she's been with me for a long as I can remember? And how come all of a sudden, you're here, telling me she's nobody—she's just a behavior? I know that Sister can't always come out, I know she and I use the same body, but she's a whole lot more real to me than you are! I mean, give me a break here, she's always been there for me and—no offense, but this is only the second or third time I've seen you people."

"We understand, Carlen. And we are not offended. Your concerns are natural ones, and of course you would consider yourself closer to the Wicked Sister persona. But it is time also for you to consider the nature of the connection with the Wicked Sister persona; how this impacts the current life, karma and evolution of spirituality."

"But you said it yourself," Carly responded, "I've never

been spiritual. Religion never seemed comfortable for me. It seemed hypocritical and—um—too drastic. I mean, everything has to be decided in one half a second about your immortal soul and where it's going to go forever: heaven or hell. Now, that just doesn't seem fair or like the God I thought of when I was little."

"Exactly," smiled the Blue One. "Consider this, Carlen: How young were you when you thought of God? Do you recall?"

Carly thought a moment, "No, not really. I just know I thought about God, that's all and I know I was pretty little."

"It is this, Carlen—" and in literally *no time*, before her mind's eyes in something like a private screening room, a scene unfolded and in the center focus was her own little self, a small Carlen. Then, without yet another millisecond passing by, she was there again, in the little body, viewing the world from her own two-year-old eyes. It was a moment before she could orient herself to the tiny body and its maddeningly limited movements, but once done, there was a surge of energy that shot through it and involuntarily, she clapped the chubby little hands and yelped with joy. Then she turned her head and saw the same Blue One and all the vastness of the Blue People, filling the tiny kitchen of a little house in a somewhere that didn't matter. She lifted up her arms to greet them all. Smiling, the Blue One said, "Dear Carlen, you do well today. Shall we speak of the One and the One Law?"

Little Carlen did not understand the words spoken, but she knew them. It was a cosmic knowing that was present in her, and as the pictures and sensations unfolded to her, she nodded her head, smiled widely and clapped her hands with each one. "Light, light."

As quickly as she had become the little Carlen again, she was thrown back into the older self. While there was a sense of self-misplacement for a second, a disorientation, she could

161

feel herself settling into the body that was healing from the incident. It was like putting on a shoe; a little constraining at first, but then the shoe becomes a part of the foot.

"Do you see, Carlen?" the Blue One spoke. "Here is the same Carlen who was with us in that time, the same Carlen who knew of God, the One Infinite Creator, and who knew of the One Law, who has known these principals since the beginning of the Soul Genus. We urge you to consider these things. We are with you Carlen. If this gathering of our souls together on this level had not been pre-appointed and agreed to, we would not be with you. It is a time of choices for you, a time for you to affirm your contract. Remember: recognize, confront, forgive and release. We are with you."

"Doris, can I ask you something?" Carly sat on the edge of the bed, elbows on the wiggle-y rollaway bedstand. Breakfast was over and Doris had just come back from her morning walk.

"Sure, I know everything. Shoot."

"Well, this is the second time this has happened and it's starting to spook me." Carly picked at the corner of the magazine she'd been reading. "You said something about me being surrounded by blue light, okay? And I didn't think a lot about it at the time, except that I'd just started seeing blue lights in the last couple of months."

"Yes, they're called 'blue pearls of wisdom' by the old occultists and even by some of the more enlightened of today's metaphysicians," Doris said, settling back on the half-raised mattress. "Ones who see the blue lights are alleged to be of the avatar class; masters in their field, if you get into that pecking order sort of thinking."

"Do you?" Carly thought she knew the answer, but had to ask.

"Not for a half heartbeat. I don't think that class lines are any more equitable there as here. I do think that of all the many souls who are capable of seeing the blue lights or the green ones or white ones or whatever, don't always see them. And I also think that those who do see them, like you, might be one of those more aware beings."

Carly let the implication sink in, then shaking her head, she smiled and said: "Well, I don't think so, Doris. I mean, we're not exactly—umm—nevermind. But what I was going to ask or, I don't know, just talk about, I guess—I've kind of had these vision things."

"Vision things?" Doris smiled. She knew what was coming.

"Yeah. They are visions, I guess. I don't really know how to describe them. I haven't got any name for them. But they've appeared here in our room, twice, since I've been in here and when I'm there with them, I feel like a million bucks. I mean—"

"Them?" Doris prodded, still smiling, one eyebrow raised. "And what's this got to do with blue?"

"Well, they are blue. I mean, not really blue, maybe, but there's always a blue glow going on around them. They have robes, kind of, and they float. There are so many of them, you could never count them all, even if you could see them all—at once, I mean. There is one who stands at the front and he's the one who speaks. And I get this—feeling, when they're around—like I'm suddenly well, I'm protected, I'm enriched and I'm asking questions about things I never ever think about anymore, or thought I had the intelligence to think about." Carly shook her head, "I don't know, Doris. Have you ever heard of anything like that in—well, in the things you've studied or done over the years? Am I crazy?"

Doris laughed out loud. "What did I tell you, pal? It's good to have someone to be crazy with. Everyone that I know who's involved in metaphysics is called 'crazy' or 'weird' or some such thing. You just have to let that stuff roll off your back." Then she sat forward in the bed, and became more serious. "It sounds to me like what you're experiencing, Carly,

163

is some serious guides. I'm not sure, really, about the exact—um—group you've described, but I do know that there are really higher echelon levels that bring forth some extreme knowledge. For example, the Brotherhood of the Light would be such a group. Elizabeth Clare Prophet, before she promoted herself to Queen Mother Empress of the Known World and got her little compound going and while her ego grew with her warchest; the Brotherhood was a regular group she channeled with. Actually, I think she was the one that stuck that handle on them, then after that, it was like they were her exclusive property. None of her followers, even, could channel with the Brotherhood-"

"Excuse me, Doris, I hate to interrupt, but what do you mean, 'channel with'?"

Doris laughed again, "Haven't I told you about channeling, yet? Well, bad me!" She paused, looking very closely at Carly, studying her briefly before going on. "Channeling is communicating on a psychic intellectual level, though there are many who will tell you that 'psychic' and 'intellectual' can't possibly be mixed. Channeling is kind of like praying, except that you get the other side of the conversation back with channeling and praying is just one end of it, yours. It's more of a discourse while prayer is beseeching, make a prayer to ask God for something. A channel, you know, is like a pipeline system from one point to another and the water or oil or in this case, intelligent thought flows through—both ways. You get the picture."

"I do! Doris, you are really terrific. I think I get what's going on. At least a little bit." Carly felt renewed. "These guys, the Blue People, could be like the Brotherhood, huh? Bringing information about the way things work. Like the Law."

"The Law?"

"Yeah, they talked about the Law of One, I remember. The One Law of the Law of One. And it was so simple! It's just a simple formula—as the Light increases, everything touching it increases in some way or another. It's the pebble in the pond theory."

"You mean the ripple effect?" Doris asked.

"Yes, the ripple effect. And it's the pebble that marks the place where it all starts—at the center and it widens and widens and goes on forever. There's so much more to it, you know? But I don't know how to say it, how to tell you. You see it, know it's there and you know what it can become. You extrapolate."

"Extrapolate?" Doris smiled. "Now there's a word. What does it mean exactly?"

Carly couldn't answer; she had never used the word before. She only had a sense of what it meant. She could see the picture of the geometric symbols, simple, clean lines that connecting, created more geometric expressions and like the Blue People, their group, went on forever. But, she'd never used the word before, actually had not known of its existence. "I don't know for sure. I don't know why I said it."

Doris smiled, "I think you were channeling, Carly. That's what happens when you start to open to your—guides. Your Blue People, huh?"

Both Carly and Doris turned when they heard a knock at the doorframe. The door was open and in the doorway stood Frank Bickham with a dozen white roses.

"Carly," he came to her side of the room, "I've been so worried about you."

Doris observed Carly with fascination as the whole of her countenance changed; her features became more svelte and shrewd and she telegraphed immediate raw sexuality. For the first time in days, Wicked Sister spoke, "Frank! It's about time! Where've you been? I need to be rescued!"

"Well, I'll be damned," Doris muttered to herself as she watched Frank embrace the new Carly, "there's two of them!"

19

There is no grace in being right, particularly. The grace comes in acknowledging when you're wrong. Yet, there is no right or wrong. Go figure.

In the moments it took Frank to walk past Doris' bed and let the flowers fall on the bed while he brought Carly into his arms, there was an amount of time that wasn't counted; that didn't pass by on the clock. Carly noted that this seemed to be something of a phenomenon with her lately and she took it to mean that it had a purpose. Wicked Sister had immediately emerged out of a cloud of quiet that had worried Carly and now, with her aggressive greeting to Frank, Carly was surprised and disturbed all the more.

"And what did you think, Carly?" Wicked Sister asked in the time-still limbo, "Did you think I was going to hang around when you're in cahoots with those goddamned blue creatures. Or that I'd just let you take us back to Victor? Or worse?"

"Sister, you have no idea what you're doing. You can't start this thing up with Frank again. It's not a relationship that's possible, don't you see? It just never can be, no matter how wonderful he is; *we* are not. We've had a twenty-two year affair with his son-in-law and whether or not he wants to be, he is married to Victor's wife's mother. This is the kind of tangle that destroys lives."

"Whether you like it or not, I'm going to have my fun with Frank. I'm not going to let you take us back to Victor and do that whine-y 'I love only Victor' shit, and beg him to take you back. I fuckin' hate him and I'll tell you what. If I ever fuckin' see him again, I'll kill him."

"Stop talking like that! I mean it, Sister. You're not going to do anything to Victor, and Frank has no business in our life. It doesn't matter how you feel or even how I feel about him, it can't possibly work and that's that. I'm the one who's gone through all this. You go out and play around and don't think about tomorrow while I'm the one who has to live it. The Blue People are not evil or even close to that. I don't know what they are, but they're just about the only thing right now that I'm not afraid of. Mother is upstairs in CCU, dying—"

"Yeah, well, that's someone else I'm going to take care of too, if I get half a chance. I'm tired of her old crap. Let old Norbie take care of her. Or I fuckin' will, if you get my drift."

"Sister, you can't just go around doing whatever you want to do and leave me to work out the details. If you do anything, I'm the one they'll come after—you'll be no better off than I will. Keep that in mind." Carly was firm and more than usually insistent, but Wicked Sister was unresponsively on a track of her own. She had waited days, wandering around in some gray aggravated fog and now Frank had come in and empowered her. She had no idea why she had to do it, but she knew she did. It was for Carly's own good, after all.

"Do I look horrible, Frank?" she asked.

He held her back, looking at her, his hands on her arms. "You look wonderful to me. I—you didn't call me, Carly," his face was anguished for a moment, remembering, "I only knew you'd had an accident."

"An accident?" Wicked Sister laughed. "I'm not sure what happened could be classified as 'accidental'."

"Victor told me that your mother called in for you; that you'd had a collision on your way to visit her." He held her again, "I'm only glad I'm here now. None of us knew anything.

167

Not how to get hold of your mother, where you were, how badly you were hurt. Nothing. It was frightening, Carly."

Wicked Sister reveled in his embrace and moved closer to him, then moved back, surprised at the pain in her breast. "God—" she said, almost turning it into her typical expletive, but she caught herself, reminding herself to be more Carly-like. At least for the moment.

"What's wrong?" Frank asked, concerned. "I'm sorry, have I hurt you?"

"Um-no," she said. "I just had a twinge, that's all. There are some things I'm not used to yet." Then she saw Doris studying the two of them. She didn't like Doris anymore than she liked the Blue People. "What are *you* looking at?"

"Not a thing," Doris smiled, and went back to her magazine. *Amazing,* she thought. *I can't wait to get home and do her chart. I wonder how it works when the other one is out. I'll have to be sure I speak only to Carly. This one is not anyone I'd want to tangle with.*

Frank seeing Doris for the first time, turned to her offering his hand. "Hello," he said, "I'm Frank Bickham. I didn't mean to be rude—it's just that—we've—been worried about Carly, here."

Doris smiled and looked sideways for a quick second at Wicked Sister who was in turn, attempting to level her with a look. "I'm Doris Patrick. No need to apologize. I understand what's going on." She extended her smile to Wicked Sister, letting her know that she knew. "I think it's time for my morning constitutional, if you don't mind. Nice to meet you, Frank."

Bickham Industries Frank, Doris thought as she took her magazine and headed down the hall for the family room. *Big money. And who's Victor? Hmmm. He must be the man who— What a snarl. I wonder what Carly will have to say about all of this when she can re-surface.*

Wicked Sister felt of her face, to check the bandages.

—

She had not had any knowledge of the conditions of the body for several days, since that first day. She could find no Carly memory of what the face looked like after Victor had finished with it. She was insecure. "How do I look, really, Frank?" she said, moving away from him, but taking his hand and leading him to a chair. "Am I hideous?"

"Never." Then he smiled, "You're always beautiful. I'm relieved to see you up and walking and talking. I wasn't able to ask Victor for any details or to ask him why he didn't ask your mother for more information. I couldn't appear too distraught in front of him. Then Mandy would hear about it and it would eventually get to Beatrice, which would upset her cruelly."

Wicked Sister said nothing, she smiled a Carly smile trying to absorb all that Frank had said, trying to be calm like Carly, too. She probably hated Victor as much as Carly loved him and hearing of his story to Frank, she hated him all the more. *What will I do to him,* she wondered, *how will I pay him back? I won't kill him after all, yeah. That would be too quick, that asshole. I'll think of something, though.* She was unused to projecting, to making a plan or having goals, but she allowed this was probably a good time to start. There was a lot to do. Finally she spoke, "I wonder what happened to my car."

"I'll buy you a new one," Frank said, stroking her face, "You're alive and there were times I—didn't know if that was so. I called everywhere trying to find you and at last, here you are. Saint Elizabeth's didn't list you as a patient at first. It wasn't until yesterday that you were listed and then they said you were restricted from having visitors. I imagined every conceivable kind of injury."

He kissed her lightly on the mouth, "Carly, I want to hold you and make love to you so badly, but I don't want to hurt you."

"The hurting part's already been taken care of," Wicked Sister laughed. "It'll be a few days before we can—I can—

———

169

um—be with you. The injuries—" *What can I say? How do you tear off your tit and ruin your twat in a car accident? Oh, that goddamned Victor, that fuckin' asshole.*

"No one has ever meant as much to me as you, Carly. I know it sounds corny, but I just found you, just discovered how monumentally profound loving you can be, I don't want to lose you now. As long as I know you want me, too, I'll be the soul of patience." He kissed her again.

"Frank, let's sit down, I've got to sit down now." Wicked Sister was surprised at her lack of strength and she didn't at all like the feeling. It had never been her burden, the body, that was Carly's. Cutting Carly off, like Carly had cut her off, didn't seem like such a good idea now. "I think I should be in the bed, maybe. Damn."

Frank helped her onto the bed and she lay back, exhausted. Her left breast felt as though it was going to fall off and the whole of her lower self was throbbing from pain it hurt so bad inside and out. Her cheekbone stabbed pains into her eye and made her face feel as if it had cracked in two. "Am I in one piece?" she asked him. "I don't—"

In the moment it took Frank to reach over her to find the call button, Wicked Sister had given over to Carly. "You made a fuckin' mess of our body, Carly," she said on her way out, "I'll come back when it's better. It's not good for anything right now."

Carly looked up at Frank's face and saw, amazed, a genuine anguish. He was worried about her, actually concerned. No one had ever shown anything like that for her before and she wasn't sure what to do. It made her anxious.

"Carly, are you okay?" He touched her face again. "I didn't mean—"

Judy Simpson was the day nurse. An efficient woman, not unpleasant, but bustling and just the slightest bit officious. Neither Carly nor Doris liked her as much as they did Karen. "What can I do for you, Carly?"

"I pushed the call button," Frank said, "she became very pale and weak all of a sudden and—it—I panicked. I'm sorry."

Judy came to the bed and took Carly's wrist. "Your pulse is good, you look fine," she said after a minute. "You okay now? Any complaints?"

"No," Carly said, looking at Frank, then back at Judy. "I just felt a little tired. I—haven't been up a lot—"

"True," Judy said, "but we'll take care of that later today, m'dear. If you're going to go home in a couple of days, we can't have you fainting all over the place, now can we?" She looked at her watch, "I'll be back in an hour or so with your meds."

She turned to go then saw the flowers. "Let me take these and get them some fresh water. They're beautiful."

As soon as Judy left the room, Frank turned to Carly. He took her hand, "I didn't mean to upset you or tire you out." He kissed her fingers, "I love you, Carly. I want to—make it better for you, not worse."

Carly felt that same surge of closeness she had felt with him the night of the incident and it moved her off balance. Her anxiety worsened. What had Wicked Sister said to him? What had happened? She could only speculate as Wicked Sister had erupted so suddenly and so powerfully that she'd been thrown back into a gray place that numbed her brain and her senses. She'd never been there before and it had been frightening. It was even more frightening to think that Wicked Sister could do that or even that she would. "You didn't upset me, Frank," she lied, "I—it's just so—complicated."

"Yes, it is complicated. I completely agree," he kissed her hand again, "but I know that loving you is worth overcoming the complications. I also know that you feel more than just casually about me, Carly. I'm not young or dashing but I'm also not an aging playboy with years of callous experience in these things; still, I felt your response to me. I said it before, Carly, this is an attraction with meaning."

171

Carly couldn't look at him anymore; to do so only further entrenched the dual feelings of anxiety and attraction. She turned her head to look out the window, which seemed to be the only way she could talk to him. "Maybe, but I don't know what to do about any of it."

"You don't need to do anything, Carly." He said, "Just let me take care of it. Let me be a part of your life."

"I can't. You can't." She was too quick with the answer and too firm.

He smiled; he knew an opportunity when he saw one. "I can and you will," he said. "The real sin, here, my beautiful girl, is not to love, to turn away from it."

She turned to look at his face again and still, she could say nothing. He bent down and kissed her very lightly and carefully and again, she was amazed that she could be stirred, that she could feel close. "This is forever, Carly," he whispered, "we're obligated to work it out."

20

Sometimes it takes the third eye to gain the workable perspective. The third eye can be anyone's as long as it has 20/20 forward vision.

Doris was intrigued utterly with the drama of Carly Worthington, but more than that, Doris sensed a connection that ran deep with them and interlaced their souls in an indelible way. When Carly had been released, Doris was still a day away from going home, but they had hugged each other and promised to be in touch. Doris amusingly reflected on the many hugs that had been forced upon her in her long career in the metaphysical arena and probably not one of them was anything other than the look-good hug. The hug that said, "See? I'm a loving new age person, everyone, and whether or not you deserve my love, you're going to get it because it's my duty." But the Carly hugs were real and Doris knew very well that they were not given lightly, which made hers equally genuine. Doris was convinced, too, that there were life interchanges between her and Carly and she meant to define them, and at the same time, cement the relationship further.

Her first order of business on coming home had been to ask her daughter to bring her cat back. Poor old Kiva, she'd been gone from home for so long and gone from the bond that sustained them both. Doris laughed at the thought and how it had played in her mind. Her daughter, Cindy, was a terrific pal, but Doris knew their contract didn't go beyond the present life. She'd committed to giving birth to her, raising her in fun and love and after that, well, there was Karma

173

okay, good Karma, but it would be their own free choice as to whether they wanted to take it anywhere beyond that. Two old souls making a pact that worked well for each. But the cat, her precious Kiva, that was different. You didn't just make a pact with an animal, it was not a two-way street, where the animal and the human could just pick up and take off and go their separate lives way after the fact. When you committed to an animal soul, you committed a tie that promised a forever contact, as long as was needed. Doris never presumed a Universal law, but she suspected that this one essence of it had something to do with the spark of a higher soul being evolved. Cat to human? Anything was possible. And not knowing for sure wouldn't stop her from treating their warranted relationship as if it had been written in celestial stone.

The minute Cindy brought her into the house, Kiva bounded from her arms and trotted into the kitchen where Doris sat at the table. Up into her lap, then to her bosom and a loud raucous purring accompanied a kiss-lick to the cheek. "Oh, you beautiful noisy old thing, you!" Doris said, and stroked the cat now lovingly cuddling her neck. "Must be you're happy to see me!"

"Say 'hi' to your other daughter," Cindy said, coming to the other side of the table to sit. "How are you feeling? Got any coffee? Shall I make a pot?"

"Hello, Cindy, dear. You are such a Gemini, child." Doris smiled, then answering her," I'm great, feeling about 40 pounds younger, I do have coffee and why don't you?"

"Well, you're looking a lot better than when you first got out of surgery, that's for sure." Cindy got up to make the coffee and as she went by her mother, she bent over and kissed her cheek. "Good to have you back, Mom. I love you, you know."

"I know, kiddo. And thanks for taking Kiva. That really helped out."

"No problem. She was good, as always. She missed you,

though." Cindy measured the coffee into the coffee maker, poured the water and turned on the switch. It obliged her by coughing into life and beginning its process. "So I see by the books on the table, you're doing a chart. When are you going to start doing that on the computer I got you?"

Doris had Kiva securely settled in her lap, purring loudly, and she went back to the calculations for Carly's horoscope. "You know I really appreciate that computer and I do like to email folks, but I don't think I'll ever trust it to work up a natal chart."

"Why not?" Cindy chuckled. It wasn't like she didn't know what her mother was going to say.

"Because it can't feel the person's essence when it does it. And when it's done, it just hands the paperwork to me cold and I don't know a thing, then I have to reach too deep to try to find the balance point. Sometimes, it just doesn't work. No matter how long you've been at it, Cin, you know that—each one of them is individual, a unique being, born at that instant in that place, in that moment from that mother's womb." Doris tapped some figures into her calculator. "It's not just the cold hard facts about a person that makes a good astrologer make a good natal chart and give a good interpretation. It's that clue you get when you're rounding the table of houses, when you discover that Pluto's in the 4th or that the Moon's trined by Jupiter, or when you discover their ascendant, their mid heaven. It's the 'aha!' the best astrology software in the world can never give you."

Cindy laughed, "Mom, you're the best!" She set a cup of coffee at the table to her left, "So; who's chart are you doing?"

"My roomie in the hospital."

"You mean the woman who'd been beat up?" Cindy sat at the opposite side of the table, "The one with the mother? Carly, isn't it?"

"That's the one."

"Well, I can see why you'd want to do her chart. I didn't

175

really see much of her when I was there, but I could feel the energy."

"The energy indeed." Doris acknowledged. "She's got a Scorpio sun and it looks like it'll turn out to be a Scorpio ascendant as well. She thought her mother said that she'd been born in Port Huron about 8 in the morning, but she also said that her mother was drunk a lot and that it was just something that stuck with her. 'I could've imagined it,' she said. But it's what I've got and I feel pretty good about it."

"Birth certificate? She ever think of getting one of those?" Cindy asked.

"I don't think she had any interest in that. She seemed more interested in detaching from her mother as much as possible, not researching her roots." Doris looked up at Cindy and smiling took a sip of her coffee, "She's a special person, somehow. I don't mean the usual New Age 'everyone's special' sense. Carly is an old soul, extremely, innately in touch, but with a huge conflict and I'm not sure just how she's going to play it out. I could do a thousand charts around that energy, but it wouldn't tell me anything more than that she's well connected, she's at a cosmic crossroads and I already know that."

"Well, what do you know about her? I mean, 'cosmic crossroads' is pretty heavy stuff, huh?" Cindy leaned forward to take a look at what her mother had done so far, "Where's her Moon?"

"It's in Capricorn, in the second house, not an easy placement for the Moon. Her sun's about a degree and a half away from being 'the accursed sign' of Serpentine and let me tell you, she's got challenges all over this baby." Doris turned the chart around so Cindy could read it right side up. "And— she has some equally profound help. Look here," Doris pointed to a glyph in the 5th house, "Look what's at 3 degrees of Pisces, right on the nose."

"Wow." Cindy adjusted her glasses. "Saturn, exact sextile

Uranus, trine Mars, trine the South Nodes, exact trine the Sun. This gal doesn't do anything by halves, does she?"

"See what I mean?" Doris said, "Look at her Venus, too, trine Moon and all the rest of her stuff in Capricorn. And Saturn at 3 of Pisces?"

"Yeah, isn't that the—um—Master thing?"

"Mm-hmm. The beneficent fixed star signifying Master of the Occult. I mean I've seen some charts with that indication, but usually on the Ascendant, or one of the quick movers, like the Moon or Mercury or Venus, but I've never found one at Saturn before this. Unbelievably propitious." Doris said, "But it only means she has the potential to fulfill that Teacher of Teachers contract, not that she will. She's got a hundred other reasons here not to."

"You mean the squares?" Cindy still studied the chart, "And the oppositions! And two quincunxes! Gee, conflict is right, Mom. You sure know how to pick 'em."

"Yes, I do, you included, my little flip flop Gemini!" Doris laughed. Then turning serious again, "But speaking of Gemini, I discovered that Carly has a second personality."

Cindy looked up, interested. "What do you mean, a 'second' one?"

"Right up your alley, huh?" Doris smiled again. "I knew that would get your little clinical psychology heart a-thumpin'."

"You're right about that. The dream of every psyche scientist/therapist from here to Jabib is a schizophrenic expressing multiple personalities walking into your office."

"Cindy, my child, you're salivating all over her chart." Doris laughed, "Don't get ahead of yourself. I never said anything about schizo. This woman is probably an alcoholic to some degree, though I don't think to the extent that it's more than pattern habitual—"

"Now, there's a new term; 'pattern habitual'. May I use

that in my practice?" Cindy smiled at her mother fondly, "You are a treat, Mom."

"Thank you. Back atcha. What I mean by that," Doris winked at Cindy, "and I use it in *my* practice all the time, so feel free—is that Carly has embraced a pattern of behavior from her mother and it's become habitual in her life. It's not like she's spiritually or mentally or possibly even not physically addicted to alcohol, it's that it's a pattern with her and she's habitually addicted. Yet, what I think is that these patterns started early on, so it didn't begin as a physical addiction at least, and the denial was so fierce with the love hate thing going on with her mother that the second personality took form. Now, here," Doris pointed, "is where it takes shape in the chart. This conflict with the mother, here in the fourth house that reflects back to her will, then follows this path," pointing again, "to the afflicted moon, the unconscious, then here past the interception, another twist, to the North nodes. Hmm? Isn't that incredible?"

"Can I have her, Mom, can I have her?" Cindy laughed. "Oh, I would be the star of the office to bring in a client like that."

"Well, you can't have her, she's mine!" They both laughed, then Doris continued in the more serious vein, "Actually, there is a connection between us that goes deep, I think, and is some past life thing. Correction: past *lives* thing. And the man who came to visit her yesterday was Frank Bickham. You do know who he is, don't you?"

"I do. He's Mandy Bickham's dad. I went to school with Mandy, remember? Well, she was ahead of me by a couple of years, but who could forget the richest girl in school, huh?" Cindy handed the chart back to her mother, "So where is he in all of this? I wouldn't have any idea how to identify him in her chart. That's beyond my capabilities."

"He doesn't show up in the chart right away. I think he's there because I sense it, but if I'm going to pinpoint his relationship with her, I'll have to do some progressions and get into things a little more deeply than I have up to this point." Doris looked down in her lap and stroked the contented napping Kiva, "There's another man, too."

"You see that in her chart?"

"Yes, I do. Take a look at how the 7th is aspected."

"Mother, you know I can't get into anything beyond the obvious in a chart." Cindy said, shoving the chart further across the table. "I can do expansive motivational studies, but I'm a limited astrologer. You'll have to tell me."

"Forget the chart. Trust me, it's in there. I don't know who he is, but I picked up that he's been around a long time, that his interest in her is not what she thinks it is and certainly can't match her loyalty and dedication to him. I told you she was conflicted. When Frank Bickham came to see her yesterday, he brought white roses and he carried his feelings for her all over his face."

"But he's married!"

"Since when did that stop anyone from falling in love with someone else?" Doris petted Kiva one last time before the cat hopped down to check out her food dish. "After all, there was your father, remember?"

"Touche'." Cindy leaned forward, thinking only briefly of her father, now living with his second wife in Arizona. "So; what do you think?"

"I think I care about what happens to Carly, about the decisions she makes. We know that being married doesn't stop anyone from falling in love, but it doesn't help the evolution of the relationship. It was when Frank walked in that the other one, the surly, brash one, came out. She as much as told me to take a walk—so I did. I didn't like her one bit and she didn't like me right back. She was so very much not Carly. I wish you'd have been there, Cin."

"So do I! And not just because I'm a practicing psychologist but—I don't know—to confirm your sighting, I guess. And to be there for you. I have the feeling that you're really connected to this woman." Cindy got up to get the coffee pot. "And I'm only a little bit jealous."

Doris smiled at her as she poured them both a second cup. The sun crested the diminishing clouds just then and streamed its elegance in a grand ray through the kitchen window and onto the table, highlighting a corner of Carly's chart that lay innocently at its edge. The moment grabbed Doris' thoughts and she felt gripped by a wedge of time that had impressed her psyche an eon ago and was now, for a breath, remembered, then gone with the intake of the next one. "Whew. That was something," Doris remarked quietly.

"What was something?" Cindy said, returning the coffee pot to its warming plate.

"I had one of those memories; you know, like a deja vu only much more electricifying." Doris picked up the chart as if looking at it now might show some glyph that the sun itself had imprinted in that moment of revelation; that would tell her what it meant. "But no. Easy come easy go."

"Okay, Mom, now you're being mysterious." Cindy sat down again and Doris saw that the clouds had once again veiled the sun.

"I'm sorry. It was just a thing. People have them all the time."

"I'm really interested in this Carly thing. You have no clue as to who the first guy is?"

"No, not in identity terms, but I have a good idea of who he is, how he is and I'll tell you this much, he makes me very angry," Doris said. "He's connected—oh, I don't know. I get about that far and I seem unable to get any further with it. I do think he's the one who beat her up and raped her though."

"What?" Cindy came forward again, "I thought she was only beaten. By a thief or a purse snatcher or something like that."

"No. It wasn't anything she would talk about, but she'd

had surgery on her left breast, they did an implant because he damaged it so badly, and I knew she'd had some gynecological things done because it was Dr. Lefkowitz who operated. She's a Gyn surgeon. So; something was going on down there. It wasn't any coincidence that she was beaten up then she just happened to have a hemorrhaging uteris or whatever at the same time. I picked it up psychically, too, and it wasn't pretty, I'll tell you. She stuck to her story about falling in the shower, though." Doris shook her head, "But when Frank came in he talked about a Victor telling him her mother had called in, presumably to her office, she's an art director at that big agency, to tell them about an auto accident. One thing I know is that you don't generally get injured in the vaginal area in an auto accident and another thing I know is that her mother has been at death's door since that night Carly came in. She told me that. So how could her mother call this Victor guy?"

"Fascinating." Cindy said, "And how do you think you might be involved with her in some past lives."

"Oh I don't know, Cin. It's just a sense of it, like I said. She feels like a younger sister or a cousin, someone close and I kind of think that there've been other relationships too, but all mutually supportive, like that, like sisters, close relatives, brothers maybe." Kiva jumped back into Doris' lap again and she stroked the purring cat absently. "And another impressive thing, Cin, Carly's been in touch with the Teachers."

"Your Teachers?" Cindy straightened up.

"One and the same."

"How do you know?"

"She told me. She called them the 'Blue People' and told me how they'd all fit into our hospital room but they really didn't; there were too many to count."

"What did you say?"

Doris sipped at the coffee while Kiva curled in her lap, "I

didn't say anything or do anything, really. I had the sense from them, the Teachers, that it wasn't an appropriate time for me to—um—intervene, to reveal anything. She asked me if I thought she was crazy and I said something to the effect that if she was, I was, but beyond describing to her what channeling was, I said very little."

"Well, yet another high metaphysician was observed sparkling in the northern sky." Cindy smiled. "Only you, Mom, could be there and recognize the Light. Isn't that something, though? The two of you ending up in the same room at the hospital as roomies for a week. What is it you're always saying to me about no coincidences?"

"Nothing is by accident; all is by divine design." Doris smiled back at Cindy, "That's a Teachers-ism. First garnered through automatic writing about 20 years ago."

"Doesn't it make you wonder," Cindy mused, "just how far and wide they spread themselves?"

"No, I don't wonder any more. I know they're out there and here and there when they ought to be. I know they manifest themselves to different people on different levels in different ways. And I'm almost never surprised when I hear about it; but I was some kind of taken aback, let me tell you, when they showed up in glorious blue surrounding both me and Carly in that hospital room." Kiva, still purring, looked up at Doris with huge green eyes, interested, alert. "Oh, I said something to make you perk up, didn't I, Kiva?"

21

Once you start expanding the mind, thinking the same old thoughts in it is excruciatingly painful. Is that also by design?

Dr. Rosen had scheduled Betta Mary's surgery for Friday morning at 10 o'clock which would have made it easy for Carly to be there. She was still in the hospital then. But Betta Mary's condition wouldn't warrant her coming through it; so it was shoved to a tentative date of Wednesday, September 9 at 10 AM. Now, Monday, Carly was out of the hospital, back at her apartment, without a car, without a job, without Victor and going crazy with all the un-drunk beer and liquor in the place. There was the issue of the rape that Dr. Steele still wanted to address with her, there was the what-to-do-about-Mother thing, there was Frank, there was Wicked Sister and now the Blue People were there, not exactly harassing her but making her feel as if she should do something. Their presence seemed to insist on an action and it was an action she was unable to identify currently. Even if she could identify it, she had no confidence that it would be something she could actually do. And she still had to find a way to get to the hospital early the next morning.

Talking with Doris Patrick had been like a miracle, pulling her out of her low mood and initiating a curiosity and an excitement of discovery and learning. She had never felt close with any woman before; and thinking about it, she realized she hadn't been truly intimate with any man until the one time with Frank and that was a frightening concept to her. Thoughts of it opened a pathway that seemed dark and

183

cluttered and strewn with gaping pitfalls that could swallow a person whole. Then there was that thought, that unnamed pain of a memory of the billy club left rolling about on the kitchen floor with her blood on it. It was too repulsive to think about what Victor had done to her with it, but jamming it away inside of a denial box was not working. And so it went, around and around and around her thoughts clamored in dilemma and turmoil in the vast new spaces of her mind that Doris and the Blue People had insisted that she crowbar open.

"If this is progress," she thought, "it isn't fun and I don't like it."

An instantaneous glow of blue developed into the group, fronted by the one Blue One and settled before her as she sat at the passthrough bar between her kitchen and living room. Their vast numbers queued well beyond the confines of her apartment, it seemed and yet, there they were within its walls. Seeing them appear like that disoriented her and she quickly wondered if she'd ever get used to them coming immediately and so much into view like that.

The one Blue One smiled a greeting. "Yes, you will assume a greater familiarity as we commune thusly. We will tell you, Carlen, that we understand your discomfort at present with the burden of growth and evolution of the mind and spirit. It is a necessary thing, however, and we would not be so impelled to encourage these sessions if there were any doubt at all about your interest in them, or your ability to assume a profit from them."

Carly felt of her coffee cup, then the cut glass sugar bowl and the spoon. They were all solid with the characteristics she was used to feeling as she touched them. Yet, here were a hundred thousand Blue People standing in her kitchen talking to her about things she had no way of hearing, and most disconcerting of all was that she was talking to them.

"We have told you of choices and commitments; we are

certain of your understanding of these things. It is important in the time consideration of the reality where such things are measured, that we move on to explore the more precise details of these as they impact the Carlen personality—"

"Whoa," Carly interrupted. "You may know what you're talking about and you may think that I know. But I don't. Precise details of what that impacts, I don't get that at all— and who's the Carlen personality? If you mean me, why don't you say 'Carly'? That's who I am."

The Blue One smiled broadly and humor was light in his tone as he continued, "Ah, yes, the nickname 'Carly.' Carlen is the name given to the entity at the time of the birth of the body, hence it is the name of the personality, a facet of the Higher Self that with the many other facets, goes to make the whole essence, the Soul Genus. If it more familiarizes you with the purpose, the shorter version of the name shall henceforth be used to address you. Does this please the Carly entity?" He smiled again.

"I guess so. I really hate the name 'Carlen.' It's a big reminder that I'm a one parent child and I don't know and I'll never know if I got stuck with the worst one or not." Carly considered the Blue One and his group. "Which brings me to why you're here, if you're really here. And why you brought up the business of how I used to think about God when I was little—"

Now, the Blue One interrupted, "We merely affirmed your memory of those considerations by providing the doorway to the Soul Genus, the Higher Self, a platform on which to display the activities that once done; are never lost by the Law and only by the Law, can they be dismissed. But it was you, Carly, who brought the subject to the fore. It is our job, if you will, as teachers, bringers of order, teachers of the discipline of the Light, to facilitate the recollection of such activities when appropriate. We will tell you further that all such recollections are at your will, Carly, for there is all of that of every moment

185

of breath drawn and Light encouraged that lies within you to reinitiate in the current expression."

"But all of what you're saying isn't the real me, it doesn't apply to me. You seem to think I'm someone who can do all of these things you want. That I have all these great abilities when the only thing I can really do is draw and well—you know what else. I don't think very well at all, I drink too much and probably am an alcoholic because I want to drink to obliterate everything; I can't do a relationship except for a bad one, because I don't know how to love anybody. I mean, you know, love anyone without it being a sexual thing. That, I can do! And even I know that when I die, that's done with." Carly watched the Blue One consider her as she spoke and it occurred to her that all of the issues she had addressed had somehow been triggered by him, by them. "Okay, I get that you're asking me in a way to look at these things, these ways I behave or think in my life, but I'm not kidding when I say, you've got the wrong person here. I'm not who you think I am."

This time, the Blue One laughed, "More to the point, Carly, you are not who *you* think you are. We are completely aware of who you are and our analyses of your Light attributes and activities remains exactly as has always been. It is our function to assist in tuning the Carly personality's vibrations to those of the Higher Self so that an alignment of purpose of the Soul Genus expression can be accomplished. Throughout the life of the Carly personality, there have been dreams and recollections of other facets of the expression, other personalities, if you will, that have given advancement to the Soul Genus. That the Carly personality has chosen to obliterate, as you so expressed, through the indulgence of alcoholic drink and the denial of interactive relationship in the life would argue for its entrenchment in these ways. Yet, the Carly personality opens with ease to greater possibilities, to higher prospects of expression and realizes as we speak thusly, that obliteration and denial has been but for an instant in the Universal measurement of these things. It is understood that these addictions and behaviors can be set aside in far less than the instant in which they have been obliged and it is only the thin thread of insistence that it cannot that prevents the Carly personality from so doing. Perhaps it is timely then, to explore one of these facets of the Soul Genus, so as to gain a perspective. Might you agree to this, Carly?"

Carly was amazed at the clarity with which she understood where the Blue One was going with his remarks. A fleeting thought of the keenness of being sober preceded the excitement that injected itself into her at knowing that they were speaking of recalling a past life. She and Doris had talked about past lives and reincarnation as a theory and how that theory had established itself in the many world religions, both past and present, but neither had entered through the personal gates their conversations at once invited and skirted. *Maybe it is easy*, she thought, *maybe this is just trading one kind of addiction for another, too.*

"Indeed, Carly, that might be the case," the Blue One interjected into her thoughts, "but that is a worthy risk to take. Logic, that highest of all thought, dictates that at the very least, the one addiction is the more judicial of the two. Come now, it is a moment of choice. We cannot impose upon you the lesson, for to teach is to learn, to learn is to teach and so the inter-reactive continues until we are all ascended to the level of the One Infinite Creator. We must do this with all wills aimed directly for the one path."

"Well, then, let's go," Carly said, knowing somewhere within and without, perhaps, that here was a moment she would not forget in whatever time ruled wherever she might be. And she smiled at recognizing that they, these teachers, had skillfully managed the direction of the interview to conclude in the way they had originally declared. Almost her last thought as the uninitiated Carly, she realized too, that all

---

187

along, her will had been synchronized with theirs and she wondered if she really was the part of them that they so insisted she was.

"And so it is, Carly."

In the next instant of saying her name, there emerged a scene before her focus. A large cellar-way made of gigantic block stones appeared, so real, and there had been shaped out of smaller stones a large alcove that she knew would be damp to the touch. She stared at it, saw the rags that made a bed in it and wondered if she was really seeing it or if it was some trick of light and focus. Carly's eyes became uncomfortably scratchy then and heavy lids fought to close or to open and she couldn't determine which. Sitting there, she felt her head jerk as if she'd just escaped sleep, and she looked all about her at the place that had been her kitchen, but the scene didn't go away. Instead, it seemed to grow larger, become more encompassing, and with warm unseen arms it reached for her and enfolded her in it. With no bit of resistance, she was there in that dank cellar-way, suddenly feeling stunted and frustrated at a kind of stupor of perspective that now came over her.

Carly struggled with thoughts as if in a murky soup, trying to bring anything to the front of her mind that would explain the awful clutch in her throat. She looked down at her hands that held a ribbon and a piece of an ivory comb. She was horrified to see that her fingers were no longer slim and artistic but stubby, plump things, strangely gnarled and with only one knuckle for each. How could they be hers? She asked that question not of the creature who she was, but of some other self that hovered above that strange grotesque body. But there were no answers from any quarter.

The comb and the ribbon she held were extremely dear to her for some reason she could only barely think of. Looking at them seemed to trigger some duty in her and she knew she had to go up the cellar-way stairs. But first, it was necessary that she take care of the prizes she held. She touched the ribbon to her face, rather ritualistically, laid it flat under the rags in the alcove and with the clumsy fingers carefully placed the ivory comb piece in the pocket of the apron she wore. Then she began her wobbly way up the wide stone stairs. Her feet felt rounded at the bottom, so she commanded the creature whose vessel she shared to look down to see them but she could detect nothing as vision was blurred and slanted, as if coming out of a skewed tunnel. There was no curiosity about this slug mind that lived in her brain and as her, Carly could no longer wonder why it would be that she could see the hands, the ribbon and the comb but she could not see the feet, only feel their stumpiness.

As the creature struggled up the steps that were too high for the bowed sausage legs, there was a great concentration on the doing of it. She did not at all hear or notice in any way, the very large woman called Minot, who stood at the top step before the scullery, holding a heavy tall mirror she'd scraped across the stone. When at last, she had found her way to that topmost step, she grunted, hauled the misshapen body to the floor there and managed to stand erect. It was in that moment that she saw the visage of the repulsive creature that she was. Instantly, she stepped back, shocked and horrified at what confronted her in the mirror. To the round asthmatic guffaws of Minot, she fell into an unbalance, lost her footing and tumbled back down the steps she had struggled so to achieve.

"Poor little ugly!" Minot laughed. Then to someone in the scullery, she said, "I told you she would! She does it each time! She is so frightened at seeing herself, she falls backward!"

Laughing still but done with the joke, Minot scraped the mirror off to its storage place and left the cellar-way landing. The dwarf couldn't tell whether she was hurt or not. The awful compacted body seemed without true feeling, but if a wrench of the heart was what Minot had wanted, she would have seen it had she stayed to watch. The little thing that Carly had become was immediately cut to the center of her being as she put that clump of a hand into her apron pocket to touch the comb but did not find it. She could not think of words, no real thoughts came. She was driven only to wail for her lost treasure.

22

If ego gets in the way here, just say the word and we'll smash it to bits and make it disappear. Then and only then, will we let you have a brand new, nice new clean one.

Carly, breathless, reeled from the stool at the kitchen passthrough, went to the living room and collapsed on the couch. She pulled a toss pillow to her midsection and held it there. Her face wounds suddenly throbbed, feeling ballooned at the storage of tears uncried. "What awful thing was that?" she asked, her thoughts wobbling as the little body had making its way up the steps.

"Ah, yes. Do you feel the empathy with the entity just experienced, Carly?" Asked the Blue One, his tone even as always.

Carly took another breath and soothed her face to take away the throbbing. Then, she looked at her hands and was grateful to see that they were the beautiful best feature she'd always known them to be. "What *was* that? Some kind of shock therapy?"

"Not at all, Carly," the Blue One smiled still. "It was simply the direction of the Higher Self that was followed. Please answer our question. Do you feel the empathy?"

Carly turned to look at the Blue One and sure enough, there he was, flanked by his group that poured its ranks out of her living room into eternity somewhere. Considering, she knew she had felt an empathy with the creature, she had been it, she had been utterly broken not by the woman Minot, but by not finding that precious chunk of ivory comb and she had no other thing to say than, "Yes, maybe."

191

"Do you wish to learn more about the little entity and about why Higher Self chose that particular expression as an introduction to this experience?"

"Yes," Carly said, hesitating only slightly. Whatever it was, whatever it might mean could only bring her closer to an understanding of who she really was and all the choices she had made. "But can we do it more gradually or gently this time?"

"Indeed we can."

Immediately, Carly felt as though she ought to be relaxed, to be in a reclining position so as to allow as little of her own Carly sensations into the experience as possible. She let herself ease back onto the couch and folded her hands comfortably on the toss pillow she kept at her midsection.

"Breathe easily, Carly, and think of the little entity. Allow the purpose of the recollection to be the overall focus and open to the worthwhile endeavor of discovery."

Carly let herself think of how she had felt as the little dwarf and it was then that she remembered the dream she'd had as being the small person in a crowd of beautifully clothed people. It was that memory that greased her slip into the little body once again. Instantly, she was there, thinking in its terms and feeling its dull-coated emotions. The Blue One and the group then, very carefully and considerately lowered her into a scene, and she felt herself being integrated into the odd little body. There was some innate momentary reluctance on her part and as she wondered at it, she set it aside. She realized then that the body she had come into was the dwarf as a child, stunted and grotesque and though she had experienced it those minutes before, it was now even more stunningly real. With no other way to be, its physical mind was not capable of the speed of her thoughts and the moments passed as she felt herself go dull. She heard only an echo of a little Carlen those many years ago wailing, "Mommy, I want to be with you!" Then, Carly was she, Julie Boit.

———

She squatted by the little river that meandered its sparkling way past the land the house sat upon. She loved to play with the stones and make them into shapes and patterns in the dirt and though she never grew tired of that, she sometimes liked to play with the fish in the river, too. They wiggled and the stones did not. When she played with the fish, she sat in the river on a big stone and let them swim around her legs and her body. She could be still as the stone itself and the fish never knew that she could move. She felt very important that she could have a secret from the fish. And it felt good to sit in the water as it made such nice noises.

She could not remember the beginning part of the day when it was in the middle of it and she was completely unaware that anything at all would take place at the end of it, even though all very like events occurred in each of her days. She played in that one spot on the bank or she sat on that one stone in the stream and the day was incidental only to itself. If it rained in the countryside of the Sainte Savin, she didn't notice as wetness made no difference to her over dryness. These were conditions that were without interest to her and as well, she had no concept that they were the conditions that changed the components of her play. When it rained, the dirt she played in became quite structured and she liked that but was not curious to know how she might effect such a condition on her own and when it dried, she didn't remember that it had been wet. She simply accepted what was when it occurred. When it rained, the fish did not swim around her but searched elsewhere than the surface of the water for bugs to eat. She sat still and waited for the fish to come. When they didn't, they simply didn't and perhaps then, she would go back to the wet dirt.

The day merely was the day. Until the end of it came and as soon as she noticed a hunger, a bad feeling came on her and there was her father and her brother. She didn't like any

193

of it when they did it to her, it hurt and she cried some, but after awhile it was done and she was given food. She remembered neither the hunger nor the things done that hurt her. She sat in the box by the cooking fire afterward and played with the ravelings of cloths that were in it. Sometimes she could make marks on herself and the box with a piece of the black that came out of the fire. If it was red, she didn't want it, because it hurt, but if it was black, it was fun. Most of the time, she could remember that.

When her mother came home to their house, she liked it, but she couldn't remember when it had happened last. "Julie Boit, Julie Boit, my precious child," her mother sang to her. Julie could smile but she couldn't yet speak many words. "Mama" and "sing Julie" were some that she spoke. Once she had known the words "Papa" and "brother" but she didn't like the words so she had lost them. If it was that her mother beat her father and brother with a stick, Julie felt no badness, but let the ravelings and the box fill the moments of that distant rage and clamor. Sometimes to sleep was good if she hadn't slept too much in the dirt, but she never knew when she did or didn't; so she just let sleep come to her when it would.

Julie Boit did not know how old she was when her mother took her with her one day to the Manse. But by then, Julie knew how to speak many words. Her mother had told Julie after she had pushed the dead baby out of her bottom, that she must come with her to the Manse. She must speak words to the great people there, as they would want to know that she could talk. Her mother told her that she must smile as much as she could, that she must clean her hair and her body once a month and do as she was told by any one and all of the great people there.

"What is a once a month?" Julie did not know. She did know that she could ask her mother but she must never ask anything of the great people at the Manse. If she did, they might not let her stay, her mother had warned.

"A month's time is when the blood comes to you, Julie Boit. After that, you will know to clean yourself." And that was that; something she could remember and oh yes, she would do it! She knew how. She would go to the river and sit in it.

The great people at the Manse frightened Julie Boit at first, and she hid behind her mother. She had never seen so many people all together ever, nor had she ever thought the Manse would be so large and have so much stone about it and so many smells. She had seen the Manse in the far off distance from her spot at the river bank for a long, long time. It was something for her that did not need remembering, for it was always there. When she got the baby in her from her father and her brother putting the seed for it in there, her mother had beat them more. When it had come out of her and it didn't move, her mother was glad but then she cried some, too. When she cried, Julie cried. She didn't know why but it hurt her inside of herself when her mother was sad. After they cried, her mother wrapped the dead baby and put it in the ground, then she said to Julie:

"I am ill and I cannot keep them from you. You must come with me to the Manse where I labor."

"What is labor?" Julie asked her mother because that's the part she could remember of what her mother had said because it was at the last of it, but something terrible had been said, too. Julie didn't know what it was, but she felt very badly again.

"Labor is doing what needs to be done and what you are told to do. The cook, Madame Laurents, will tell you to fetch things and carry things and sometimes, you will be made to clean the food, or chop it or peel its skin from it. The peelings then, must be taken in buckets to the swine in the yards in back of the Manse and that will make you dirty, so you will

195

have to clean yourself extra in those times. Monsieur Bernard who rules the whole of all the servants, will tell you to carry linens sometimes so you must be clean for that. And he will tell you to help Mademoiselle Jeannette and Madame Beauvard with the dusting and cleaning. Then others like Paul, Gabrielle, and Minot will make you take up some of their chores. You will always be made to scrub."

It was all too much to remember, the words came too fast and became just sounds of noise, so Julie Boit never remembered what labor was, nor could she even think to ask her mother what "scrub" meant. And that moment in front of all of them, she forgot everything and could not speak a word.

The very large bosomed woman who was the cook, Madame Laurents, was most annoyed with Julie Boit, but moreso with her mother. "How am I supposed to make this wretch understand me if she cannot speak," she bellowed, "if she does not know more than two words? As you are ill, Marcianne Boit, and you are going to die, you cannot expect I will take this creature to replace you in the scullery. No indeed! I will ask for another from Sainte Savin."

"Oh please, madame," her mother cried, "she will do all you ask. She is only shy at so many people here now. You may beat her every day. Please, madame."

"And what good would that do? Am I to wear myself thin trying to beat some brains into her? I should say not! She is stupid, *I* am not. I shall find another who is not so dull nor so ugly."

Julie understood many things the cook had said. Strangely, her mind had opened at that moment and she became clearly aware that she was thought to be unacceptable. She did not like that, it pierced her in her heart and her throat and brought far more pain than making the dead baby come out. But the one meaning she understood that so wrenched her soul was that her mother was to die. To die meant not to move like the dead baby did not move no matter how much she poked it. She knew about die. Her mother would no longer hug her and sing, "Julie Boit, Julie Boit, my precious child." All warm words would be gone and warm arms never moving around her again to make her feel close and cherished.

She began to cry, standing behind her mother. Julie touched her mother's clothing and patted it. "Julie do, Mama," she whispered. "Julie do." She stepped from behind her mother then and knelt before Madame Laurents. "Julie do good. Please, woman."

The cook was beside herself, not sure how she should feel about the ugly misshapen girl in front of her or about the mother who had served her so well over the years. It was not easy making these choices. She would have much preferred that Marcianne Boit had never brought the poor miserable child to them, but on the other hand, she understood the instincts that had driven her to it. Estelle Laurents was a mother, too. Now what to do? She did not want the girl stumbling about, spilling slop that was meant for swine, being unable to tend to even the most simple details of daily life in the kitchen of the Manse of La Petite Monde. What to do? There was no question of course; she would look to Monsieur Bernard. It was his domain; he would have to decide.

"I can find no reason not to take her," Monsieur Bernard had said upon the petition being put to him. "She will not eat much, she will not know enough to run away and she is so fearsomely ugly that never will a young man come along and give us trouble with her. If she does not do well, Madame Laurents, we will put her in the fields. She will sleep with her mother in the cellar-way alcove."

"Julie do good, man." Her mother patted her and pulled her to a standing position. Her mother was happy, then, and Julie smiled at all the great people. "Julie scrub."

Julie Boit had no sense of time passing. She knew though, that she had been apart from her mother for a time so long that the terrible sadness and loneliness had begun to move

197

quietly away from her. Julie remembered her mother well enough, though, and was grateful for images of her. She treasured the two of her mother's possessions left there in that little alcove where they had slept, and because she had them and kept them with her in the night, she was able to know what the cook wanted of her in the day. The broken piece of ivory comb and the beautiful red ribbon were the enchantment that made her understand with her mother's mind. Julie used the comb in her hair as her mother had shown her but she could not do the ribbon up to stay on her head in the special way her mother had done, so she kept it straight and neat under the pallet of rags in the stone alcove. Best of all, she remembered it was there and she loved it being there in the night. It made her feel happy. Only once had the comb been lost after Minot, the charwoman, had scared her again with the ugly witch she carried about with her, but Julie had wailed so loudly at its loss, that it was Msr. Bernard who had come to find it for her. Mlle. Minot did not show her the witch ever again.

The cook was alternately kind and mean to Julie, though Julie was unaware of any changes in the woman's treatment of her. Julie performed consistently the best she knew how. She was now capable of remembering which buckets were the slops, which buckets were milk and which held the scrub water. She could even remember most of the time where she had scrubbed and when it dried, she remembered not to scrub over an already scrubbed place. She could fetch water and clean buckets, she could carve the skins from the potatoes almost as well as her mother had done. Monsieur Bernard never made her carry linens, and she was made always to stay out of the way of the Masters, they who were even more grand than the great people of the kitchen. Julie was unaware that this was because she was considered too hideous to be looked upon by their fine eyes.

When Julie came to the edge of the kitchen and there

was before her all that monstrous space of rooms and walls and stone and marble beyond, she was overwhelmed with the abundance, depth and breadth of it and cowered at the threshold. Even if Monsieur Bernard had wanted her to carry linens or to scrub in the great places where the Masters walked, she could not have done it. But again, she was unaware of what were her limitations as well as her capabilities. When she became confused about these things, when she was struck with an inkling of a consideration of any of it, she simply touched the ivory comb in her pocket. With that, goodness came to her and she remembered the feel and smell of her mother. Except for that one time her mind had opened to the cook's remarks, she thought nothing about anything, she simply went about the day until the night came, then she went about that until the day came again.

Julie Boit could not get up from her bed in the alcove one of those days advancing from the night. She could not make her legs move. Her throat hurt mightily and her arms tingled down to the very fingertips that held the red ribbon to her cheek. But she did speak when later, Cook came to find her and scold her for being a lazy slug. "Julie die, woman," she croaked. And with that she smiled, happy with her red ribbon near her face, the piece of ivory comb in her hand, and the light went out of her crooked body.

11155-BARR

23

Complications exist only as perceptions. The trick is, simply, to simplify perceptions.

Carly lay on the living room couch, coming back to herself with the essence of Julie Boit still a part of her and she wept. She cried for herself, for being Julie Boit and because, being her; that was all she could do. She tried to find words to use in her mind to express how she felt but she could not, they were no longer at her command. She had lost her vocabulary, that most precious gift of language the intellect uses to make itself known in its world. It was a horror, feeling so completely shut off. She felt choked, claustrophobic, imprisoned. Even the Little Carlen with the broken life could inventively speak and make her dislikes, fears and joys known. Julie Boit was a thing, a flesh and bone object without mentality or any prospect of it, whose only possible happiness was the kindness of a forlorn mother, a broken comb and a red ribbon. Carly wept again, at once wrenched with the pathos of the poor dwarf, her stupidly brave acceptance of her tragedy, and vexed that she would have chosen such a venue for herself. She was, too, stung with an almost embarrassment at the horror of being so grotesque in the eyes of others. If these lives were choices, why would she choose something like that for herself?

"Ah, that is the question and in the question, as always, lies the answer." The Blue One's voice was even, gentle and a shade unceremoniously upbeat. And again, Carly was annoyed with that seemingly cavalier attitude when she was confused and wrung out from the pitiful creature's inability to communicate. Carly may have been annoyed, she may have been gripped by the sorrow of such a situation, she may even have felt to some extent a kind of empathy for the dull thing—but to have chosen to be less capable of thought than an animal? And so voraciously ugly that she was not fit to look at? No. She surely had not chosen that life, she knew it. It was someone else's authority at play there; some Lord of Karma like Doris had described, some Higher Being that had made her do it to live out some sort of punishment.

"It was your authority only, Carly." There they were again, still even, still upbeat.

"No, not mine! Why would I ever want to—to develop into that dirty, thinkless piece of meat?" Carly shuddered. Then, in a swift moment, she listened, utterly involuntarily, without a will, as the whole of what she had just said and thought played back to her in very carefully enunciated tones, as if it wasn't her voice at all, but a caricature of it, aping the worst of her. Slapped broadside with her own offensive feelings, her mind flinched at the notion that she had such capacity for arrogance and intolerance. She had always thought she had no right to superiority.

"You do not," the Blue One hummed, "nor does any entity on any level. We understand completely your aggravation and shock at having become acquainted with the choices of the Soul Genus in that circumstance. We trust, also, that you will come to find the answer to our question. We ask you to consider this life and those with whom the Julie Boit entity interacted. There is within it, a most defined thread that loops and winds around the others in the Carlen tapestry."

"There is a tapestry? A thread? What is it?" Carly couldn't imagine it. She didn't want at all to go there again, to look into that hapless being, suffer what she suffered and have it compact her into that loathsome useless creature again. She wanted them to tell her, to make it quick and be easy.

No tone changed, nor did their tempo, not one intellectual inflection was a fraction different than it had been. "You must

201

find the expression for yourself, Carly. If we attempt to increase your light for you, we are no brighter for it and you remain dim, at best."

"But it's so *hard* to do this by myself!" Carly moaned. "I don't like doing it. I don't like being alone. Why have I given myself this then?"

"Sleep, Carly. And dream. You are not alone. We are with you."

She realized she was tired, that sleep was needed; and in the moments of warm giddiness when it came, she realized that she had cried for the first time in 37 years. What did that mean? How would it change her?

"You're a big fat bawl baby!" Wicked Sister said. It was the first time Carly had ever seen this pretty little girl who was in the living room with her. She had just come back from her mother's bedroom where Mommy and Horehay were playing in the bed. She had wanted to play too, because she didn't like to be alone but they didn't want her to play so Mommy hollered something awful and Carly was pierced through her heart with it. She sat on the floor of the living room in the tiny house and sobbed and sobbed and sobbed. She couldn't stop the hurt inside of her until the pretty girl sat across from her, slapped her leg and called her that name. Carly was surprised and didn't know what to say at all. But she did stop crying.

"Who are you?" Carly asked, finally, wiping away the itchy tears with the back of her hands.

"I'm Sister." The dark haired girl with dark eyes like hers smiled a pretty smile. Carly thought she had never seen any other little girl so pretty, even on TV.

"Where'd you come from?"

"Same place you did, dopey. I'm your Sister." Wicked Sister came closer to Carly and put her arm around her shoulders. "You know how sometimes Mommy gets pissed and she hollers 'Wicked Sister'?"

"Uh-huh. I 'member." Carly absorbed this other little girl's warmth, thinking how lots better this was than going in there and playing with Mommy and Horehay anyhow. "She just did it," Carly said.

"Well, that's me. I'm Sister, but I'm not wicked. I don't like that." She smiled again and kissed Carly's cheek.

Carly was so pleased to have someone who loved her. She kissed her back. "I thought it was a bad me when she says that."

"Nope. It's me but I'm not bad. She don't like me 'cause I piss her off 'cause I'm prettier and smarter and better than her."

"You sure are pretty," Carly said. "But how come I never seen you before if you're my sister?"

"I dunno for sure, but maybe it's because the old bitch don't want anyone to know 'bout me." Wicked Sister looked off toward the bedroom where the rocking and squeaking noises were overwhelming those from the TV. "So she doesn't have so much trouble when she wants to get rid of us, you know, like going to Aunt Laura Lottie's. If she's only got one kid to drop off, it's easier. Then she can go off and fuck her brains out, ya know? It's the only thing she knows how to do."

"What's 'fuckerbrainsout'?"

Wicked Sister laughed a pretty little laugh and she took Carly's hand and squeezed it. "That's what they was doin' in there, you dopey," she said, "when you thought they was playin' and rompin' on the bed."

Carly's face got red. She felt stupid. "Well, okay, but what is it? What—"

"Oh, he's got a little weeny on his front bottom that gets all big and red and hard when they start rubbin' and kissin'. Then he puts it," Wicked Sister sighed, as if she'd recited the process a hundred times, pulled up Carly's dress and pointed to her genitalia, " in there on her and they go at it."

"But how! What for?" Carly shook her head, not sure she could ever understand why anyone would want to do that. "I'd rather draw, I think. Glad they didn't let me play too."

"Yeah, me too." Wicked Sister looked at the drawings of the rabbits Carly had finished before she'd been ordered out of her mother's bedroom. "Boy, you sure draw good."

"You want to draw?"

"No, I can't draw." Wicked Sister didn't seem unhappy about that, it was stated very matter-of-factly. "I'm real good at games, though. Wanna play somethin'?"

"Sure, I got—umm—we got all kinds of stuff. You pick." Carly watched Wicked Sister go to the games pile that she had neatly arranged in the toy box.

Wicked Sister came back with the Old Maid cards. "You know how to play these?"

"Kind of." Carly began to count the cards out. "You get some and I get some, we put some in the middle, then we match the pictures and make 'em into pairs. But the Old Maid, she's the ugly one—she don't have a pair. She's alone."

"She's ugly like Mommy, the old bitch." Wicked Sister laughed again, loving her joke.

"Yeah," Carly laughed too. "But I bet she don't 'fuckerbrainsout', neither."

Wicked Sister squealed her appreciation of Carly's joke and they rolled on the floor, laughing and scattering their card piles.

"She don't have a pair," Wicked Sister crowed. "She don't have no Horehay weeny!"

They threw their cards down as the squeals of laughter overcame them until they could barely breathe. Wicked Sister stomped her feet laughing so hard and Carly fell onto her back and kicked her legs and both of them whooped their laughter over the TV sounds and the rocking bed squeaking sounds. They were together and it was such fun and they hugged and Carly wasn't alone anymore. She wouldn't ever be pretty, maybe, but she wouldn't be ugly like the Old Maid, either.

"I love you, Carly." Wicked Sister said, "We'll *always* be together."

"I love you, too, Sister. And I won't cry never again. I promise."

But she did cry again. And she knew that was wrong.

A dream is like a playlet, sometimes. Badly written, but nonetheless personally entertaining in whatever genre it focuses. That is, until you wake up from it and have to assess it and evaluate it and in the agony all of that creates, to dismiss it appropriately so that it doesn't completely maim your perspectives for the rest of the week. Oddly, in thinking about the dream she had awakened from this early Tuesday morning, Carly was surprised to find the memory of that other dream about being small and with wooden feet. The details of it exploded before her in the very front of her mind; being in the forbidden place with the beautiful people, being chased by the two huge women and then, being alone by the river and knowing they were coming, threatening. Waking up sober was a unique help in remembering it and she noted that with some satisfaction. That, too, was something she hadn't done consistently in over twenty years. While she marveled at that she marveled also at the sensations so similar in each dream, though standing alone, they couldn't be compared. Then she added the Julie Boit raw unspoken sensations and click, click, click, all the feelings settled themselves into one single category. Alone as opposed to being not alone and she was once again stabbed with a poignancy she couldn't identify.

Carly curled the covers back from her body and sat up on the edge of the bed, her feet felt for slippers while she checked the digital. 7:02 AM, red squared data numbers contrasted

205

against the black. She stood up and grabbed her robe from the chair and putting it on, headed toward the kitchen, trying very hard not to be aware of the yet unpacked luggage that Frank had brought to her bedroom that night. There was so much to think about, there simply was no time to think about that. About the smell of him, the way he put his arms all the way around her and held her, happy with a long, sweet kiss instead of throwing her to the couch every Wednesday night and insisting himself into her before their clothes were off. Indeed, no time to think about that at all.

First things first. There was coffee to be made, teeth to be brushed, scars to be checked and then what? Sort out who she was? Who she might become? But how to do that? It seemed an impossible task, now, the farther she was in moments and thoughts from the slick chute into which identified feelings similarly arranged themselves. At the final scar-checking ritual, the one around the left breast, she was distracted enough from the burden of thoughts to be pleased at what she saw. Several of the stitches had voluntarily fallen away and hung by the teeniest thread, some had disappeared altogether, lost in the shower perhaps. There was no soreness anymore, not even any tenderness and she wondered about that, remembering the way the Blue Ones had shown her how to move her hand across the area and to think it healed. What had the one Blue One said? "Thought is the creative force," he'd said. "To whatever extent you imagine the tissue healed; the body will follow likewise, as that is its promise and it never fails—" But no matter what they said, in the light of day, in the everyday reality that was her life, healing anything was Jesus Christ's domain, and she was only a pretender.

Too much to think about all alone. She missed Wicked Sister awfully. The dream that was real had brought that sentiment to her as a knife thrust. And maybe, after all, that's why she was healing so well; to get Wicked Sister back, to entice her back to a whole healthy body so they could argue and laugh and make up. Maybe that was the thing she was supposed to do. Then they would be back together and Wicked Sister would always know that Carly would have Victor on Wednesday nights and she could crab about it all week long. And it would all be unchanged and steady again. After awhile, after things got back to normal, maybe they could go with Frank on a weekend or something.

A blue light showed itself in her vision as a quick neon-like flash and then it was gone. What did that mean when it came and went so quickly and didn't bring the Blue People? She wondered if it was an admonishment or a reminder, perhaps. Or was it a key to a doorway she ought to go through? What had she been thinking about when she saw it? Frank. She'd been thinking about Frank, about being with him for a weekend. Thinking about missing Wicked Sister and wishing everything was back the way it had been. And knowing that was a foolish, foolish waste of a thought, of a 'creative force' because here she was, home in the apartment with only depressing thoughts to think and depressing chores to do. The kitchen floor needed to be properly cleaned, she'd only wiped it up before she'd left last week, feeling weak-kneed at that. The toilet needed cleaning, the shower should be scrubbed. "Julie scrub, woman."

Carly smiled at the thought, remembering Julie Boit's eagerness to show she could do the work for the cook and make her mother proud. "Isn't that strange how I find that amusing when I'm so damned depressed?"

"We are with you, Carly." She heard the words on the inside of her ear just as another blue light flashed at the corner of the refrigerator and perched there for a millisecond. She turned around on the stool at the kitchen passthrough to see if they were floating there, but there was no great mass of Blue People queued past her walls and into infinity. What then, was the meaning of it?

207

"Have you explored the Julie Boit lifetime? Have you asked who loved you in spite of ugliness self-perceived? Have you found the inside of your dream, yet?" Whispers of thoughts tickled her mind and she sat quite still for a moment, trying to hear more clearly, or receive more adroitly. Was it the Blue People insisting on her learning what they wanted to teach? Or was it simply her own curiosity?

It was in that instant that Carly made the decision. She got up from the stool at the passthrough and went into the kitchen with her coffee cup. She would clean up her little messes in the apartment, get dressed and feel good about herself all the way out to the farm. Then she could be with all the wonderful old ghosts that still lived there and since little in her life was real anyway, it seemed the most acceptable way in the moment to escape the awful mundane of how this had all turned out.

24

Scorpios are great secret keepers. They take a secret and they put it in the farthest, darkest corner of their lair. Then, they can never find it. Especially when it's theirs.

It didn't take Carly long at all to realize she had no car. She could hardly drive to the farm with no car and that dilemma brought another one that made her heart sink—where was her car? Had it been towed away? If so; where had it been towed to? What did they do with unclaimed vehicles? Would they sell them? She had no idea of what to do. She couldn't even remember how many days it had been since she'd been in and out of the hospital. It seemed an insurmountable problem and faced with it, she collapsed in a fugue. There was no use in trying to solve it; as one solution would simply create another problem. If the car had been towed and she found it, how much would it cost her to retrieve it? She had parked in a handicapped spot, so that would be an extra fine. Why hadn't she received a ticket? It was all just too much and it hurt her to think. It would be easier and even helpful if she had a drink. Just one to make her relax. She always thought better when she had a drink, things were better defined, they became manageable.

She went to the refrigerator where there was beer. "Good to start with a beer. No, wait," she thought, "I said 'just one', so I'd better make it a good one. Scotch it is." Cheered by the thought of the scotch and the great blast of warmth and support she knew she'd get with the first swallow, she took the bottle cap off and reached into the cupboard for a tall glass. Ice to tinkle and one little peel of lemon to enhance the edge and there it was, the golden nectar, the pale liquid sun that lit her nights, her days, her mind. One good sip and so nice, warmed through and through. *Who cares about a stupid old car anyway?*

A blue light descended from somewhere above the ceiling and landed for a half second of visibility on the telephone. Carly turned her gaze back to her scotch and her thoughts back to the delicious warmth gathering inside of her. It had been a long time since she'd had anything alcoholic and it felt better than she'd remembered. Better than chocolate. Better than sex. Well, more nutritious, anyway. She laughed. "Sister would have liked that one," she thought, "I wish she was here. I wish she'd come back. I'm done crying. I'm never going to cry again."

The blue light, now grown larger, came to sit at the counter next to her scotch bottle. This time she looked directly at it and in the second of its existence she said, "Go away. I don't like what you've done to me. I want Sister back. I want to be the way I was."

The telephone rang and Carly turned to look at it for a moment, considering its ring, then deciding it wasn't a special ring, she went back to her scotch, sipping it and feeling the strength of it pour through her with each satisfying swallow. She heard the machine click into its message taking mode. It seemed to whir forever and ever as somewhere inside the machine, a soundless mechanical voice was being recorded. And whose voice would it be? Someone terribly long-winded. They talked and talked and talked and now, she had finished her drink. That didn't seem right. There was something wrong with time, because she hadn't had enough of it to finish a whole tall scotch, she hadn't even chewed the twist and followed it with an ice cube chaser. Well then, nothing left to do but pour another. "I know I said 'just one' but it wasn't fair that somebody made me waste it when they stirred up the clocks." She smiled at her picture of stirring a half dozen different clocks in a pot, then going faster and faster, round and round, until all their little hands and numbers and digital beams boiled into steam and evaporated into the air. "Gone. So; it's not a sin to try again—poetry, ah poetry!"

"Sister!" Carly said aloud. "You've got to come here right now. The body's better, it's all fixed up with new important stuff, ready to go back on the market and—" Carly snickered, "I need to know how you knew about Horehay's weenie!"

"That was pretty funny," Carly conceded to herself, laughing more. "Come out, come out, wherever you are!"

"Who, me or Horehays' weenie?" Wicked Sister laughed with Carly, as she came around the back of the stool at the pass-through and tickled Carly's back.

"Yow! You dickens! God, where have you been?" Carly smiled brightly, "I thought you were gone forever."

"Nah. I just didn't like all the blue shit and that Doris. Jesus Christ, what a pokey nosey meddling bitch!" Wicked Sister sat on the stool beside Carly. "No car, huh? Well, we gotta do something about that!"

"Yeah, but what? I haven't a clue where it could be. They probably had it towed, but—"

"Not to worry. I'll take care of it. Could be at the cop impound. Could be at the far end of the fuckin' hospital parking lot. Could be a lot of places, but I'll goddamned find it."

"How do you know about that kind of thing?" Carly asked, feeling once again confident that things would be taken care of. Then smiling broadly she added, "which brings me back to my original question. How did you know about Horehay's weenie and where it went into?"

Wicked Sister laughed. "Me to know and you to fuckin' find out."

"Come on! Quit that." Carly's smile lessened. "Come on, I want to know. How could you know and I didn't? Why would I think they were in there playing a game, but you knew what they were doing—"

"Well you know now. That's what's fuckin' important, right?" Wicked Sister was playing with a pencil on the counter top, moving it in circles with her finger.

"Sister, tell me how you knew. Was Horehay like Uncle George? Did he try something when Betta Mary wasn't around?" Carly took a long sip of her drink, not sure what she felt about Wicked Sister's coyness, but she did feel alive, interested.

Chaos.

"What?"

"I didn't say anything," Wicked Sister let the smile fade from her features, too. "What did you say?"

"Nothing. I thought you said something." Carly turned to see if there were suddenly Blue People filling the living room again, but it was still and dim, shaded against the early afternoon light. She turned back to Wicked Sister, "Okay, I must have been hearing things. But nothing's going to distract me from the Horehay thing. How did you know about—him, them—and—it?"

"You mean his schlong and her twat and fuckin'?" Wicked Sister whooped her laughter. "His dick, her cunt and doin' the nasty? His johnson, her pussy and—"

"Okay, that's plenty! I know you have the vocabulary—what I want to know is how you knew about all that stuff and I didn't?"

"You did know. Jesus Christ, whaddya think, I'm a fuckin' wizard or somethin'?" Wicked Sister was getting exasperated, "I can't keep a secret from you that you fuckin' want to know, but I'm really fuckin' great at keeping them from you if you don't want to know."

"What does that mean?"

212

"That means that—oh, shit! I don't want to do this!" Wicked Sister flipped the pencil across the kitchen. "How come all of a fuckin' sudden, you have to know everything? How come we can go on for forty fuckin' years and not ever get into this shit? And now, all of a fuckin' sudden, after that goddamned Doris and those blue assholes—you gotta know this fuckin' minute!"

Chaos downward.

"What?"

"You heard me! Jesus Christ—"

"No, I mean, yes. I did hear you but there was that sound again or words or something," Carly said, looking at the air around her, as if there would be a voice box there, set to whisper and she would see it and find out what it was saying. But there was air, followed by wall studs, countertops, a refrigerator, and a pencil still spinning on the countertop by the sink. Nothing else.

"What're you looking for?" Wicked Sister sat on the edge of the stool, one foot on the floor. "If those goddamned blue assholes show up again, I'm outta here!"

"They—won't show up. I—uh—well, I don't know what I did, but I think they took the hint." Carly once again turned back to the Horehay matter. "Why are you so reluctant to tell me how you knew? I got what you said about keeping secrets but really, Sister, I don't think that applies, here. I mean, you knew all about the auto impound, about where the car probably would be and you just go take care of it and it's done. How do you know how to do that kind of thing when it absolutely baffles me and I don't have a single notion where to begin with it?"

"Oh, that stuff is simple. You just figure it out. You just know it's got to be somewhere and you look in the phone book and there you go. Duck soup."

———

213

"What does that mean, duck soup?" Carly laughed. "You say the damndest things and that's another thing. I don't know where you get them from."

"From you. Where in the hell else would I get them from?" Wicked Sister now had the pad of paper that the pencil went with and she was tearing tiny pieces off the top sheet. "I don't know what the fuck 'duck soup' means. It's just something you say when something's easy."

"Did you get what Horehay's penis was from me?" Carly's heart thumped as a tiny gleam of a picture of that organ came to her.

"Yes, goddammit! Now are you fuckin' happy?" Wicked Sister did not look up from her task of shredding the paper into teeny pieces. "You gotta know every goddamned thing. What is this—school? A test?"

"How did I know?" Carly was relentless, now. The scotch put her right at that acme peak of brilliance, where she could reach anywhere and touch anything and command it to appear. "I'm seeing the pictures, Sister. I'm seeing something. How did I know?"

"Look at the goddamned fuckin' pictures and tell yourself, huh? Yeah," Wicked Sister snarled, "you know so goddamned much, you don't need me. Tell your fuckin' self. Look at 'em, look at the fuckin' two of 'em on that fuckin' bed. Goddamn them! Goddamn her, that bitch!"

Chaos downward spiraling.

"Let's not argue, Sister," Carly said, pulling back, putting the pictures away while she poured another scotch. "You know she always does that, Betta Mary does."

"Oh yeah! And you don't?" Wicked Sister held the paper up and tore the tiny pieces off in front of Carly as if emphasizing her words, then letting them curl on little air drafts down to the floor. "You are the goddamned one, you are! Miss Hoity Toity! Miss Prissy Butt! Too goddamned fuckin' good to be the one to touch it, making me do it. Bawlin' your stupid face off! Too goddamned fuckin' wimpy to be the one to stop it. Yeah, that's right. You're a fuckin' wimp! A soft know-fuckin'-nothing worthless mewly little kitten who sat right there and let him and every one else diddle ya because you couldn't say 'no'! It was me that had to stop it. Me that had to fuckin' bite the fuckin' thing to save your ass. You'd of just fuckin' choked on it, that's what. Yeah, that's right. Old Horehay shows you his dick and wants you to suck it and you just bawl and run away, and then you want to go play in bed with 'em.

"Yeah, not so nice now, huh, Miss Priss! Well you wanted to know." Wicked Sister let the pieces of paper fall like snow and Carly was mesmerized with how each one seemed to match a horrid picture of Wicked Sister's description; and she couldn't stop it anymore than she could stop real snow. "He gets it going in her while he's got his hand on you and the old bitch is too hot to give a shit—she just wants to fuck. That's all she ever did. And who had to make it stop? Not you, you fuckin' bawl baby! It was me, that's who! And now, all of a sudden, you and those blue assholes are out to get rid of me. Well where in the hell would you be if it wasn't for me, huh? Huh? You'd be at the fuckin' funny farm, that's where!"

Chaos downward spiraling tangled.

Wicked Sister pulled another sheet off the top of the pad and began the tearing again, "Want more? Huh? 'Kay, I'll give you some fuckin' more! It was Uncle George, it was the fat fuckin' deacon at Aunt May's church, it was always some fuckin' rummy or stinky old greaser who wanted in our pants. I bit dicks, I twisted them, I punched balls, I did everything I could to save your ass and what do you do, you moony pussy? You fuck Victor, that's what! You let that slime-y user break

215

your fuckin' cherry. And do I get a say in what we do? When finally at last, someone comes along that I could get hot over and time comes to fuck him—who gets to? Huh? It wasn't me that got to be with him—all I got was the aftermath and then I fuckin' had to beg for that. Please Carly, let me see him, let me have him. And what the fuck do you say? I'm tired. I can't. It won't work. I'm done.

"You know what I figured out, Carly?" Wicked Sister had put the paper down and had arranged little piles of the torn pieces of it; some of it had made snow on the floor. "I'll tell you what I figured out. I figured out that Victor isn't the problem. Betta Mary isn't the problem. Frank's being married isn't the problem. *You're* the problem."

"That can't be," Carly breathed. "I'm the one who's out there taking the beating. Making it nice for you. I went to school and worked two jobs to make it through. When things get rough with Betta Mary, who takes care of the problem? Who drives? Who works? Who makes it happen? Who covers up for you? Just because Frank thought I was you or he couldn't tell the difference isn't my fault. That was an accident. It—just happened too fast."

"Oh yeah, fuckin' oops! You had plenty of time to get out and let me in. Don't give me that Miss Martyr shit—nice for me, my ass! You just wanted your cake and wanted to eat it, too! You wanted Betta Mary dead and you didn't mind if I hated her for you and beat her up some. You wanted to fuck Victor and get even with him at the same time; so what do you do? You go out and get every old fart you can find to fuck and I'm the slut, not you. You; you wanted to play the purist, the virgin, the loyal lover of 22 years, the demure innocent. And you're giving me all the crap about you can't have a relationship with Frank because of Victor, but you decide he's hot because I like him and all of a sudden, I'm standing at the bedside with Victor watching you fuck my man."

Chaos downward spiraling tangled negative.

"You knew Victor was there! You—you *are* wicked. What were you thinking? That he'd beat me up and kill me for you? Did you call him and tell him to come over and watch Frank and me like you called in sick that morning?"

"Don't be stupid! I can't get more than an arm's length away from you. Ain't that a pisser, though? Victor was already there; there wasn't anything I could have done about it any more than I did. You were the one that begged him not to go and rode his goddamned leg all the way to the fuckin' door. Jesus Christ, I thought I'd puke. Then wah-wah-wah I can't live without Victor! Oh, poor me! I just wanna die."

"Stop it!" Carly turned her head and looked the other way. "I want you to get out. Go away now."

"Ha! Fat fuckin' chance. You were the one who wanted to know all that shit. Now you do and what's your answer? You want to waddle back into all those puddles of tears. Oh yeah, that's real fuckin' cool. Those blue guys give you a sob story about a shitty retarded bitch and you're all fuckin' brilliant and doing all this fuckin' self analysis and you're gonna go to heaven and be a fuckin' saint, huh? Yeah. You are pathetic! You want to get rid of me? *You* leave!

And oh yeah, the car? Frank said he'd buy *me* a new one."

Utter chaos downward spiraling tangled negative misery.

217

25

Insight's in the eye of the insightful. Is that an acquired skill? Can I do that?

Doris knocked on the door of Carly's apartment. Bruce, the maintenance supervisor stood behind her. He had let her in the building after she called. She was concerned about Carly she'd told him, which was true enough; she simply omitted the part about the Teachers suggesting that it would be productive if she were to visit Carly and make it snappy. Bruce had been the maintenance supervisor for the complex for the past 15 years and Carly was the only tenant who had remained throughout his tenure. Of course, he would let a friend in who was concerned about her condition.

It became obvious after resolute pounding on the door for 3 minutes brought no one forth. Doris turned to look at Bruce with his fistful of keys. "What do you think?" Doris asked.

"She could be gone somewhere," he suggested. "Her car hasn't been in her carport stall for over a week."

"I know, that's what I told you. She has no car at the moment, it was probably towed from the hospital last week when she came in." Doris looked back at the door, its blankness aggravated her. "I have to have called her twenty times in the last day and a half and I've got no answer to any of my messages and now the machine is so loaded with them it won't take anymore. There's got to be something wrong."

"Okay," Bruce said, "I just have to be sure, you know. If the deadbolt's on, we're not going to get in, anyway, though."

He put the key in the lock and turned it, pushed against

the door and it opened freely, no deadbolt. "Well, I guess I don't have to remove a door anyhow."

Bruce went in first. All the blinds were closed in the living room and it was dim. Doris followed him in and closed the door, making it even dimmer. They looked around but the living room and the kitchen and dining area seemed to be empty of any person.

"Carly!" Doris called in a moderate voice but firm enough to be heard. She repeated her call four times, but no answer. Then to Bruce, "Is this a one or two bedroom? How far back does it go?"

Bruce walked over to the kitchen to find the lights. "It's a two bedroom. All of 'em on this floor are but it goes back there to the master bedroom at the end. She could hear you, though, if she was in here. I think she's gone out."

"I don't," Doris said, coming toward the kitchen. As Bruce snapped on the lights, Doris saw the confetti of tiny pieces of paper all over the floor at the kitchen passthrough and the smell in the place was that of stale liquor. *Not like in a bar,* Doris thought, *but like it's permeated the air.* She doubted that Bruce could smell it. She wondered what significance was in the hundreds of little paper pieces.

Bruce was now watching her more than he was considering where Carly might be. He was making sure she didn't steal anything. Doris smiled to herself, conceding that was, after all, his job. She went around the passthrough to the kitchen, saw the pencil out of place in the middle of the otherwise clean and barren countertop. There were no knickknacks, collectibles or other standard kitchen paraphernalia like mug trees or cannister sets, cookie jars lined up along the splash back. And that was no surprise to Doris, having already determined that Carly was something of an obsessive about cleanliness and appearances, but what did surprise her in that context was all of the paper confetti on the floor and the pencil out of place on the countertop. There was no

219

wastebasket in plain view but that was also not a surprise as she knew that Carly would never allow so ghastly an object to be exposed to view. It would be under the sink, most likely and she went immediately to that cupboard and opened it.

"You shouldn't snoop," Bruce warned.

"I'm not snooping. I'm looking for something," Doris said, tipping the wastebasket she'd found under the counter out into the light, the better to see its contents.

"Same thing," Bruce countered. "Snooping and looking's the same thing."

Doris saw the empty scotch bottle almost immediately, drew it out of the wastebasket and held it up. "Here's what I was looking for."

"That's a scotch bottle. So what?"

"Carly's an alcoholic who hadn't had a drink in better than a week, Bruce." She looked him in the eye, "This means she probably didn't quit with this one bottle. There's no empty glass and nothing else to suggest that she had a couple of drinks out of that almost empty bottle and went on her way to shop. With no car."

"Maybe, but I don't know how you get that from one old scotch bottle."

"I'm psychic," she said, meaning it, but Bruce smiled at her joke and she thought to herself that it was unfortunate that she wasn't quite psychic enough. Doris left the kitchen and hurried back to the large bedroom at the end of the hall. The Teachers had sent her here, or more accurately, had politely insisted it would be good if she came here, and something was up, that she knew. The bedroom was empty. The bed was made and had not been slept in. Everything was tidy including the nightstand. A clock, a small lamp and a phone was all it bore.

"Is there a bathroom off this bedroom?" Doris asked, looking around but not seeing a doorway.

"Yeah, through the dressing room here." Bruce pointed at a small doorway through a kind of walk-in closet.

Doris got a part of the way through the little walk-in area that served as the "dressing room" and saw Carly's legs dangling over the edge of the bathtub. "Oh good God!" she said, "What have you done, Carly?"

She went to her quickly and saw that there was no water in the tub, scotch had been spilled from a partly full bottle and it was now sticky ooze on its way to the drain. A glass with a dried out twist of lemon sat on the edge of the tub and Doris began to breathe more easily, instinctively knowing that Carly was drunk, probably dangerously so, but she wasn't dead. She could see the pulse beating slowly in her neck. "Bruce, you'd better call 911, then help me get her up and out of here."

Carly was mortified that the 911 people, Bruce and Doris had seen her in that most exposed position in the bathtub. She would have slept it off, probably, and suffered badly from a twisted neck and sore bones and a hideous hangover, but she would have done it all very privately and quietly. There had never been a time when she was in trouble and she let Doris know that.

"I just didn't count on the fact that I hadn't had a drink in a while, that's all." Carly said 12 hours later and almost sober, giving Doris a look that didn't thank her for her trouble. Her head reeled still from the alcohol residue left in her brain as the heart banged the blood through it, tormenting each individual cell with a drumming pain. It was hard to remember what she had done at the last of the drinking session, how she had wound up in the bathtub, but she did remember that Wicked Sister had come back. That made her stomach churn all the more. Disaster was in having to throw up; it was innately bad. Flash a picture of Uncle George holding her up to Aunt

---

221

May for inspection, his semen all over her dress, calling it "puke." It was bad. Almost as bad as crying.

Doris had accompanied Carly to the hospital, stayed with her during the treatment and talked to Dr. Steele about her condition, who released her to Doris. It had been a long afternoon and evening, but now Carly had finished sleeping it off, she'd been injected with vitamins, soundly lectured about alcohol abuse and given pamphlets on clinics and therapy groups. And Doris was with her at the kitchen passthrough now, waiting to see what other work the Teachers had in mind for the remainder of the evening. She knew there was something and it didn't matter to her that all Carly offered her was a morose look of unappreciative disdain.

"I should tell you first, Carly, that they rescheduled your mother's pacemaker procedure again. It's supposed to be this Friday at 10 AM. They seem to be stuck on 10." Doris smiled encouragingly. "I downloaded a few of your messages from your machine so it could take more. I erased all the ones I left."

Carly looked up. "You listened to my messages? Why would you do that? Those are personal." She was thinking about Victor calling, how his apology would be private and for her only to embrace. Then she smirked inwardly at the notion, knowing very well that he hadn't called and he wasn't going to. "Sorry, Doris, I'm just a bit cranky yet—the hangover, you know. As much as I like scotch, I don't know why I have to suffer from such awful hangovers."

"I wonder. Do you really *like* to drink, Carly or do you do it for another reason?" *Too bad Cindy isn't here,* Doris considered her daughter's expertise, *she'd know where to go with this.*

"What other reason? Why would I do it if I didn't like it? I mean, that doesn't make any sense." Carly sipped at the coffee Doris had made. The sandwich sat untouched on the plate.

"Carly, I know about the other personality who—um—

co-exists with you." Doris wondered how that had made its way out of her mouth, she hadn't been thinking of it at all. It had simply slipped into existence as from some unattached place and into her vocal mechanisms that now seemed to be on automatic loudspeaker. The Teachers.

"What other personality?" Carly looked up again, an involuntary acknowledgement written on her features.

"I saw her." Doris concluded that since the cat was out of the bag, she might as well follow the path the Teachers had set out for her. "It was when your friend, Frank, came to the hospital to visit you. She just emerged."

"Frank came to visit?" Carly asked, perplexed, remembering now something Wicked Sister had said about Frank buying her a car.

"Yes, who did you think the roses were from?"

"I thought they were yours. I—I just—woke up from—my nap and there they were. Nobody said anything so–but wait! Maybe I remember something–He walked into the room and–and I felt–shoved away–yeah, I remember a little bit." Carly looked back at her sandwich, absently running her finger along the edge of the now hardening crust. "You could tell she was there? How could you tell? She looks different, doesn't she?"

"Yes she does, but it's not so much a difference in features, it's a difference in inner demeanors. I mean, you're both very attractive, but she has a harder, slick look about her—" Doris thought, "No, that's not it either. I don't know. It's really difficult to describe."

"She's beautiful and I'm plain. She's exotic and I'm common. I'm a mess and she's organized." Carly said, still tracing the sandwich crust with her finger. "She's strong and I'm weak. I drink and she isn't a drunkard. She has solutions and I have problems."

"Carly, that's not so." Doris reached over and touched Carly's arm. "She's simply another facet of you, for whatever

11155-BARR

reason she is. All those things you say she is and you're the opposite—while it's true that we all have oppositions within ourselves, that's what makes it interesting to find the balance. But the final word is that you are the things you give her the credit for. It's all you."

"No! Not all. She threatened me, Doris. She threatened to take over our body all by herself. Now, why would I do that to me? I mean, I know we share a body, but she is real. She's my sister." Carly was struck again by Wicked Sister's cruelty earlier when she had been there, talking with her. It was a sharp slash at her insides. Carly had been so happy to see her, but then they had argued, worse than ever before.

"What's her name, Carly?" Doris asked, remembering the oppositions in Carly's horoscope; remembering the blankness in the seventh house of relationships with Taurus on the cusp and the empty third house, siblings, where only Uranus, the planet of explosive change, aspected it. Where there should have been so much, there was nothing.

Carly was surprised by the question at first, then she realized this was the first time she had ever spoken aloud to anyone about Wicked Sister. And except for the Blue People and their broaching the matter; she didn't think about Wicked Sister in any context except as always being there, her hero, her rescuer, her witty companion, a co-conspirator. "Her name is—well, she's Sister."

"She has no regular name?"

"No. I know what you're thinking," Carly said, "I know you're thinking that if she has no name, she can't be real. But she is. She's Sister. She's a lot stronger than me and I think she's planning somehow to take over."

"How would she do that? Yours is the will that is the force in your life, not hers."

"You know, I think that's what the Blue One said. Something like that anyway. He called her a 'Shadow Entity'." Carly smiled, remembering, "I told him he'd better be careful what he called her, she can get awfully touchy sometimes. Mother called her Wicked Sister, but she hates the 'wicked' part. She hates Mother, too."

"Do you hate your mother, too?" Doris now felt that she was deliberately moving the direction of their conversation, but she had no idea what path might unfold. Each question seemed more of a surprise to her than to Carly, yet she was compelled to ask.

"No, I don't hate Betta Mary," Carly lied. "I put up with her. I take care of things because I have to. I'm the only one who will, who's left to do it. Wicked Sister would kill her if she got the chance she hates her so much. And a couple of times, she's come close to actually doing it, I think, but she pulled back." Carly smiled at Doris, "You know, this is making me feel a little better. What's in the sandwich?"

"Just baloney and cheese with a touch of mustard. That's all I could find and besides, I'm not known for my culinary skills. I thought eating something—" Doris left it there while Carly took a bite of the sandwich. "What did you feel when Sister was 'almost' killing your mother?"

"Mmmm, this tastes good." Carly took another bite, "I had no idea how hungry I was. It must be the vitamins they gave me."

Doris was certain that Carly was avoiding having to consider her question and by becoming involved in an activity that would please her interviewer, eating the sandwich, this activity would also serve to distract the interviewer from pursuing the topic. "Do you remember how you felt, Carly? I mean when Sister was doing whatever she was doing to your mother?"

Rage. Hit. Choke.

"No, I actually don't. I don't even remember what she did to her. I could have been drinking," Carly said, trying not to chew and speak at the same time. "If I was drinking, then, I wouldn't remember. Sister might because there's a lock box of memories she gets into and she's never affected by alcohol or drugs, actually. Isn't that strange? And I'm such a sop."

"Hmmm. I wonder how that works." Doris said, thinking that Cindy might have some answers.

"How what works?" Carly asked. "The fact that she's unaffected by substances? Yeah, I wish I knew."

"If Sister remembers, then, can I talk to her?" Doris' adrenaline began to pump, thinking that she really had little fortitude for confronting Wicked Sister again. She also thought she had absolutely no business getting into the situation in the way that she had—she was on completely shaky ground. As she thought the thought, a large glowing blue light quivered on the edge of the coffee cup that Doris had set forth between them on the passthrough counter. Doris looked at Carly, wondering if they could both see it at the same time. Carly in the same moment looked at Doris, knowing she saw it, too. She smiled a closed lips smile, her mouth full of sandwich that she quickly chewed and swallowed.

"No. In the first place, the only memories Sister has are mine, at least that's the way it's been until recently and don't ask me how that works, either. It's a lock box and that's all I know. Besides, I'm not going to let her come out," Carly said. "The Blue People are here and she hates them, too."

"Remember what I told you about having someone to be crazy with?" Doris smiled.

Carly laughed a tenuous laugh. "Yes, I do. And this is really crazy, isn't it?"

"Yes but it's a lot better than being crazy with Sister, don't you agree?"

"This sandwich is really good, Doris. Thanks. Will you stay with me tonight? I don't want to be alone."

26

*Who's afraid of the big, bad Wicked? 'Not me,' says the first
little Piggy. 'Me neither,' says the second and the third little
Piggies. How about you, Carly? And Carly says, 'Yeah,
I'm scared right to Death.'*

Doris called Cindy to let her know she'd be staying with Carly
overnight. "Just in case," she said. "And I know you're
probably all snuggled in, but would you mind going next door
to check on Kiva?"

"There is no convenience like having your daughter right
next door, is there?" Cindy chuckled, then she said, "Sure,
Mom, I don't mind. But it's going to cost you. You will have
to tell me all. What's going on?"

"Quite a lot, actually. But for the moment, suffice it to
say that I'm staying the night because Carly doesn't want to
be alone. And I don't want her to be, either." Doris thought a
minute to form an articulation of what she sensed about being
there. "Plus there's something going on with the Boys. It's a
big night somehow. Well, day, night—time. Yes, time for this
crisis to come to an outcome."

"Like how?"

"Like I don't know how. I wish I did. Well, no, that's not
true. I don't wish I did, because if I knew, I wouldn't be having
to learn it—and to learn is to teach—"

"—and to teach is to learn." Cindy chimed in, her voice a
smile, "But you will have a rundown of it all for me tomorrow,
won't you?"

"I promise." Doris said. Doris hung up the phone on the
kitchen extension. Carly had given her a nightgown and a

227

robe and slippers and she went into the small bedroom now to change into the nightwear. Doris was shorter than Carly, but wider in the twenty years she had on her, so the loose clothes fit her quite well. Carly's feet were a size larger, too, but with slippers it didn't much matter.

"Forgive me," Doris said when they were back in the kitchen, "I'm shuffling."

"You're supposed to shuffle when you're in slippers anyway. It gets you all set for bed."

"How does it do that?" Doris was amused.

"It just puts you in the mood, you know? Like warm milk and the last donut hole."

"Where did you have warm milk and the last donut hole before bed?" Doris asked. "I can't imagine out of that childhood, your mother or your aunts taking the trouble to see that you were even comfortable, let alone, give you any treats."

"They didn't," Carly admitted, smiling. "But Grandma Kuhns did. I mean it wasn't a long time that I got to be with her, but it stood out in my mind. Grandma made the best donuts I've ever, ever tasted. And she saved all the donut holes for me; they were mine and nobody else could have any unless I wanted to share, you know? It was great! Of course, I always shared with my grandpa and that was our— little routine. Before bed, we had warm milk and I always got the last donut hole." Carly laughed, "Even if it wasn't the last one, we called it the last one, then the ones that were left were the next-to-last, the next-to-next-to-last and so on."

"And shuffling in your slippers went with that, huh?"

"Always." Carly's eyes showed the warmth of her memories and Doris, watching her, wondered how Carly had come to this place now as a relatively functional person with only that small bit of human nourishment to sustain her over the years.

"Because of who she is and where she has been in lives

prior to this one." And the Blue People simply appeared this time, their ranks defying the restrictions of the walls, the one Blue One smiling benevolence as his presence came to the fore and rested there as he spoke. Carly looked at Doris, a tinge of guilt coloring the glance. "Can you see them?" she asked, "Because if you can't, I'll tell them to go away."

"Yes, I can see them," Doris said, a bit breathlessly, "but I've never seen them like this. My view of them has always been different, but I recognize the energy."

"Indeed you do, Doris, as we have been with you in your times, as well. We will tell you that your perspectives will be other than that of the Carly entity. Again, the difference is in the levels of perception from within to without, if you will. Meaning that no level is greater than another, simply that it is other. You are given to other work in this life, Doris, which normally insists upon other perceptions; but here we are in this level phase, and conveniently, we present the visage that occurs here. You are, of course, quite able to adjust to this. You may be advised and know also that there is no mean purpose in your connection with the Carly entity at this critical time."

"Can you tell me what specific purpose that is?" Doris asked, then looked at Carly who was raptly interested. Then as an aside to her, "You're certainly not going to be alone tonight!"

The Blue One smiled, "That is fact. We are here; we are with you. To you, Doris, we say that the specific purpose is known to us at this current sliver of time; but it is subject to your individual options and may change tenor after a moment's passing. So you see, it would be misleading to speak it in terms. Our interest in this gathering is to allow the Carly entity a review of the Julie Boit expression and to collect about her, the shielding and strengths that will be needed in the times soon to come. We ask that you become involved in this, Doris, as you have come through a passage similarly and there is a

229

bonded cord between the Soul Genus expressions, but again, it is your choice."

"You know very well I'm delighted to be involved." Doris was excited, she had never experienced the group as so defined. "That's why I signed on twenty years ago," she added, smiling.

Carly looked at Doris, cocking her head and raising an eyebrow. "You know these blue people? I thought you said you didn't know who I was talking about when I described them to you in the hospital."

"I didn't. Believe me, dear, I've never seen them like this before." Doris spread her arms to encompass the vastness of the vision. "But know them, yes I do!"

"We will tell you this, Carly," the Blue One spoke, his tone warm and encouraging. "Doris and all others will see us in different perspectives, as we outlined a moment ago. Not simply because of tasking on different levels but because each personality is given uniquely distinct gifts of sight, if you will. Prior to this time now, Doris was able only to see us as an inner vision and at that it has typically been more auditory than visual, although there were moments in deep meditations where we took a form as out of a nebulae. We do not control these factors, but are present etherically in whatever ways are commanded by the entity. It is unimportant to our work and to those with whom we work how we are perceived, only that we are. These manifestations with Doris have served and served well, we might add. However, here, the ruling presence of the Carly entity, and we use that terminology in the most bland context, is in force, hence, the vision of our group is as the Carly entity images. Because of the gift of sight the Carly personality possesses for the purpose of expressing a profession, we manifest as quite detailed." He smiled. "Thank you. We enjoy detail."

"Who is Julie Boit?" Doris asked, suddenly centering on the mention of the name during the group's explanation several moments prior. The Blue one and the group were silent for that moment, their waiting was an urging to Carly to respond.

"I—um—she was—I guess—me, kind of." Carly stammered, being embarrassed to bring up the subject of a past life, even to Doris. "I don't know. It seemed very real, you know? Real while you're there in it, but—oh, who knows? Is any of that stuff real?"

"Does it matter, Carly?" the Blue One interjected. "A good beginning for our session, actually. A most important point to remember, Carly, is that the details of these sessions, of any dreams or visions expressed, and as presented to your perceptive mind, are always valid, for there is the true reality. In the intellect, which is the direct heritage of the One Infinite Creator, the sensibilities and endeavors of the essence lie. Is it for a co-worker, a neighbor or even a relative in the life, in the society in which you live in the current moment and which you and others call reality, to give sanction to your truths, your virtues and practices, by their standards? If you have visited a life and a facet of the Soul Genus for the purpose of coming to a deeper understanding of the opportunities of spiritual evolution; whose essence does such a visiting impact? Only yours, hence, only your thoughts regarding it are valid. We ask that you consider this and especially when in concert with the Doris entity, be unafraid of rebuke or disparage."

Carly looked at Doris and smiled, a little sheepishly, "I have a ways to go, I guess." Then she continued, encouraged, "Julie Boit was a retarded girl, a dwarf. She was unbelievably misshapen and dull-minded, but I think she had a heart a whole lot bigger than mine—" Carly stopped because somewhere in her was Julie Boit's heart swelling to the beat of her own and Carly couldn't speak for a moment with the realization. Tears came and dropped onto her arm. She wiped them away and Doris smiled, also knowing this was an expanding moment

231

for Carly. The Blue People were simply there, a pleased and pleasant presence.

"Anyway, she was with her mother, a beautiful person," Carly continued, finding her way more perfectly as she remembered the sensations of being Julie Boit. "The mother was incredibly protective of Julie and encouraged her every word and opportunity. I remember not being able to speak, to say anything. Not because I didn't have a tongue or a voice, but there were simply no words in my mind. Later, those that came to me were the beautiful ones of the mother when she sang, "Julie Boit, my precious child, my precious, precious child." I felt so special—I mean, I can't explain it—I can't." Carly let the tears fall again and tried to think of what made them come; what grand swelling of the essence of her created them. It went beyond emotions, she knew, it was a higher thing she couldn't yet identify.

"But you are at the threshold, Carly," the Blue One said, "and so goes the evolution. As always, these things are to be explored, discovered; then it is the higher endeavor of recognize, confront, forgive and release. Doris is understanding of these things and is a teacher."

"To be called a teacher by those who Teach is high compliment indeed," Doris said. Then a thought came and she expressed it, "It occurs to me that I'm to be some kind of director or something here. With Carly, I mean. Because I've been at this for awhile. But she really has me beat, doesn't she? I mean,—um—her expression is much higher than mine, isn't that right?"

"Ah, even you, Doris, do continue to create an echelon; what is it called?" the Blue One smiled as did the group. "Yes, a pecking order. It is quite immaterial to the moment and the task as to what expression level the Carly entity occupies or that which the Doris entity occupies. Again, let it be said that all are equal in importance; even to the level of the youngest soul for there will you be again in some future cycle; and there will you be seeking with us as it was intended. But to answer your question without admonition, indeed, Doris, you are the 'director' of the process, that process being to assist the Carly entity to her best Karmic threshold. Again, that is if you choose to do the work."

"And me?" Carly's eyes shone for the first time in weeks and she felt a movement within of great and propitious moment, as if having been blocked and confined in a box for forty years and the top had just come open. "Do I choose? Have I chosen?"

"Yes, Carly," The Blue One seemed to turn to her though she knew he had never turned away. "You have chosen and it was always so. If your choices had been made differently, we would not have urged ourselves here thusly, nor would the Doris entity be so entangled as now happens."

Doris laughed. "'And the moving hand writes, and having writ'—keeps on writing! But the story can change as we speak, can't it?"

"Precisely. Do you see, Carly? Do you understand how the flow of events, of the time space grid; that which surrounds the earth and beyond, is moved by a thought, a force of the intellect, a mere choice of one being amongst the vast many?"

"It's hard, but I'm getting it." Carly allowed herself to be amazed at the mass of knowledge she had absorbed in just the past hour, but she couldn't wonder now at how much more she might invite in the future. If she did, she knew she would be overwhelmed. "Let me ask this: at that first—um— meeting in the hospital, that nothing, absolutely nothing, you said, was by accident but all was by Divine design. And then I woke up and there was Doris, and I've never felt so close to anyone in my life—I mean that—I didn't have anyone to feel close to, except Sister. Was this arranged?"

"I think I can speak with that authority, Carly," Doris smiled and touched Carly's arm, a quick touch and Carly noted that it was not only welcome, but it sang to her. "I knew the minute you were brought in that something was up. I felt your energy in spite of the fact that you were out like a light—" Doris laughed, "—no pun intended. I picked up on it but they, my Teachers, your People, didn't let me in on it and now I know why. As I said to my daughter earlier, 'I don't wish I knew, because if I know, then I don't have the opportunity to learn what I ought to out of the teaching.'"

"Exactly and well considered, Doris." Again the Blue People seemed to turn to Carly, yet without moving at all. "It seems only a glimmer to you now, Carly, but in the days and in the weeks to come, now that the choosing has reached the time of its articulation in the life, the glimmer becomes the glow and the glow a star. So Light is increased. We will tell you that the mother entity, Betta Mary, perches on a thin edge and a terrible chasm on either side of that edge gapes bellowing and she is afraid. Fear is a violent nemesis and is the antithesis of life and light. Think what flight could lift her, Carly, out of the grip of this dire threat to soul and essence. This we give to you to eschew and to you, Doris, let us tell you, we are honored with your joy and knowledge. The one shall lead and the other shall follow and perhaps these roles will alternate from time to time." And smiling as they vanished, they said, "We are with you."

"Wow!" Carly made the exclamation, knowing it was equal only to a whisper in scoring their impact. "It doesn't make any difference what room they come into, where you're coming from, when they're done, you are changed."

"And then they come back and you've changed some more." Doris said. "Shall I make some hot chocolate or tea or something? I don't have any donut holes, dear, but I know we'll have to do something to calm down before bed."

Carly laughed, acknowledging that she was excited, vibrating almost. "Yes, tea would be nice. There's some honey in the cupboard over by the sink and the tea bags are—"

"—in the cupboard with the rest of the dry to wet

beverages, I would bet." Doris smiled, "and I'll bet too, that the honey is with all the other sweet products, am I right?"

"Are you—um—remarking about my need for organization, by any chance?" Carly asked.

"Yes, by some chance." Doris once again surveyed everything that wasn't on the kitchen countertops that should be and thought of all the aspects to the 7th house in Carly's horoscope that should be there and weren't. "One thing I would like to see is you feeling secure enough to let some clutter happen on the outside—then we'll know that the clutter inside is being purposefully rearranged."

Carly looked at the starkness of the kitchen, at the clean shapes of the cupboards angled to the countertops. Neat. Like the fastidious games pile in her toy box, like her desk and drawing board at CSG. It was the first time ever that it looked empty to her, too clean and not warm and cozy, maybe like a kitchen ought to be, like Grandma's kitchen, like her hugs, like her loving mind.

"Hey Doris," she said, "I think that Julie Boit, that retarded girl, or at least the Blue People's leading me into the experience, was to show me about unconditional love. I mean, there it is. Her mother loved her so unconditionally and she absolutely returned that unquestioningly. And the beauty of it is that she could. She wasn't hindered at all by any of the kind of garbage I'm carrying around. She was so stupid, she was brilliant, so ugly and malformed that she was the epitome of the beautiful essence. No strings, trust that it's there, you know? And Julie Boit is showing me how to do it."

"Bingo." Doris turned around smiling. "And they said you were retarded!"

Laughter and tea with honey. Good for what ails a spirit.

___

27

Beginnings are the damndest things. How do you know where to or what with? Who provides the spark, the seed, the initiative? Good news; endings are worse.

"Did you say Friday was Betta Mary's surgery?" Carly asked. Doris was in the kitchen finishing up the breakfast dishes. It surprised her that Carly didn't have a dishwasher. It shouldn't have.

"Yes, that's it. Friday at 10 AM. Tomorrow, I think, though who would know how much time passes when the Teachers are shifting us around so." She turned to Carly who was making notations on a calendar. "September 11, right?"

"Right." Carly looked up and smiled at Doris. "I can't begin to tell you—well, I don't have the words. You've just been such a friend. I never knew about friendship before."

"Those are good words, Carly, you seem to have them just fine, and you've put them all in the right places." Doris leaned on the counter to peer at the calendar. "You know, one thing that will happen to you in communicating with the Teachers—"

Carly smiled still notating on her calendar, "You mean the Blue People."

Doris chuckled, "Yes, a vision of vast numbers by any other name. But what I was going to say was that you'll begin to notice that your vocabulary will improve—um—expand after these sessions. Your mind opens to all kinds of possibilities and energies and once you have the crux of it, the seed of Light, they've called it, there are no boundaries.

I know that sounds corny, but it's true and I'm dedicated testimony to that."

Carly set the calendar aside. "It doesn't sound corny at all. In the past two or three weeks, so much has happened, but now I can sort out that my thinking is improved, I mean, the pathways that my thoughts follow. There's more—um—responsible logic, I think. Before, what I would do is just collapse and let Sister take over. I know I have miles and miles to go yet, but I really can see headway. Believe me, I believe you."

"And speaking of Sister. What do you think? What will you do about her?"

"Nothing right now. I don't feel threatened at the moment." Carly reached over and squeezed Doris' hand. "Don't worry, I'm not 'collapsing' again. But I do have practical considerations I've got to deal with. I have no car. I have to find one of those, probably at the impound lot. I have no job and I really have to find one of those and right now, and I don't have a clue where one of those might be lurking. And I have to deal with Mother—I don't know—without all the turmoil or something. You know what they said. I've got to think about how to get her off that edge before she falls. Do you suppose they mean hell when they're talking about the two chasms?"

"Something like that only as I get it, what they're referring to, the chasms, are created by your mother, as that's how it goes. Every individual creates their own reality and in a case like hers, I would think, the reality she's created has been chaotic and like chaos, it grows without order or reason. Now, the chasms are huge and out of control, and there they are looming at her as she faces the great passage of death, overwhelming her. She's a young soul, probably, and has no inkling of how to change the situation, most likely believing she's squandered all of her chances."

"There's so much to think about, so much to learn." Carly

237

sighed, feeling more than a little overwhelmed. "I guess I have to take it one step at a time."

"Aptly put," Doris smiled. "Like the 12 steps."

"12 steps? What's that? A movie?" Carly looked up from her staring into her coffee cup.

"Oh Carly, you're so funny. You don't know honestly what the 12 steps are?"

Carly held Doris' eyes. "Look at me. Do I look like I'm hiding the fact I really *know* what you're talking about?"

"No, I guess not," Doris laughed. "The 12 steps—AA, Alcoholics Anonymous. It's an alcoholic recovery program. I guess maybe you wouldn't know. That would be one thing Sister would keep you away from for sure."

"You must think I'm pretty dense or a socially challenged or something," Carly said, a look of appeal on her features. "There's a lot I don't know. A lot I've never had an interest in knowing. I tell you it was Sister and me at the bars every weeknight but Wednesday, then the weekends were pretty much spent rescuing Betta Mary then going out and–um–treating ourselves afterward. I've always kept to myself at work. I was just never good at being cute or clever like Emily Hanford, for example. I was never a tease like that. If I talked to someone, I meant it. I mean, a touch to me was as good as saying I'd go to bed with them or give them my gold or whatever. And I never went back on my word, if I had control over it. That's the way it was."

"Carly, I don't think anything about your social graces or lack of them." Doris came back over to the passthrough counter and leaned against it once again. "You are a Carly just becoming to me. I don't see any of the baggage you claim to have, no pun intended. Remember what the Teachers, your Blue People, said about letting others dictate who you are by caring about what they think of you?"

"No, did they say that?"

"Well, I paraphrased, dear, but yes, they did. That was

the beauty of our little Julie Boit, wasn't it? She could not have cared less, let alone even been aware that others were thinking anything about her at all—"

"She did once," Carly interrupted. "Once when she heard cook say something about her mother and that cut her right to the quick. It wasn't that Julie was ugly, it wasn't that she was stupid, but Madame Laurents said something about her mother being sick and that she would die. It was such an opening that I wondered, in it, if it was me, Carly, doing the thinking for her, because she totally understood everything in that one moment. And that one moment of clarity changed her life, actually. She came out from behind her mother and she stood right up to them, to Cook and the others and she said, 'Julie do, woman. Julie scrub.' Just like a soldier, in compliance with an order from another quarter. And of course, she got the job." Carly laughed, "Now, there's where I could take some instructions from Julie Boit, huh? I sure need a job and not having interviewed in some 25 years—"

"Oh, yes, that'll work nicely." Doris laughed with her. "I hear Maids International is looking for help. You could go and assure them that 'Carly do. Carly scrub.'"

"I'd rather find a place that was looking for an artist then I could say in all truthfulness, 'Carly draw, man. Carly paint,'" Carly laughed. "That ought to get me a big salary, huh?"

The phone's muted jingling, a sort of a bell-purr, insisted itself in their fun, bringing both of them back to the day's hour and moment. "The phone's ringing," Doris said. "And I think I'd better get dressed and get home to Kiva. She's probably going nuts about now."

"Maybe it's her calling," Carly smiled as she reached for the phone. Doris went off to the little bedroom as Carly spoke her 'hello' into the receiver.

"Hello, Carly." Victor's voice sounded unreal in her mind; but depressingly real in her ear. With just those two words, he had begun again the bondage of the years of their lust reforming itself into steel bands around her psyche and what was worse; she recognized it happening. She turned to face the inside of the kitchen, feeling that if she couldn't hang up on him, she had to hide the call. She waited to hear his voice again. That was the match that lit the addiction.

"Carly? Are you there?" He sounded just like he always had, not at all like the awful Victor of the night of the incident. Had it really happened?

"I'm here," she said, trying not to sound like anything; like there was nothing between them, good or bad. "What do you want?"

"You." He said it like he always did, glibly, but full of intention, his deep voice playing over her body as if he was touching her, prepping her. "I am so horny for you, Carly. I– didn't mean anything I said the other night. I just–I guess I went a little crazy. I–um–you know–that was a shock–and um–it hit me pretty hard–um–watching you–and him."

His words were words that were without meaning, the only thing comprehended was the tone of his voice and she let it play with her, feeling it willful in her, wondering from somewhere above herself why she was letting it. Then, not thinking about it in any way, allowing old conditioning to move her, she listened to his breathing and felt herself become aroused.

"Carly," he whispered, knowing he'd gained the necessary ground, "I need you. If I go one more day without being with you I won't last. Carly, tell me you want me. I–oh God, Carly, I'm so sorry. You're the only thing that means anything to me."

Carly breathed a tremulous sigh, "Victor, please don't say these things–I don't know what to think."

"Baby, don't think anything. Just let me be with you," he soothed, his voice low and masculine, creating reactions. "Carly, it's you and me–it's always been you and me–there'll never be anyone else for you. No one can do it to you like me, baby. Let me fuck you. God, I want you so bad, so bad Carly."

Her silence emboldened him, knowing he had the foothold, he took the final initiative, "I promise I won't hurt you. I'll be so careful of you, Carly. Just let me fuck you. I'll give you your job back. Then we can do it every day, baby. C'mon, baby, let me do it, let me in again?"

The wash of desire was like sinking into a warm bath and drowning for the last time; she had no will to resist the fatality of it. She swallowed, then whispered, "Yes."

"I'm on my way," he said, "I am going to fuck you so good, baby."

Carly put the receiver back in its place on the counter and dazed, she let herself not think but only feel the lush yearnings his voice had incited. There was that passion remembered, that breathless almost painful need to be satisfied and until it was, there was only that motivation, that force, that need. She had blocked off any clue to her behavior, she didn't even question whether or not she was physically able to be with him; she couldn't think about Frank except in the context of making it up to Victor for having cheated on him with Frank. As she had done for so many Wednesday nights for so many years, she closed out any other factor in her life.

Doris came out of the bedroom with her purse and realized immediately that the phone call had changed Carly. "Carly, are you alright?" she asked. "You look glazed."

Carly looked at her blankly, but smiled, trying to pretend. "No, I'm fine. Just tired. A lot on my mind."

"Would you like me to stay?" Doris offered. "I can let Kiva wait; she'll be okay."

"No," Carly said quickly, then, more measured, "I just need to get at the car thing and the job thing. You know."

Doris knew she was lying, but she also knew that there

was no use in trying to fix someone else's gait; that to meddle would only break it more.

"I trust you, Carly," she smiled simply, hoping, intending the words to paint an aura of protection around the moment.

"I know," Carly said, closing off. "I'll call you later."

28

Living a life of intemperance and orneriness will surely lead to death. Living a life will surely lead to death.

The phone rang again just after Doris left. Carly thought about not answering, letting the machine get it, but she couldn't think quickly enough to make the decision. Her body was alive with the anticipation of again consummating the enduring passion she and Victor together owned. His voice was still crawling around her flesh, touching her, exciting her. Even Doris had been an interruption. And now this phone mewing, bleating at her, insisting on a nice 'hello.'

"Hello." Not so nicely, maybe.

"Carly Worthington?"

"Yes?" It was more a question for the caller than that she was unsure whether or not she was Carly Worthington.

"Carly, this is Dr. Mitchell, your mother's doctor. I've just been called to Betta Mary's room. She's not doing well at all. I—uh—should ask about your condition, too, but I've got to hope you feel well enough to come in to the hospital." His voice had that somberness about it that she supposed was typical of these kinds of calls. Hadn't that been how Grandma's doctor had sounded? "I think she's probably undergoing the last crisis here. Could you come soon?"

No, I can't come soon. I can't make it there until I have raging passionate sex with the man who brutalized me just two weeks ago after watching me make love to his father-in-law. Why is this happening just at this precise moment? Why is Betta Mary opting to die just at the critical instant that I'm about to get back what I gave away? Why must I make this unkind sacrifice for this woman

243

who left me every day of her life to do what I want to do this one time? I can't come there at all and watch her die; I won't be any help and I want more to have Victor with me again. She can die alone; that's how she's left me. But can I do that? How will I be changed if I do?

"Yes," Carly said at last, grinding out her words from a throat clenched with frustration. "I'll be there in fifteen minutes."

She hung up the phone and immediately wondered how she'd get to the hospital. In that moment of saying 'yes' to Dr. Mitchell, she had released her lust for Victor, that moment of triumph of restoration and of control over him through submission. It was, she saw, a hideous thing that had almost happened; and realizing, she let it out of her self and watched it diminish in her interest. She replaced it by simply calling the taxi company and concentrating on the strength she would need for the task ahead. Releasing Victor would be the easiest thing she would do that day, she knew.

This was what the Blue People had said would happen; she hadn't thought it would be so soon. She didn't feel anything about the moment; about finalizing the madness of reincarnating a relationship with Victor; about the import of someone's death. What she felt was the puzzle of the two chasms, what the Blue People had told her, and what she might do to pluck the woman from the precarious rim between which she wobbled. Then she wondered again, why should she?

In the next few minutes, Carly went through the movements of putting makeup over the newly formed scar, changing into her grey slacks and turquoise blouse, then hurrying out of the apartment before Victor arrived. She would meet the taxi on the corner of Michigan Ave and Hamilton Street over by the Jewish Synagogue. Victor would not see her there and by the time he realized she was not at the apartment she would be on her way to the hospital. Her mother's impending death was an interception that was perhaps the saving of her life. That, she reasoned, was why she should.

The taxi stopped for her and she got in, casually telling the driver to take her to St. Elizabeth's. It was a beautiful day, sunny but not hot, the air moving easily in the trees and sending a nurturing waft of freshness into the streets. She seemed not to have telegraphed any urgency to the driver as they moved through the afternoon traffic at an unhurried pace. Carly looked out at the familiar blocks and intimately known landscapes as if she might be a tourist, seeing them all for the first time. Maybe it was a guard against thinking about how she would still have to deal with Victor some other day, and thinking about little Betta Mary and her frightening death episode. But at the same time, she felt no need to shift her focus. She would simply go to the room in CCU where Betta Mary would be and she would see what might come to her. "We are with you," the Blue People had said. And Doris had said "I trust you." She believed them and the corner of her mouth lifted in a tiny smile as she noted their hand in her litany of choices made in the last half hour.

It was upon walking into the room and seeing Betta Mary, her gnarled fingers grasping at the sheets, working them in some sort of involuntary death grip, her body arched and mouth open into the mask, that Carly stopped, stunned, feeling now the imperative of a plan, of knowledge. She could not make herself move closer to the bed where her mother lay and to herself, in carefully articulated words, she thought, "I can't do this. I don't know how."

Blue light descended on her, veiling the room and she felt herself nudged gently forward. She moved toward Betta Mary's bed as if on a moving platform, like the Blue People, it seemed she floated there. There was no thought of intent, no communication with them, she knew though, that this was what they had told her about and what she had the strength and the knowledge from somewhere within her to do. *How*

245

does one snatch a person from the gaping maw? One does it, that's all, one simply does it.

She looked at her mother's eyes, glazed, open only half, with lids swollen and red, unable to descend to closure with the bottom lids, stilled by the morphine. The smell of feces in the room was an afterthought, yet it was everywhere. It was mixed with an unappealing sweet odor, something that had once been wonderful but was now sticky and cloying, like corrupted fruit. Carly was sure that this was the odor of dying flesh Dr. Mitchell had spoken of and that had come to Betta Mary in the last few days of hanging on. Why had Betta Mary hung on so? Was she trying to get to a place where she could get the Pacemaker and have rosy cheeks again and dance until dawn like Dr. Rosen promised? Or was it that she was just afraid to move either forward or back—the two chasms flanking her. Raspy breaths were muted in the mask and Betta Mary's tongue lolled in her open mouth. There seemed to be no life but those short gasps, no spirit left and Carly wondered how long she could sustain the wait and what was it for, anyway?

She looked at this little pebble of a woman, someone who had incidentally given birth to her and who had then begun the long enduring discipline of abuse and abandonment. Had Betta Mary ever come to rescue her? To hug her or speak to her kindly or understand her awful fears? Not ever once. Ever. It was Wicked Sister who'd done that.

"Carly. You came." Betta Mary sat up then, and with hands that were now relaxed and supple took off her mask and laid it aside. Her eyes were alert and the lights in them shone. Carly looked around for the Blue People to tell her what was happening. This was as unreal as they were and she wasn't sure what to do. "I was so worried," Betta Mary said, her countenance that of the woman Carly remembered from forty years previously. "I didn't think you'd make it in time. You know I'm in trouble. I sent the message."

The Blue People. "Yes, I—got it, I think," Carly said. "I've never done this before, you know. What were you expecting? I mean, do you know what we're doing?"

"No." Betta Mary said, her eyes widened. "I thought you did. That's what they told me."

"Who told you that? Why would I know anything about death? Or dying. Or anything?"

"I'm not sure exactly who they were, but I know they were your people. It was not more than—oh, twenty minutes ago, maybe." Betta Mary reached for Carly's hand. "You got to help me, Carly. I don't know what to do or where to go. I been so bad and the others are going to get me."

"Who's going to get you, Mother? Who are 'the others'?" Carly narrowed her eyes to see if she could see any blue beyond the white of the pillow or in the back of room in the dimness by the machines. There was nothing discernible as blue, nothing discernible at all, only grey dimness at the corners of walls and ceilings. Where were they? "I don't think anyone can just come and get you unless you let them. I mean, if you're so afraid they're going to do it, aren't you sort of inviting them?"

"I don't know." Betta Mary's voice had a tinge of panic to it; she spoke quickly as if not to would end her chances of speaking at all. "I was hoping you'd tell me. I'm afraid. I did so many bad things, Carly."

"Yes, I know you did. You did them to me." Carly looked away, annoyed at herself for being annoyed, for bringing up something she could never change. "Look, Mother, I don't know why you did that stuff. I don't want to know. I mean, it's not like it's my burden or anything. I don't know why I'm here and I can't imagine who told you I could fix things."

Forgiveness.

"You said something important," Betta Mary came closer to Carly. "What was it? I didn't get it."

Carly looked around again for the Blue People. She had heard the word and she knew they had urged it into her inner hearing. "It was 'forgiveness.'"

"Yes, that would be it." Betta Mary looked as good as she'd looked in Carly's memory and that's how Carly knew this had to be an altered reality; a place where Betta Mary said whole sentences repeatedly without a demanding blasphemy or a corrupted word. It was one of those Blue People things where lessons are learned and lives are changed.

"I have to go now, Carly. Come with me. Don't let Them get me, Carly, please. Your people said you could be with me; that you'd help me, show me what I need to do to be good again."

Forgiveness comes after confrontation.

"Mother, I can't show you that. I barely know how to manage my own self. I can't be responsible for you, too." Betta Mary tugged on her arm and as if she was in tow, a boat on the water with no sail of its own, she floated after Betta Mary, out of the CCU room and into the hall that was no longer the hall. Betta Mary didn't know where she was either. She turned to Carly and asked: "What's this place?"

Carly looked around. It was definitely not the hallway, but she couldn't really identify what it was. It was a place, the floor or road or whatever it was they stood on was like a regular black topped road, paved. To their left, the tarmac spread itself, moving until it stopped at a grassy place where trees grew. Carly looked to her right and the image repeated itself except it was different grass and trees, then in front, the pavement of the road continued, beginning an upward slope and suspensions and railings that would be parts of a bridge began to form along the edges. And sure enough, the veils of the image receded as a fog would lift, revealing a bridge structure. It was like one of those Disney animations she had been so fond of watching as a child where the brush came onto the page and as it made its bold swath across it, images of forests and rivers and birds appeared. Only this was a bridge and as she focused on the center of it, she could see that it was an unfinished one. Whose brush was it waiting for?

"Do you see that, Mother?" Carly asked.

"Do I see what?" Betta Mary's voice had changed, too, Carly noted. It was gentler and struck some long ago chord of baby memory. Had she sung to Carly, had she cooed her to sleep as a child? Perhaps. That which hadn't seemed possible was now a fact of her perceptions; possibilities were endless.

"You don't see the bridge?" Carly pointed Betta Mary in a forward direction. "There it is, a bridge like the Mackinaw Bridge only it hasn't got a middle." At that moment, saying that, she realized it didn't have a middle but that it did have another end and it spanned a beautiful body of water, a river of turquoise, its current moving its surface to sparkle in the sun.

Betta Mary said nothing, astounded at the vision. She looked back at Carly, then she spoke: "I never saw a thing so beautiful. I knew you could help me, Carly. When your people told me you were the one, I was so proud. I says, 'To think I gave birth to her.'"

Forgive follows confront follows recognize.

And there it is, Carly thought, understanding the unfolding of it all at that moment. There is the bridge that crosses the river that flows between realities. There is the bridge that spans the waters of forgiveness that flow throughout eternity;

you cannot cross over the River of Forgiveness until you're ready to go to the other side. It was so simple, so straightforward. Just forgive, that's all. It doesn't hurt, it doesn't cripple, it doesn't make you a chump, Carly smiled, it also doesn't make you a saint. What it does do is let you do it some more and you get really good at it after awhile and you are offered peace and freedom.

And where does release come in?

In an unbelievable instant, great black birds with wings of fire and ice and tears swarmed overhead and swooped down toward them in a cloud of frightful noise and Betta Mary wailed, "There They are, Carly! They're coming to get me! They'll burn me and cut me and pluck my eyes out! Save me, Carly, save me!"

"I can't save you, Mother. You save you. Let them go!" Carly shouted to her mother over the whirring metallic noise of the wings, "If we forgive each other together and forgive ourselves together, they'll be released and they'll fly away."

"I don't know how!" Betta Mary cried. "I knew They'd be after me. I've done so many awful things. Oh Carly, help me! I don't want to get snatched off to hell!"

Carly turned to her mother and grabbed her arms, then turned her so that she had to look at Carly. "Just do this, Mother," Carly shouted, "Do this one time, just one time and don't pay attention to their noise and the wind of their wings! Believe me, it will go away. Now, say this: 'I forgive myself forever, for everything I shouldn't have done and did and all the things I should have done and I didn't. I forgive Carly and Carly forgives me. Forgive opens the way to the Light.' Say it! And know that what you're saying is as true as God."

Betta Mary held onto Carly's hands, the blast of the swarm above them swirling around their words, but they held on to each other and spoke loudly and knew as they repeated the words of forgiveness that it became theirs. Miraculously, the black swarm above them reduced in size, the last flap of the awful wings urged off with the final twist of a wicked wind and quiet came again. Carly looked around her and smiled, "It worked," she said. "It really worked."

"Carly! You saved me!" Betta Mary squeezed Carly's hands.

"No, I didn't, Mother. You saved you. I couldn't possibly have done it. That's the Law. You have to do it yourself or else it doesn't work—and this worked so you had to be the one who did it." Carly looked at the bridge then, the middle that had been missing was now completing itself. As this was done, people appeared on the other end of it and began moving toward the middle. "Mother, look!"

Betta Mary looked where Carly pointed. "Well, look at that! Come on, Carly, let's go see who it is." She began to pull Carly along. "It looks like some from Independence, you know? If I didn't know better, I'd swear that was my brother Joe. He was killed in the war. I told you about him, didn't I?"

Carly was astounded to see all the people, the closer they got, the more excited she became. *This is the Bridge,* she thought, *the Bridge the Blue People talked about. This must be the Bridge Plane, then, the place in between where you dream and where you find old friends.*

"It *is* Joe!" Betta Mary cried out, "Oh Joe, brave Joe! Where's Dad, have you seen Mom?"

Joe and Betta Mary hugged and he led her into the crowd of people, all excited and talking happily together as they might have at a reunion at the farm. There was Grandma Kuhns and Grandpa waving at Carly, smiling and blowing kisses. Beside them stood Aunt Laura Lottie, her hair, dark as dirt when she lived at the farm, was now blonde and piled on her head like she was a movie star siren. Carly smiled

251

warmly at this capriciousness, so like Laura Lottie. "I always wanted to be blonde," she hollered at Carly, waving, "and now I am!" Her purple sequined dress seemed quite unexceptional to the rest of the crowd but to Carly it spoke of Laura Lottie's dreams of glamour that she could finally realize. Carly longed to run up to her and give her a hug, but she knew she that would be forbidden for now. This was not her party.

"Come here, Carly." Betta Mary shouted happily, "I want you to meet Joe and Teddy and Bill, my brothers! They're all here, Carly. Teddy has his legs back! Come on!"

"I'm sorry, Mother, I'm not allowed just now." Carly sadly gave a little wave, "But I'll be back; will you meet me then?"

"Oh yes! We'll all be here, Carly!" Betta Mary turned to her brothers and said: "You've never met her, my daughter, but she's really something, you know. I was surprised when her people came to tell me that I should get ready, you know about that. But they said, make sure you get Carly to take you, she knows—"

And the group began to fade into the veil that descended over the bridge and Carly suddenly felt forlorn. That was the part about death that was so reprehensible for the living; the block, the great wall that came down between places and you couldn't get through it. She had never seen her mother like she'd been as they'd come up to the bridge, sober and responsible and even thoughtful. They had forgiven each other for all those mass of hurtful actions over the years, but there was still something missing; something incomplete and it left Carly hollow and undone.

"What do you think it might be that would fill that vacancy, Carly?" The Blue One whispered to her. She turned to look and he and the rest of the People were lined up behind her, winding down the paved road she and Betta Mary had walked to get to the bridge.

"I don't know," Carly said, a little agitated. "It went very well up until they all began to fade out. See? They're almost gone now and it—makes me sad, I guess. I'm thinking of all the years I missed with my mother. Maybe things that never would have been, ever, but you think about them, you know? And why was it so easy coming together at the end? It just seems such a waste now and so futile."

"Ah yes, but think of the one thing that the simple act of forgiveness opens and no wall can block or diminish, Carly," he said quietly. There came a sweet humming from the vastness of the Blue People. It sounded like violins muted and the breath of flutes in the distance.

At that moment, Carly saw her mother at the edge of the crowd of people on the crest of the bridge. She was waving as if to blow away the descending fog and Carly heard her crying out: "I love you, Carly! You are my pretty fruit, the best thing I ever did!"

Carly felt the surge of these sweet words coming at her and they filled her wholly as she received them. "That's it!" Carly said, "That's what follows forgiveness. Love. Light, the increase of the Light." Then she waved back at Betta Mary and sang out, "I love you too, Mother. I *will* be with you!"

"Ah, perfect, Carly." The Blue One spoke, a hum, "There are some who can penetrate the veil that obfuscates; there are some who cannot yet do that. Those who can shall assist those who cannot and that of course, is the ever upward spiraling pathway to Union with the One by enacting that simple thing that was intended, increase of the Light. Be well, Carly. As you are with the mother entity, we are with you."

Carly woke to the sound of the flat-line warning on her mother's monitor. She lifted her head that had somehow rested its forehead on the side of the bed. Betta Mary's hand, still warm and dry, was in hers and Carly saw when she looked at her mother's face that the mouth was closed with a slight

253

smile at the corners of it and a look of peace covered the features. The nurse's hand touched Carly's shoulder gently. "She's gone, Carly," Nadine said.

"Yes, I know," Carly smiled, one lone tear trailing unabashedly down her cheek, "I was there when she went with her brother Joe who was killed in WWII and my Grandma and Grandpa and Aunt Laura Lottie."

Nadine, having heard many versions of a relative's passing simply didn't acknowledge Carly's remarks, instead she said: "I've notified Dr. Mitchell, he'll be up in a minute. Is there anything I can get for you, Carly? Anyone I can call?"

Carly smiled at her obvious sidestepping of the description of Betta Mary's passing. *Like Doris said, probably something I'll have to get used to*, she thought. Then, to Nadine's question, she answered, "Yes, actually, you can get in touch with Dr. Rosen and tell her, 'Sorry, your little surgery party's been cancelled. Betta Mary got a better offer.'" Carly smiled a little and squeezed Betta Mary's hand for the last time.

29

They say that death comes in threes. But who's counting?
One, two, three—

The rains during the night had refreshed the whole yard all the way down to the bottom driveway, then the meadow beyond the barn and as far as she could see. Carly was amazed still at the homely beauty of the old place, carved out of southern Michigan's generous rolling hills by seven generations of the Kuhnsmeuller family. Shortened to Kuhns by her grandfather's grandfather, the name had substance in that part of the county. John Taylor Kuhns had been poor but industrious and honest as had all of his family before him and that family had come to be a fortification of tradition and means in the small community of Independence. Carly let that poignant fact grip her heart, realizing that this was no more; that she was the last of the Kuhns and that the final two generations had not particularly phased out as champions of the family honor. It was sad but to mourn it was a foolish and wasteful endeavor, just as she knew that to mourn the wasted years of the relationship with Betta Mary would be, to everything she had come to learn in the past few months, uniquely counterproductive. The Blue People and Doris were equally fond of reminding her that "what is, is." And that seemed immensely satisfying to Carly, fitting in just the right spots in her insides, filling holes and caulking cracks with its substance. It was so righteously true.

255

Keep it simple.

"If the Universe can have such a simple straightforward basis for its being, why do I have to make mine so complicated?" Carly had asked the Blue People. And as always, there they were and quick to answer:

"To learn simplicity is a most complicated task," the Blue One smiled his usual mystical smile, "The energy of Universal dynamics, it being so vast and infinite, would seem to argue for deep thought and sacred knowledge to be understood only by those of a highest etheric echelon. When in fact, it is its very simplicity that signifies its divinity and as it is divine, that premise of simplicity, it is thus for the greater understanding of it by all who will to seek it. As a human in the physical expression, committed to a process of learning all of the many things you have already known, it is natural that the essence is confused; so it is that the need for simplification is a primary motivator. Moreover, the current society supports only a hierarchy of intellect, wisdom, organized and dictated education to behold the mystery of the Godhead, a situation that is neither simple nor intended. So again, it is natural that confusion and complication in the individual perspective would be the standard. It is no accident that these societies have evolved in this way; there is great Karma there, but that is another matter to be addressed another time. Again, what is, is and at the moment, it is the very thing we are interested in exploring."

Carly walked now down to the bottom yard, turning on the path to the machinery storage sheds and the old schoolhouse where Grandpa Kuhns had kept the big threshing machines. She thought about the complications and the simplicities and the discourse given her by the Blue People. It was easy to see it all and to grasp it and hold onto it when they were there with her or when she and Doris talked and went over these concepts; but by herself, she felt small and ineffective. The day was chilly even though the sun filled the cloudless sky and she brought her jacket closer around her and buttoned it. The wind snapped its way over the hill, moving the grasses in a swirling pattern as if some giant invisible sidewinder was making its way across the slope and down the lane. Complications, indeed. Tasks to do that didn't want to be done and she most of all not wanting to do them.

"Like now," she thought, "though the walk is lovely and even sentimental, I don't know what to think about the machines; what to do with them, how to evaluate them. Where do you sell an outdated threshing machine that nobody can use again? Or a 1953 Farmall tractor? Or great Grandpa Kuhns' old steam engine?"

To get rid of them seemed cruel beyond belief; it seemed a sacrilege. It was the end of all these things, of this place, but in practical terms; what would she ever do with any of it? She had no job as yet, and she certainly wouldn't find one living out here in the last bastion of rural America, 45 minutes to drive to any town of size in any direction. Victor's offer of her old job back had gone back to the office with him the day that Betta Mary had died and, she presumed, his passion for her with it. She saw that episode now as a gift, and she gladly received not having to deal with Victor–at least, for the moment. Yet, she had no money to pay the impound fee for her car so she was driving Betta Mary's old Chevy that stank of smoked tobacco and other offensive odors now indelibly fixed in the upholstery. There was one month left before she would have to make her apartment lease payment and there were the mounting electric bills, phone bills, hospital bills, car payments and the piece de resistance; Betta Mary's funeral. She was without any means as to how to prepare a resume', it was something she had not done in over twenty years. And now, she must inventory tools and machinery with which she wasn't familiar and felt guilty even doing. Someone had to do it, she knew, and that someone was only her because there was no one else anymore. That thought itself seemed to drag her back into a familiar but dreaded pit.

There had been no will. Betta Mary had not lived that way, details had not been within her capactiy. The complications of the resolution of this oversight were sometimes more than Carly could think about. Many times she thought of Frank and his legal knowledge but once she let that door open, her thoughts went to other things about him and to wanting to explore more than she knew was healthy for a tenuous dedication to a path. And then, thinking about him, no matter for how short a duration, she couldn't help but wonder why he had made no further move to contact her. She tried not to be hurt or to wonder what he thought of her. More complications. Yes, indeed, it was very difficult to learn to keep things simple.

Once at the smaller of the two sheds, she saw the cultivator under its tarp, then moving on to the larger shed, there was the disc plow and the spreader. She peeked under the tarps to see the condition but little was revealed as the light was dim. She felt of the seat of the plow, remembering how cozily it had surrounded her backside as she sat on it on a summer's day, the sun having cooked its metal to a warmth that defied even the covering of her blue jeans. The seat's surface was now a rough texture and her fingers came away with rusted flecks of metal. It was such a shame, she lamented to herself, but there was nothing to do but get on with it. A few tools were scattered around the dirt over to the sides of the shed but they too, were rusted. No use to count them; she would simply have to come with a basket and gather them up for the trash. Finally, she made her way up the lane the other 30 yards to the schoolhouse; the old building great Grandfather Kuhns had moved up onto the hill to store the marvelous old machines. Easier than building another barn was his philosophy and much sturdier in the long run. So true. There it was, standing still, circa 1880, greyed siding and cedar roofing and still some wavy glass left in the window mullions. How venerable. Carly went inside and skirting the great monster thresher, traced her fingers along the blackboards many times painted over by Grandpa Kuhns whose children had defaced their neat blankness with childish doodling and cartoons. Somewhere on one of them, she'd drawn a beautiful princess with a gold tiara and skirts and ruffles and a precious feathered fan that she'd had the princess hold coyly to her face–something like the dream of the celebrants in the marble place. Carly remembered she had worked on it for a good week, between chores and schoolwork with Wicked Sister kibitzing, making her laugh with her sardonic remarks about what kind of underwear princesses should wear and what she used the fan for. Even in the dimness, Carly could see that Grandpa had painted over that drawing, too.

Her attention went back to the threshing machine. As near as she could see, it looked to be in good shape, but again, she couldn't think who would want it. It was a dinosaur. And at that she smiled as she remembered thinking how much the separator looked like a Brontosaurus standing out in the field after a day's work, frozen to immobility by lack of a crew. A wait in stasis until dawn when the crew came back and then it became the chaff spewing dragon as all its minions fed it the stalks of grain to separate. It was easy to remember these little bits and pieces of life when the mind was sober; it was fun and even rewarding. Still, that didn't get the task accomplished.

Inventory taken per order of the court; or per her understanding of the Probate Court's requirements, Carly sidled by the thresher and out into the sunshine again. It felt good on her cheeks and she could feel it through the jacket on her shoulders and back as she turned north again and began her way back down the lane to the bottom driveway. That task done, she could now submit her lists and order an appraisal

259

so that the court could determine a value on what to probate and to whom, what would go to her and what would go to the IRS in inheritance taxes. She rounded the corner at the bottom driveway and started back toward the house, but she did not feel the sense of accomplishment that she should have. There was more needing to be done, to be recognized, confronted, forgiven and released. She could feel it, but she couldn't or wouldn't yet identify what that something was.

Keep it simple.

Carly came up the hill to the house and there, all of that world was shaded by the huge Box Elder tree that had stood as an umbrella over the back porch, the old stone house, and the well curb for all the years she could remember. She once again pulled her jacket around her and raised her shoulders to the instant chill of moving from sun to shade. Still nagged by the unidentified, she determined to go inside and call Doris Patrick to ask for her help in discovering what was left to do; what refinements out of the thousands ahead of her needed doing right now. It was a bare moment later that she heard the crunch of tires on the gravel of the bottom driveway and she turned to see Doris' car making its way past the barn. She was not dumbstruck by the coincidence of it as she might have been a couple of months earlier; but she remained amused and even imitated unconsciously the Blue One's Quixotic smile.

Doris put the car in park and turned off the engine. Carly stood at the bottom step by the porch and waited for her to get out of the car and come up. They would go in the house together.

"You called?" Doris pitched a large smile.

Carly laughed. "Yes, I did, but as usual, I wasn't aware that I did until just a couple of seconds ago. I'm always the last to know."

"Scorpios are." Doris came to the porch steps and put her arm around Carly's shoulder. "That's typical of the pre-flight mode."

"Pre-flight mode?" Carly went ahead of Doris into the kitchen. "Want some coffee or tea?"

"Yes, tea would be nice. Crisp fall days require the comfort of hot tea." Doris set her purse down on the pantry cupboard, a moveable storage pantry that was twice as old as she was. She did not think to remark to herself that she had grown so accustomed to these visits with Carly at the farm that she felt an intimate part of the memories there. "Cindy sends her love and wants to know when she can dissect your brain."

"Oh any day will be fine. Just make sure that she slices off only that part of the 75% I'm *not* using." Carly clattered the cups and the teakettle in the small kitchen and opened and closed the cupboard doors looking for a tea tray. "Tea will be out in a minute. What did you mean by 'pre-flight' as it has to do with Scorpios?"

"Oh, that," Doris said. "Only that often the Scorpio typically blocks all preliminary sensations prior to its flight out of the pit. You know, the flight of the Phoenix, the eagle soars and so on. These are just remarks I can't resist, Carly, don't take them verbatim. Although, that one is pretty straightforward. And come to think of it, the flight of the Phoenix is about to launch."

"Does that mean I'm about to fly up out of the pit?"

"Something like that. The myth of the Phoenix signifies a rebirth; the new, rising up out of the ashes of the old. It's what you've been working on for the past year, whether you noticed on a conscious level or not is immaterial to the facts."

"So? Do I just start flying or what?" Carly came through the door to the small kitchen with the tea tray. Her grandmother's clock chimed the hour, eleven bongs and Carly noted Doris' look of interest and pleasure at the sound of it. "That's Grandma Kuhn's Seth Thomas mantle clock that

261

belonged to her grandmother. I brought it in from the parlor this morning. I don't believe you've seen it before. It's a venerable old thing and it's good company when I'm alone here at night. It ticks so loud it sounds like a courting cricket and every time I hear it, I smile. Good memories."

"You didn't have very many of those, did you?" Doris asked, taking her tea cup and adding the sugar. The smell of fresh sliced lemon piqued her nose.

"Maybe not, but the ones I did have are all the more precious for that." Carly stirred her tea, looking at Doris pointedly. "Two things. You said I 'asked' you to come here this morning and you said I was about to make a flight? Out of my Scorpio pit?"

"Yes. First, I was simply sitting at my kitchen table enjoying a bowl of oatmeal and a piece of toasted cinnamon bread from the Continental Bakery when I got the call. The horns sounded and drums drummed and I knew immediately who it was and where I should go. No blue this time, though. I think they are trusting us enough to interact independently of them." Doris sipped at her tea before continuing. "Second, the flight of the Eagle or the Phoenix, from the Scorpio's dark pit is imminent for you. But I thought that was a given; that you knew that from our earlier talks."

"I guess so, but it becomes murky sometimes, all covered over with that veil again when I try to think what I'd be best off doing. It's just an awful lot to have to consider. I mean, there are so many things that are–here–um–and real. Or at least, they are things that demand my attention first." Carly gestured with her right hand, an open palm in a semi-circle sweep of the room. "This, the house, the things, Grandpa's equipment, probate. All of that takes months, maybe even a year or more to find out if there are any others who have any claim to the property. In the meantime, I don't have a job, I don't see how I can live here and try to find one, although the rent's very do-able."

Doris chuckled. "I guess I'd think about that first, huh? After all, what do you need the apartment for? At least for the duration, until you find out what you'll be doing and where you'll be doing it." She smiled softly, "It's tough, I know, a lot's been dumped on you in a very short period of time, but you know what they say: 'that which doesn't kill you makes you stronger'."

"Well, I may be dead, then, and not know it. I don't feel very strong right now." Carly looked at the north window, the panes of old glass, wavy and dimpled, let the late morning sun through to play on the boards of the kitchen floor. She sighed, then smiled, "That's funny. I'm sighing like my grandmother used to. She could sigh more expressively than anyone I ever knew. When the burdens were just too much, she sighed a sigh that would rattle the dishes in the cupboard. I called it the 'terminal sigh'. It ended everything she felt, I guess, and sighing it, she let it go and got on with her life."

"You know, Carly, I don't think it's any accident that you've had to come back here to this place, the scene of the only normalcy you had in childhood, to get your bearings about your future. I also think that, no matter whether you feel it just yet or not, but, listening to the ghosts of your past, these memories, is the preliminary to saying goodbye to all of it. You are, after all, at this jumping off point. It's a choice again. Fall or fly." Doris waited a moment for Carly to consider her words. "Have you heard from the Blue Guys?"

Carly brightened. "I have. I do. They are here whenever I ask for them and when I don't, too. They are wonderfully supportive and informative but, they won't tell me what to do."

"Yes, I know," Doris laughed. "Isn't that maddening?"

"More than I can say." Carly smiled with her. "But I know there is something in particular, a specific thing, that I have to do or I should be doing and they can't tell me and it won't come to me. It's a nagging thing. There is so much I have to finish up, so many loose ends and all the time I hear 'keep it simple, keep it simple' which always reminds me about what they said regarding simplicity and why I should."

"Well, then, there's an avenue right there." Doris said, tapping the side of her cup with the spoon, "attention, attention! If they're pounding the simplicity thing into you, that's your clue. Think about it, Carly. What in your life is the most complicated thing you've entangled yourself in?"

"A lot of things," Carly began her answer. Then she thought a minute, running her forefinger around the rim of the teacup. "Too many, sometimes. It's overwhelming. But maybe I need to categorize these complications and define them, then set priorities, huh?"

"Exactly. So; think about it." Doris thought she knew the answer, but she knew too, that if she did, it wasn't hers to dictate. She smiled at the thought of the Teachers and all they had taught and all she had learned. "Especially," she thought to herself warmly, "Etheric Protocol." Still smiling she went on, "Just consider the duration of each of these complications. Then, perhaps, which one of them is the one you would least like to confront and resolve–that's probably the one that is the most needing of resolution."

Carly laughed. "Oh you are clever, you are. You get right to the heart of it every time."

"I am led," Doris responded with neither humility nor arrogance. "It's what is."

"And that's it. That's the clue," Carly said. "There's only one thing in my life that qualifies as the most needful of simplification and as the one thing I don't want to have to deal with. Sister."

"Yes, Sister. I think so, too." Doris was very serious then, and her voice was soft, "And how will you set about resolving this complication?"

"I wish I knew. It's hard enough to think about her without choking up. She did so much for me over the years and we had a lot of fun together. She was–well, my sister." Carly stared again into her tea and said, dreamily, "She won't come out, you know."

"And why would she, Carly?" Doris asked, softness still a tenor in her voice. "If she comes out, she's going to have to face the music, so to speak, and she knows it. Her ploy is to lay low, be quiet and maybe things will be forgotten, then she can come out later and take up where she left off–growing into a full sized real personality ego, crowd you out and really make a mess of things."

"That sounds like she's got more of a plan than me."

"Up to this point, that's probably been the case." Doris reached for the teapot, to refresh her cup. "You're the one who has actually done all the things you give Wicked Sister credit for; you're also the one who's done all the things you've disassociated yourself from and laid on her."

Carly looked squarely at Doris, her eyes large with realization. "That is wickedly true. I let her become what I wanted to be, an unbound spirit, not having to answer to any authority or be anything more than what the moment dictated. Then, I let myself, me, Carly, be the martyr, the one who did all the right things, even when I didn't want to and even though the right things weren't always so right. She could talk filth and be brash and that was okay, because it was her, not me, and I didn't have to take responsibility for it." Carly shook her head. "No wonder Mother wasn't sure who I was. And of course, I kept her away from Victor all those years because of the way I had set it up. She would do the hating of Victor and cheat on him with all those men and I could continue to be the long-suffering me who loved him perfectly while he treated me like a disposable object. And the old men..."

"Keep going, Carly. What about the old men?" Doris held Carly's eyes, encouraging her with her own.

"The old men–yes, the old men were a double hit. I could get back at Victor and get back at the father who didn't choose me, who I never knew, by conquering these old men with the only thing I thought I had to conquer with, my sexuality, the same weapon my mother used on her men. And finally, it was the same weapon I used to control Victor while I suffered his controlling me." Carly closed her eyes and shook her head quickly, as if that motion would throw the images out of her mind. "That's really ugly, Doris. I don't know how I can ever get rid of that."

"Whoa! Let's not talk *that* way. That's a negative, if ever I heard one." Doris lifted the teapot and refilled Carly's cup. "Take a sip of tea, dear, and re-think your approach. You're doing very well at this analysis, but you can't embrace guilt. If you do, you own it."

"You sound like the Blue People. And thank you for that!" Carly took the cup, raised it to Doris and sipped her tea, thinking how many times she'd done the same gesture inanely with alcohol. "Getting rid of that is a part of the process and I don't embrace the guilt–almost but not quite. I am doing a lot of recognizing and confronting. Maybe it's time for me to forgive and release. Maybe confronting Sister will help me to confront Frank, as well. Just because I don't know what to do about him doesn't mean I can sit back and not do anything."

Carly paused a short second then went on, "You know, it's amazing how all of this can drag on for months and months on end and suddenly, when you get it; it's faster than the speed of sound."

"Or like the speed of Light, hmm?" Doris smiled a Kiva smile, satisfied.

30

There are always mysteries in life that might go unanswered. Like, did Lizzie Borden really do it? If you have to know, you must make up your own answers. Then, it's no mystery anymore.

It was in the midst of the morning's chores of finding the storm windows that Carly remembered she had dreamed about Wicked Sister. In that moment, standing in the old stone house, contemplating the upper storage shelves and whether, in the dimness, she could determine if a few of the storms were stacked there, the dream unfolded to her consciousness. Wicked Sister had stolen her body and left her to live in a speechless place, in a stone cellarway alcove in a French manse on the river in Sainte Savin. Secure that Carly couldn't get out of Julie's body, Wicked Sister had redecorated the Carlen body with all sorts of trashy clothes and jewelry and had gone to Frank to make love with him. Carly could follow her all the tantalizing way to Frank's arms but then there was a blankness of self that overcame her senses and whatever was done was not known or felt and she was alone again, without the ribbon and without the comb.

Immediately there followed a blue light, enormous this time and it became the Blue People in a moment so fast her eyes could not relay the process to her brain. "Ah Carly," the one Blue One spoke, the rest of the group again queued into infinity. "The storm windows you seek are on the upper shelf, two here and the rest lay in the barn loft, though you will find that none are catalogued as to which fit one window or another and so, none at all will fit as you would want."

267

"And good morning to you, too, with all that encouraging news," Carly said, rather saltily. "Then if there are none that fit, why would I care where they are?"

"You may care or not, as you please; it is a small thing but points up an anomaly of action in which you currently indulge."

The Blue One remained smiling and there was no impatience in his tone, yet Carly felt an admonishment. She tried not to sound defensive, but she knew that attitude permeated her essence at the moment. "And what anomaly would that be?" Then within the instant of formulating the question and it coming to the forefront of her mind where she presumed they picked it up, she saw the connection they were making. "Wait, I get it," she said, moving out of the old stone house into the patches of sunlight the de-leafing Box Elder allowed. They followed in a blue wave. "I think what you're getting at is the storm windows, never having been marked for the windows they fit, are like the episodes of my life that have never been marked for the times they fit. And so; they're all stacked here and there and not being marked, can't fit even the windows, or the times of my life, that they used to fit. They've all gotten warped." She laughed, "Bent out of shape for real."

"Excellent perceptions, Carly," the Blue One hummed, "And now, what keeps the Carly entity from gathering the old, forgiving the warp and releasing to the new?"

"Well, if you're talking about storm windows," Carly said, "Money for one. I can gather them up all I like but that's not going to get new ones. This is real life where people just don't go around turning water to wine and rocks to loaves and fishes or old rickety storm windows into new vinyl ones."

"Oh, is it?" The Blue One's smile was infinite.

Carly stood by the back porch, hand on the railing of the steps, allowing the realization of what she'd said to come fully on her. It was like the time after the experience of being

Julie Boit and all the horrid prejudicial things she'd said about the dwarf whom she'd been.

Change your attitude, change your reality; change you.

"I guess you're getting at my owning the negative stance, huh? Yeah, like Doris said, 'embrace the guilt and you own it' or did you say that?"

"No matter; it was said and remembered as was intended. Yes, we do ask that you address the attitudes coming out of the dream of this morning as these signify your continued reluctance to forgive the Shadow Entity, to release and move away from these chaotic times. Again, we remind you that choices are imminent. It is not that we have ordered up the timing of these things for that is not within our authority to do. It is that Higher Self and the Mistress of the Soul Genus in concert with the current personality expressing, the Carly entity, has by prior commitment set these series of events in motion."

"So; what do I do about it? You never tell me what to do."

"Again, we have no authority. You must make the choice to create the appropriate action and undertake to express it. We would ask that you consider the formula for achieving the path's goal; recognize, confront, forgive and release. In this moment, you are nearly accomplished in this with but a short distance left to end the cycle and begin anew. We offer all support, understanding and Light as you move through the last of it. There we will be with you, as well, when you reach the other side of it."

Carly sensed they were finalizing something and an edge of panic came to her consciousness. "Wait. You can't go! What do you mean, 'the other side of it'? Am I crossing the Bridge, like Mother did? Am I going to die?"

"Very like that, Carly. It is a passage that unfolds to a greater expression and like a death of the body, renews."

269

She saw then the image of Betta Mary among all the people who had loved her and whom she had loved in spite of herself; she saw the bridge unfolding into manifest passage and she felt the beautiful warmth of understanding descending to her. "I see. I really do see now what is required. What I am requiring of me. Or we, maybe Julie Boit and I, are requiring of us, to die out of the old and get to renewal. You can't do one without first having done the other."

"This is Law, Carly. All must and will do it, in whatever time concepts and within the framework of whatever precepts they will to express. All may reach for it, touch it and be of it; some in one time, some in another; but all surely will, as that is intended by the One. It is our joy and delight, Carly, that you are thusly poised; and that we have participated in this opening with you. We do not leave you ever; for we are bonded soul to soul, Light to Light; that is our commitment one to the other. It is only that we must seem to be gone from you for this brief breath of time, for you to do what you must do. We are with you here and there."

Carly felt the rush of them leaving; as gently as they had appeared in her life, they left it now as abruptly. At first, she was bereft, wondering how many more of these losses she would have to suffer before she got to that place where it wouldn't matter. Then she took a deep breath and made herself remember the moment, the words they had spoken to her, and the recognition she herself had accomplished. Attitude, it was all attitude.

Still with her hand on the railing of the porch steps, she turned then and went on into the house. It would be a good place for her to begin to die.

"Sister," Carly said firmly, "You know there's no putting it off any longer. Come here and talk with me this last time, please."

There was no sound, inside or out. Even Grandma's

clock's noise had been drowned out by the silence. Silence of the wind outside, silence of the trees and the birds, silence of the inner humming of the personalities of Carly and Wicked Sister, that had been so entwined for the forty years of their relationship. "Come out, Sister. We can't put it off. It has to happen if we are to survive, however we do."

When she came, it was with a rage of herself. Carly was moved by the proprietary sense of it and it brought to her again the moment so similar when Victor had announced his reasons for marrying Mandy Bickham. The force of it, then and now, was physical.

"What the fuck did you think, you cunt!" Wicked Sister spewed. "You're too fuckin' good to get mad? To stand up for your fuckin' self for a change?"

Wicked Sister was a swirl of energy and Carly was momentarily thrown from her plan, and the commitment. She felt herself easing into that familiar place where she could balance; a place of soothing the fury by denying it, blaming Betta Mary or Harold Seckinger or even Victor and leaving the responsibility there. "Habits are hard things to break," she made herself say, "but we have to do it."

"What the fuck's that got to do with anything?! Jesus Christ, Carly, there you go again! Blaming me for every fuckin' crappy thing you do! I'm not the one who has the habits–it isn't me that's the goddamned souse, it isn't me that's the goddamned whore, either. Just because I like to fuck…"

"That's what I'm talking about. Exactly. It is me that is the souse, that is the whore. I'm not going to blame you for anything I do ever again. Sister, I don't want to say goodbye, I want us to be together always, but I know that the only way we can do that productively is to agree to come together and take the finest of each of us and meld it into one. Both of us, as we are, will have to die…"

"Oh god, Carly, I don't want to die!" Wicked Sister, always intrepid, was now wavering, her voice a quivering reed, "I'm me. I want to live and be *me*. I want the fun of being beautiful and bringing the asshole pricks to their knees by ruling their goddamned dicks from wanting me so. I want to laugh at grabbing little wimp's balls and making them cry. I want to enjoy wrecking Victor, goddamn him! I can't die! I'm your only strength! Carly don't make me do it, please."

"But look, Sister. Just listen to what you're saying. Everything is negative rage–all the things you want to do are things that aren't wholesome. There's no profit in those desires; we both lose. You have to die, Sister, and so do I. I have to have your strength, your heart and courage but you need my intellect, my sensitivity and thoughtfulness. Somehow, we came to be two separate halves where neither of us could sustain an existence without the other but the existence could never be whole. If we agree to die, we can be reborn as one whole person. It's our only chance, Sister."

"Does it hurt to die, Carly? You know I can't stand pain. That's something you've always been good at, taking it."

"Yes, too good. I thought it was my place to take it, like Julie Boit, who hadn't the intellect to question it. But dying? I don't think it hurts, Sister. If it's anything like dying out of Julie's body, I don't think so. It was so quick. There was just the oncoming realization and then it was done. And the actual part of dying for Betta Mary was the easiest of it all; it was the suffering she underwent beforehand that was so excruciating."

"If I didn't agree to this, what would you do? Would you kill me, Carly?" Wicked Sister reached across the table and touched Carly's hand. "How will we be when we're dead? If we're made into one, how will we talk to each other? How can I touch you or how could you touch me? We'll be alone, just one alone."

"We won't be alone, we'll always have each other. The best of each other." Carly felt a stricture in her throat; tears were coming to her and she smiled. "And I wouldn't kill you,

I love you, Sister. I want the best of you to live and I want to be a part of that. We had an experience, you and I, and not many get to look at ourselves the way we've been allowed to."

"I know. I really do know, Carly. And you're right, I've never allowed myself to have the intellect or the sensitivity because I didn't have to; you had it. Anymore than you had the balls to bare the lion in his den, huh?" Wicked Sister laughed in contrast to Carly's smiling tears. "What will we be like? A laughing, crying lunatic who forgets to keep 'fuck' out of her vocabulary every once in awhile?"

Carly laughed a little, too. "I had a dream a few months ago about going down a long hallway with all the doors and then to a marble plateau where I saw the Blue People. On the way back, I saw a statue of a beautiful woman that was not a statue after all, and when I got closer to her, she came close to me and I knew her from eons and eons ago. She looked like you."

"I remember," Wicked Sister said. "I mean, I got into your memory box and found it. I didn't know what to think about it. I do know that you and I look different, but I didn't know who she was or why she would be in that dream."

"I'm not sure who she was, either, but I think she's someone who kind of rules us. Maybe she's the Mistress of the Soul Genus, like the Blue One said. Perhaps she's who we will be more like as the one whole person. And I'll tell you, I will have no problem looking like you."

Wicked Sister smiled again, and ran her finger along Carly's hand. "And our pretty hands, we'll have to keep them and I hope we can still draw like you do. You are so good, Carly, brilliant even. You're probably wasted at CSG, but you already knew that, huh?"

"Yeah, I was getting there. But we'll let those things evolve as they will. Our first priority is to do this. It'll be over in a minute, Sister. Let's just do it, please?"

273

"Carly, I'm scared of this dying thing. Maybe you've done it before, but I haven't." Wicked Sister sighed then, knowing it was the only way any part of her could survive. "How do we start?"

"I'll take your hand and we'll go to the Bridge again. We'll cross over it together. The Blue One said he and the People will be waiting for us."

"Okay, let's do it before I fuckin' chicken out on ya."

31

The other side of the bridge no longer exists in the way it did once you get to it. Then, the other side becomes the side you're on. Humans, you might consider personal disagreements and other wars with that mindset.

At first Carly thought she wouldn't remember anything about the saga of the Carly and Wicked Sister interface; but she remembered everything as if nothing had changed. It, she had changed, though, and markedly. Wicked Sister had walked with her to the middle of the bridge and, without warning or clatter, she had simply integrated into her. The only pain Carly felt was that one second of letting go of the ego and that was more a stab of nostalgia than a physical pain. "After all," she had asked herself at the time, "isn't all pain a condition of the mind more than it is a physical response?" Her answer had been a knowing 'yes' and in that, she was comforted that Wicked Sister had transformed without the pain she so dreaded. As Carly together, she felt sturdier, and more whole.

It became evident to her that as she crested the mound of that strange bridge, very like the one her mother had crossed just weeks before, the Blue People waited for her there as they had promised. A heart-stopping blue light bathed all in its glow and the group of People in it and emanating it spread their numbers out so vastly beyond her previous perceptions of them that Carly was again surprised at its enormity. From what seemed to be to Carly their center, there shone a pillar of brilliant white light that moved within itself with such powerful force that Carly knew immediately that she was seeing the Force, the connection between the People and the One Infinite Creator. Even on that level, which she knew not to be a physical expression, Carly was overcome with chills and she immediately associated the sensation with what Doris had called "the old ladies' chills of truth". The Blue One was instantly in front of her, smiling and even laughing a bit.

"Yes, it is so. The expression 'old ladies' chills of truth' is descriptive of a phenomena experienced on more than one level and we laud the Doris entity for borrowing such a charming phrase for this application. Indeed, that is the purpose behind the work. We teach that which we know to the many who seek the knowledge and they in turn are pleased to go about and speak of it, teaching, in their uniquely individual manner, giving it a more common acceptance. As an outcome, there are many levels of these teachings, yet we seek more. Again, it is the Law of One; Increase the Light. We greet you."

Carly felt herself being drawn into a cosmic embrace that was unlike any expression she could have imagined. It was at once, warm, loving and supportive and she understood that she had attained something new and important. She had made a passage. "Will she be safe?"

They knew immediately that it was Wicked Sister about which she inquired and they answered, "She was always safe, but now will be more safe within the embrace of the whole Carly personality, expressing all that was her grace and releasing all that was not. It is primary in the metamorphosis of the Carly entity, that the Sister personality, even tenuous as it was, be a strong fiber of the new expression. It is important to note, also, that these changes initiated by the Carly entity and agreed to by the Shadow Entity are those of a nature of will and of choice to do; not as a dictate or burdensome admonition from a so-called outside source. One ought to be mindful that when doing those activities one perceives as *having* to; that all is done joyfully and voluntarily, for only then will the energy apply."

"Do you mean," Carly asked, sure that she knew but still, new to this understanding, "that when someone has the idea that he's *supposed* to do something, that it's some kind of an order from God or whatever, it probably isn't and he'd ought to get his attitude on straight? Like, a fellow who thought he had a call to evangelism; that it was God ordained and he took it as a burden, sighing his way through it and not setting a good example. Like that?"

"Exactly," the Blue One laughed at her freshly plucked example, as did the People. "In the teaching into which you are to be again initiated, you will find a burgeoning clarity of these precepts and you are charged, by your own delightful commitment, to carry them with you as in baskets to give to those who will to find such gifts. And in each basket is a flavor of the Carly entity, who has set about to define in the way of her singular expression the declaration of simplicity which she has found to be a truth. In these definitions and refinements of the understanding now embraced by the human society in the earth experience, the truth expands wider and wider afield, to come to all who will to own it."

"Initiated?"

"Ah yes. It is this, Carly; you, on a level of high standing, prior to your entrance into the present body and personality, Higher Self and she who is Mistress of the Soul Genus, have contracted to undergo an Initiation of the Fifth Level. This is a process you have previously experienced in a time of a long ago past; and it has been deemed necessary that you undergo this Initiation once again..."

"A refresher course?" Carly asked, feeling now much more quick and able to comprehend their direction. "And I agreed to this. Yes, I know I must have; otherwise I wouldn't have been so able to come to the Bridge or to ask Sister to come with me."

"Indeed. And let us explain to you once again, that the Fifth Level we refer to is only that of another or different level of expression than that of those who occupy the Fourth Level, for example or the Sixth. Neither is higher nor is it lower; it is merely of a different communication, necessary to the completion of all souls' highest expression so as to enter Union with the One Infinite Creator."

"I know. At least I think I know," Carly said. "I shouldn't be arrogant about attaining any level, whatever it is, right?"

"Yes, that is correct. We do admonish you in this small way, Carly, to be mindful of your verbal approach to articulation of ideas and thoughts, for these will tell the energies of the soul and will declare such to be so. Be mindful that there are things that are appropriate, there are things that are truths, there are presumptions that outcome as correct, but in the overall aspect of energies, there is no right and there is no wrong. We have seen that in the human society as it exists currently, there is an emphasis on right, righteous versus wrong and wrongful. This, in elemental impression, equates to a certain superiority of one entity or group of entities and its discipline and oppositely, a wrong and wrongful equating with the negative. And in particular, the evangelist's ploy of emotional control through the threat of declaring one to be sinful, having an original sin that was unfairly but nonetheless inevitably inherited through no fault of the entity's current expression. This would be a dilemma indeed, if throughout the eons of evolution of the individual soul, it continued to acquire this same black sin at the beginning of each incarnation. And thereby having to spend its energy focus on ridding itself of this one incessantly dogged 'wrong' each lifetime, never gaining beyond a demise of the one cursed inheritance."

Carly laughed with them. It was again an essential warmth that she felt, a camaraderie of spirit. "In these times of Initiation, we will be with you thusly, for though it may seem to be an undemanding task, the very act of transference from one level to another will cause consternation from time to time. It is essential to the overall good of it that we assist and support. There are yet two issues of import that we wish to bring forth at this time. One is that the rules of Initiation are such as to preclude any intimate human interacting, or any over-indulgence in the more addictive substances such as alcohol, drugs, caffeine and the like."

"You are aware, aren't you, that I haven't had any alcohol since that day before mother died?" Carly was quick to speak, "And it's not likely I'll have an opportunity for sex, if that's what you're getting at."

"Yes, we are aware of your determination to be alcohol free and we applaud your discipline. However, we apprise you of these rules only because we must; it is imperative that you adhere to them, else ground gained is lost at twice the rate at which it was gained. And it is well to be mindful of the natural inclinations of the flesh, hence temptations can be upon one before recognized. In the culture in which the Carly entity resides, the urge to copulate is strong, but the motivation to such union and its soul rewards is little understood. Not simply because of the innate command of the animal to reproduce its kind; but such activity, when appropriately prefaced, is a force that enhances spiritual Light unlike no other and is a sacred intent of the One. Just as wine acts as a systemic cleansing when drunk, it can also obliterate the senses because of its alcoholic content when overindulged. So; we caution, as the sexual coming together between humans creates a greater Light upon fulfillment; because of that very urge to fulfillment, the act is abused to ruination of the spirit. Hence, it will undoubtedly be necessary for you to carefully draw about you a line of demarcation for a duration of the Initiation."

"In other words, no booze, no sex. I have that." Carly

279

said, "But what about duration? What is the duration or 'a duration'? A couple of weeks, a month or two, maybe?"

"It is that, yes, but it will be for as long as it is. There will be those who will come to you, Carly, to seek a truth they think you have; and it will be for you to position each to find what they need of your truth so as to better find their own. This, in the beginning, will take focus and endurance on your part. Again we remind you that you must choose this, for we cannot insist upon it nor may we choose it for you."

There was no question in Carly's mind that she would choose what they held out to her. It was a given, and had been since she had crested the bridge and headed down the slope to the other side of it. "One question," she said. "Have I died? How will I be when I go back? Will I be one of those walk-ins that Doris spoke of? Will I be able to draw? Will I still be Carly?"

"Hmmm," the Blue One mused while the others mused with him, humming like a soft breeze, "we count several questions beyond one. But we will answer each in turn. You have completed a phase of life that is very like dying, but you have not, technically, if such term is applicable, died. You have undergone a metamorphosis of the essence; there will be only a minutely noticeable change to the physical body and its countenance, but it will be poignantly manifest within the essence. You will not be what is termed a walk-in, though these occurrences, however rare, are valid. Indeed, you will continue to be able to draw and because of your enhanced awareness, you will be pleased to find this tasking property greatly improved in scope and application. You will, after all and without fail, be Carly forever, for the Carly entity is now an indelible expression of the Soul Genus."

Carly smiled, pleased, feeling she had reached a plateau that had been unavailable to her previously. "Well, this is Carly Forever, then, signing out; ready to go back to the farm and make a beginning at this business."

"But not so fast," the Blue One chuckled, then explained. "There is yet one thing more we ask you to consider."

"What one more thing?"

"A simple exercise."

"Keep it simple, huh? But it always seems that the simpler I keep it, the more expanded it becomes."

"Ah, but it remains basically simple; a key." The Blue One waved a berobed arm in front of the group. "Here you see the many of our essence. We have grown far beyond questioning our heirarchy and we go forward to the Light, teaching, as is our task. What we ask of you, Carly, is that you begin the Initiation in this level by coming to know that Higher Self, the Mistress of the Soul Genus, she who is the sum total of all you have ever been and all you will to become. The adventure unfolds before you; you come to it with grace and keen perception and it will be all that much simpler and well-defined if you proceed hand in hand on the pathway with she who advances you."

It must have been, Carly acknowledged, that she granted their counsel as in less than an instant, the beautiful tall woman whom she had seen at the last of the hallway dream stood before her.

"I am Ahn," she said, "let us walk together."

And they went out of the glow of the blue and into kitchen at the farm, the bridge fading far away and into the diminishing fog on the other side of the barn.

"What do I do now?" Carly asked, watching this tall figure glide about the kitchen, staring, poking at all the common things in it; as if she had come to appraise them.

Ahn turned and smiled at her, "I have come to appraise in a sense, but not these possessions you have arranged here. I have come to appraise our opportunity of managing the Initiation; of coming through it appropriately learned." She moved to the kitchen table, fingered Grandma Kuhn's oil cloth that covered it, then slid into one of the mismatched oak

281

chairs around it. "Sit, Carlen, if you please. And yes, I know of your aversion to the name 'Carlen' but while we enjoy the shortened version, we must attain a sense of value to the formal one."

"But I don't feel so much of an aversion to it anymore. Isn't that strange?" Carly mused.

"That is as it should be," Ahn said, sitting tall in the chair but still, not out of proportion to the rest of the kitchen. Carly supposed it was because of her new perspective. Things that mattered, mattered; other things were easily dismissed and that was what set the priority of consideration.

"You asked what you were to do now," Ahn went on, her exquisite eyes lustrous with intelligence, "and I will tell you. Now, this time now, henceforth until we are complete, you are to focus your efforts both spiritually and in the physical aspect of your existence on the Initiation, its requirements, its offerings, even its hardships."

"Hardships?" Carly asked, wondering how many more there might be.

"Only in the most definitive sense; perhaps 'difficulties' or 'challenges' is more an accurate descriptive for you, Carlen. This is the first we have spoken and I am clearly not familiar with the nuances of your vocabulary as of yet." The sound of her words were smooth, but rich and sweet like a cello. "It is imperative that you concentrate on the doing of the Initiation; even though I am the first and the last of us and we are as one, I may only guide you, counsel you and comfort you in times of exasperation and confusion. I may not reveal to you any quick or experienced answers or methodology beyond what is innate in us and that you absorb through recalled knowledge."

"If I understand you correctly," Carly said, returning the direct look, "what you're saying is that just about covers everything except you actually taking over for me." Carly paused, watching Ahn. "And didn't the Blue One say that I'd already done this Initiation? Did I do this as someone in another life?"

"In a sense, yes," Ahn replied, now touching the oil cloth again. She seemed fascinated with it. "And that will come to you, as well. As the Teachers Group told you, there are those who will seek you out in times to come and when this occurs, we must be ready. To be complete and prepared, we must know ourselves and see our pathway to the One clearly and unwaveringly. Do you understand this?"

"If you mean, do I get what you're saying, yes, I do," Carly smiled, "but do I understand? No, I understand very little of this."

"It will come to you. Our first step is one that is a determination. You have been shown one of the lives that have shaped us indelibly in this cycle and in being shown you have moved into the life in a practiced way, remembering innately the methodology, we are certain. Each of these expressions that will be critical to examine as we make passage through the Initiation will render us a module of learning that, like a puzzle piece, will fit with others to form the larger and most comprehensive picture, the key to our more perfect future."

"But what do you mean? Will I be asked to go into hiding? What will I do with this, the farm? What about a job? I've got to have a job, don't I?" Carly knew she probably shouldn't be addressing such mundane concerns, yet it was a part of her existence here and was necessary to her survival. "There won't be any use to learning if I can't pay the bills and I get hauled off to debtors prison."

"Work for you is in the offing," Ahn replied soberly. "But if it were not, there would be no lessening of the effort, for this temporal plane will slip away while our soul, this home of ours with the long hallway you saw in the dream we gave you, expresses forever. It is a part of the Initiation energy that you learn to negotiate these concerns."

283

Ahn touched the oil cloth again and stood, "One last thing for this moment of our meeting, Carlen," Ahn said. "You must to discover and identify the mother energy, she who loved you as Julie Boit. This will be a stepping stone to other levels of the Initiation." She smiled at Carly and said, just as she faded out of vision, "We will give you a dream then, to herald the beginning of the Initiation. Learn that our cycle numbers the first of the Ascended Numbers, 11."

"But wait," Carly said, a pitch too loud, "I have to ask a question! It's important."

"Ask," came the round melodious voice.

"Why me? Why am I, us, we—singled out for this Initiation."

"We chose it and in choosing, we qualify."

"So; anyone can," Carly said, musing. "Anyone can."

32

Footprints in the sand are inevitably changed by the elements.
Look back at them. If they are your footprints, you should
take a care to command the elements.

Carly hadn't really considered her progress from any vantage point; she'd been too busy living it and dodging the challenges she had now come to understand that she herself had created on some other level, in some other time grid. "Time grid?" she asked herself, amused, then answering herself aloud, "It's true what Doris said about changes in vocabulary and articulation as the effects of pal-ing around with the People." She could marvel all she wanted, but it was now indelibly programmed into her mind and resulting activities and communications came to her almost as naturally as any other expression. So; she had reason and logic, that marvel was fading, but a rich satisfaction had overtaken and added color where there had been little.

She woke now each morning from a dream; remembering its details had become a part of her morning routine. She had begun a journal at Doris' urging and wrote in it about the dreams, about her conversations with the People and about her own self-discoveries and the rising of a surprisingly strong intellect out of the ashes of her old behaviors and self-denegrating beliefs. Thinking of it that way, too, amused her. "There it is," she thought, "exactly how Doris had predicted it would happen; the Phoenix rises from the ashes, the Scorpio rises out of the pit and it was time." The dream Ahn had promised to send her had not yet come. She knew she would recognize it when it played out to whatever of the myriad of

285

levels of consciousness she was finding available to her. It would be impactful, she was certain, and that would identify it. In the interim, time seemed to be speeding up; there was none of it to waste sitting around waiting for a dream when there were loose ends to tidy up, strings to clip and choices yet to be made.

It was such a morning, a dream awakened to after a long chain of them all night long, that she knew before she ever indulged her journal, that this was the day to confront Victor at last, once and for all. To finish that so that it would never come at her again in any form. If she must deal with Victor for her health and her progress; she was sure that dealing with Frank wouldn't be far behind. And better to get these tasks to completion all at once. Carly smiled again knowing that was the Scorpio talking.

"Scorpios don't just accomplish a thing; they put it in their sights, consider everything else in the vicinity of their target fair game and good or bad, they devour it," Doris had said. "Then they look around for more. 'Appetite' might be a classic description of the Scorpio nature rather than 'desire.' I have yet to see a Scorpio person who merely quietly 'desired' anything."

Carly was always entertained by Doris' view of matters astrological and metaphysical, for she went about her craft with a tongue in cheek, almost irreverent attitude but she was all the more accurate in her interpretations for it. Carly presumed that her cavalier approach was one that was innately designed to detach Doris from her subject matter and her subject, as well. Carly was learning a lot about detaching, or more to the point, she mused, about having been most uselessly attached.

The tick-tock of Grandma Kuhn's mantle clock made its cricket sounds more loudly than ever it seemed, as Carly went through the chores of the morning. It was a noticeable and welcome accompaniement to her considerations for the day;

it was a cute noise, comforting in its steadiness and it fed her reason as she set about defining her feelings about Victor. What, she asked herself, would she need to get rid of and what would be necessary to keep as a part of her lesson? Did she hate him for what he did to her? How pro-actively had she invited such an attack? And why, after all the years of living in denial of the unwholesomeness of the affair, would she so suddenly ask for it to be flung into her face and so violently? Why indeed?

That Scorpio thing again.

She smiled widely as she heard the thought inside of her mind and recognized that she was doing exactly what she and Wicked Sister had done for years except now she was doing it more productively. She was having discourse with herself as a way to consider her dilemmas, to reflect all the aspects, to encounter what she must and activate a release. There had been so much of her relationship with Wicked Sister that had been worthy; but so much, too, that had gone awry. Now was the time to focus on the Victor dilemma and taking an action that would release the ugliness of it. Today was the day to do that. Procrastination was not acceptable. Grandma Kuhn's clock agreed as it reminded Carly of the time, a count of nine bongs–9 o'clock. Do it and get past it.

Carly had at last, retrieved her car from the impound lot and was glad she was driving it into town versus driving Betta Mary's old clunker. Driving a more reliable car, one that didn't smell of tobacco and alcohol and urine, left her free to cement her plan of excisement while she drove. She had not heard from Victor again since the day her mother died. Even going through the funeral arrangements, there had been that unbidden flap of a hope that he would see the obituary in the paper and call or send flowers. Something, anything to acknowledge that they had once meant something to each other. That hope had fluttered in the breeze of those times with consistent and annoying reminders that her ego was still quite afflicted. She had not questioned why she had not heard from Frank, but she had the sense that it had to do with Victor, with his manipulative hand. In the last analysis, she dreaded thinking why Frank hadn't contacted her more than why Victor hadn't.

The sun shone almost glaringly out of an outrageously blue sky, making every tree and every bush and bird stand out in singular beauty. No clouds in the sky and no breeze leaving all things unmoving contributed to the day's crispness, and this in turn, seemed to invigorate her determination to secure all the loose nagging ends of this current state of things in her life. The Blue People had continually urged her to this place and the encounter with Ahn had only confirmed it as an imperative to moving on. The other strings had not been difficult to snip at all and she'd needed no encouragement from the skies or a smile from the earth to get them out of the way. Once she accepted that the apartment was only a unit of rooms that would not serve her particularly handily any longer, she could let go and she did. Once she found that she would lose nothing by releasing the objects collected during her 20 years there; she sorted out useful from not useful, sold what was not useful and moved the remainder to the farm. There she had been for the last three weeks, nicely settling herself into its pace and learning how to make a mess in the kitchen and leave it that way for a bit. Doris had been very pleased and Carly was warmed now at the memory of her comments.

"I like you here, Carly," Doris had smiled looking about the comfortable clutter, "I really like you anywhere, of course, but here, you especially fit and by that same token, 'here' fits itself better with you in it. The walls seem more hospitable, the sun shines more brightly in the yard. It's a good match, I think."

Carly had sensed that about the place and herself, even when she'd first gone back to the farm to stay after Betta Mary died. It had been a place to hide in then, a place to regroup and lick her wounds; but somewhere inside herself, she knew she'd found a good solid platform for the jumping off she knew loomed before her. And now, the first of the leaps without a net was about to manifest. She turned the car onto New Britain Road, the last stretch of country before town started turning into city and traffic and no relaxed thinking or review could be tolerated.

Had she made a plan? Not really, yet she knew the outcome and that was enough. The rest of the activity would be something to trust; just as she'd confidently headed for the center of the bridge with Wicked Sister, yet knowing the center of it didn't exist. She'd trusted it would build itself and it did. She knew what was waiting for her on the other side and she wanted to be there more than she was worried that the route to it might not materialize. She would go directly to the CSG office and trust that Victor would be there. She knew that the element of surprise would lend itself to modifying any untoward behaviors toward her. Not quite formed yet, but lurking somewhere around the middle of her unarticulated priorities list for the day, was the demand package that would find its way front and center and land, splat, bullseye in the midst of Victor's morning. It consisted only of a modest severance settlement and a release from the non-compete contract standard for creative staff of the agency. These things were there in her, slightly hidden, but showing enough of themselves to give her courage. It was a part of the gift of Wicked Sister.

The elevator to the executive floor was vacant and she was glad of that. She wanted to focus; distractions of knowing people and making small talk would be counter-purpose and might lead to the degeneration of her determination. She presumed the small elevator to be free of people because on some level, she'd necessarily commanded it to be so. It was the same when she reached the reception area. No salespeople, no clients, no interviewing hopefuls were left to sit in the reception area, studying the sweeper's patterns in the grey carpet. Carly slid past the reception desk, not looking, hence not knowing whether or not it was manned, and to the open area of the conference rooms and executive offices rotunda. Eyeing the double doors, now closed, that entered into Harold's old and Victor's new office, Carly headed directly for them, knowing very well that she would not 'hear' Millie's protective cries about not having an appointment or other violations of protocol. She would staunchly move past her so resolutely the air would move in great gasps and set Millie down to wonder about morning office storms.

While Carly did these things on some level in her private self, she was unsure exactly how they were playing out on the level of popular reality. Was that Millie frantically punching Victor's number on the interoffice line? Was that Harold who'd come out of his smaller office on the Michigan Ave side of the building to see who Millie was raising her voice at? Carly considered these possibilities on that other level, but none of it really mattered–she was intractable on her path.

"You *may* not go in there, Carly!" Millie warned, her voice strident and robust with indignation.

Carly said nothing but went there anyway, not violently, not even staunchly, but with focus. She opened the one door that she knew would not be bolted from the other side. It was an easy gesture yet one that might have been like a twig snapping in an otherwise quiet forest. Victor looked up at the sound–he'd been reaching for the receiver. "Nevermind, she's in there," they both heard Millie say. Harold had moved to a position beside Millie, both now politely jockeying for the best vantage point. Carly turned, smiled at them, and closed the door on their curiosity.

Victor's sanguine countenance was now distressed, but he rose nonetheless as though he had ordered her there, and was now prepared to begin negotiations. "Carly," he said, his voice so casual as to be awkwardly so, "what's on your mind?"

"Very little," Carly said, still smiling. "I've come this morning because I thought it was a good time to clear up a few things–in my life, Victor. It only has to do with you because you were once in it, my life, that is; and there are now some issues that need to be looked at and dealt with in perspective."

He held up his hand. "Now, look, Carly, I tried to make amends for that–mistake–I mean, I–would have been willing to continue where we–where you left off, but when I got to your apartment, you weren't there. There was no one to let me in, and I—uh–had given back the keys, so–I–there was nothing else to do but leave. I figured you were sending a message and I don't have a lot of time to waste on people who say one thing and do another." He allowed an injured look to pass across his features. Carly recognized that ploy so often used in past situations and she wondered idly how many times it had worked and why it was particularly without impact now.

The Grace of Forgiveness.

"Of course," Carly said, realizing the innate strength of that thought and she added immediately, "I forgive you, Victor."

"What?" He let a sardonic smile strike the innocent injured one. "*You* forgive me?! Come on, Carly. I wasn't the one fucking someone else in our bed. Just because I tapped you a couple of times—"

"It was hardly our bed, Victor," she laughed at the outrageousness of his reasoning. "I'm not here to argue with you or rehash old actions–or attitudes. You probably should know, however, that whatever disgusting thing you did with that billy club ruptured a lot of my insides; twenty stitches over my eye, a cracked cheek bone and breast replacement surgery is not a few incidental taps. Not that you will consider these things; I know how you are about taking responsibility, but it's fair of me for both of us that you should know the extent of the injuries you inflicted that night." Carly was still smiling as she talked. It was a sincere smile, soft almost and sweet and it unnerved Victor as much as if she'd held a knife to him. "As for my not being there a few weeks later when you were on your way over; that was because of a phone call from the hospital I received shortly after I spoke to you. Mother was in a bad state at that point and in fact, died about an hour after I got there."

"I'm sorry, Carly–but how was I supposed to know?" His eyes shifted, their focus just slightly to the right of her face. It was obvious that he couldn't meet her gaze. A telling lack of sincerity would be in those light blue eyes, she knew and she looked instinctively at her watch, realizing it was over. The time was 10:45 AM and there was nothing more that would be necessary to do or say to erase everything and let go.

The matter is ended; the matter is released.

"How swift and simple it is when you can grasp the meaning," she thought. Just one more thing to do and then she could leave. "I have no idea what you've told Frank beyond the absurd story that I was in an automobile accident and that my mother called in for me."

Victor started to say something, his face a parody of the stricken lover, but Carly held up her hand, palm open to him. "Don't!" she said. "Don't bother to tell me, Victor, whatever story you've told him is something you will to have to deal with, not me. The only reason I brought the subject up at all is because I intend to let him know what I will be asking CSG because of lost employment. He's an attorney, he'll understand CSG's options more than you."

Victor now had clear vision of what potential for disaster lay before him; and he instinctively did the one thing he didn't have to think about; and the one thing that had always worked unfailingly in every instance. Before Carly could step back or react in any way, he had her in his arms, holding her breathlessly tight and he pressed his mouth over hers to stop the flow of awful rhetoric he didn't want to hear. He put the palm of his hand on her lower back and pressed her abdomen into his automatic erection, fully expecting the usual surrender to begin. Instead she began to laugh into his open mouth and his tongue met her teeth. Her surrender was humor and he was utterly taken aback; he didn't know what to do next. His erection was now a diminishing promise and he dropped his arms and stepped back, letting her cave in to her laughter.

"This isn't funny, Carly," Victor said, dismayed and confused.

"Oh yes, it is!" she managed between spasms. She thought about Wicked Sister and her dedication to getting even with Victor, through mayhem, if necessary and there they both were, joined now, their best humor discreetly killing him. She laughed for both of them and for the delectable irony of it. "It's just absolutely perfectly funny."

"Stop it, Carly. Stop laughing," he said, his voice dropping to that monotonal quality it had taken on the night he'd beaten and raped her. "You'd better be serious, Carly. I'm not going to fool around here."

"That's all we ever did, Victor, was *fool* around. We certainly never wised around." That struck her as even more amusing and she laughed all the harder. She turned away from him for a moment to try bring the swells of laughter to a minimum; then turning back to face him, she saw that he was quickly assuming the strange attack mode that had overtaken him the night of the beating. Suddenly, Carly realized that this, too, was a pattern; one she had seen only once before; but she knew in some deep new way of knowing, that Mandy had seen this vacant and violent behavior many more times than once. Carly thought it was very like a soul keeper had misplaced his soul, and while trying to find it; it being a very small, young thing, the robotic body reacted to its commander's last perceived insult. She saw nothing in his eyes and wondered in that moment, what substance there had ever been there. She knew immediately why she hadn't recognized this flaw in him. She had chosen not to. It had been convenient for the life of her own dysfunction.

But now she spoke, "No, Victor. You can't do that again. Especially here in your office but more than that, I won't let you. It's important that you get a grip on yourself and on your life. It seems to be a time of options and change for everyone. Why should you be any exception?" She reached into her coat pocket for her car keys, "I'll tell you briefly that I'm going to visit Frank next; I will put my demands for a severance settlement on the table and in addition, I'll tell him everything. Perhaps then, he can ignore me for real reasons and maybe he can influence you to get some help."

She turned to leave his office and as she did, she saw the mask of blankness drop from his face and a look of painful bewilderment replace it. It was good to feel the empathy his look triggered in her and she recognized that she had attained a foothold on the pathway. She opened the door to the outer office, remembering briefly how her hand had been shaking the last time she'd touched the door handle after her encounter with Harold. She smiled making the comparison.

"Carly," Victor's voice was forlorn, "don't go."

She went.

33

Yes, dreams can be something else–and anything else or everything else. In between and all around them is Learn; Teach; Enjoy.

Finding Frank was not as easy as finding Victor, nor was she as confident in being able to muscle her way into an office she'd never been in. Carly was certain Victor would have called to warn him and probably to concoct some outrageous story about why she would be seeking him out and what she might reveal. After a visit to the fourth and last of his potential locations, offices in the various operations of his conglomerate of companies, if she didn't find success there, she promised herself, she would give up for the day. She had an instinct, however, that she had commanded the energies, and it was imperative in her to accomplish this last cleansing; so Frank would be found and found that day.

She was not wrong. She found him at Bickham Paper in an executive wing of offices that was much less imposing than those at CSG. There he was, standing at the copier in the reception area, like any one of his hundreds of employees might, pushing buttons and reviewing the results of the miracle of toner and the electromagnetic drum. The receptionist saw Carly heading directly for him and she said, rather loudly: "May I help you, Miss?" In other words, "don't bother the big man." Frank looked up from his task.

"Carly." He was surprised. Perhaps Victor hadn't phoned him after all. He turned to his receptionist whose body language was painfully in the alert mode, "It's alright, Charlene. No appointment is necessary for Ms. Worthington."

295

"Hello, Frank," Carly said, half-smiling, not really sure what her demeanor should be. "I won't take up much of your time."

"No problem." He was friendly but distant. He stacked his copies and reached under the lid for the paper he'd copied. "I always forget the original and then wonder where I put it. Come on back, Carly."

He walked ahead of her with an easy stride, but his back was stiff and his shoulders set, signaling a mindset that Carly didn't want to think about. This was going to be a lot more difficult than the Victor encounter. She tried to think only of what the People and Ahn had said about getting past this block in the pathway, about re-creating Carly through Initiation and that in order to do that, she had to do some difficult peeling away first. Surely, they would help her keep the memories of this man's incredibly electric touch at bay; they would darken the light in her mind that illuminated their one night of closeness in its sweetly exotic detail. Or would they? So far, they had not; and it came to Carly that this was probably a part of the process; learning how to categorize her feelings and prioritize the more pressing and critical directives. Not having thought about Frank as one of those strings to be tied up, she reasoned, the strength of his presence was an influence triggering her reactions. His polite coolness, too, impacted her emotions and made her question what she remembered. What had happened between the moment of his declaring that their relationship was intended, that it was inevitably forever, and this aloofness now exhibited. Whatever it was had Victor's name all over it.

She followed him into a small-ish office with one desk, a wall of bookcases filled with what appeared to be law books, one window, a plant and one guest chair. Carly smiled as she thought how much it reminded her of her own no-nonsense office at CSG. Frank went around to the other side of the desk and indicated the one guest chair to Carly. "Please sit down," he said, his tone businesslike. "Now, what can I do for you, Carly?"

He had not smiled once, his look was almost bored, so distant it was and it stabbed her hard that he could do this. Yet, even as unprepared as she was for these feelings mounting against her, she was determined to see it through. "I'll get right to the point, Frank," Carly said, her voice much stronger and even than she had hoped it might be. "I've just come from CSG where I intended to give Victor my requirements for a settlement. His reactions to my showing up there weren't unexpected but I found it necessary to–remove myself before I'd conducted all the business I'd set out to do." She tried to identify any reaction on his face but there seemed to be none; she went on. "I thought he would have called you and mentioned I might be stopping by—"

"He did." Frank's features did not change, his look neutral and almost disinterested.

"I see," Carly said, which wasn't exactly true. She didn't see, but she had to move forward and quickly or she knew this block of immovable Frank would soon diminish her resolve. She felt hurt and she wanted to get it done and get back to the farm where she would be safe. She would call Doris, she promised herself, and they would talk about it. That would help. But now, Carly stood up, an instinct of movement not thought out at all, but having its effect on Frank. His eyes came a little more alive as he looked up at her. That slim reaction pushed her into a declaration.

"Actually, I don't see," Carly said honestly. "I don't really understand any of what Victor does or has done and I don't want to. I only want to get past it. And I want to get past this. More than likely, Victor has given you some very unattractive scenarios regarding my activities that made his firing me necessary. Some of them may even be true; but that's beside the point. The point is, Frank, that he fired me without cause, certainly none in the eyes of the law, expecting I'm sure, that I would simply be quiet and crawl back in my hole as I had done for him all the years of our very long and tawdry affair."

Frank flinched, his look that had signaled distance changed now to one of disbelief, then an awful dawning of a reality suspected but denied followed. He opened his mouth to say something, but Carly shook her head, "Please let me finish." She took another breath and went on, "It doesn't matter what he told you, you'll have to come to understand that, Frank. You'll probably also do well to trust that what I'm telling you now is the actual reality, the true fact. I have nothing to gain by lying, less than nothing, actually."

Carly felt a surge of energy and began to move around his office, to the window, then turn again toward him. "I expose myself to even more disdain in your eyes with the truth than anything Victor could have invented to save himself. He and I have had a relationship since high school; I helped him through college both financially and acedemically and we were to be married. He met Mandy and that was the end of it until they returned from their honeymoon. Then he came back and every Wednesday for the next 22 years would become my night to be married to Victor. I allowed nothing to get in the way of that. Then when you and I–came together, I still vowed to let nothing disrupt the commitment to Victor, the commitment as I perceived it, anyway–it would have gone on. But that, of course, was never intended. I have no idea how it was that he found out it was you I'd gone with that weekend and I never would have imagined that he would use his keys to my apartment to lie in wait for me. I'm not really sure that he did know it was you until you came through the door. Then, our—making love—must have pushed him over the line."

Frank was visibly disturbed, but he said nothing, waiting for Carly to finish. His eyes closed briefly and he passed his hand across his forehead as if he had a headache.

"After you left, he beat me very badly and raped me. Even then, I wouldn't have gone to the hospital except that my mother had been taken there for an emergency heart condition. Once there, I passed out and they did the surgery to patch me up. So; I did not have an auto accident and my mother would have been incapable of calling Victor to tell him of an accident anyway, as she was in desperate circumstances herself at the time. This was just one of his inventions to save himself, his job and his life. You're probably now starting to put the pieces together about the many 'falls in the shower' Mandy has had over the years." Carly sighed, almost smiling as she reminded herself once again of her grandmother's 'terminal' sigh. "Victor 'fired' me just before he beat me up and he did it out of a rage he's hidden from himself for all these years. I'm not going to go into any details about my injuries or anything related to Victor. I'm not seeking vengeance, reinstatement of my position at CSG, with Victor or with you. I'm asking for a severance settlement to sustain me while I find another job or court some clients who will give me free-lance work, which means also that I have to ask that my non-compete contract be voided." She stopped pacing and stood in front of his desk again. "There, that's it."

"Carly, I don't know what to say. I had no idea." He stood up and started around the desk. Carly could see that he intended to embrace her. She backed away.

"You were not supposed to have any idea of it, Frank," she said. "I don't care if Victor gets help or if he doesn't. But I care about you and what happens in your life."

Frank brightened, but once again Carly shook her head. "It's true that I—uh—feel deeply about you, and I'm finally in a position to know the difference between what I care about and what I'm supposed to care about, but I'm yet unable to trust any 'feelings', yours or mine. You have to concede that the entanglements and convoluted relationships in our

299

lives have made it nearly impossible for us to establish any sort of a wholesome connection."

"Carly, I'm so sorry I let him influence my feelings for you. He said—"

"No, Frank. I don't want to know what he said. It doesn't matter, really it doesn't. I'm at a huge crossroads in my life and I have an immense amount of work to do to make myself whole again. It was just too easy for you to say to whatever Victor told you that 'yes, this is the truth about Carly' and allow that to destroy what you had previously found by your own instincts. As I said, maybe some of what Victor told you is true but true or not, it would surely come up again. We would be continually disrupted, trying to find the love that once was a shining thing and being sad and bitter to see it so tarnished." Carly paused again, momentarily considering whether she was finished. She wasn't. Just one more thing: "I also don't need to remind you that you're a married man, and no matter how much of a non-marriage it may seem to you, it is an unresolved issue that would come between us ever more ugly each time it did."

"I feel terrible, Carly. Isn't there something I can do to— bring us back together?" Frank's look of bewilderment struck her heart. "What if I–divorced Beatrice? Provided for her care. There are things I can do, Carly. Maybe I should have done them already, but—"

"I know. But Victor said, or Mandy said or Beatrice had an interlude. Don't you see, Frank, these are excuses we make for ourselves. Heaven knows I've done plenty enough to recognize this in others. Why did it take a violent beating for me to see the danger to my inner self in my affair with Victor? And even then, it took unparalleled help from–uh, outside sources for me to see things clearly. Then, just because you and I have a strong attraction for each other doesn't make it okay to forget our other obligations–mostly, the one to honor self. There it is, Frank, it's up to you to make your life work, with me or without me; that shouldn't matter."

"If it doesn't matter, then why can't it be with you?" He came close to her and reached to embrace her, but she backed away again.

"Maybe it can. Someday. But for now, there's too much work to do separately before we can even think about a successful togetherness. I admit that we had a good start in the physical aspects of a relationship, but that can't be criteria; and it would only serve to distract both of us from making the kind of commitment we ought to make and for the clearest of reasons. I'm headed in a direction, Frank, and I want to stay on course."

He reached quickly across the space between them and touched her face. "You are so beautiful, even more than I remember."

Carly sighed, then smiled. "Thank you, Frank. That confirms that I'm becoming a whole person." There was so much more to tell. But was there? Maybe not, maybe all of that could sit still inside of her and be quiet while she healed. Maybe so. She laid the manilla folder she had carried with her from the car on his desk and felt his masculinity as a solid energy as she went around him. She hurried away then, to the office door. "Look that material over, if you would, please. It's not unreasonable at all. As an attorney, I'm sure you'll agree with the premise. There is no litigation signaled and I have no interest in pursuing any. I've given up the apartment but my new address and phone number are in the folder there. I have an answering machine. Let me know what CSG will do as soon as possible."

"Wait, Carly," Frank said, "You didn't mention your mother. How is she? Why did you leave your apartment? Why did you wait so long to contact me about this? I would have seen that you got some work, at least."

"I didn't contact you earlier because I had other matters

to deal with. Myself, mostly. Mother died, there was the funeral, there was my healing and ending an intense addiction to alcohol–there were a lot of reasons, I suppose. But, as some friends of mine are always reminding me; 'what is, is' and here we are, Frank. I've contacted you now. I'm confident work will come and as for CSG, I simply want what's fair."

"I'm sorry about your mother. Naturally, I didn't know–I—uh, would have, I suppose, if I'd followed through in spite of Victor."

"One thing I've learned is that we attract to us the challenges in our lives, in this case, for both of us, a big one was Victor–but as soon as we receive these challenges, they're ours to deal with. Victor has his own set of problems, I'm sure you'll agree." She turned toward the door again. "I really have to go now."

Frank stood near his desk for a moment, then almost as an affirmation, walked resolutely across the room and to the door where she stood. "Will I ever see you again?"

"I don't know," Carly said, trying not to think about how good he looked, to think only of the clear pathway. It still glimmered before her. "Things evolve, I'm told. People do, too. You never know what your choices might be tomorrow."

"Then there's hope," he said and bent to kiss her. She turned away once again and he smiled slightly and set his jaw.

"Always," she said, close to tears. "Always hope. Someday." They both felt the wrench as she walked through the door and closed it, the click of the latch bolt a finality heard on both sides of the wall.

When she got back to the farm and checked her machine, his voice was already waiting for her on its tinny little tape. In spite of her motivation to set him aside and focus on the more productive pathway, she vowed to keep the tape and listen to it every once in awhile, just to remind herself of perspectives, both hers and his.

"Business first," came his voice, rich to her ear in spite of the plastic speaker. "I've issued an order to the head of Bickham Enterprises payroll department and he will see that the first of 60 monthly checks in the amount of 75% of your regular salary will be sent out immediately. I would do more but reading your request it sounds like you'd be uncomfortable with that. I have also dictated a stipulation of release from your contractual obligations regarding the non-complete agreement you signed with Harold Seckinger last year. Any one of our CSG clients will be delighted to have your services, Carly; you are a creative and skilled professional. I've also directed Harold to include you in the CSG projects you would normally have headed up as they surface, on strictly a freelance basis. We will both gain from such a relationship. Whatever Victor does about his personal life with my daughter is up to the two of them, and as a father, I have to respect their privacy and right to make their own choices. But using an advantage as an employer, I've offered to remove him from his position if he doesn't seek at least cursory help. I've also made certain he understands that, as concerns any future work you will be doing with CSG, he is to keep hands off distance.

"Now, this is me, Frank, personal to you, Carly." His voice softened, lowered, "Someday is an exciting time and Hope is a most powerful engine that drives us toward it. I look forward to its inevitable arrival and in the Meantime, that other promising interlude, I will work on my 'earn Carly' skills. I'm going to fix my life and offer what help I can to those close to me who want to fix their lives, too. We'll all get our heads out of the sand at the very least, thanks to you. If Hope works and Someday comes tomorrow, I'll be ready and if Hope is slow and Someday doesn't come to be for a decade, or however long it takes, then I'll be patient. Knowing you're in the world with me, as you are, is comfort and encouragement. You are my one, my best beloved."

The door opened from the hallway and she knew that to pass over the threshold meant a commitment of the highest kind; one that encompassed all of life and wisdom and planets and every star becoming for now and forever. Yet, it was such a simple little room, very unassuming, bland and in some respects she thought it almost childlike. There was the ivory comb and the red ribbon on a night stand near the bed. Over the bed was thrown a ridiculously ruffled coverlet with flounces of rich French lace decorating its hem that was completely out of character with the rest of the room's décor. Three exquisite china dolls, also out of character, rested like sisters hand in hand in the bend of a rustic wooden chair. The rest of the room had very little to distinguish it from any room in any impersonal institution anywhere. She saw, however, that there was a well-kept collection of drawings, toys and games in a box at the end of the bed and, she was surprised to remember it as being hers. It brought Wicked Sister to mind.

"Do you like the room, Carlen?" The voice came from behind her and she was so startled that she jumped forward beyond the threshold. Then she turned to see that it was Ahn who had spoken. Or was it?

This visage had no blue robe, no sacred jewels, no sheen of gold jewelry turning the light in sparkling flashes. Her hair was no longer a fall of black onto her bosom but short, rather, and with a flip to the side, something like her own hair; the 'do' that Wicked Sister had so loved. Maybe—

"Yes," Ahn spoke. "Maybe I came to you as Wicked Sister; maybe there was a need for this being to enter your life and to qualify it for you by playing the foil, the pathway to unconditional love. Could this be so? What do you think, Carlen?"

"I–yes, I guess that could be so." Carly looked very closely at the woman before her and as one can in dreams, she insisted the face close to look at it as if she were looking in a mirror. So many

times she had done this with Wicked Sister; so many times. And, she was there but not there. Ahn smiled.

"Look again, Carlen, who else do you see in my eyes?"

Carly studied her face again. Everything she did in this place was instantaneous, yet she felt as if she'd spent 100,000 years in that moment, finding a world of souls behind those eyes. There was just one who looked back at her out of the Universal soul and Carly was immediately overwhelmed with joy. Marcianne Boit sang exquisitely, caressing her little Julie, "Julie Boit, Julie Boit, my precious child, my precious precious child." Carly began to cry; her tears were sweet honey, so happy she was to find her mother. For the first time, she felt almost priveleged to be the little dwarf, to be held by one who loved her so, not minding at all that she couldn't think very well, not caring about stupid cruelties others had inflicted on her. So much it didn't matter that her heart swelled with forgiveness, naming them in her mind by seeing their faces. Mme Laurents, Cook, who was kind some and cruel some, but who did what her level demanded. Forgiven. Mlle Minot, huge charwoman, so unhappy with her size and her place in the world that all she could do to tolerate it was to torment someone who could not torment back. Forgiven. M'sieur Bernard, Master of the Kitchen and the Scullery and all the world beyond, so distantly responsible he must order the beating of a simple idiot so she would learn not to go where she would discover her utter ugliness reflected. Forgiven.

"Who is Marcianne Boit, Carlen?"

Carly felt as if she could finally open her eyes, that they'd been only slits before with limited vision and scope. Seeing Ahn's face, knowing now who she was, it was easy to make the connection. "We were Marcianne Boit, a Mother of the Soul Genus, is that correct?"

"Yes," Ahn smiled, "We were the embracers, the loving support for a difficult life that could seemingly find little lesson or little profit for having been. But now you know, Carlen, of the possibilities for experience on all levels. Now you understand the urge to repeat the warmth and comfort that you yourself gave to you in that life, a

---

305

necessary thing then, but also necessarily bringing forth the Wicked Sister personality in this current expression."

"I do see. But what am I to do now?"

"Absorb this clarification, allow it to open you to more rooms of this your soul's mansion, step across the threshold and take from it only what you need in the moment. Do not linger, but dream forward."

"I see. If I linger, I may get caught there, correct?"

"That is correct. To dwell in the experience for its sake is to allow purpose to become diffused. Knowledge is swift, as swift as Light, and there is no other force; receiving it fulfills all desires, all hungers of the soul, and once received, it is forever, it is Increase of the Light, the One reason for being."

"One? Just one among all the many I can think of? What about the joy of finding a friend? What about the recognition of a soul mate? Or accomplishing a challenge you once thought could not be accomplished?"

"One is the One Law of the Law of the One. There is no other." Ahn smiled that same encouraging smile the People smiled, *"All of the other laws subsidiary to the One are aimed at completing the One, as it was intended."*

"So it all comes back to the One Law—simple." Carly smiled, too, knowing that was a truth and feeling the fullness of having been able to acknowledge it. *"This is a wonderful dream!"* she declared to Ahn, *"This is the one I've been waiting for, isn't it?"*

"It is."

"Is there more I need to know? Something I need to do now?" Carly asked, seeing a long, long hallway manifest before them. It was the hallway, the one Ahn had called "home" and the one she had dreamed of all those months before when she'd first seen Ahn. How many doors were there? How many doors to consider? The Julie Boit door was now open forever, but she couldn't stay in the room, no matter how sweet the mother's caresses, how great the knowledge that a loving self was always at hand. Move on and

discover how to simplify the complications; how to make the Light Increase.

"There is nothing to do now, Carlen, but move with the winds of the Universe. All will right itself and all will become clear and meaningful."

Carly woke to the feel of a smile forming around her whole being. It had simply become a real thing, a fact of her reality that she could do this life and do it well. The day came onto her as a thing of gold, a treasure of sunshine against a beautiful sparkling cover of snow that had come in the night. The window's picture an incentive, Carly turned back the covers and immediately got out of bed. She could smell the coffee aroma coming to her from the kitchen. Doris had stayed the night after their long session of poring over a stack of books she had brought and, always an early riser, she had started breakfast. It was the morning of Carly's 44th birthday, a fourth cycle of 11. She knew she wasn't quite whole yet, but she had all the means to complete herself and the awareness to take the task in hand. She felt rich with a sense of purpose as she looked down that long hall with all the promise and fulfillment Light gives as it Increases. She was with friends.

"The Initiation begins," Ahn said, the People humming agreement. "We are with you."

11155-BARR